BY

Ilya Ehrenburg

A Change of Season

I. THE THAW

Translated from the Russian by Manya Harari

II. THE SPRING

Translated from the Russian by Humphrey Higgins

Ilya Ehrenburg

A
CHANGE
OF
SEASON

NEW YORK

Alfred·A·Knopf

1962

L. C. catalog card number: 62–11045

THIS IS A BORZOI BOOK,

PUBLISHED BY ALFRED A. KNOPF, INC.

FIRST AMERICAN EDITION

The Thaw was first published in volume form in Russia by *Sovetsky Pissatel* in 1954, and in the United States of America by Henry Regnery Company in 1955. *The Spring* was first published in Russia in *Znamya* in 1956.

CONTENTS

I. THE THAW

PRINCIPAL CHARACTERS

In Russian *a person may be addressed or referred to by his surname (e.g. Zhuravlyov), his first name (Ivan), a diminutive of his first name (Vanya), or his name and patronymic (Ivan Vasilyevich). For the convenience of the reader, the main characters in the novel, particularly those whose names appear in several forms, are listed below.*

Koroteyev, Dmitry, Dmitry Sergeyevich, engineer
Zhuravlyov, Ivan (Vanya), Ivan Vasilyevich, factory director
   His wife Lena, Yelena Borisovna, schoolteacher
   Their daughter, Shura
   Lena's mother, Antonina Pavlovna Kalashnikova,
     Kolkhoz chairman
Sokolovsky, Evgeny Vladimirovich, chief designer
   Maya Balabanova, his former wife
   Masha (Mary Vandervelde), their daughter
   Fomka, his dog
Pukhov, Andrey, Andrey Ivanovich, schoolteacher
   His wife Nadezhda (Nadya), Nadezhda Yegorovna
   Their son Volodya, Vladimir Andreyevich, a painter
   Their daughter Sonya, a student
Savchenko, Grisha, a young engineer
Saburov, a painter
   Glasha, Glafira Antonovna, his wife
Scherer, Dr. Vera, Vera Grigoryevna, physician

3

GOROKHOV, another doctor
TANECHKA, actress friend of Volodya Pukhov
SERYOZHA, pupil of Andrey Pukhov
BRAININ, an elderly engineer
YEGOROV, chief engineer
KHITROV, an engineer crony of Zhuravlyov
DOBZHINSKY, club manager
USHAKOV, secretary of the Party Town Committee

Surnames often take *a* in the feminine (e.g. Chizhov, Chizhova).

1

THE LIBRARIAN FELT NERVOUS.
Her spectacles had slipped down her nose and her pepper and
salt curls danced about. She announced:
"I call on Comrade Brainin to speak next. Comrade Koroteyev
will speak after him."
Dmitry Koroteyev slightly raised his thin dark eyebrows in an
expression of surprise. Yet he knew that he would have to speak
at the readers' meeting. The librarian had asked him well in advance and he had accepted.
Everybody at the factory treated Koroteyev with respect. The
director, Ivan Zhuravlyov, had recently admitted to the secretary
of the Party Town Committee that without him the release of the
new precision-cutting tools would have had to be put off to the
following quarter. Nor was Dmitry valued only as a brilliant
engineer—people were impressed by his many-sided learning, his
intelligence, and his modesty. Even Chief Designer Sokolovsky,
who was known for his sharp tongue, never said a word against
him. As for the librarian, who had had a discussion with him
about literature, she told everyone: "His feeling for Chekhov is
unique." It was evident that the readers' meeting, for which she
had worked more than a month like a schoolgirl for a stiff examination, could not possibly be held without him.
Engineer Brainin spread a pile of papers on the table. He
spoke too fast, as though frightened of not having enough time,

with painful hesitations while he put on his glasses and searched among his notes.

"In spite of the defects, rightly pointed out by those who have preceded me, the novel has, so to speak, great educational significance. Why did the agronomist Zubtsov fail in his afforestation scheme? The author has, so to speak, posed the problem correctly —Zubtsov underestimated the significance of criticism and self-criticism. It is true, of course, that he could have had the help of the secretary of the Party Organisation, Shebalin, but the author has clearly shown the results of neglecting the principle of collective leadership. If the author heeds criticism and alters certain incidents, the novel will be worthy, so to speak, of inclusion in the golden treasury of our literature."

The club was crowded; there were people standing in the aisles and against the doors. The book chosen for discussion, a locally published novel by a young author, had made a stir. But the audience was worn out by Brainin's long quotations, his "so-to-speaks" and his dreary bureaucratic voice. Everybody brightened up when the librarian announced:

"I call on Comrade Koroteyev. Comrade Stolyarova will speak after him."

Dmitry spoke well and was listened to attentively, but the librarian frowned: it was not like this that she had heard him speak of Chekhov. Why did he attack Zubtsov? You could see he did not like the novel, yet he was praising it. The characters of Shebalin, the conceited secretary, and of Fedorova, the honest young Communist, were realistic and Zubtsov himself was quite alive.

"Frankly, what I didn't like at all were the author's revelations about his hero's private life. To begin with, the incident he describes is improbable; there is nothing typical about it. Are we really to believe that the agronomist, an over-confident but honest man, falls in love with the wife of his colleague, an empty-headed flirt who has nothing in common with him spiritually? It seems to me that here the author sought nothing but a cheap effect. Surely

6

our Soviet people are more honest and more responsible than he has made them out to be. This love affair might have been lifted straight out of the pages of some bourgeois novel."

He received prolonged applause. There were those who liked his wit: he had spoken caustically of young authors commissioned to write a creative work, who arrived at the prescribed place, whipped out their notebooks, briefly questioned all of a dozen inhabitants, and then declared that they had "collected enough material for a novel." Others were flattered at the thought of being more high-minded than the hero of the story. Still others applauded Koroteyev because he was "a clever fellow."

"He beat him good and proper, there's no doubt about it," said Zhuravlyov loudly to the librarian (he was sitting in the praesidium). She said nothing.

Zhuravlyov's wife, Lena, a schoolteacher, was perhaps the only one who had not clapped. "Lena has to be different," sighed her husband.

Dmitry had sat down and was thinking confusedly: "I must be getting the flu. Nuisance . . . with Brainin's project on my hands . . . I shouldn't have spoken. Only fed them the old platitudes." His head was aching. The room was stuffy.

He had not been listening to Katya Stolyarova and was startled by the applause that interrupted her. He knew Katya from the factory. She was a cheerful girl with a white skin and flaxen hair, no eyebrows, and a permanent expression of delighted astonishment at life. He forced himself to listen:

"I don't follow Comrade Koroteyev. I wouldn't say the novel was a classic. It isn't *Anna Karenina*. But it holds your interest and I don't see what bourgeois novels have to do with it. The way I look at it, a human being has a heart, and so he suffers. What's wrong with that? I'll say straight out, I myself have experienced such moments in my life . . . The book grips you; it's no good just brushing it aside."

Dmitry thought: "Who would have imagined that giggling little Katya has had time for tragedy? 'A human being has a

7

heart.'" All at once he ceased to listen, ceased to see the room, the librarian, the books, the spiky, grey-brown potted palm under the window. He gazed at Lena and all the torment of the past few months revived in him. Lena had not once looked at him; he longed to meet her glance and was afraid of it. That was how it was between them nowadays. And yet last summer they had talked, joked, argued unconstrainedly. He had often visited the Zhuravlyovs. In his heart he did not like Ivan; he thought him too complacent. He went because he found it interesting to talk to Lena. She was intelligent; Dmitry had not met her like in Moscow. Of course, here in this provincial town there was less bustle; people had more time to read, to think. Yet even here, Lena was an exception. You could feel that she had depth. It was even difficult to understand how she could live with Zhuravlyov; yet they seemed to be on friendly terms, and they had a daughter who was five years old.

In those days Dmitry had known a peaceful pleasure in Lena's looks. Savchenko, a young engineer, once said to him: "She is a real beauty." Dmitry shook his head: "No, but her face is memorable." She had gold-flecked hair that turned red in sunlight, and green eyes; their expression was elusive, at times teasing, at others sad, but most often incomprehensible. Sometimes he felt, another moment and she would vanish, be caught up and lost in the dusty slanting ray of indoor sun.

"How good it was in those days," thought Dmitry. He came out into the street. "Whew! What a snowstorm!" Yet earlier, when he was going to the club, it had been calm and fine.

He walked half-consciously, without a thought of the readers' meeting or of his speech, his head filled with Lena, the havoc in his life, the feverish dreams of the past few weeks, the helplessness he had never known before. His friends thought of him as a lucky fellow for whom everything worked out right, and indeed in the past two years he had gained wide recognition. But there were other years behind him. He was thirty-five and he

8

had not been often spoiled by life. He had had to struggle. He had a strong will; you could tell it from his long, dry face with its domed forehead, his grey eyes, which could be either cold or gently condescending, and the stubborn lines about the mouth.

Dmitry was in the tenth grade at school when he had to face his first great trial: in the autumn of 1936, his stepfather was arrested. The following morning outside his house he saw his best friend Misha Gribov and called out to him. He would have liked to share his grief, to ask advice. But Misha grimly pursed his lips without a word and crossed to the other side. A few days later Dmitry was expelled from the Komsomol. His mother wept: "What has it to do with you?" He comforted her: "You mustn't think of it like that. This is just an individual case." He went into a factory. Neither embittered nor shut in, he made new friends, he was contented with his work, and at night he studied, saying to his mother: "You'll see, one of these days I'll go to the University."

A few years later, in stifling August weather, he was marching, gloomy but not disheartened, across the steppe; his division was in retreat. He happened to be the one on whom the general chose to vent his rage, cursing him for a coward and threatening him with court martial. Dmitry calmly told his friends: "Good thing he's cursing, means we'll be all right." A little later he was wounded in the shoulder; he spent six months in the hospital, then went back to the front and stayed for the duration. He fell in love with Natasha, a signals officer. Not until Breslau did he discover that she also loved him. She told him: "You look so cold, I was even frightened of you; but your heart I knew at once." He dreamed of happiness after the war; but Natasha died senselessly—a mine exploded in a Leipzig street on the tenth of May, when nobody was thinking about death any longer. Steadfastly he lived down his sorrow, letting no one guess what he was going through. Only much later, when his mother asked him: "Why don't you get married? You're over thirty; when I'm gone there won't be anybody to look after you," he confessed: "I lost my happiness in the war, Mother. Now marriage doesn't even enter my head."

He had one remedy against desperation—work. He took a course in machine construction. His thesis was well received and there was a plan to keep him at the Institute, but somebody pulled strings and the position was given to another man; Dmitry was sent off to a factory in the Volga district. This was where he suddenly became the clever fellow who was destined to succeed in everything. Zhuravlyov, normally distrustful of young people, recognised his gifts at once. He was elected to the Town Soviet, where he often spoke. The workers trusted him and talked to him freely; they looked upon him as an honest man, unspoiled by his position.

And what had happened to him now? Why had he lost his self-possession? Why was he striding bleakly through the snowstorm, his head filled with thoughts of Lena?—Not thoughts even, rather a feeling that he could never oust her from his life. How stupidly it had all worked out, how childishly. And how out of keeping with his past.

The wind blew; the snow was blinding, deafening. There was nobody about, yet Dmitry stopped suddenly, raised his eyebrows slightly and burst out laughing. "Isn't it comical!" he thought. "I get up on the platform and calmly prove that these things simply don't exist. The novelist thought up Zubtsov, made him fall in love with his friend's wife, shamed him publicly, and to tie up the ends, sent him to the Arctic. Naturally Koroteyev can't put up with that! 'It's a cheap effect. It isn't typical.' Well, well, just bear that in mind, Dmitry Sergeyevich. People like yourself and that Zubtsov just don't exist. You're inventions, puppets; there simply aren't any such people.

"What must Lena be thinking now? That I'm a bureaucrat? a cheap liar? She must guess, even if no one else does. Women understand these things. I hardly dared say anthing to Natasha almost till the end, and yet she told me afterwards: 'I knew right

from the beginning. At Sozha—remember?—there was an air
raid but you insisted on shaving—that was when I guessed.' I'm
all right at figuring out machines, but when it comes to feelings
. . . Surely Lena must be laughing at me.

"But what's the good of thinking about it? Lena is Zhuravlyov's
wife; our paths are different. This nonsense can be dealt with.
But why did I say: 'Such a thing can't happen'? I don't know.
Certainly not to mislead. After all, my feelings are my own affair,
my private business. A book is different, that's a public matter.
Why write about such things? They can't help anyone. Zubtsov
messing up his job—that's something the reader can get hold of.
He can draw conclusions from it that are useful to him. But as to
what Zubtsov feels about a colleague's wife—that's just a question of absurd morals. Love is a cement—everybody says it is,
but this is a corrosive. I was right in what I said. That's not the
trouble. The point is that I must take myself in hand."

Near the bright round street lamp the snow was like a flock
of startled or excited birds, fluttering up and falling and fluttering
up again. Underneath stood a pair of lovers lost in an embrace.
Was it perhaps Katya, thought Dmitry. The girl gave an exclama-
tion and they walked on. Dmitry smiled. "Katya or another . . .
That was how Natasha and I wandered in that park outside
Berlin. There was a grey lake in it, and water lilies, and once
the major swooped down on us . . . Fine, so long as you are
young. I must get this nonsense out of my head, once and for all."

The streets were empty. Everybody had gone home—whether
they had sat in judgment on Zubtsov, or been to see *The Lady
Vanishes,* or heard the lecture on cattle breeding, or spent the
evening visiting friends. The new houses, dreary in daytime,
now looked like a theatrical set, their golden windows struggling
with the snow. Inside there were people—sleeping, quarrelling,
suffering, rejoicing—there was everything that goes on in life.
But all that was secondary; the important thing was work.

Feeling that only work could save him, he hurried on, and as
he struck matches on the darkened stairs, he thought happily:

"Now I'll settle down to Brainin's project." He spread the drawings on the table. The heat was on full blast; he couldn't breathe. He threw open the casement, the snow whirled in. "Must be getting the flu . . . But perhaps that's also nonsense? Must work."

Usually when he worked he sat motionless; he could sit like that half the night. But now he kept shifting restlessly, leaning back, moving the position of the ash tray or the lamp, getting up and striding up and down, his big shadow like a frightened stranger, darting over the whitewashed walls.

"Brainin is right, a lot depends on the welding; the danger is the warping. Tomorrow I'll talk it over with Zhuravlyov. Now they will be having tea. Lena will say: 'Koroteyev spoke like a stuffy clerk.' She'll laugh, and he'll defend me: 'Novels aren't in his line, but then he's all right at his work. That's the important thing.' Quite right, Ivan Vasilyevich, it's work that matters. When Lena laughs her eyes darken; sometimes when she laughs her eyes are sad . . . Rubbish! Must tell Zhuravlyov about the reduction gear . . ."

At five he told himself contentedly: "With these modifications, Brainin's project can be recommended . . . Not worth going to bed now. But to stay awake is difficult—all that nonsense will crawl back into my head. Shall I put down the modifications in the form of an official note? That will make it more convincing to Zhuravlyov, and it will kill an hour. . . ."

When he went out, the snow was still drifting but the streets had come to life; people were hurrying to their work. The street lamp shone as brightly; the same white birds fluttered. Only the lovers were no longer there. Snatches of conversation were flung at him:

"A wonderful film. I couldn't sleep all night."

"Tell Yegorov. He'll let you go. Silly to wangle sick leave . . ."

". . . and such crowds. You can't get through . . ."

Dmitry was thinking: "What nonsense it all is! And yet how it sticks! Will it ever leave me? I've read about it in books, seems you have to live it." Unexpectedly he smiled: "It's absurd, but I think I'm happy."

2

AT HOME, AFTER THE READERS'
meeting, Lena laid the table and went into the kitchen to fetch the tea and the cold cutlets left for supper. She managed to talk, yet Ivan noticed that she was not herself. Fortunately, instead of asking her straight out what was the matter, he suggested: "Worrying about the bad marks you handed out today?" Relieved, she answered: "Yes."

Ivan picked up his newspaper (he had not had time to look at it in the morning). Reading as he ate, he commented from time to time: "Nikiforov got a good dressing-down," or "There's a shortage of compressors, no doubt about it." Lena hastily agreed.

She was glad that he was reading. It gave her time to think. She had just realised that what had happened to her was irreparable. It was terrible to have to live through such a thing alone.

As a student Lena had had many friends but nowadays she at times felt lonely. There seemed nobody at the factory for her to talk to. She felt drawn to people with more experience of life than she had (she laughed at it—a teacher and still wanting to be a pupil!). At the school, until a year ago, there had been Pukhov, who was one of the most remarkable people in the town. An old Bolshevik who had fought in the civil war and a gifted schoolmaster, he was universally respected. Lena looked upon him as her saviour. He had guided her in her work and comforted her when at first she was bewildered by the noisy, self-willed children. He had treated her as his own daughter and she had come to rely upon him more and more. But last winter he had fallen ill; the doctors had diagnosed *angina pectoris* and forbidden him to go on working. He was better now and sometimes visited the school—he could not bear to stay away—but Lena thought it wrong to bother him with her difficulties. She told herself crossly she was not a little girl, she would soon be thirty, it was time she stood on her own feet. All the same, she found it hard to have nobody with whom to talk things over.

Another of her friends was Dr. Vera Scherer. She had met her just about the time Pukhov fell ill. She was never to forget that meeting, for it was that day she realised that her husband was a stranger to her. After it she cried all night. Lena was attracted to Vera but she saw her seldom; Vera was always busy. And she was locked up in herself. She had lost her husband in the war. She told Lena: "It can never work a second time." It was embarrassing to intrude on her—she had her own sorrow.

With Dmitry Koroteyev, Lena had made friends at once. He told her stories of the war, of Germany, of his friends. He made them seem alive; Lena felt she knew them. They argued over books. She could not believe in Voropayev's luck; Dmitry thought it was convincing. He was fond of Listopad; Lena thought him soulless. Of Grossman's novel Dmitry said: "He writes honestly about the war. That's exactly how it was. Only his heroes reason too much; that's why sometimes you can't believe in them." She laughed: "As though you didn't reason!" He blushed and muttered: "We mustn't be personal. . . . I expect I've bored you . . ."

He never told her anything of Natasha or of his childhood, but she felt that he was not as lucky as her husband thought him. She guessed in him an inward strength and a profound though hidden restlessness; to her this was a real person.

At the time of the Korean Armistice she had heard him read a paper. It dealt competently with the failure of the strategy of the United States and the conclusions to be drawn from it: this war had ended differently from the war in Spain. The aggressors would have to think again and the friends of peace the world

14

over would raise their heads. As they came out of the club together, Dmitry had said to her: "At our Institute there was a Korean girl—a tiny little thing, like a child . . . I keep thinking of her . . . She had such a wonderful smile. Isn't it wonderful that she can smile again, after all they've been through . . ." Lena wondered if perhaps she was the only one who knew the whole of him—both the Dmitry who had read the paper and the one who told her of the Korean girl.

But there were also things she could not understand in him. One day she told him of a tenth-grade girl, Popova, who had only just escaped disaster. "Can you believe it, they threw her out of the Komsomol. Never heard her story; never worked it out properly. In the end the Party Town Committee intervened and she was reinstated. But can you imagine what it means to go through this at seventeen? A real tragedy. Fomin's fault, and he hasn't ever been reprimanded. Isn't it intolerable!" She had expected Dmitry to agree with her, but he said nothing. He seemed to be remembering something. Had it been her husband, she would have thought: "He's frightened." But Dmitry she respected; she told herself that there were still a lot of things in life that were beyond her.

Imperceptibly she became attached to him. If he stayed away she missed him and asked her husband: "Are you sure he isn't ill?" That was last summer, when her relationship with him still seemed good, straightforward, simple. Then he went on vacation to the Caucasus. He came back looking so gloomy that she wondered: "Did he meet a girl he liked and then it came to nothing?" He began avoiding her. Twice she met him in the street; he said he had a lot of work but he would be sure to drop in soon, sure to. She made wild guesses at what was keeping him away and suddenly caught herself wondering: "Why am I thinking of him such a lot? Can I be in love with him?" She reassured herself at once: at her age people didn't do such silly things. It was simply that there were so few people who were interesting to talk to, and after all, they had been good friends.

She had been unwilling to go to the readers' meeting. It bored her; there would be speeches read from notes, quotations from reviews, and endless summaries of the story. But Ivan had insisted that she must go: the secretary of the Town Committee would be there. "Everybody is going. What's the point of making silly demonstrations?" Besides, she would be interested—the librarian had said that Koroteyev would be speaking. Lena lost her temper: "As if I cared." Ivan chuckled: Women! Almost hero-worshipping Koroteyev one day and not caring to listen to his speech the next! . . .

Lena had no idea of what that evening was to mean to her.

As soon as Dmitry began to speak, she longed to run out of the room or hide her face . . . Wasn't it to her that he was saying this? He had decided to explain why he had stayed away. "Now it's all quite clear. He considers me an empty-headed flirt like the heroine of that novel. He has made up his mind I am in love with him, and now he's lecturing me! He is a decent man, he has other things to think about, and anyway I must understand that this sort of thing simply doesn't happen. It's a lesson to me. But why does he have to say it publicly? Couldn't he have come and told me? He has thought it out—this way it's more insulting. He wants to make quite sure that I'll stop pestering him. He needn't worry. He'll never see me again."

Afterwards, when they went out into the snowstorm and Ivan wanted to call a taxi, she insisted on walking home. She thought the walk would do her good. All the way she seethed with indignation against Dmitry. But as she came into the house, suddenly she understood: there was no reason for her to be angry or indignant; the trouble was in herself. Only now did the realisation come to her that she loved Dmitry, that all these weeks his absence had been a torment to her, that there was to be no happiness for her, no peace of mind. She hurried into the kitchen. The kettle took a long time to boil and she could grieve a little without feeling Ivan's puzzled eyes on her. She was no longer angry. Dmitry had been right. He had to warn her; the form in which he did it was immaterial. He had only done his duty. He had seen what she had failed to understand and he had made a clean break. Now she had to go on living. But how?

She served supper in the dining room and sat watching Ivan eating while she pretended to drink tea. Lucky that he was reading and that the article was a page long . . . She asked herself in astonishment: "Can this really be my husband?"

Lena met Ivan one evening at her Institute when the students had put on a play. She was finishing her teacher's course and he had recently arrived in town; he said that he was never happier than among young people and often visited the Institute. Lena had a small part in the play (she wasn't a good actress) but afterwards, when there was dancing, Ivan asked her to dance with him. They danced and talked together all evening and at the end of it he saw her to her hostel.

This had been six years ago. Since then Ivan had greatly changed. He was stout, flabby, loose-cheeked, and a little bald (people thought of him as middle-aged, though he was only thirty-seven). His eyes, which had been dreamy, were now calm and confident; his voice was peremptory; and his laugh was such that nobody felt like laughing with him. Everything in him had changed.

Or did it only seem so to his wife? In the beginning he had attracted her by his cheerful zest for life, his optimism. He was never downcast; even in the darkest moments he always said there must be some way out. In this he was unchanged, but now it angered her. A few days before, Yegorov, the chief engineer, had come in looking as white as linen and told them, hardly able to control his voice, that his wife had cancer. Lena forced herself not to cry and Ivan said: "You mustn't worry. She'll get better. Medicine works miracles these days." And a moment later he was asking: "Tell me, Pavel Konstantinovich, how are the machines for Stalingrad; what's the position? This is the third time they've been after me about them."

There was another incident she could not forget. Last summer the secretary of the Town Committee had told him in front of her that the dilapidated hovels and hutments of the workers were a disgrace. The building fund had been approved a year ago, and what had it been used for? "The new precision casting bay," said Ivan unruffled, "was an absolute necessity. Without it we could never have fulfilled the quota. We'd have disgraced ourselves; there's no doubt about it. Weren't you the first to clap us on the back because our output was sixteen per cent above the target? As for the houses, don't worry, they'll outlast us all. I've seen worse in Moscow."

"Nothing upsets him," Lena thought. "He has one answer to everything—'We'll get by.' He's selfish through and through."

In his youth, his light, good-tempered gaiety had given him charm, but this had left him with the passing of the years. He had had his troubles in his work. Three years ago there had been rumours that he would lose his job; twice he had had to go to Moscow. He had got by. But perhaps it was because of this that he smiled less often? Or did he now feel crushed by his responsibilities? Or had he simply put on weight? Though even now he brightened up when he was talking of multiple lathes, or of the welcome he had had in Moscow, or of Nikiforov, who had tried to ruin him and had himself got into trouble. Lena thought this only smugness. In reality he was devoted to his factory and proud of it. He felt at moments that the factory and he were one —if he received a friendly handshake it seemed to him it was a welcome for the whole collective and if the output were below the target, it was his, Ivan's, personal misfortune.

He had one hobby: going off to fish on Sunday mornings, or arguing with Khitrov about the bait, he suddenly looked seventeen. It got on Lena's nerves. Couldn't he read a book or go to see a play? No, his greatest joy was to sit for hours gazing at his line.

Nor could Lena understand his friendship with Khitrov. Competent at his work and comfortably married, Khitrov was pink

and fat like a grown-up baby, and had a way of telling the same
funny story for the hundredth time, laughing in a pleasant bass.
He had an unshakable belief in Ivan's brains and in his lucky star.
Together they fished, or they went shooting, or played drafts
over a cosy pint. Ivan remarked: "He knows his onions." Sokolovsky, the chief designer, commented nastily: "Khitrov never went
near a river; now he swears that he's loved fishing all his life. He
even says: 'It's harder to catch a pike than a gudgeon, no doubt
about it.'" Khitrov disgusted Lena. She thought he was a boot-
licker and asked Ivan crossly: "How can you talk to a yes-man
like that?" He shrugged his shoulders: "Khitrov is no fool. Sometimes he has the most original ideas. You always judge things
lightly; you don't know him."

Ivan was fond of her and of their little girl, Lena was sure of
that; but it was not of such a feeling she had dreamed when she
decided to become his wife. He thought her high-falutin'. He
mocked: "They say in the old days the cabby used to ask a rouble
and accept ten kopecks. That's like you. You make demands on
life. But life is simpler. And harder."

In their first years together, Lena had tried discussing love, the
aim of life, what happiness is made of. He would smile tenderly
but always cut the conversation short, saying he had work to do.
He considered her a good wife; he was happy with her. True, she
had a weakness, she always wanted him to talk about his feelings, but a woman might have worse defects than that.

Ivan was pleased when she made friends with Koroteyev. He
felt no jealousy: Lena was sensible. She simply wanted somebody
to talk to, perhaps even to flirt with—that was natural. He himself had neither time nor talent for keeping her amused. Dmitry
was sound enough, just fond of showing off his knowledge. It
flattered him to have Lena listening to him open-mouthed.

When Dmitry stopped coming, Ivan was puzzled. Could Lena
have got sick of him—of such a clever fellow? He thought: "The
trouble is, she is too fond of me, no doubt about it."

Lena had made it a condition of their marriage that she would go on teaching. It was not to become a housekeeper that she had taken her degree. She found her work enthralling and tried to share her passion for it with Ivan, showing him the children's essays, going into raptures over old Pukhov, complaining of the headmaster. Ivan said: "Do you think I haven't enough troubles of my own? Of course, teaching is not an easy job. But a factory isn't a small thing either."

About his work opinions were divided. There were those who said he was just a formalist and an opportunist. If the factory had got on, it was thanks to Dmitry, Yegorov, Sokolovsky, Brainin: Ivan had only hindered them. Others said he was a good administrator, an honest man, and that this mattered more than anything. Nobody put any passion into defending or attacking him; he did not arouse strong feelings.

Lena thought him self-assured, and yet he often lacked self-confidence. But he never shared his doubts with his assistants. He believed that the responsibility should rest on him alone. Dmitry thought Ivan's reports to the Ministry were too rosy. Ivan shrugged his shoulders—Dmitry might be good at his machines but of the mysteries of management he understood nothing. Ivan knew what would happen if he were to mention his difficulties to Moscow. They would only frown up there and say: "Zhuravlyov is panicky." People liked honey and if they were served with pepper instead it made them cross. He told his wife: "You have to know when to say nothing." To Lena this was cowardice. And yet Ivan had served three years in the army. He had fought in the defence of Rzhov at the hardest moment and was remembered by his comrades as a man of courage. Talking about the war, he said to Lena: "Yes, you could be killed, no doubt about it. But, then, to die, that's nothing much. It's not as if you were put on the carpet and told: 'Now give an account of yourself.' That's a different kettle of fish."

Whatever his opponents said, the factory was in good standing —not a single stoppage in six years. True, the deputy head of the Ministry had told him that in using the money earmarked for the workers' dwellings to build the foundry he had acted outside the law, but Ivan thought: "That's only for form's sake. The Ministry, like myself, is interested above all in output." Naturally he hastened to reassure the deputy—all the workers had their proper space allocation; there was nothing catastrophic in the situation. In any case, preparations were underway for building three new blocks of apartments. Indeed, plans and estimates were passed by the New Year, but Ivan wasn't in a hurry to start building. After the Plenary Session of the Party's Central Committee, Sibirtsev, the chairman of the Works Committee, asked him cautiously: "Have you seen, Ivan Vasilyevich, what the papers say? . . . They think it's high time the workers were given the space they were allocated." "They'll get it," replied Ivan, but he gave no further thought to Sibirtsev's words. Ivan was not a fool, but his mind was not remarkable for its suppleness.

That autumn *Izvestia* had published an article about the factory. Ivan had said sternly to the correspondent: "No point in writing about me. I've given you the output figures—stress production. You might mention Koroteyev; he deserves it. Above all, interview the workers. Here's the list." All the same, the journalist had written up Ivan, "one of those managers of Soviet industry in whom daring is combined with sober calculation and great experience." The chairman of the Town Executive Committee telephoned to congratulate him. At the Eve of the Revolution celebrations of November 6, Ivan sat in the praesidium next to the regional military commander. "Zhuravlyov is on his way up," said the town.

No wonder that the artist Volodya Pukhov (son of the old schoolmaster), who a year ago had returned from Moscow, was doing Ivan's portrait for the yearly exhibition. "I only back winners," Volodya liked to say. He chose Ivan so that his subject should ensure his success. In its review of the exhibition, the local paper would devote a column to Pukhov and the portrait would be bought by the museum. Ivan was depicted wearing all his decorations and seated before a huge table on which stood the

model of a machine. Lena, catching sight of the unfinished portrait, made a face—Ivan looked rather like a turkey cock.

It seemed to Lena that she saw right through her husband; in
reality there was a lot in him she failed to see. Thus, he was genuinely upset at the death in agony of Yegorov's wife, even though
he kept repeating cheerfully, almost until the last day: "Don't
worry, she'll get better." In the same way, his expression darkened as he peered into the damp, bleak hovels that sheltered his
workers. They recalled his childhood to him—he came from a
poor village in the Kaluga district. It saddened him that people
lived in such conditions. But he reassured himself: "The houses
will last a while. And if we hadn't built the foundry we'd have
been in a nice mess, no doubt about it. Anyway, the men aren't
so badly off—you can't compare it with the way their fathers
lived. Next year we'll build three new blocks." He believed that
if you said everything was all right, that in itself would make
things better. "The great thing is not to get demoralised. Yegorov
must have wanted to be reassured when his wife was ill. That's
the great secret—the less you look at the dark side, the less of it
there will be."

Once a fire broke out in the assembly shop. Ivan showed himself at his best; he kept his head and took all the necessary measures competently so that the fire was quickly dealt with. Afterwards, to make up for the loss of time, he worked a whole
night-shift with the men, encouraging them by his presence.
Talking of this event, which caused excitement throughout the
factory, Dmitry said to Sokolovsky: "Didn't Zhuravlyov astonish
you? Here's a man without the least initiative, yet he didn't lose
his head." Sokolovsky, who invariably made fun of the director,
now said thoughtfully: "That's true. You know, gardeners talk
about a dormant bud. It can stay dormant for years, but if you cut
off the main shoot, suddenly it comes out. That's like Zhuravlyov
—he's a very ordinary bureaucrat, it needs a storm to wake
him up."

The turning point in Lena's attitude towards her husband had

come not over Dmitry but a year ago over a conversation that
had passed unnoticed by Ivan. That day their daughter, Shura,
ran a temperature. It happened that the pediatrician, Filimonov,
was ill himself. Lena panicked; she was convinced Shura had
pneumonia. She phoned Ivan and he suggested: "Send to our
own hospital for Dr. Scherer." Vera Scherer came and said that it
was ordinary flu; the child had nothing on her lungs. Lena was
overjoyed, but in her agitation she insisted: "Are you sure? Her
breathing is so odd." Vera unexpectedly lost her temper: "If you
don't trust me, why did you call me in?" Lena blushed: "Forgive
me, I don't know what I'm saying. Truly, I didn't mean to hurt
your feelings. This is awful!" Vera's eyes had filled with tears;
she said quietly: "It's you who must forgive me, it's my fault. My
nerves are on edge. Sometimes people say such dreadful things
. . . It's since the announcement . . .[1] It's very bad—a doctor
shouldn't behave like this." Lena blushed a still darker red. She
took Vera home. From that day they became friends.

And it was also from that day that Lena despised her husband.
He came home late, tired and hungry; he asked how Shura was
and Lena told him of her conversation with Vera Scherer. Ivan
said nothing. She insisted: "But don't you think it's quite outra-
geous? What's it got to do with Scherer . . . ?" Ivan said soothingly: "Don't get so upset. I told you to call her in myself; she's
supposed to be very good. I've got nothing at all against her. Still,
you've got to be careful whom you trust, no doubt about it."

Lena left the room without a word. Everything that had been
seething in her suddenly boiled up. Sobbing, she kept repeating:
"And that man's my husband."

Months later, after the fire, listening to Dmitry praising Ivan's
conduct, she could hardly keep herself from crying out: "If you
only knew how cowardly he is, how heartless."

When the newspapers announced the rehabilitation of the

---

[1] The announcement in *Pravda* of the arrest of a group of doctors
accused of conspiring to poison several Soviet leaders.

Kremlin doctors, Lena rushed immediately to the hospital, asked for Vera, and threw herself into her arms.

That evening Ivan said yawning: "Turns out they weren't guilty after all. So your Scherer needn't have upset herself."

If she stayed with him, it was not from pity, though she knew he was attached to her, nor because hardship frightened her—she had her job and could always make enough to keep herself and Shura. She stayed for Shura's sake. Shura loved her father; and he, too, became quite different when he played with her, younger, more light-hearted. How could she part them? "It isn't Shura's fault," she told herself. "It's my fault. I chose him, now it's up to me to pay."

She tried to tell herself that love was not so necessary after all. She had her work, her friends, her daughter. These were not the times for personal drama. True, Ivan was selfish, cowardly, but he was not a traitor or a thief. And if she stayed, Shura would keep her father.

Her friendship with Dmitry had distracted her from her bitterness; and when he had ceased coming, she was consumed by her uncertainty and thus gave little thought to her husband. Outwardly, nothing had changed; she went on pouring out her husband's tea and asking him about the factory. She was convinced that she was living only for Shura and the school.

Only now, after the meeting at the club, did she understand that her heart was given to Dmitry. So little had she expected it that the knowledge stunned her. She sat wretchedly, waiting for Ivan to finish his last glass of tea.

Putting aside his paper, he said abruptly:

"Why didn't you like Koroteyev's speech? I thought it very good. Not that I have read the book, but he was right about the Soviet family, no doubt about it."

She answered with unusual calm:

"I hardly listened. I told you I didn't want to go. I'm worried about the seventh grade. The program is overloaded and a lot of children can't keep up. You've finished? I'll go look at Shura."

The child was sleeping. She had thrown aside her comforter. Lena covered her and, sitting by her, burst into tears. Would Shura, too, have to go through this? "It's easier for a man. Of course, I have my life, the school, the schoolchildren. But if you knew how hard it was . . . Just to get through the day . . . Shura darling, what are we to do? I don't know, I just don't know."

3

THE EVENING OF THE READERS' meeting was also memorable for the family of the old schoolmaster, Andrey Pukhov, though none of them went to the club. His daughter Sonya had meant to go, but it was Andrey's birthday—he was sixty-four—and his wife, Nadezhda, said that whatever happened, they must give a party. For three days Andrey listened to Nadezhda's lamentations—flour was scarce, there was not a turkey or a goose in any shop in town, and, as though on purpose, eggs were unobtainable as well.

Andrey chuckled: that's what she was like, to hear her talk you'd think there would be nothing, yet the guests would eat so much that they could hardly get up from the table.

Nadezhda wanted to invite her cousin and her husband, a contemporary of Andrey, the former headmaster now pensioned off, but Andrey said: "Let's ask Sonya's and Volodya's friends, let them have a good time; you and I will enjoy ourselves looking at them."

Andrey was sociable. He liked Brainin and the former headmaster and sat for hours listening to his wife's cousin talking about her rheumatism, her mud baths, and her new bee-sting treatment. He often visited the widower Yegorov, who lived nearby, and comforted him in his recent loss. They discussed machines, or Eisenhower's latest speech, or Yegorov's daughter who taught music. But he was never happier than among young people. It may have been that he had kept a youthful fervour, or perhaps that he had taught for over thirty years and really knew the young—there was nothing he couldn't understand about the terrors of examinations or the tragedies of first love or youthful dreams of fame.

Only in his own family he at times felt lonely.

He had lived happily with his wife for thirty years. In her youth she, too, had been a teacher—she had taught in an adult school. Their first child, Volodya, was born in 1920, the year of the famine. When Nadezhda took him to headquarters to show Andrey, the sentry stopped her: "Look out, little one, don't drop him"—small and thin, with her short-cropped hair, she looked a child herself. A year later she had a daughter, who died within a month; Nadezhda was dangerously ill and had two operations. When Andrey went back to schoolteaching, she devoted herself to the duties of a wife and mother. By the time Sonya was born she had long forgotten the dreams she had had as a girl, the diary she had kept then, the books that she had read; she had grown fat and soft. On the rare occasions when she recalled her youth she was amazed: it seemed to her that it must have been another woman who had addressed those soldiers' meetings, galloped, while she was pregnant, across the steppe, or helped her husband to print leaflets. How long ago it was! Her world had closed in around her and grown compact.

When Andrey fell sick Nadezhda felt that she must save his life. She complained to everyone that he did not follow the doctors' orders, that he behaved like a child unconscious of danger. In reality, Andrey knew he had not long to live and because of this refused to be an invalid—he felt the moment he surrendered the engine would stop.

He announced that he was well and would return to work. For

the first time in their married life Nadezhda became frantic. She screamed, wept, ran to see the doctors. Vera Scherer said: "Of course he ought to be in bed, I've told him that. But sometimes a man knows better than his doctors. He told me he couldn't live without his work. If I were you I wouldn't worry him." Nadezhda did not give up, she went to see the headmaster, the school director, and the secretary of the Town Committee. Andrey did not go back to work.

He was not idle. He looked after his former pupils, those whose fathers had fallen in the war and whose circumstances were particularly difficult. One had a mother who was a speculator and sent him to the market; another had to nurse a younger sister who was ill; a third had been neglected and kept bad company. Andrey would help the mothers and do their homework with the children, telling them of long-past days: how the Revolution was started, how he once saw Lenin, how the Whites were driven back.

Nadezhda watched her husband growing weaker and every day she begged him tearfully: "Couldn't you stay in bed at least a day?" He reminded himself that her eyes, cruel in their concern, were the eyes of love and hid his suffering, forcing himself to smile, instead of groaning, when he had a heart attack.

Volodya had been Nadezhda's favourite from his childhood; he was a handsome boy with clever, mocking eyes. She told her neighbours: "He looks so quiet and yet he worries me." He was never naughty, never fought with other boys, but, always with the same meek voice and courteous smile, behaved impertinently to his father, whom he nicknamed "The Old Guard." He teased his schoolfellows, composed rude verses about little girls, and drew caricatures of the teachers. His love of drawing was evident when he was small and his mother asked herself with joy: "Perhaps he's really gifted?"

He studied painting in Moscow. Spending his holidays at home, he would tell his mother funny stories about his teachers, about first nights, about the girls at the Red Poppy Restaurant,

27

talking like an old man tired of life. Horrified, Nadezhda begged her husband: "Do talk to him. He must have got in with the wrong kind of people." Andrey sighed; he had long ago tried everything—arguing, begging, scolding. Fate was making fun of him. People said: "Pukhov is even capable of re-educating criminals." Only with his own son he could do nothing. Volodya never disagreed; he only looked at him mockingly through narrowed eyes, and Andrey knew the boy was laughing at him.

After finishing at the Art School, Volodya painted a big canvas called "The Feast at the Kolkhoz." [1] It was greatly praised. He was given a studio in Moscow; he sent some money to his mother and wrote that he intended to get married. The girl threw him over for a movie producer. Volodya was offended. He was equally offended when the jury rejected his picture, "A Meeting in a Workshop." His nerves got the better of him. Unexpectedly even to himself, he lost his temper at an artists' meeting and verbally thrashed the venerable masters, laureates twice and thrice over. Then it was discovered that he had been assigned the studio by mistake; that it was required for an artist who had recently been made a laureate. At the same time his commission to paint the portrait of the distinguished steel worker was inexplicably cancelled. Volodya realised that he had said the wrong things. He set about retrieving his position. He lavished praise upon the artists he had insulted; he ran down his own work, calling himself a boor and a bad comrade, and finally announced curtly that he was leaving for the provinces to gain experience of daily life at an industrial plant.

Thus, after his long absence, he was again at home. Of his failure he had said nothing. On the contrary, he made his mother happy by telling her he had been sent on a creative assignment and that his whole being was full of a great work upon a "shock" theme.

Six months later, the editor of the local newspaper, looking at

---

[1] Collective farm.

Volodya's painting of two workers reading a newspaper, was filled with admiration: "Immensely talented! Look at the expression in those eyes! We must have a feature on it!" It was said that Pukhov's name would be put forward for a Stalin prize. His mother congratulated him on his success. He shrugged his shoulders. "You like it? I think it's trash. Not that they do better than that in Moscow. On the whole I prefer not to think about it."

Nadezhda confided to her husband: "That girl Volodya meant to marry must be terribly stuck-up. You know how easily he is influenced . . . Do you like his painting?" Andrey replied unwillingly: "It's the way he thinks that I don't like. Yesterday I heard him arguing with Sonya about some book or other. Sonya said there weren't any ideas in it; Volodya told her a writer wasn't paid to have ideas. 'All that happens to you with ideas is that you break your neck. What you're meant to look for in a book is ideology. If it's there, what more d'you want? It's lunatics that have ideas.' You know you're wrong in saying he is influenced; he's much more likely to corrupt others. Even as a boy he was the same. It's that frightful cynicism . . ." Andrey's voice shook and Nadezhda became alarmed: "You mustn't get excited."

Nadezhda thought Andrey, as always, misjudged Volodya. He was always taking Sonya's side. She could not realise that though, indeed, he worshipped Sonya he now felt painfully estranged from her. He thought it was his own fault—it must be that he no longer understood young people, that he wanted her to be the same as he had been at her age. It was well known that fathers never understood their children. "Volodya I have the right to judge. He's a careerist. There must be many people of his own age who disapprove of him. But what can I blame Sonya for?— Nothing. If occasionally we misunderstand each other it must be because I talk the language of the past. The only thing that's strange is that I don't feel this barrier with my pupils, or with Savchenko, or with Lena. Perhaps the more you love people the harder it is to understand them."

Sonya was exceedingly reserved. She hardly ever showed any

enthusiasm and she never opened her heart to anyone. Her parents knew, of course, that she was not indifferent to Savchenko, a young engineer who often came to see her, but when Nadezhda tried to talk to her about him she answered quietly: "He's nice, but you mustn't think . . . He's only an acquaintance." Several times, her mother had invited Savchenko to dinner—once on Sonya's birthday, once to celebrate Volodya's homecoming. Sonya treated him the same as all her other guests. Only when she was alone with him did she change: her face softened, her eyes grew warmer. One day last autumn they went together for a walk in the country. All around them the September woods were full of sad and brilliant colours. Sonya stopped to pick some gold-leaved branches; then they walked on in silence. All at once Savchenko took her in his arms. For a moment she lost her head and kissed him. Then she was herself again, hurrying back to the path. That evening she said to him: "We'll have to wait. I'll know in February where I'll be sent to . . . Not much good getting engaged if we're to be in different places . . . Or perhaps you'd like me to be a kitchen wife! Anyway, you couldn't get an apartment. Zhuravlyov would never give you one; you haven't been here long enough." Savchenko went away upset—why was she so sensible? He was not to know that after he had gone she threw herself face down on her bed and cried. "Was I very stupid? I must have been. But you have to think about the future! Usually the man is practical. But he's a boy, so it's I who have to talk about these things. Can't he understand I hate to do it! He doesn't understand a thing, but I can't do without him."

Was she as coldly logical as her father and Savchenko thought, or did she only try to look as if she were, believing that anything else had to be written off as "nonsense," "idealism," "quixotic foolishness"? She loved literature but she studied engineering—her father could not make her out. She told him: "It's more useful. It will make it easier for me to get an interesting job." Once she had started on her course, she became genuinely enthusiastic about electro-technics, but she went on saying: "This is what is called for nowadays." She liked poetry, particularly Bloch and Lermontov, but she told her father: "If there is any room for poetry at all, it can only be for Mayakovsky's." She helped her mother with the housework—she felt sorry for her. She was far more competent than Nadezhda; she always managed to get to the counter in a shop, however big the crowd, and knew how to stir up the manager of their apartment house. When her mother worried about her father's doing too much, she said: "He has to have an interest. It keeps him going." And listening to her father's stories about Misha's progress or Senya's chemistry, she thought: "How old I am compared to him!"

When she congratulated him on his birthday, Andrey smiled: "What is there to rejoice about? I've lived long and done little." Sonya laughed: "You seem very young to me."

Guests arrived for the birthday dinner. They were Volodya's friends, the artist Saburov and his wife, and an actress from the local theatre, Orlova, who was generally known as Tanechka. Nadezhda had naturally asked Savchenko but he said that he was speaking at the club and would drop in afterwards.

At dinner, Volodya gently pulled Saburov's leg. Saburov tried to hold his own, but he mumbled so that nobody could understand a word he said.

Volodya and Saburov had been friends at school but life had parted them. Volodya dreamed of fame, of money. He always knew which were the "shock" themes, what artists had been rewarded, and who had been told off. All this time Saburov diligently painted landscapes that were never shown. He seemed to care for nothing except his painting and his wife, Glasha, who was delicate and a cripple. Glasha was a proofreader and they lived mainly on her very small earnings. Needless to say, they lived badly. Judging from the way Saburov swallowed chunks of pasty that Nadezhda kept piling on his plate, he didn't often eat his fill. Glasha looked at him with adoring eyes. Since his marriage, he painted, in addition to landscapes, portraits of his wife. He made her ugly but gave her ugliness a charm. Volodya often told his parents that Saburov was talented—perhaps more talented than the rest of them—but that he had a screw loose: "Simply hasn't an idea of what is wanted at the present time. He'll never get anywhere."

He was making fun of Saburov now:

"Still trying to win over our era?"

Saburov mumbled heatedly about Raphael, colour sense, composition, until Nadezhda said: "Do eat, your pasty will get cold."

She had kept the champagne until the last, waiting for Savchenko. When he came in she stole a glance at Sonya, who was arguing about some play with Tanechka and did not so much as look up.

Pukhov asked how the meeting had gone off.

"I was surprised at Koroteyev," said Savchenko. "I've always thought he was intelligent and sensitive. Yet he spoke according to the book of rules. Have you read the novel?"

"I haven't," sighed Pukhov. "Haven't got round to it. They say it's good."

"I don't know if it's good or bad, but it stimulates you. There's an unhappy love affair; that's what Koroteyev couldn't stomach. It seems that private tragedy won't do in novels—'Why delve into emotions?' and so on. If it had been Brainin now, it wouldn't have surprised me, but I didn't expect it of Koroteyev."

Volodya grinned:

"He's clever. Why should he say what he really thinks?"

Andrey could not contain himself:

"Not everybody thinks the way you do. Koroteyev is an honest man. That doesn't seem to have occurred to you."

There was a moment of embarrassed silence—Andrey had spoken with unusual sharpness. Then Savchenko began again:

"I was sorry the speech I made at the meeting came before Koroteyev's, but there was a girl who answered him; she was very good. I think you are mistaken, Vladimir Andreyevich, everybody spoke quite openly. Perhaps you haven't been to these discussions recently, things have changed a good deal . . . This

32

novel touches on a raw spot—so often people do one thing in their private life but say something quite different. The public is longing for such books."

"It's the same with plays," Tanechka exclaimed. "Think of it, three new plays we've had, and every one a flop . . . There simply isn't a play worth acting . . . Art . . ."

"You are right," broke in Saburov. "It's high time we remembered there is such a thing as art. Say what you like, Volodya, I can't argue with you. But Raphael isn't colour photography."

Volodya answered lightly:

"Raphael wouldn't be admitted to the Artists' Union. We can't all be like you, painting masterpieces for the year 2000. Not that I'd bet on your masterpieces arousing much interest in the year 2000."

"Don't say that, Vladimir Andreyevich," murmured Glasha. "If you saw his latest landscape—it's quite extraordinary."

"All the same," insisted Savchenko, "I can't make Koroteyev out. I've been working with him close to a year. He's a real live person, you can feel it in his every word. Why did he attack Zubtsov?"

"I've read the novel," said Sonya, "and I quite agree with Koroteyev. It's not enough for a Soviet man to control nature. He has to control his own feelings as well. Zubtsov's love is somehow blind. A novel has to educate, not to confuse the reader . . ."

Savchenko overturned a glass in his excitement:

"It isn't blind, it's big. And you can't put everything neatly into pigeonholes . . ."

Nadezhda thought: "He's in love with her, all right. How cold she is. Whom does she take after? Not after Andrey or me . . ."

It may have been the wine—everybody suddenly talked at once, shouting one another down. Saburov was yelling something about "the force of colour." Tanechka had leapt up and was repeating: "Love is love, say what you like." Volodya, mimicking her, wrung his hands.

Andrey was standing by the window. Looking out at the snow

33

flooded with a white acid light, he thought: "I can't make Sonya out. Did she say it only to tease Savchenko? No, she talks like that when he isn't there. She must be right in her own way. Who am I to judge? I am too old."

Sonya, taking advantage of the noise, slipped away unnoticed to her room. She sat down on the bed without putting on the light. She felt she had to be alone, if only for a moment. She thought: "I've really lost my head. It's enough for him to look at me and I become unnatural. I can neither talk nor think. It's frightful! I must control myself. I must behave towards him as I do towards all the others, or he'll despise me. He insulted me again tonight, telling me you can't put everything into pigeon-holes. How stupid! If that's what he thinks of me he doesn't understand me in the least. I feel as much as other people do—I even feel too much. But I hate emotionalism, I really hate it."

Savchenko walked into the room. He could not see her but stretching out his hand he touched her shoulder. He took her in his arms and kissed her.

"You're mad. People might come in."

"When will you stop being so logical? If you love me . . ."

She got up, switched on the light, and looked at him furiously:

"Well, this shows I don't. And I'll tell you what, don't let's talk about it any more."

"Wait. I'll tell you . . ."

"You've told me quite enough. Now we must go back or they will notice . . . Father will be hurt—it's his day."

Soon the party broke up. Sonya did not once look at Savchenko and never said a word to him as he was leaving.

Savchenko walked home morosely, plastered with snow, remembering that he had hurried from the club to the Pukhovs', dreaming like a fool of happiness. "I'm twenty-five. My youth is finished. Koroteyev says I'm a romantic, I exaggerate, I let myself be swept away. He's right. It isn't possible to live like that. Perhaps he's altogether right? Why should love be so important? I've got an interesting job. Koroteyev trusts me. Ahead of me are

many tests; we live in an extraordinary time. Just imagine a
young man like me sighing over his unhappy love in the spring of
forty-one! And a little later defending Stalingrad! But perhaps
the one doesn't exclude the other? I remember Uncle Lenya coming home on leave. I followed him about asking how to work a
mortar and build pontoons; he showed me a girl's photo and said:
'Grisha, I've found my happiness.' And six months later he was
killed. How complicated it is to live . . . Here am I, thinking all
the time of Sonya; it's because of her that I remembered Uncle
Lenya. And now I can't even go to see her. Can she be in love
with someone else? She'd never say she was in love, she's much
too proud. I'm not, I'm ready to admit to anyone—I found my
happiness and now I've lost it."

Sonya told her mother the champagne had given her a headache. She would get up early and tidy the place, but now she
must go to bed.

She lay down without undressing and thought about Savchenko. "Clearly, I've lost my head. He has, too, I think . . .
But why is it we always end by quarrelling? Our characters are
too different. Love alone is not enough. How can you share your
life with somebody who doesn't understand you? I mustn't think
about him. He's good, straight, honest. That isn't the point, either:
I love him. But one has to subjugate one's feelings. He's right in
one thing; worst of all is to say one thing and do another. It
would be best if they sent me far away—to the Urals or to Siberia. Then the problem will vanish, I'm sure of it. But this is weakness. Let them keep me here and I'll still manage. This is like another examination—to see if I can control myself. Of course I can.
But how wretched it makes you feel."

Volodya said to Tanechka he would see her home. She lived
far away and they had missed the last bus. Volodya longed to
take a taxi but she said that she had had too much to drink; she
needed some fresh air. Volodya was annoyed—a pleasant pas-
time, walking in a snowstorm! Tanechka talked incessantly. She
had liked Volodya's father. He was kind and handsome—she

wasn't being funny, she meant handsome—distinguished. She hadn't understood a word Saburov said but she liked him, too. It was not a good idea to drink too much; afterwards you felt sad. She felt unhappy—that was clear as two and two—but she wouldn't think about it. It wasn't worth it.

Tanechka had kept a child's directness, though she was thirty-two and had spent nine years working in theatres in the provinces, among people who shied at nothing so violently as ingenuousness and sincerity. She worked conscientiously. She was considered gifted and had gradually made her way. Now she often played leading parts. But deep in her heart she was unhappy.

As a child she had thought of acting as a life of tragedy and splendour. You would expect what followed to have sobered her. She came to realise that she had no talent and that indeed talent was not often met with. Other people were content with craftsmanship. She saw intrigues, cliques, ham actors, little rooms in dirty hotels, light affairs, and a weight of misery. Tanechka had grown sad; her face was covered with little wrinkles (it's the grease-paint, she comforted herself). Outwardly she was resigned, but at the bottom of her heart there survived a dream: somewhere there must exist a bigger, better life, and Tanechka had simply lost her way.

Long ago—some seven years—she had decided to take poison when the actor Gromov, whom she adored, told her: "We ought to part. We're getting on each other's nerves." Gromov was her first real love; she looked upon him as her husband. Afterwards there had been others—Kolesnikov, Borodin, Petya. She learned to give herself without illusions and to part without much grief. Volodya she had accepted out of loneliness, without asking herself if she loved him. Besides, he had been so insistent—he had argued, pleaded.

He was nice to her, he teased her only moderately, and often cheered her up—he had a lightness that she lacked. When she complained she had no talent, there were no decent parts, and she was sick of everything, he distracted her with funny or malicious stories of famous actors he had known in Moscow. Sometimes his views on life annoyed her, but at others they made her laugh. He said that everybody did pot-boilers, that that was nothing to be surprised at; and that turnips were more necessary than art; but nobody ever thought of spelling turnip with a capital T and nobody made a drama out of forwarding the cause of turnips, they just planted them and served them. You had to live as best you could. And life contained a few good things—a ragged piece of sky seen through a window or a ship's siren heard at night.

They were used to each other. If Volodya stayed away Tanechka became upset; and Volodya told himself in surprise: "There's nothing to her, and yet I like her."

It was a long walk. The storm roared, Volodya raged, and Tanechka talked on.

"Tell me, what are Saburov's pictures like?"

"One house and two trees. Or two houses and one tree. He doesn't believe in any other kind."

"Why?"

"He says that's painting."

"And what do you say?"

"I say he's a schizophrenic. Nobody has ever bought a single sketch of his."

"I'll tell you why you say that. It's because your own pictures are pot-boilers. Oh yes, they are. He's not a schizophrenic, he's an artist, you can tell at once. I want to see his pictures. A house and two trees, that isn't at all funny, stop being so pretentious. And don't tell me I'm drunk. Of course I've had a lot to drink, but I'll say just the same tomorrow. You do paint pot-boilers. What d'you want with such a lot of money? Now Saburov . . ."

"Are you in love with him?"

"Don't be disgusting. But I envy Saburov's wife. He loves her."

"No, he paints her and she loves him. That's their division of labour. He must have somebody to praise him and he's found Glasha. She gazes at his masterpieces and squeaks: 'It's simply marvellous!' "

"That isn't a bit funny. It's touching. And it's a good thing she's ugly and lame . . . Now you could never love me . . ."

"Ah! Now we come to the point. Psychoanalysis and fortunes in the teacups at three a.m. By way of tea leaves, snow. The hero is an aging producer of pot-boilers. The heroine is an honest actress a little tattered by life."

Tanechka stopped and frowned at him: "You know, I'm sick of your affectation. If you can't talk like a human being, you'd better not talk at all."

They remained silent until they reached her house. Volodya wanted to come in but she banged the door.

She sat in her fur jacket without taking off her scarf. The snowflakes melted and ran down her face together with her tears. "That's the champagne," she told herself. "Saburov is a remarkable man. He must look down on me. I tell Volodya he does potboilers, and what do I do? Tripe! Only Volodya has even less excuse. I'm just an average actress, what they call a cog in the wheel, but he's somebody they discuss, they write about, they take seriously. Nobody knows he's empty, he has nothing inside his heart. That's why he laughs at everything. It wouldn't be a bit surprising if he hanged himself. And I can't help him—I'm empty, too. Glasha loves Saburov, but do I love Volodya? That's not love. We've just made a deal because it's too frightening to be alone. He doesn't love me either. How badly everything has turned out. When I was at the drama school I used to walk along the street and think: Just there, just round the corner, there is happiness . . . Time to go to sleep, there's a rehearsal early . . . They say drink makes you sleepy; with me it does the opposite. How can you sleep when you start thinking about everything . . . Try counting up to a thousand . . . All the same, Saburov is right, there is such a thing as art."

Volodya sat gloomily in his taxi. "When Tanechka drinks, she's insufferable. All the same, I like her—that's a fact. She must have known I didn't want to be alone tonight; that's why she didn't let me in. Beastly evening. Beastly arguments about art. Saburov is talented all right, but only a schizophrenic can paint and put away his paintings in a cupboard. Who's he painting for? Perhaps his cripple? Everybody's shouting about art and nobody cares a fig for it really, that's the sign of our time. No wonder Tanechka was impressed. In her heart she dreams of Art with a big A. Nice if she could fall in love with someone solid—a chemist or an agronomist—she needs desperately to be happy. Why did she have to go for me like that? I do pot-boilers; so does everybody else, though they don't all admit it. She thinks I'm fond of money. Well, you have to live, that's a fact. Those were terrible days in Moscow before I left . . . It's funny, if you have money you get invited out and entertained, and during that time nobody so much as looked at me. I was lucky to scramble out so soon. But was that a crime? Did I hurt anybody? If it were up to me, I'd show Saburov's things at once. He's very talented, but that's not the point. There isn't any justice, and I bet he also wants to live. Why did I say he was a schizophrenic? He's just an ordinary man, only as stubborn as a mule. Comic when Savchenko drank two glasses of champagne and fell on Saburov's neck. Savchenko is a blockhead. What can Sonya see in him? She isn't a fool. It's all right when Father talks about ideas—that's his right, he grew up in that sort of time—revolution, romanticism. But Savchenko is an ordinary engineer. His business is with machines, not with ideas. Why should he get up on a soap box? Idiot. Everybody trims his sails, manoeuvres, lies, only some are smarter at it, some less smart. I'm sure Savchenko must envy me—I don't clock in, I can get up when I feel like it, and when I sell a picture I make four times as much as he does in a month. He probably thinks I'm happy, but he's much happier than I am because he's much more stupid. I'm sick of everything. Incidentally, must get up on time —Zhuravlyov's last sitting. He's got a face like dirty cotton wool. I've made him a fine figure, though—leader of Soviet industry, chin up and a glance expressing an iron will. If the museum really takes it, as Maslov said, that's twenty thousand. Shall I buy a Pobyeda?[1] Nice to speed on the road, everything flickers past, you haven't time to notice anything. Not worth it, perhaps, better give half to Mother, she doesn't say she's short, Father keeps giving everything away. Zhuravlyov has a handsome wife, I see her painted by Tintoretto—red hair, pale skin, green eyes. But what's she really like? Probably swears when she goes to market and babbles rapturously to her friends: 'The Commission Stores have shoes from Paris.' Nuisance Saburov finished off the vodka; I could do with a drink now. At the hanging committee in Moscow Kryukov cursed the painters for being pessimistic and shouted: 'We must have optimism' and then took to drink and was taken off to the hospital . . . Why is there such a lot of snow? It makes you feel so wretched you don't want to go on living . . ."

Andrey Pukhov sat in his armchair, his eyes closed. He remembered Volodya's words with horror. "It's some kind of double talk! Addresses activists, demands significance in art, paints workers, and then calmly tells you everybody is a liar. No, I mustn't think about it. What a joy that Sonya is honest. Of course, I find it easier to understand Savchenko . . . But she is honest, that's what matters. One mustn't expect everybody to be the same—why should Sonya be like Savchenko? That's what I wish for sometimes, but that's bad, that's grousing at youth. I'm in a bad mood. Birthdays are nice when you're a child; now they frighten you. And then this wretched heart . . ."

He had told his wife he felt in splendid health; it had been a fine idea of hers to celebrate his birthday; the party had been wonderful . . . Now he must lie down.

Recently he had become afraid of night, as of a journey to a distant, enigmatic country. He felt worse when he lay down—he was troubled with palpitations, pains in his left arm, dizziness.

---

[1] Like the newer Volga, a medium-sized Soviet car.

I · The Thaw

He couldn't make himself comfortable and didn't like to turn for fear of waking his wife.

Pity to have lived to endure this, he thought. "It isn't death that's frightening, only this. And you forget. You want to do something and you find you can't." He was invaded by depression. It arose not from his mind but from his body; he felt like yawning loudly or crying out. Nadezhda was asleep and her even breathing made him feel still more afraid. There was a moment when he felt: "I'm dying. I mustn't make a noise. Nadya is asleep."

He forced himself to think of easy, simple things. Tomorrow he must see Seryozha's mother. No wonder she was having a hard time; as a typist she would earn less than six hundred roubles a month. But Seryozha was exceptionally gifted in mathematics; he must not leave school. Andrey had spoken to Nadezhda. They would try to help a little.

For some reason, the image of his wife as a young girl came into his mind. Her hair was like Seryozha's, even to the top-knot. She wore a soldier's coat. "Nadya was brave. When we were surrounded at Rostov, she begged for a rifle. How long ago was that? It's terrible how long a life can be; you look back on it and you can't believe it. And, after all, you remain unchanged, and you forget that your age is different. Nadya is still brave. She's only afraid for me. And I for her. How will she manage by herself? All our life we've been together."

Now the sound of Nadezhda's breathing roused a quiet sad tenderness in him. It occurred to him that he would like to live a little longer, even though he was ill and weak. The pain in his heart eased, it became the normal tedious pain to which he was accustomed. He realised with relief that he would probably fall asleep soon. Suddenly the world was cosy, and drowsing off, he thought: "I'm glad it isn't for tonight. It seems you always want to live. Right to the very last."

4

LENA DIDN'T FALL ASLEEP UNTIL
the early morning and woke up late; it was Sunday. She thought
at once: "I must tell him everything today. There mustn't be any
concealment; it isn't honest." But when she went into the study,
she found Volodya finishing the portrait. Ivan insisted on her seeing it.

"It's a good likeness. I'm stouter, really. But the expression is
exactly right, no doubt about it."

Pukhov smiled condescendingly:

"Your husband's features don't stand out, he's difficult to paint.
But I have tried to convey the inner man."

Lena said nothing and left the room. "Why did he say 'inner
man,'" she wondered, "with that little smile? . . . Strange that
Andrey Ivanovich should have such a son. Can there really be a
lot of people in the world who lie continually? Like me . . .

"I'll go and buy some honey; Shura loves it. I must get some
air; my head feels heavy; I can't concentrate. And it's so fine, in-
credible after such a night. When I come back the painter will be
gone . . . I'll say: 'I must tell you everything.'"

It was clear and frosty, with a pink sun as in a picture-book
and snowdrifts—so dazzling that it hurt your eyes. At other times
such weather made her happy, but now it weighed her down.
There was snow everywhere. "How far away the spring is," she
thought; "endless! And what will have become of me by the time
it comes?"

She did not manage to see Ivan alone. Khitrov came and they
announced that though it was a little late they would go hunting.
Snorting gaily, Ivan said: "Perhaps I'll bring a hare for dinner."

She felt relieved: "He'll come home late. I'll have to put it off until tomorrow . . . After all, I haven't yet decided anything. I don't know what I'll say . . ."

The following day there was a long committee meeting and she again put off the conversation.

Each morning, as soon as she woke up and heard her husband's little cough, she remembered everything and thought: "I must make up my mind. I can't continue in this state." Then she went to school, urged Misha Lebedkin to learn his lessons, argued with the education officer, read Nekrasov's poetry to her pupils, trying to convey the melancholy resonance of his words, and was herself carried away by it. After the last break there was usually a parents' meeting, or a seminar in Marxism-Leninism, or a meeting of the amateur theatrical group. So the days went by.

Ivan frowned: "Lena has no sense of measure. Is it possible to overload oneself to this extent?" At breakfast and in the evening he attempted to distract her—Brainin, famous for his absent-mindedness, had come to the office that morning wearing his wife's sweater and was terribly upset thinking he had lost a lot of weight: the sweater was much too big. Then his wife rushed in. They nearly died laughing . . . Ivan laughed loudly and without humour. Lena tried to smile.

"I am acting dishonestly," she told herself on the way home from school. "How can I go on living with a man whom I have ceased to love or even to respect? I should have told him long ago. But he'll never consent to give up Shura. There will be endless scenes. The child will suffer. I do not have the right to spoil her life. Then what am I to do?"

In January there were more snowstorms. The snowdrifts grew and as she picked her way between them she felt: "I can't bear this weight, I think another day of this and my heart won't stand it."

As soon as she came home she would go to Shura's room. If Shura were asleep or playing with her father, she would wander listlessly about the apartment. The rooms felt strange, as though

43

she hadn't lived in them. She looked round her in astonishment at the curtains she had sewn with so much care, at the knick-knacks she had collected, the armchair placed under the lamp, all this comfort which she had created and which now seemed hostile.

She assured herself that none of this had anything to do with Dmitry. She wasn't thinking of him. They had stopped seeing each other—what of that? In reality she was thinking of him ceaselessly. "That was the chair in which he sat as he told me how in Breslau they occupied the top floor of a house while the Germans were still below. That was when Lieutenant Babushkin was killed; he had been a pianist. Then we talked of music." Suddenly Dmitry had stood up and said in a low voice: "You are too young, Yelena Borisovna. It is difficult for you to understand . . . There are times when the heart is frozen, and all at once something stirs . . ."

Why did it all have to end so badly? It was her fault; it was she who had disturbed their friendship with something frightening and irreparable. He had stopped her just in time. But now she would never see him. And yet so little would be enough to save her: let him drop in for half an hour—let him talk of what he liked, say that it was cold outside or that there were no good novels—that would be enough so long as she could feel his presence . . . No, this was stupid and degrading. This was the way heroines in novels behaved in the old days; they had nothing else to do. She was a Soviet woman, she had a sense of dignity, she didn't need his charity. The problem was not Dmitry. If they met by accident in the street or at the club, she would smile and say a friendly word or two so that he shouldn't think she was offended. Her problem was her husband.

She refused to see any connection between her feeling for Koroteyev and what she felt about her married life. Had she not met him long after she had ceased to love Ivan? In reality, Ivan's nearness had become unbearable to her after that evening at the club when she realised that she loved Dmitry. Last summer she

44

had looked on Dmitry as her friend. Now she felt she had no friends and knew that if she left her husband nobody would understand or comfort her. And yet it was precisely now—since she had lost Dmitry—that she thought insistently of breaking with Ivan, telling herself that only making a clean breast of it to him would cleanse her of something dark and shameful. But every time she reached this point she thought of Shura and put it off. If only there were somebody with whom to talk it over!

She laughed angrily at herself. She was thirty and she could not make up her own mind; she wanted others to decide for her. "It's shameful. If somebody had told me on the day I joined the Komsomol that I would come to this, I would have been the first to say: 'Throw me out at once.' " And still she longed for somebody to confide in, somebody to ask whether she had the right to dispose of Shura's future.

It did occur to her to write to her mother: she had thought of it as early as last autumn. But she decided not to; she wouldn't say anything even if she went to see her parents. "Mother is wiser than I am—she knows people better—but she would never understand a thing like this. She would only be distressed at having such a daughter."

Lena's mother, Antonina Pavlovna Kalashnikova, was the chairman of the Red Way Kolkhoz. She was intelligent and masterful. She had married early. Her husband was a gentle, dreamy man who adored babying the children and spent his evenings carving little wooden animals. "What's that, a pig?" Antonina asked. He smiled shyly: "An elephant. For Lena . . ." He was always apologetic—if he carved toys, it was only for the children. And when Lena and her brother Seryozha grew up he tamed a flock of other children to whom he gave his beasts. Lena treated him as an equal and pestered the life out of him. When she was too naughty he whispered: "Don't, darling, I'll tell Mummy." From her early childhood she was accustomed to regard her mother as the real head of the family. She loved her passionately and jealously (she believed Seryozha to be her favourite), but was a little frightened of her.

Lena was quick at lessons and read voraciously. She would recite *The Demon* [1] to her father and tell him: "When I'm grown up I'm going to write books." Her mother's brother worked in a town, and after finishing the seven-year school, she was sent to him.

This was shortly before the war. Lena's father was called up at once; Seryozha went in forty-two. Antonina was left alone. She was elected chairman of the Kolkhoz. The times were hard—nothing but women and old people. There were no potatoes—the crop had failed. Some of it was frozen, some never sown. Antonina now revealed her gifts—she was excellent at managing, good at planning profitably, at encouraging and, if need be, at scolding people. She started bee-keeping in the Kolkhoz and, on the advice of an evacuee from Lithuania, induced the farmers to grow early vegetables for the town market long before the papers began urging it. The Red Way paid off its overdraft and became one of the best kolkhozes in the district. Antonina was mentioned in the newspapers. She was indifferent to fame and when she read the article she said: "What's interesting in that? . . . They'd do much better to write about our boys out there."

Great trials were in store for her. In the summer of forty-four Seryozha was killed near Minsk. Her husband was shell-shocked and came home an invalid, with shaking hands and head. He asked timidly: "Tonya, will you take me back like this?" She threw her arms around him and broke into loud sobs.

The only joy left to her was Lena. She was proud of her daughter and there was nobody who did not know that she had finished high school with distinction and gone on to college. The moment she came home on holiday, her mother would bake cheese-cakes, ask the neighbours in, and make her tell in detail about her studies, her fellow students, the plays she had been to see. Lena

---

[1] Poem by Lermontov.

joked and laughed and yet remained vaguely frightened of her mother.

After getting her degree she came to tell her parents about Ivan, but hesitated for two days—her mother might be angry; in the end she told her father. Antonina threw up her hands: "Lena darling, what a joy! Now I shall see my grandchildren. But why didn't you tell your mother?" It was decided that next winter she would spend two weeks with the newly-married couple.

Antonina did not take to Zhuravlyov. Naturally she didn't say a word of this, but Lena noticed from the way her mouth was narrowed to a thread. Ivan was on the contrary delighted with Antonina. "Your mother has a statesman's brain," he said to Lena, "no doubt about it." When she said good-bye her mother kissed Ivan but Lena felt that she did not approve of her choice.

In fact, she stayed away at the time of Shura's birth and waited until Lena brought the child to see her two years later. By then Lena was beginning to be disappointed in her husband and admitted it to Antonina: "I imagined he was different. Perhaps I always find things more attractive from a distance." Antonina shouted at her: "You put that nonsense straight out of your head. I've lived a lifetime with your father and I've never had such thoughts. Take hold of yourself. You've got a job—Shura. What else do you want?" Lena was furious with herself; what had possessed her to tell her mother? Her mother was a remarkable woman. If there were more like her, Communism would come very soon. But feelings she neither could nor wished to understand. She might be right—this was not the time for them . . .

Now Lena sighed: "It must be nice to have a mother you can confide in. Sonya Pukhov must tell hers everything. But how could I write to Mother that I wanted to get divorced? She'd say she brought me up to be a decent woman. As for Dmitry, I'd sooner die than tell her that."

One particularly troubled evening she finally decided to speak to Zhuravlyov. She even had her opening sentence—"Please hear me out calmly"—but she had no time to bring it out. Ivan's desk was heaped with files; he took a notebook out from under one of them and said smiling: "Look, that's Shura's portrait of a cat." Lena ran out of the room; she was afraid of bursting into tears.

Too wretched to sit at home, she decided to go to Vera Scherer's. She would tell her everything. Vera, who had been through such a lot, would help her.

5

IT WAS RARE FOR VERA TO HAVE visitors. Occasionally Chief Designer Sokolovsky would come to see her and sit shyly, with long silences between his words. Vera gave him tea with jam. Then a patient would call her out or Sokolovsky would get up in mid-sentence and say: "Forgive me, I must have tired you . . ." Every time after he left she asked herself: "Why does he come?" She considered him interesting and honest and at times surprised herself by thinking: "His ideas are just the same as mine"; but it troubled her that perhaps he came out of curiosity, just because she was unsociable, to observe "the hermit crab," as Yegorov called her. Or did he pity her because she was so much alone? That would be absurd; she was not a child. Or was he simply bored at home? She couldn't make it out. It was now three years since he had started calling, and the nurse who lived next door, talking to Nurse Barykhina, never spoke of him as anything but "the *fiancé*"; yet it never entered Vera's head that he could be in love with her . . .

Vera was forty-three and her blue-black hair was turning grey, but Sokolovsky was not alone in finding her attractive. She had the charm that years of hidden suffering give a woman who is no longer young; a faint, hardly noticeable smile softened the strain of her expression.

She was considered a good doctor. She understood her patients and knew how to comfort and put heart into them. Last winter, when two of the patients at the hospital made a scene, shouting that doctors, particularly doctors like Vera, should not be trusted, Engineer Yegorov came and held her hand and said repeatedly: "Oh, oh, oh, what a disgraceful business. Don't let it get you down. Everybody loves you." About that time she was sent a pot of cyclamen with a note pinned to it: "From a group of workers."

Yet, although she had been practising at the factory for seven years and everyone respected her, she had made no friends and, apart from Sokolovsky, only Lena ever came to see her.

Lena thought that her reserve must come from having lost the man she loved. It was true that before the war Vera had been constantly surrounded by people, and although this was due chiefly to her husband's character, she herself had not then shunned the world and had even allowed herself at times to be infected by his high spirits. Yet even he would sometimes wonder: "What makes you silent all the time?" She said, confused: "I don't know. I wish I weren't. Sometimes I think I was born a monster, like somebody with four fingers." He laughed and kissed her: "You a monster! Be as silent as you like. I don't need your words to understand you."

She had been reserved since childhood. Her father, a small-town dreamer, a buffoon who had spent his life at his shoemaker's last singing an absurd song about Mariette and her beads of jet, said about his daughter that an angel had sealed her lips with sealing wax. She suffered by her timidity and repeatedly promised herself to change, to make a friend in whom she would confide. But Katya or Fenya or Marusya, whom she tried to hero-worship, would turn out to be an ordinary little girl and she would enter in her diary: "There is too much lying everywhere. Or do I only think so because I'm morally a monster? It is all my fault. I have no right to be alive."

She left her native town to become a student. Those were years of change, of heart-searching, of turmoil, of lofty flights as well as tumbles into muddy depths. Other girls of her own age, early matured, married and divorced with equal ease. Vera was known as "touch me not"; her friends made fun of her. She was dreaming of a great love. There was already a strain, a bitterness in her expression, and at moments a look of anger came into her dark eyes.

Vasya, a fellow student, was attracted to her. (Only Vera called him Vasya, everybody else's name for him was Vaska.) [1] He had a round face, freckled even in mid-winter, and a jolly, ringing voice. He would wait for her by the entrance to the University and come to see her at the hostel. To Vera his insistent, tender words sounded like an accusation. She told herself: "I must be a monster. I can't go on being an exception. I must live like other people." She gave in to him, not because she fell in love but because she had resolved to force herself into acceptance. Perhaps in time they would have grown attached to one another, but Vasya was young and ignorant emotionally. He ruined everything by the childish words he spoke at a moment when Vera, lying with her head buried in her pillow, did not yet dare face what she had done. Straightening his hair before the mirror, Vasya said gaily: "Now let's go have some ice cream." Vera went through months of torment and resolved never to give herself again.

She broke her resolution four years later. At the age of twenty-seven she fell in love with Yastrebtsev, a geologist. They could not have been more different—it was hard to understand how they could live together. Yastrebtsev was noisy, talkative, expansive, quick to show his feelings. He swore roundly and

---

[1] She called him John; to everyone else he was Jack.

brought home a crowd of friends, with whom he argued half the night. Everything about him was astonishing to Vera, and everything delighted her. She told him: "I never thought such happiness could exist."

They were separated by the war. On the fourth day Yastrebtsev went to Kiev. Vera stayed and worked in an evacuee hospital in Moscow. Later she was sent to Krasnodar, which was at that time far behind the lines, and when the rear became the front she found herself in a medical battalion. An officer she met told her that he had seen Yastrebtsev on the first Belorussian front. Six months later she got additional news: he had been killed at Darnitsa. She went on hoping—there could have been a mistake. Not until V-day, rejoicing with the crowd that the sorrows of the war were over, did she finally understand that they would never meet again. The black sky streamed with crimson and yellow fires. Her tearless face expressed such torment that a doctor who was standing next to her said: "Go to bed. I'll give you something to make you sleep." She spoke to no one about her grief. Nor did she talk about her mother or her younger sister, whom the Germans had killed at Orsha. She worked calmly and was thought to be imperturbable. Nobody could guess that Army Doctor Scherer, when she was alone, asked herself in desperation: "What have I survived for?"

Suffering did not make her callous. Long ago, while she was still a student, she had asked the head surgeon if nothing could be done to help a patient who was in pain and was told that medicine wasn't magic: she must get the better of her nerves or she would never make a doctor. Many years had passed since then and Vera had learned self-control. The army hospital had been a cruel school: she had seen torn bodies, burned faces, the blind, and those who had been driven mad; every day people were dying on her hands. Yet even now she was tormented every time she saw that she was powerless. Examining Yegorov's wife and realising that this kindly, cheerful soul would soon be faced with pain and death, knowing that Kudryavtsev's boy was doomed and that nothing could save Pukhov, she felt hemmed in, crowded, stifled by other people's sufferings.

The day Lena decided to confide in her she came back from the hospital after watching the accountant Fedoseyev die. He had had pneumonia, had been given penicillin and was off the danger list—he had told his wife she could expect him home the following week—when he was suddenly killed by an embolism.

Vera was moving restlessly about her room when the doorbell rang. She thought it must be Sokolovsky. Usually she was both annoyed and glad to see him, but now she thought with irritation: "Today of all days."

Lena came in.

Vera forced herself to be pleasant. She knew that Lena was as easily embarrassed as a child and that it was easy to hurt her feelings.

"How lovely, Lena. It's ages since I've seen you. Tell me your news."

Lena began telling her at once that the headmaster had no sense. The literature program was badly planned; a lot of it was over the children's heads. The seventh grade was very difficult; naturally there were loafers but that was not the point. Pukhov had had an individual approach to every child. She was no good at it and the headmaster applied the same yardstick to everyone. She spoke too fast, on a single note, as if reciting something she had learned by heart, and suddenly broke off.

Watching her, Vera felt disturbed—she looked ill, her eyes were brilliant, her cheeks flushed.

"You haven't caught a chill, Lena? There's a lot of flu around."

Lena got up and hurried to the door. "No, no, I'm quite all right. Forgive me—it quite slipped my mind, we've got a meeting . . . As it happens, about the seventh grade. I'm so sorry, please don't be annoyed, I really must have lost my head . . ."

She was already in the lobby. Her voice was tearful.

Vera shouted: "Lena darling, wait!"

Barykhina called from the landing: "It's no good. She's gone."

"How could I have let her go," Vera reproached herself. "All this time there has been something wrong with her. Has she quarrelled with her husband? She's very honest. She takes things to heart—like the time last winter when I got to know her. And Zhuravlyov is a real bureaucrat. She doesn't ever talk about him but it can't be easy. Or perhaps she's having difficulties at school. The headmaster made a bad impression on me, too. He's a Chekhov character—the man in the glass case. Poor girl . . . There I go, criticising others when it looks as if I'm in a shell myself—I seem to have turned to stone. How is it I couldn't make her talk, I didn't comfort her? I should never have let her go in such a state."

She picked up a medical journal, read a page, and realised she hadn't understood a word. It had not been a good day.

In her pale face, her dark eyes under the overhanging brows looked darker and the lines at either side of her fine-drawn mouth, which gave her an austere expression, stood out more sharply.

The doorbell rang again. This time it was Sokolovsky.

6

WHEN ZHURAVLYOV WAS APpointed director, his predecessor, Tarasevich, who was transferred to the Ministry, said as he described his staff: "Sokolovsky has a head on his shoulders; he's a good worker. He's got a sharp tongue as well, but don't take any notice of it. He is original." Zhuravlyov often recalled these words. He could not see anything original in Sokolovsky—he thought him merely impudent. He complained to Lena: "Sokolovsky asks me to keep Krapiva on, says his wife is ill, she's got some sort of functional disorder. I tell him Krapiva has been late four times, and it's no good being quixotic. You know what he said? 'Ivan Vasilyevich, have you really read *Don Quixote?* I'd never have believed it.' Just like that. In front of everybody. He's insolent enough, no doubt about it." He would have got rid of Sokolovsky long ago but he knew that at the Ministry he was considered a good designer—somebody was sure to take his side, and Zhuravlyov detested trouble.

Sokolovsky's colleagues, like his former chief, thought him an eccentric. Even his looks were odd. He was tall almost to excess, with grey, close-cropped hair, blue eyes in a copper-coloured face that even in winter looked as if he were just back from the South, and a scar across one cheek. A short pipe, its stem half bitten through, was always stuck between his teeth, though he smoked little and only when he was at home. He worked in silence. Listening to Brainin arguing with Yegorov as to whether the Americans would succeed in taming Churchill, he said nothing. He drank vodka and he still said nothing. It is true that nobody tried particularly hard to make him talk—his crotchetiness was well known.

People who had worked with him for years knew hardly anything about his background. It was thought that he was from the North. His father was a fisherman. He had got his scar in the civil war. He seemed to be fond of music and of astronomy. He had a family, but his wife had been unable to stand him and had run away. He kept a small, nasty-tempered dog. He was to have received a prize but his invention was pirated. Only one thing was known for certain—his last job had been in the Urals. There he had quarrelled with his chief, who had then blackened his name. There had even been a newspaper article headed "A Falcon Without Plumage"[1] which described him as an ignoramus making himself out to be a sage. The affair had taken a long time to straighten itself out in Moscow and in the end he had been transferred.

---

[1] This is a play on Sokolovsky's name: *sokol* means falcon.

I · The Thaw

Among his oddities—and he had many—perhaps the strangest was his habit of occasionally drinking vodka with Volodya and even condescending to make conversation with him. There was nothing strange in Volodya's appreciating Sokolovsky's company: he believed that after Moscow he had got into a jungle where hardly anybody else had an enlightened outlook. Sokolovsky's mocking comments delighted him and he thought that he looked down on everything, as he did himself. But Sokolovsky not only saw what was bad around him; sometimes he was pleased and even filled with admiration. At such moments he blinked his bright blue eyes and puffed fiercely at his unlit pipe. But of such things he said nothing in the belief that the good was seen by everyone, whereas about what was bad there was almost a conspiracy of blindness. And how much rottenness there still was! That was why he liked to "have a try at it" and it was this that so endeared him to Volodya. But how could Sokolovsky like Volodya, when even Tanechka in her ingenuousness had seen through him?

Volodya was unlike himself in Sokolovsky's presence. When he was talking to his father, he denied ideals. With Tanechka he mocked at love; with Saburov he made fun of art. But neither his parents nor Tanechka nor his Moscow friends had ever seen him in that mood of diffidence and meekness which came over him with Sokolovsky, who was moved by his inward restlessness and discontent. When Sokolovsky asked to see his paintings, Volodya answered in confusion: "I wouldn't show them to you for anything—they're hack work. Perhaps one day I may yet succeed in doing something real." Only once did Sokolovsky lose his temper with him. It was when Volodya asked: "Is Zhuravlyov any worse than Brainin or Yegorov?" Sokolovsky shouted at him: "You're not twenty, Vladimir Andreyevich. Is it your ambition to be a cynic? I'll tell you straight, that's a terrible thing to be. In ancient times the cynics looked down on worldly goods and wandered from place to place telling people unwelcome truths. But I'm afraid it isn't worldly goods that you despise but, on the

55

contrary, the people who are willing to do without them."
Volodya blushed, thought a little, and then admitted that he
sometimes talked a lot of nonsense for the sake of being clever—
it was true that Brainin and Yegorov were honest men. Sokolovsky grunted: "All right, drink your vodka."

Pukhov had every chance of testing the truth of Sokolovsky's
rumoured eccentricities. The mongrel, Fomka, was indeed revolting. Not only did it tear a hole in Pukhov's new trousers, but it
bit him painfully, so that he limped for a whole week. Sokolovsky
grinned: "He tried it twice on me." Volodya ventured: "That's a
curious character, your little dog. They don't usually turn against
their own people." Sokolovsky said that he had found Fomka in
the street and did not know what sort of life he had had before:
"Must have been rotten, to turn him into such a fool. He's a good
dog really. He's devoted to me, a splendid watchdog. Only now
and then he gets a black-out—doesn't know whom he is protect-
ing against whom. That happens to human beings, too—quite
often. People mean to help, and turn against their own . . ."

It was also true that Sokolovsky cared for music. One evening
when Volodya called he found him sitting by the radio set, too
engrossed even to greet him. He was listening to Shostakovich's
Tenth Symphony. When the broadcast ended he remained silent.
Finally he said: "Fine piece—mathematical, limitless," and said
no other word that evening.

Volodya found the most unexpected books lying on his table—
a fat astronomical atlas, a history of India, *Problems of Crystal-
lography*, Petrarch's poems. "When does he have time to read all
that?" he wondered; "and why does he? Must be bored. Like
me . . ." What finally staggered him was that Sokolovsky was
learning English: "At my school German was the foreign language. Feel like reading a few things in the original . . ."

Brainin, who never missed an article on international affairs
and who adored arguing about diplomacy, once came up to
Sokolovsky (he could see nobody more suitable in the clubroom
at that moment): "Do you think these Franco-American differ-

ences have any real basis, so to speak?" Sokolovsky smiled: "You know best, you're the specialist on international affairs. The French have a saying: 'If youth but knew, if age but could.' It seems to me the Americans could but won't and the French would but can't." Brainin could make nothing of it, but to be on the safe side he laughed.

There were times when Sokolovsky spoke out first, not waiting to be asked. That was when he boiled with indignation at botched work, disorder, or a heartless attitude towards people, and then he didn't care who heard him—Brainin, young Pukhov, Zhuravlyov, the workmen. Then he cursed the union organiser— why hadn't he raised the question of the canteen, it was in a disgusting state; or Zhuravlyov—the tenements would tumble down at any moment; or Dobzhinsky, the club manager—why was there never a concert or a decent lecture? Whenever you dropped in, it was either Brainin making a report and everybody snoring, or three wretched couples dancing to a squeaking record; or Lopushkin—why did he turn out such a mass of rejects, it made you blush to see them, and afterwards people blamed it wrongly on the design; or the journalists—what did they mean by writing up the factory as if it were a paradise? Zhuravlyov would soon grow little wings. Such were the remarks that made most people a little frightened of him.

Lately for some reason his attacks had grown more rare, and Zhuravlyov reflected with satisfaction: "Sokolovsky's aging, he's cooling down." As he read his newspaper, Sokolovsky now quite often said: "That's right." Only recently Yegorov had complained to him of the director: "I told him Vasilyev was indispensable and that I wouldn't give up Namulyan. We need another staff unit now we're turning out conveyor belts—he knows that perfectly, but would he admit it? Said he wouldn't dream of putting in for it. We must reduce our staff, not expand it. What can you do with him?" Sokolovsky smiled: "My idea is he'll soon be fired." Yegorov brightened: "You've heard something?" Sokolovsky shook his head: "No, I haven't heard anything. But I feel it coming. I've read the last two resolutions twice—it's absolutely right, what they say about the footwear, the pots and pans. They mean people to live properly."[2] Yegorov looked bewildered: "What's the connection?"—"The one follows from the other," answered Sokolovsky and wouldn't add anything.

On the wall of Sokolovsky's room there hung the photograph of a pretty girl. Volodya was intrigued by it but never dared to question Sokolovsky. In fact, only Clava, who cleaned his room, had been told by Sokolovsky: "That's my daughter. Twenty-two years I haven't seen her."

In 1928 Sokolovsky had married a pretty blonde called Maya, a student at the faculty of literature. He had been captivated by her melancholy looks and her pensive shyness. Was she really as he believed her to be, or had he embellished her in his imagination? He was working at a Moscow factory. The times were hard; he had no leisure. It escaped his notice that the timid dreamer had turned into a vain, shrill woman. "Bored?" he repeated after her in astonishment. "Why don't you work?" Maya sobbed in answer. They had a daughter, Masha, and Sokolovsky thought their life would right itself, but Maya didn't change. Every night he listened to the same grievances—his friends were each more boring than the last and he was himself as dry as a stick. She had seen real life only once, in an American film given at a VOKS[3] party. She must leave the baby with its grandmother and go south; if not, her doctor said she would have a nervous breakdown. Back from Kislovodsk, she announced that, first, she was not yet well, though she had taken the baths—she had been through a dreadful tragedy. Second, they must be divorced at once or she would die or lose her reason. Third, she had met a most attractive man. At present he was in trade—he was buying furs—but he had been to college. He was a lawyer. He was not, of course, a Communist, but he was a sympathiser. He had a Belgian passport and lived in Brussels but was a Russian, so he had made inquiries, and she could get an exit visa and was leaving with him in a week. Masha they would, of course, take with them. He adored children; the little girl would get a good education. In general, it had turned out for the best for Maya, and for Masha, and for Sokolovsky. Sokolovsky asked her only to give him news of Masha. His wife was touched and kissed him, leaving two red streaks on his unshaven chin.

After she had left he realised that he had never loved her. He soon forgot her but he often thought of Masha. At first Maya regularly sent him picture postcards of Gothic castles and churches, informing him that the child was well. The last postcard came shortly before the war. Maya wrote that Masha was devoted to her stepfather, that she still knew Russian, that they called her Mary—it was prettier than Marie, that she was doing well at school, and that she could not add a postscript because she had gone to the movies with her governess. Sokolovsky said aloud: "Mary," and himself shuddered at the sadness in his voice.

For many years he received no more news and had no idea whether his wife and daughter were alive or dead. Then, three years before, an engineer who had been to Belgium with a delegation brought a letter. It was from Mary. She wrote that her mother had died, long before the war was over; that it had been terrible in Belgium—the Russians had saved everybody and she was proud to be a Russian. She had taken courses at the university but given them up for modern dancing. Everybody said that she was gifted. This form of dancing combined modern rhythm with the plastic beauty of ancient Greece. She hoped some day to come to Russia and show people her dances. The future was with the Soviet Union; she never missed a Russian film or a report on Russian life. She enclosed two photographs, one taken at the university, and the other a snapshot of her dressed in a Greek tunic at the dancing school. Sokolovsky crossly hid the dancer inside his desk, then long and tenderly puzzled over the other photograph. Afterwards he hung it on his wall and every time he looked at it was amazed: how extraordinary that this sweet-faced girl should be his daughter, that she should be called Mary, and that they should have nothing at all in common. He wrote back. A year later she sent him a hurried note: she was just rushing off to Paris; everything was wonderful. With that the correspondence ended.

After his unhappy marriage Sokolovsky lost all confidence in himself and whenever he was attracted to a woman he stopped seeing her. Growing more and more attached to solitude, he no longer dreamed of love or friendship. Thus he lived till he was over fifty, when one evening at the factory club he met a woman who disturbed his heart. He could not remember afterwards what he and Vera talked about that first time. It might have been of music, perhaps of Bach. A little later he met her in the street and asked her if he might call. So he started seeing her, the need growing in him ever sharper to watch the smile that softened her austere expression, to listen to her quiet voice, to feel her presence.

He slept badly—he would drop off at once, then he would awake in the early hours, unable either to go to sleep again or to get up. At such times he recalled his every meeting with her— their grateful, astonished joy at finding that so many of their tastes, judgments, inclinations were alike; their misunderstandings, her withdrawals, her coldness, her angry brows and gentle eyes, warm, enigmatic, like a stormy night at the end of summer. It took him a long time to realise how deeply he was attracted to her. Then one morning, waking before dawn, he told himself: "She is my love, my only love, come to me so late. All my life I have been dreaming of her, waiting for her. I'll never tell her that. I'll see her—tomorrow or in a week—and I'll sit silently, or talk of Zhuravlyov, or people on Mars, or Churchill, or the devil, of anything but that. My joy, my evening love, Vera, as I will dare to call you in my heart, how glad I am that I have lived to know you!"

He would not let himself see her often. He was afraid of boring her, and every time it was as if he inwardly prepared himself with joy and anguish, feeling that no burden was heavier than unspoken words. So he would come in and sit down, and then Vera would be called away to see a patient, and even if she was not he would soon get up—it was time to go and there would be more weeks of anguish, fever, waiting.

This time he saw at once that he had come at the wrong moment. Vera was distressed. He would never know the reason; he was powerless to comfort her.

She told him about Fedoseyev's death, about Kudryavtsev's little boy, who today seemed better—his mother was so pleased —but who wouldn't live. Of course, many new discoveries had been made in these last few years and yet . . . People believed in medicine, looked at you with hope, waiting to be saved; it was terrible to feel so helpless!

Sokolovsky said that men were only just beginning to learn to think. The splitting of the atom seemed a miracle, but to our children it would be as old and obvious as the fire-flint or the wheel. There was a steady forward movement, so there must be hope.

"That's true," said Vera, "but it's too abstract. I have to deal with living people. It's these people I want to save and can't. You told me last time you came that you were interested in astronomy. I thought afterwards—it must be comforting. Probably you'll take a look at us one of these days from Mars or Venus." She smiled. "That should give you peace of mind."

"How can you? It's just the opposite. If you think about infinity, or, if you like, about the greatest of all concepts, as we were taught at school, does that shorten or impoverish the present moment? To me, it seems to make it infinitely more significant— both that it will pass and that beyond it there is an infinity of other moments, epochs, worlds, lives."

Vera listened, but his words fell short of her. She remembered
Lena's restless eyes. "How could I have let her go? How difficult
it is to understand another human being, much more difficult
than to see the oceans on a distant planet. There's Sokolovsky
feeling he must help me. As though I were Lena . . . How depressing and unnecessary!"

"What a frost we're having," she said for no reason.

He nodded.

"According to the weather forecast, thirty-five degrees later tonight."

They both fell silent. Sokolovsky sat looking at Vera. He
couldn't take his eyes from her. He felt that there was something he must tell her and knew he wouldn't. His gaze troubled
her and her expression grew still more bleak.

He was almost on his feet to go when he began suddenly:

"The other day at the Botanical Gardens in Moscow I saw a
plant, an aloe—you know the kind, people have them in their
rooms, there's one at the club. I've read somewhere that they can
be used medicinally . . . Well, anyway, they told me it was a
Pioneer [4] who had brought it to them . . . When he found it he
took it home and put it in a pot too small for it; he hadn't any
other flowers and he didn't know how to look after them. He got
a book that said the aloe grows in desert places, so you must
hardly ever water it and you must only give it very poor soil.
Well, he liked his aloe and it annoyed him that he couldn't lavish
care on it; so he threw away the book, transplanted the aloe,
watered it, fertilised the soil—he treated it just as if it were an
orchid. And what do you think happened?—a miracle. The aloe
grew. It grew to such a size that he couldn't keep it in his room.
He had to take it to the Gardens, and they put it in the hot-house.
I can't think why it came into my mind just now . . . Please
don't be annoyed. I've bored you with all my talk . . . I very
much wanted to see you . . ."

---

[4] Pioneers: Communist Youth Organisation for children between
the ages of 11 and 16.

Vera turned away and said tonelessly:

"I don't believe it . . . about the plant, I mean. If it was used to the desert, such a change would kill it. Though actually I don't know anything about botany . . . Forgive me, I'm very tired. I've got a headache . . ."

He left hastily. Outside it was the kind of moonlit cold when your breath seems to turn to ice at once and birds, frozen in their flight, fall to the ground like stones. In deep sadness Sokolovsky paced the empty street flooded with useless light; his lips moved, puffing little clouds of steam. Was he saying anything, or did he only move his lips, quietly and sadly, without dreams or words?

7

AFTER THE LAST LESSON LENA found Andrey Pukhov in the staff room. Almost for the first time that month, she smiled with pleasure. Needless to say, she told him of her anxieties: the children in the seventh grade who lagged behind; Burkov, Chizhikov with whom she could do nothing—he cut school, he smoked and had fallen in with hooligans.

Pukhov comforted her. He advised her to see Misha's mother and said he would speak to Chizhikov himself: "I remember him —a provoking child, but not bad."

They left together. Lena said she would see him home; she wanted to stay with him and she wasn't in any hurry. She was always looking for excuses nowadays to be out till Zhuravlyov had had his dinner.

Many days had passed since she realised that she must leave her husband, yet nothing in her life had changed. She could decide on nothing. In despair she cursed herself for being a wet rag, a good-for-nothing. "And so I will be all my life. Shura will despise me more than anyone when she grows up."

Pukhov was telling her:

"I've got wonderful news. You remember Kostya—you taught him, he left last summer—not Punin, another Kostya, Chernishev, he was a red-head, a desperate character always in trouble, but he's a good boy, very gifted, reads a lot and thinks. His background is terrible—father killed in the war, mother took up with some scoundrel of a storekeeper who drinks. Kostya made an application to the Institute—though there wasn't any doubt they'd let him in, he's an honor student. Well, imagine, they turned him down—said they hadn't enough vacancies, he would have to wait until the entrance exam. The boy was in despair, and to add to everything the storekeeper threw him out. A real tragedy. I told him to work as though he'd been admitted, then I went to the director—but you know him, he listens, says yes to everything, and does nothing. I called on the Town Committee. They said it wasn't possible to do anything in the middle of the academic year. Why not? I said. Kostya has been following the course by correspondence; he won't need to catch up in anything. They said that in exceptional circumstances the Ministry can decide. The Ministry wrote that they saw no objection but the decision lay with the director. I go back to him, he looks at the letter, nods, says yes, it's a shame to see the boy go down the drain, but as the Ministry hasn't given any instructions, he has no right . . . Well, then, I got down to it and wrote straight to the Minister, told him I'd taught this boy, he was enormously gifted, it was an injustice that he hadn't been admitted, told him about the background . . . That was last year. And now, today, my wife brings me a letter—it's from the Deputy Minister to say they've given orders for Kostya to be admitted. Just imagine, Lena! Think what an accomplishment!"

Lena looked at him and smiled: he was an amazing person. She knew that he was very ill. Vera had told her there was nothing that could be done for him; he might last out until next year if he kept strictly to his diet—only he wouldn't. She said his illness caused him pain but he never said anything; he didn't want anyone to know. And now he was completely happy because Kostya had been admitted to the Institute. "Now I understand the people who made the Revolution," thought Lena. "If only I could learn from him. Just to walk next to him makes you feel a better person."

"I'm off to Kostya's now to tell him," said Pukhov. "A friend of his took him in, Sannikov, another of my old pupils. They've got a room in Lenin Street."

Lena was troubled. "It's a long way. Should you walk so far? Why not let me get him and bring him to you?"

"Why should you? I'll get there fine; might as well look in on Sannikov at the same time. Don't think of me as an invalid, I'll creak along! When I got that letter this morning I felt ten years younger, honestly. To tell you the truth, I didn't have much hope. I thought they'd just forward my letter to the Institute. That often happens. But you see, they've straightened it out themselves. It's a tremendous achievement!"

He stepped cautiously as though first feeling the ground with his feet, although his eyes were good. Now and then he stopped in front of a shop window and pretended to be looking at a dummy ham [1] or an ancient poster. "He finds it difficult to walk," Lena thought fearfully. She took his arm.

He laughed. "I tell you I'm young again—like Faust, walking arm-in-arm with a young woman."

He was in splendid spirits, laughing and making jokes, and his face did indeed look younger.

Going home after she left Pukhov, Lena went on thinking of him. Ordinarily as she neared her house, she began to fidget, glancing at her watch and wondering whether Zhuravlyov had yet gone out. Now she forgot that it was early and he would be in.

---

[1] In Russia, for reasons of hygiene, only imitation foodstuffs are displayed in shop windows.

Zhuravlyov was sitting in his armchair, the lamp-light on his newspaper. He nodded:

"Nice that you've come in. I was just thinking I'd have to dine alone again."

She stood stock-still, as if turned to stone, neither answering nor going through into the kitchen. He asked her in surprise:

"What's the matter?"

She sat down in a chair opposite to him and said calmly:

"Nothing . . . That is to say, I have to talk to you. It's a good thing I found you in. I have been meaning to say this for a long time, but I kept putting it off . . . We are no use to each other any more. Don't be angry . . . I am sure you feel the same way. I have been hesitating for a long time—because of Shura—but I see I mustn't any longer. Do you understand?"

Her voice broke but she mastered herself at once and went on quietly as before:

"This is terribly painful, you must believe me, but I have thought it all out. I can't go on. It would not be honest."

Zhuravlyov thought at first that Lena did not mean it. He considered her somewhat unbalanced and occasionally told himself she was hysterical. He tried to shout her down, but she said there was no sense in having a scene, they must understand each other, they should part as friends.

They dined in silence. Zhuravlyov said he would not go to his office, he would work at home on Brainin's project. Lena left him. He sat thinking over what had happened. The reason for it must be that Lena was in love with someone else. For weeks now she had hardly been at home. "Must have found somebody. Could it be young Pukhov? He has a familiar manner with her. A man like that in Moscow must have had a hundred tarts, no doubt about it. I'm too decent. I trust everybody. Just imagine how she must have been laughing at me."

Lena came home late. Ivan had waited up for her and met her with a probing glance; she turned away. "Must have come straight from him," he thought. He felt like calling her some filthy

name, but he held himself in check. She was right in one thing:
it would be stupid to make a scene. He said calmly, gently even:

"Lena, are you perhaps in love with someone else?"

She turned on him furiously:

"What's that got to do with you? It has no connection . . . I've
told you honestly I can't stay with you. I've tried to and I can't
. . . Not because of anybody else . . . It's with *you* that I can't
go on, do you understand?"

"Don't get excited. This is a serious matter. We'll talk it over
tomorrow. Otherwise we'll both start shouting and no good will
come of that."

Once again he spread his papers on the table and bending over
them tried to think what he would have to do. He no longer
doubted that Lena had a lover. "She's turned out to be a worthless flirt, there's no doubt about it. Still, I chose her myself, so
nobody's to blame. Actually, there isn't even anything to be surprised about—people are brought up badly, without firm principles. And then they find it's dull—the town is a long way off,
and there aren't many amusements even there. Khitrov's wife
manages all right. She's busy with her house and children. But
then she is a responsible woman, not an empty-headed flirt. I've
been unlucky . . . All the same, it would be silly to divorce. I
have a daughter. How can I leave her fatherless? I simply can't
conceive of such a misfortune . . ."

He got up and went into the room where Shura was asleep.
There he stood a long time looking at her, wiping with his
sleeve the perspiration off his baggy cheeks and breathing loudly,
plaintively. "They'll not take my daughter."

He lay awake all night and in the morning he said to Lena:

"Live as you like. I won't say anything. But we can't divorce.
We must think of Shura."

Lena said she thought of Shura all the time. Zhuravlyov could
come and see her, or she could bring her to him. Lena would
keep her job at school; she wouldn't leave the factory settlement; she would try to find a room nearby.

Zhuravlyov said nothing. He went to work, but all day long he could think of nothing but Lena's words. "She really must be off her head. She's frightened of being parted from *him*. The scandal of it! The director's wife moves into her lover's apartment. I'd be laughed out of town. And then they don't like things like that up in Moscow, not at all."

He tried to reason with her. "When I was a boy, people rushed to the registry as easily as to the post office—married one day, divorced the next. Now it's different. The law has changed. Nowadays that sort of thing is frowned on. People might say: How can such a person be a schoolteacher? Not to speak of myself and what I have to lose—I'm a Party member; I'm in charge of a big concern. Feelings or no feelings, you have to think of that as well."

Lena was silent.

She did not refer to it the following day. A week went by. Zhuravlyov calmed down a little: "Looks as if she's going to be reasonable. She's seen that there are certain standards . . ." He behaved considerately, asked no questions, and burdened her as little with his presence as he could. "Who knows, we might still get by. After all, nothing terrible has happened. I've got my job and I am trusted, no doubt about that. On the whole, I am not very interested in love affairs. I'm fond of Shura, and the child won't change towards me. It's a good thing that there will be no scandal. There must be many families where the same disgusting things go on and they don't wash their dirty linen in front of everyone. Koroteyev was quite right in attacking novelists—we are living in historical times. Decent people have no time for intrigues . . . Sensible of him to be a bachelor. These things can't happen to him. He's a sensible fellow altogether. His comments on Brainin's project were very much to the point. They took account of production specifications—though, of course, the whole thing will have to go to Moscow—let them do as they think best up there . . ."

68

I · The Thaw

Just as Zhuravlyov had quite recovered his peace of mind, Lena announced:

"I've found a room—it's only temporary, till the summer—at Fedorenko's. He is being sent on a further training course. On Sunday I'll tidy everything and then I'll go."

Zhuravlyov realised that she would not be moved from her decision. It would be silly to quarrel—things were hard enough without that—better not make complications . . . He said quietly:

"Do as you think best."

Lena moved on Monday. That evening when he came in, the house felt uninhabited, although everything was neatly in its place. He walked from room to room peering nervously at the familiar knick-knacks: "Strange, she's taken nothing. She was very fond of that wooden box. I brought it to her from Moscow. Yet she hasn't taken it . . ." In the dining room he came suddenly upon Shura's broken doll. Had they forgotten it? Or had Lena thrown it out?

He picked up the doll and he felt quite suddenly that he couldn't stand it. Another moment and he would cry. "It's bad, it's very bad the way it has worked out. And I thought Lena loved me. Last New Year, I said to Brainin: 'Let's drink to Lena. She's a wonderful wife.' You can never see into another heart, no doubt about it. But how dull the house is, and Shura isn't there. I'd like to go out somewhere and have a drink."

Grusha, the cleaning woman, brought in a tray with tea, salami, bread, and cheese. He quickly hid the doll. "Have to take myself in hand. Worse things can happen. Yegorov has lost his wife, but he's got his work. My life is in the factory. Sokolovsky can snarl; the fact remains it's me that Moscow trusts, not him. Anyway, his reputation is a little mouldy . . . Zaitsev said last autumn there was talk of transferring me to Moscow. Well, that wouldn't be so bad. After all, the factory is one of many units, while at the head office my experience could be used on an All-

Union scale. That is, of course, if Zaitsev didn't invent it. But why should he? . . . I wonder what the Ministry will say of Brainin's project?"

His thoughts steadied and when Grusha asked if she should clear the table he told her to leave the tea. "I'll be working late. I might get thirsty."

Lena settled down in her new room. She went to bed early and yet was almost late for school the following day. Hurrying into her clothes, she thought: "It was eleven when I went to sleep. Now it's eight, and I am still sleepy." She felt immeasurably tired, as though she had chopped wood all day or walked thirty miles.

"How did it happen? I can't understand. It dragged on and on and then suddenly out it comes. Left school with Pukhov, looked with him for Kostya's room, went home and never even thought of saying anything . . . How extraordinary!"

She walked fast, hurrying to be on time. All at once she smiled: she remembered how Koroteyev had said: "You're very young, it's hard for you to understand." She had aged since then and she had lost her happiness, but she had not surrendered. She had acted as her conscience told her to. She thought: "He doesn't love me—he may despise me even. He thinks I tried to foist my feelings on him. Well, let him. All the same, it was he who helped me. He lifted that heavy burden from me. The moment I think of him I feel better."

"Lena!"

Vera was waiting for her outside the school.

"I kept on worrying how you were. I came over twice but you were out. Well, you look more cheerful; I saw you walking along smiling. You must be feeling better!"

"I've got a new address, Vera Grigoryevna. I've moved to Fedorenko's, block G. I think you know them; his wife said she was your patient."

Vera understood at once. Her severe expression softened, be-

70

came gentle almost to the point of helplessness. She pressed Lena to stay with her until she found a permanent room.

"You'll be much more comfortable. It's a big room, we can divide it up, and it's near school. I know Fedorenko's wife. You'll never be happy leaving Shura with her; she agreed only because she wants the money. I've got a nice old woman next door to me, Nastya, Dr. Gorokhov's assistant. We'll arrange it with her; she'll look after Shura when you are out. I insist on it—we'll move you in tonight."

It was a cold February day but the sun was already a little warm, and as she came into the classroom, noisy like a poultry-yard, and saw the blackboard grey with chalk and the sunlight dancing on it, Lena thought: "It will soon be spring."

8

AFTER HIS EXCITEMENT OLD PU-khov had to stay in bed. He had had a heart attack during the night. He concealed it from Nadezhda, merely telling her that he was tired and would like to rest for a day or two. She called in Vera Scherer, then Gorokhov, urged her husband to take the drops the homoeopathist had prescribed, smothered him in blankets, and at intervals sighed loudly. Pukhov blamed himself; he should have made an effort and got up.

Volodya came and brought the news: Zhuravlyov's wife had left him. He told it laughing—well, wasn't it a funny story! Pukhov was so delighted that he missed Volodya's comments.

"That's a good thing," he told his wife. "I never did understand how she could live with him. I know her; I've worked with her for two years. She has a conscience, she puts her heart into what she does, and the children like her. I've often heard my little boys say: "Yelena Borisovna helped me." As for Zhuravlyov—he's a typical bureaucrat. Bitter tears are shed because of men like him, but what do they care? If ever one of them gets stamped out, a dozen new ones spring up, just like mushrooms after rain . . . It's very odd. I saw Lena recently, the day the letter about Kostya came, and she didn't tell me anything . . . You can't think how glad I am . . ."

Volodya went into Sonya's room; he asked her:

"Do you know Zhuravlyov's wife?"

"No. That is to say, she's been here several times to see Father, but I've never spoken to her. Do you?"

"A little. You know I painted him. I've seen the likes of her in Moscow. It's funny how Father idealises everybody. I expect he still remembers girls who went among the people or plunged into the Revolution—anyway, to hard labour. Now they go and marry movie producers, or generals; or a factory manager like this one. Father is in raptures because she's left him."

"Where did you get hold of that?"

"It's a fact—the latest local sensation. I should think there's not much to choose between them. Wouldn't you agree?"

"I tell you I don't know her. I hardly know him either. Opinions are divided about him. Savchenko, for instance, says he lacks initiative. Anyway, I'd take Father's word."

"So you are pleased?"

"Oh, stop pestering me. I've told you I don't know either of them. But if Father has a good opinion of her, so far as I'm concerned that means a lot. Only it's disgusting when people get divorced—talk, gossip, newspaper announcements, court decisions. In the old days it was probably natural; now it's shameful, somehow. After all, people aren't children when they get married. They can choose; they can think it over."

Volodya burst out laughing. "And have analyses made, and consult experts?"

"What's so funny in that? How did you find Father?"

"Better, I think. When I told him about the Zhuravlyovs, he positively leapt for joy."

"That's just what is so bad. He's killing himself. It turns out he walked three days running to Lenin Street—some first-year students' get-together. He went to talk to them. Isn't it awful! I know I used to tell Mother his nervous energy keeps him going, but now I see how right she was. We simply must get him to be sensible whatever the cost."

Volodya stopped smiling.

"I don't agree with you. Father is not like other people. Besides, he belongs to a different generation. Nowadays, a man overworks a little and before you know where you are he's had a stroke. Those old people are cut out of a different pattern. I often ask myself where they get their strength . . . Of course, it's frightening; I'm worried about Father, too. I laugh, so perhaps you think I'm not afraid. The trouble is you can't do anything—he's lived in his own way and he'll die in his own way, too."

Volodya went out. His mother dropped off to sleep (she had stayed awake all night worrying). Sonya looked in on her father; she found him reading. She decided to have a talk with him.

She had been getting ready for this conversation. She believed her mother was unable to persuade him because her only argument was his health; he only joked or said nothing, and an hour later he was off again to see his "protégés." It was sheer childishness. He was spending his remaining strength on a dozen schoolboys. He had twice been asked to write an article on his experiences as a teacher. He could have written it in bed or if that tired him he could dictate to Sonya. Honestly, that was more important than dragging himself to Lenin Street to chat with adolescents.

All of this Sonya, her voice shaking a little with nervousness, now told her father.

73

Pukhov listened attentively. There was a moment when she thought that he agreed with her. In reality, his whole being was filled with indignation. It was with an effort that he forced himself to listen to the end.

"What a stranger she is," he thought. "Chernishev, Sannikov, Savchenko, all of them understand me, so it can't be just a question of age. Nadya urges me to stay at home, too, but never would she say that it's absurd of me to go and see my boys. She knows it's necessary. After all, we've spent our life together. She hasn't any arguments. She's just frightened, and I, too, am frightened—for her, thinking of how alone she'll be. But Sonya's different. To her what I do seems childish, that's what she said: 'childishness.' She talks to me as if she were older than I am. I can't make it out."

"I can't understand you, Sonya," he said at last. "You say one thing is more important than another. How do you weigh them? Perhaps I ought to write an article. I often think of it; I've even made some notes. But does that mean I should neglect my boys? Try and understand it, they have no father; Chernishev virtually hasn't got a mother either. You stand firmly on your own feet today, but don't you remember how you used to run to me for advice? Don't you see, these are living people, tomorrow they will go on building what we began. And you suggest that I should abandon them?"

"I'm not denying it's a serious problem. But what can you do alone? These are questions that should be solved on a State-wide scale; if not, it becomes amateurish. Say you help Chernishev today. Tomorrow you won't be there and he'll fall under the influence of some bandit. I mentioned the article because that's really necessary. You told me, for instance, that you have some arguments against segregation.[2] I've read about it in *Litgazeta*—there's a discussion going on. If you state your point of view, that

---

[2] Segregation of the sexes in education: co-education has recently been re-introduced in Soviet schools after much discussion in the press.

can lead to something practical, and not just for a dozen boys—
for a dozen million. And instead of that you put your remaining
strength into arguing with Seryozha's mother, or discussing
physics with Misha. Honestly, it's senseless."

"No, Sonya, it does make sense. The community is made up of
living people. You won't get anywhere with just arithmetic. It
isn't enough to think out wise measures; they have to be applied
and for that everyone is answerable. You can't reduce everything
to a committee formula—'This has been approved; that has
been resolved.' It's on the way you live and work, on your relations with other people that the whole future of society depends.
Why do you say ironically: what can a man do alone? I can't
make you out. Years ago, six or seven years before the Revolution, I remember I used to go to see a student, a friend of mine.
There was a group of us who read Lenin, Plekhanov. I told my
father. He was a quiet, almost timid man—he worked in an office,
he was used to reprimands—he asked me: 'How many are you?
Eight? You're crazy! What can you possibly do with eight people?' That was an old man. In him it was forgivable; and the
times were different. But you're young, you're in the Komsomol,
you should be daring, not evading things. I know you have a
great spirit. Why do you put chains on it?"

He looked at her and broke off: her eyes were shining feverishly, her lips moved—she wanted to reply but could find no
words—there was such confusion in her that he forgot about the
argument and took her in his arms.

"You aren't a bit like that really."

She left him troubled. He had not convinced, only disturbed
her; she felt his words carried a remote, even enigmatic power.

"How difficult it is to live, how very difficult!"

She picked up a book and forced herself to read. Gradually the
light faded—everything in the room was grey. She went over
to the window. The snow looked purple. She thought:

"Father thinks I'm so sure of myself. He said: 'You stand firmly
on your own feet today.' In reality I keep on stumbling. I see

75

nothing, it's like twilight, neither night nor day. Everything is puzzling. It must be nice if you can laugh things off, like Volodya. Though I don't envy him; I think he feels lost . . . Zhuravlyov's wife has an attractive face. Why has she left her husband? In the old days it was understandable: people were married off against their will, or they married for convenience. Now it's all quite different and yet people still divorce . . . It's frightening that you can never read another person's mind. You walk in darkness, you think happiness is in front of you, and yet one more step and there's a precipice. What a terrifying game! Like with Savchenko and myself . . . That's another thing Father doesn't understand; he always takes Savchenko's part. It's natural in a way—they are very much alike. Though when Father gets excited and exaggerates you can't help feeling respect for him; after all, he's proved by his whole life that what he says isn't just empty words. But when Savchenko does it, it's comical—he hasn't lived yet. I haven't either, I don't understand a thing. Father seems to be convinced I love Savchenko. The other day he said: 'When the two of you have settled things.' Of course I love him. I expect it shows however much I hide it. But we'll never settle anything; I'm convinced of it. I think of him too often. It's silly and pointless . . ."

She switched on the light and finished reading the article she had begun on the latest generators for Kuibishev (real giants!). The bell rang. She remembered her mother was asleep and went to open the door. It was Savchenko, the last person she had been expecting.

They hadn't seen each other since her father's birthday. The first few days Sonya had waited for him. Every evening she had listened for the bell. Of course, he had been very rude to her and their friendship would never come to anything. All the same, it was absurd to end it in a quarrel . . . But Savchenko had stayed away.

He stuck it for a month, though he found it difficult. Every evening he started out to the Pukhovs' and turned back when he reached the chemist's at the corner. For some reason it was always outside the chemist's that he invariably asked himself: "What am I going for? She told me plainly she doesn't care for me. She doesn't even want to talk about it. And a simple friendship, that I can't accept even if I wanted to, better not try . . ."

He would go home or to the club, or he dropped in on Koroteyev, who was his neighbour.

At the beginning, when Savchenko was sent over from his Institute, Koroteyev took him under his wing, showing him his work and generally putting heart into him. "It's always difficult at first. Theory is one thing and the potentialities of a factory are another." One evening he asked Savchenko to his room. "Let's sit up a little while over Brainin's project. He's altered it." When they finished working, Koroteyev told Savchenko about the factory in Leningrad where he had had his practical training. They sat up almost until dawn and as Savchenko took his leave Koroteyev said: "Drop in again. I never go to bed early. We might talk of other things besides machines." After he had gone, Koroteyev smiled: "That's a good boy. I was older at his age. Then there was the war . . . Now it's different. He still looks unfledged."

When Savchenko came again, he told him about the war, about the battle on the Don in which a poet lost his life—he was a boy affectionately known as Pushkin who had recited verses starting with the line: "When I remember you in my old age"— about a small museum in a devastated German town where among the antlers, the stuffed birds, the Nazi banners, he had seen a remarkable portrait of a young woman by an unknown master of the sixteenth century; and about his own youth. Sometimes they discussed the news, Mossadegh's trial, the strikes in France, the Conference of the Foreign Ministers, or some recently published book. Savchenko listened to his friend entranced, forgetting his unhappy love. He was easily entranced. When he laughed he threw back his head and showed big white

77

teeth sparkling in his swarthy face. He looked rather like a gypsy,
and said laughingly: "Granny must have visited the gypsy camp.
She was full of mischief, Grandfather used to say."

Last night they had talked of literature. Savchenko had asked
suddenly: "Why did you make such an attack on Zubtsov that
time at the club?" Koroteyev grinned and didn't answer. Later, he
took down a book. "Do you like poetry?" Savchenko's face lit up:
"Better than anything, I think." Koroteyev read aloud:

"They parted in proud and silent sorrow
And saw the image of their love only in dreams.
Then death came, and beyond it, the encounter,
And in that world, each turned unrecognised away."

Savchenko was delighted. Then all at once his face dimmed as
though a candle had been put out, and his smile vanished: he
thought of Sonya. "We meet and talk, but she treats me like a
stranger . . . And yet, that day we were in the woods, I
thought she loved me. She kissed me and looked at me in such a
way that even now, when I remember it, I want to run to her
and say: 'It's me, Sonya, it's me. Don't you know me?'"

He looked up at Koroteyev, who was sitting motionless, his
book lying on the floor. There was a long silence. Then Savchenko plucked up his courage:

"Dmitry Sergeyevich, do you think that if a man feels that he
loves a woman, he ought to fight for his happiness? It seems
humiliating . . ."

Koroteyev smiled almost imperceptibly:

"He has to fight . . . There are times when you have to tear
right through the fog."

Savchenko smiled again.

That was how he came to visit Sonya. He meant to tell her
everything, to tear his way out of the fog, to find his happiness.

"Let's go for a walk, Sonya. I want to talk to you about a lot
of things. I don't feel like being in here."

I · The Thaw

"It's cold outside. But if you want to, all right."

It was freezing hard again; the wind was from the north. People walked rapidly. Only Sonya and Savchenko dawdled; there was nowhere for them to hurry. From a distance they looked like a happy couple, but they were arguing the whole time. Savchenko spoke of Koroteyev, of the automatic drive, of the Berlin Conference, of an Italian film they had both seen at the club, and whatever he chanced to mention, Sonya contradicted him (only about the machines she made no comment).

"It's a wonderful film! When the little boy lost his temper with his father, I nearly cried."

"It's sentimental. Parts of it are good but there is no solution. I never did find out what that unemployed man would do in the end—would he join the Communists or remain politically unenlightened?"

They walked a hundred yards. Savchenko was enthusiastic about France:

"The French will never agree to ratification."

"Who are you talking about? The Communists or the Chamber of Deputies? You have to consider who holds the real power. You always let yourself get carried away."

"I am talking about the real power. Haven't you learned that when ideas reach the consciousness of millions they become a material force?"

"That's in the future. We are talking about what exists today."

They walked another hundred yards.

"Today Zhuravlyov cursed a machine operator for no reason. He said he was ham-handed. He's a real scoundrel."

"You're always exaggerating. Father says he's just an ordinary man, a bureaucrat."

"Koroteyev thinks so, too. But in my opinion he is a scoundrel. Now, since his wife has left him, he's gone completely off the rails. Have you heard about it?"

"I've heard, though I don't like gossip. I'm not interested in his private life."

"I am. I'd like to understand—what sort of a woman could have been in love with him. I asked Koroteyev today what he thought of Zhuravlyov's wife—he used to see quite a lot of them. But he didn't answer; he was in a hurry. I am convinced she is better than he is and that it's a good thing she left him."

"I don't see anything good in it."

"Even if he's a scoundrel?"

"She might have thought of that before."

"Didn't your brother do a portrait of Zhuravlyov?"

"I believe so. I haven't seen it."

"What made him paint such a scoundrel?"

"I don't know. I suppose he was commissioned. You'd better ask him."

"No, I won't ask him. I liked what Saburov said about art. I find your brother's opinions very strange. Do you think he meant it or was he putting it on?"

"I don't know. He is like you. You both live only by your impressions, only he sees everything in black and you in rose."

"And you?"

"I wasn't talking about myself. I see things as they are."

They had walked many times past the chemist's shop and back. Now Savchenko was talking about a book he had read lately and hadn't liked.

"It isn't realism at all. It's just degrading man."

Sonya had herself disliked the book, but she was cross.

"I don't find it so. I consider it an interesting novel that raises an important problem. But don't you think this literary discussion might be put off? It's too cold. I believe you meant to tell me something. If you don't, let's go home and have tea."

Savchenko was silent. They were near the red brick house. He told himself: "It's now or never. How idiotic to have lost the power of speech, just as though I'd lost it in the snow."

"I'll tell you, Sonya . . . Don't laugh at me, but there it is, without you I can't . . . Come fog, come snow, anything—I don't care . . ."

Sonya said nothing. He took her hand and touched her cold mouth with his lips. She whispered sadly:

"It's no good . . . There is an abyss between us. Such an abyss that it makes you giddy."

In another second she said in her normal voice:

"I've told you our characters are too different. Let's leave it . . . Are you coming in to tea with the family? Well, why don't you say anything? You don't want to?"

Savchenko said angrily:

"You haven't told me yet that two and two make four, and that money should be kept in a savings bank."

Later, Sonya's mother called her:

"Sonya, come and have your supper. Your father said Savchenko was here. Why didn't you keep him?"

"He had a meeting. I walked along with him a little way. I've got a headache, Mother. I won't have any supper."

She locked herself in her room. She felt bitter—hadn't she just rejected happiness? If she told her father, he would say: "You must be mad, you love each other, why torture yourselves?" "I can't explain it to him but I am certain that we can't live together. It isn't just this quarrel. How stupid he was about the savings bank; for that alone I ought to hate him. He's a schoolboy; by now he may be sorry he lost his temper. I see it very clearly —we could make up tomorrow or next month, but nothing could ever come if it. How can two people live together if they don't agree on anything? He thinks I am too practical, that I only believe in the multiplication table. That isn't true, but I do live on the earth, I don't know how to soar. The only thing that puzzles me is why we are so drawn to each other. He couldn't keep away this time; and I can't do without him either. He has just insulted me, yet if he came, would I have the strength to drive him out? What is this? When he kissed me outside the gate, I thought I'd cry or throw myself into his arms. Father says I've chained my heart. How I'd like to go to him and say: 'You were right. I should not have spoken as I did. And you were right about me, too . . . Such dreadful chains, they stop my heart from beating, it's destroying me . . .'"

9

VOLODYA HAD BEEN IN A BAD mood all these weeks. He kept away from Sokolovsky and, meeting Tanechka in the street, told her frankly: "Don't imagine that you've hurt my feelings—that's all nonsense—but I'm in a bad way. I don't feel like seeing anyone, not even you . . ."

"I wouldn't do you any good," she answered. "I feel bad myself. Our first night was a flop again, I've had a row with the producer, and I've got a toothache—I ought to go to the polyclinic. So on the whole I'm not exactly cheerful." Tanechka always suspected Volodya of making too much of things, but he had really meant to go and see her. Only each time he had changed his mind: he knew she was depressed and needed to be comforted, and in his present mood he felt he could do nothing but infect her with his own misery.

"Why on earth have I gone to pieces?" he asked himself. Sometimes he thought it was because he was far from Moscow, sometimes because he was short of money, and at times he merely sighed: "I'm getting old."

It was true that he had money difficulties. Zhuravlyov's portrait pleased no one except Zhuravlyov. A small hack job had turned up just in time—decorative panels for an agricultural exhibition featuring pedigree cows and hens. The cows were easy—he was supplied with good photographs, but the poultry gave him endless trouble—they were white and altogether different from the local breeds. Volodya was offered the chance to go to a State farm and paint from nature. He lost his temper: was he to travel fifty miles for some wretched hens? In the end he obtained appropriate magazine illustrations, finished the panels, and was paid 4,700 roubles.

But he still felt low and this confused him altogether. Evidently it could not be money after all. It was nice that he could give three thousand roubles to his mother, but he still felt miserable. Something horrible was happening to him. He hadn't been in such a state even when he lost his studio in Moscow— not even when Lyolya sprang on him the news of her engagement to Shaposhnikov. He had felt hurt: he had believed himself to be attracted to her. But that same evening he had gone with Misha to the Artists' Union. There he had met Schwartz's wife and at once started to flirt with her—he did not allow his depression to get the better of him. Now it was as if he had been knocked on the head—and yet nothing had really happened. Tanechka wasn't even cross with him. If he called on her she would welcome him as in the past. She had said: "When you're out of the dumps, come and see me"; but he didn't feel like going. He had told Sonya he was bored in this godforsaken hole, but if the truth were told, he wasn't pining for Moscow either. There you had to cater to other artists, watch who was on the way up and who was slipping, calculate and fight ceaselessly for your piece of the cake. He had done all that. He hadn't done it badly. But he didn't feel like going on just now. It was too early at thirty-four to feel too old, but he must have aged considerably. Here, nobody did him any harm. Locally he was the foremost artist; he had an intelligent companion—Sokolovsky; and there was Tanechka. His father was better, that was a good thing. He hadn't realised how attached he was to him. It must be admitted that he had teased him wilfully, that was silly. The old man's views were out of date, of course, but he was a remarkable old man, an exception—one shouldn't hurt him . . . What, finally, was the reason for Volodya's dejection? Perhaps it was due to

83

thinking. In Moscow he hadn't time. There he turned round and round like a mouse in a treadmill. Here he had a lot of time, and so, willy-nilly, he had started thinking. It had always seemed to him that only madmen could just think—not of anything in particular but of things in general—and now he was doing it himself. It was a revolting occupation.

Volodya made fewer jokes and his glance lost the provocative sparkle that had so exasperated his schoolteachers and only recently reduced Tanechka to tears. Now he spoke with a polite indifference. Once he found himself on a bus next to Savchenko; they talked together and Savchenko told him about Sokolovsky's new machines. Volodya didn't like machines but he noted that Savchenko wasn't such a fool as he had thought him. That evening he told his sister: "I ran into Savchenko, he was very interesting . . . On the whole, he seems intelligent." Sonya gave him a surprised look, then scowled: "I don't see why you have to report this to me."

On that cold night when Sonya and Savchenko were walking up and down the street, Volodya left the house without a notion of how to spend the evening. Catching sight of them, he grinned and crossed to the other side—no point in startling the young people. Where should he go? "Sokolovsky's sick of me. Last time I was there he wouldn't talk at all, just screwed up his face as if he'd swallowed a mouthful of vinegar. I wonder what he does, sitting all alone with Fomka. Probably they growl at each other . . . All the same, where am I to go? At the Volga Restaurant people on official missions will be sadly chewing cutlets and the drunks will be roaring and knocking back vodka laced with madeira. Not very interesting. And outside it's beastly cold."

Suddenly he remembered Saburov. Why not go to see him? He hadn't been there since his leave from Moscow in fifty-one, three years ago. "Might look at his masterpieces. Poor devil, probably lives disgustingly. Better get some food. Crazy he is, but he likes a drink and a snack, judging from the way he fell on Mother's cooking."

Volodya went into a shop, bought masses of food, vodka for Saburov and wine for Saburov's wife, and took a taxi to the other end of the town. The little street straggling down to the river was impassable. He got out and with difficulty found the small, crooked, pink house. It had once belonged to a merchant and was now shared by four families including the Saburovs.

Coming into the squalid little room, Volodya made a face— what the devil! He had known they could not be comfortable, but this was beyond anything he had imagined. At one time Saburov had had a room in the art-school building, but he had been turned out of it. Just before that, he had got married and a room was given to Glasha—the house was allocated for use as a publishing office. Two bunks, a stove with a saucepan on it, about a hundred canvases—all so tightly packed together that you couldn't turn round.

The visitor was offered the armchair that had lost its stuffing, from which Glasha swept a pile of cardboard, rags, newspapers, and chipped dishes. Saburov was as delighted as a child.

"Thanks, Volodya, for coming. It's a joy to both of us. Just imagine what a coincidence: it's the anniversary of our wedding —two years already. I'd hoped to make it an occasion. I said to Glasha: "Let's invite Pukhov," but it didn't work out that way . . . It's the end of the month. To tell you the truth, I don't seem to bring anything off. They said the theatre might take me on, but that was only talk. Well, anyway, all that isn't important . . . It's wonderful to see you. We'll have tea; Glasha has some jam . . . Just think, Glasha, he and I were at school together for ten years. And now he's come. It really is a piece of luck."

Volodya was smiling.

"Congratulations. We ought to celebrate. I've brought a little wine: let's drink to your happiness."

Glasha was flustered; there wasn't any bread. It was the only thing Volodya hadn't thought of bringing. She said she would run out for it—the State stores would still be open. After she had gone, Volodya said:

"You remember the time the Kamerny Theatre came and I had had a disagreement with Father. I didn't have a penny and I wanted to take Mira, so you lent me twenty roubles?"

Saburov laughed.

"You said there was enough left for a lemonade for Mira. You couldn't have one yourself. Pretty girl, she was. Do you know what happened to her?"

"Wait a bit, I meant to say something else. Now you haven't any money, that's a fact. Here's a thousand. It's all I have at the moment, but I have absolutely no use for it. You'll pay me back when they've made you an academician. I'm in no hurry. Take it, I tell you . . . Listen, if you don't look on me as a friend, I'll feel insulted."

Glasha came back. Saburov suggested they should eat at once, but Volodya asked to see his paintings. Saburov protested:

"What's the point? You probably won't like them. Let's drink instead, and talk about old times."

Volodya insisted. It was not so much that he was eager to see the pictures as that he thought Saburov was being modest and would secretly be hurt if he didn't see and praise them. Glasha backed him:

"Indeed he must show them to you, Vladimir Andreyevich. His latest landscapes and the portrait of me—the one in the green blouse—they're simply marvellous."

Volodya loved painting though he admitted it to no one, and though whenever conversation turned on art he was either silent or played the fool. A few years ago he had spent a week in Leningrad; every morning he hurried to the Hermitage to look his fill at the old masters. As soon as he came out of the museum he dropped back at once into his customary life—wondering where to rustle up a commission, how to get into the good graces of Blandov of the Art Department, and what present to buy for Lyolya.

He gazed silently at Saburov's landscapes, his expression neither mocking nor approving. Glasha looked in vain for some sign of what he felt about her husband's work. All he said was an occasional curt: "Wait, don't take that away" or "There's a reflection on it" or "Show me some more." Had Saburov improved a lot these last three years, or was Volodya in an unusually receptive mood? He felt crushed. He forgot everything else and it was useless for Saburov to protest: "That's enough, let's have supper."

Looking at great paintings in picture galleries, Volodya had the sense of joy and lightness he experienced when gazing lovingly at a tree in leaf or at the beauty of a woman's face. In his opinion art had once existed but had long since vanished. No wonder that in a museum there was always something a little dead—the cleanliness and the faint cold and the whispering of the visitors. He was profoundly shaken by Saburov's work: this, after all, was his contemporary, his schoolfellow. And what was so difficult to grasp, he had done that landscape in this slum room, sitting with his cripple, looking out of that small window. How simple it all was and how far beyond his understanding —the full tones, the depths of the dove-grey and blue sky, the clayey heaviness of the soil! Saburov showed him his latest portrait of his wife and again Volodya was overwhelmed. Glasha asked him if it was like her; he didn't answer. He only saw the painting—the ochre of the highlights in the hair, the olive-shadowed face, the green blouse. And gradually, just as in the landscape nature had revealed itself in its poverty and splendour —the melting snow, the blackness of the naked branches, and the light blueness of the sky—the miracle of the northern spring —so now he saw a woman in her ugliness and her beauty. A whole lifetime would not be too much to understand her timid, plain, unnoticeable smile.

Silently he sat down at the table. Silently he drank a glass of vodka, and only then remembered that he must say something. He rose and, with a solemnity which sat oddly on him, proposed:

"To your happiness! To your happiness, Glafira Antonovna! I have seen you in his portrait. I have seen your works, Saburov. To your happiness. That is all."

He emptied his glass. A little later Glasha asked him: "Vladimir Andreyevich, tell me frankly, do you really like it?"

Again he answered nothing but, after thinking a little, said to Saburov: "You know, envy is a rotten feeling, but I envy you."

He drank another glass, and looked again at one of Saburov's landscapes. The earth was the colour of bright rust. There were rowan trees, a small grey house, and a very high and empty sky. Volodya looked at it a long time. Then he said with a sad smile:

"It's magnificently painted. That's a fact."

Saburov protested.

"The trees aren't right. They are and they aren't. I painted it one day in autumn. The weather was extraordinary—the clay was a special colour. I remember seeing it another time, in forty-one, somewhere near Kaluga. We were retreating. Stepanov was with me; he was a remarkable man, an agronomist. I kept meaning to paint him . . . You can imagine how we felt. All at once I looked—there was a cottage and a little stream with a steep bank, and the earth was that same rust colour. I said to Stepanov: 'Look.' He couldn't think what I meant at first. Then he saw. Suddenly he roared: 'We'll drive them out to hell.' He was killed near Maloyaroslavts."

For a long time he talked about Stepanov. Volodya wasn't listening. He might have been looking at the landscape, or he might have been sitting in a daze. Finally he got up:

"I'll go. I don't feel like it a bit, but I'd better go."

After he had gone Glasha tidied up the room. Saburov was sitting on the bed, his hands over his face. She thought that he was dozing and walked about on tiptoe. He called softly to her. She came and put her arms round him.

"You see, Pukhov also says it's marvellous. You must go to Saratov. They'll see it, too. They won't be able to help it. They must arrange an exhibition."

Saburov shook his head.

"Those trees are no good at all. Volodya can say what he likes;

I know. It's right and it isn't. And that top right-hand corner is
unfinished. No, I must work some more on it."

He saw Glasha's sad expression and broke off:

"Glasha darling, don't be upset. Rodionov said I'd get something at the theatre after the first of March—work from other
people's sketches. Then we'll be all right."

"I don't want you to be taken away from your own painting.
Why should you think of such a thing? That wasn't what I meant.
What I want is for everybody to see your landscapes. Don't worry
about the money—that'll come. And if it doesn't, we'll do without. I'm so happy tonight. I know Pukhov is a poor painter himself, but he understands painting—you can tell that at once."

"And do you think he doesn't know how to paint? Nothing of
the sort. In fifty, when he arrived from Moscow and came to see
me, I was stuck on a flower piece—some nasturtiums—couldn't
do a thing with it. And he painted it—just like that. And if you'd
seen it! I couldn't take my eyes away; a dark jug and big, bright
flowers. Very restless, like himself. I can't think what is the matter with him. He's particularly frightening when he makes
jokes. I've behaved badly to him—never went to see him since
that evening when they invited us. I thought I bored him. And
you see, he didn't want to leave . . . I don't know what he
needs . . . Perhaps if he met somebody like you."

Glasha was confused and her plain face, lit up by a faint,
hardly noticeable smile, became beautiful as in Saburov's portraits of her.

Towards morning, climbing up the slippery street with a
wicked wind pushing him, he thought: "Must have sounded
silly . . . Saburov lives abominably—in a pinch you might put
up with that, but nobody even knows his work. He said I was the
first painter who's been to see him. At the union they think he is
abnormal. He is, of course—you have to be a schizophrenic to
work as he does, not to compromise, to do exactly what you

feel . . . Yes, it does sound silly. All the same it's fact. I do envy him. I can go to Moscow and sweat a little and make up to people a little, and they'll arrange a show for me and I'll get a prize and everybody will say Oh! and Ah!—and I'll still be envious of that madman. Tanechka was quite right. It's a good thing he's married his cripple—a portrait like that you can't do to order, and skill is not enough, you have to feel it. There I go again, thinking about nothing, it's enough to drive you crazy. But if I did go crazy I would still not paint like Saburov. I haven't enough talent and the talent I have had I've thrown away. I'd sit in a mental hospital and I'd paint pedigree hens according to instructions . . . Is that what you wanted, Vladimir Andrey-evich? You did? Well then, you've got it."

Next morning his mother came into his room.

"There's a piece about you in the paper. I'll read it to you . . . Here it is: 'It is impossible not to single out the deeply realistic pictures by the painter Pukhov, carried out with his characteristic skill. Next to them should be noted . . .' No, that's about the carpet . . . Aren't you pleased?"

He wanted to curse but remembered his mother would be offended. He nodded, then said:

"It's good that Father is feeling better, I was worried."

His mother was touched and kissed him. Her husband was unfair to him. Volodya had a good heart; he was only reserved.

Volodya stood by the window: there was nothing to be seen but snow. The room was warm but he felt so cold somewhere inside him that he went and got his overcoat out of the hall and put it on. Even then he couldn't get warm.

10

Dinner was over. The dining room was almost empty. Only Koroteyev remained sitting with a cooling glass of tea before him, absorbed in a long article on the Berlin Conference. Savchenko sat down next to him.

"Zhuravlyov wants to fire Semyonov. Gave him a prize a month ago and now says he's a waster. Semyonov is an excellent milling-machine operator. I was watching him the other day teaching some of the young ones how to set the lathe. It's just that he is independent and Zhuravlyov can't stand that. Though I don't suppose it's even that—he's just working off his rage . . ."

His mind still on the article, Koroteyev asked without interest: "And why is Zhuravlyov in a rage?"

"Haven't you heard? His wife has left him. That's why he is so furious."

For all his habit of self-discipline, Koroteyev paled and turned away.

"Why can't they put up some shades? That lamp is 300 watts, hurts your eyes."

Savchenko noticed nothing. "Tell me," he asked, "you know her. How did she stand him all this time?"

Koroteyev got up, glancing at his watch. "Yegorov is waiting for me. I lost count of time reading that article. Interesting session yesterday—in the end Bidault had nothing to say. A silly situation for him. After all, he is a Frenchman. Yegorov is worried the boiler brackets won't fit. Have to check up."

He quickly pulled himself together, and for three hours talked boilers, brackets, welding, warping, with Yegorov. At the end of it Yegorov said: "You aren't looking well. You should get out more. Gorokhov told me—at least two hours' walk a day. I don't manage that, but I've taken to walking home."

Koroteyev walked home thinking of Lena. He told himself that there was nothing to think about; it had nothing to do with him. He must live his life and forget what he had long ago labelled as nonsense.

But why had Lena left Zhuravlyov? After all, she had lived with him for more than five years. It must have been a difficult decision for her to make . . . "I'm out of my mind," he snapped at himself. "What is so surprising about it? The surprising thing is that she stood it for so long. I often wondered last summer what they could find to talk about. It isn't that Zhuravlyov is a scoundrel as Savchenko says; he's just an ordinary man, a rubber stamp. Savchenko is a young romantic, and after all, everything is new to him. I've seen plenty of Zhuravlyov. But perhaps he's better in his private life. Perhaps she was touched by his feeling for her. Or perhaps their little girl drew them together. Whatever it was, it was a weak link and now it's snapped; it's not my business. Naturally, if this had been last summer I would have gone to see her at once. I'd have tried to cheer her up, see if she needed help. Then it was so easy to be natural. Now, even if I met her accidentally, I wouldn't dare to talk to her—I'm too frightened of giving myself away. It's hard enough for her as it is. Why upset her with my unwanted sentiments? I'm not Savchenko. At my age you have to know exactly what you're doing, you have to be as meticulous as a line drawing."

He stayed up late and by the time he went to sleep he thought he had brought himself to his senses—there would be no more such absurd and wretched nights. But his first thought on waking was of Lena. Where was she? Even if he made up his mind to see her, he wouldn't know where to find her. She might have moved to another town, or to the country, to her parents . . . No, she would not have left her job in midterm. But he couldn't go to the school. If only he could meet her by accident, go up to her, look at her without saying anything.

How long had this been going on? He had begun tormenting himself when he returned from leave—six months ago. The nonsense had proved stronger than his will. But he could not give in to it, he simply must pull himself together.

"But why *has* she left Zhuravlyov? After all, I don't know anything. Suppose she is going through all this herself? No, that's rubbish, I would have felt it. She doesn't know how to pretend. That's the sort of thing that happens in novels—she misunderstands, he doesn't realise—the novelist tangles it all up to make it interesting. Real life is much simpler. That kind of misunderstanding might happen to somebody very young—like Savchenko—no wonder he has to ask what he is to do. I'm past that age. It's absurd to comfort myself with illusions; and it isn't even decent."

During the midday break Zhuravlyov asked him to his room to talk about the brackets; he was seriously worried. Koroteyev told him of his conversation with Yegorov; the welding system must be altered. Then Zhuravlyov suggested they should have lunch together. They talked about the German question, the elections, and the chess tournament. Koroteyev made an effort to be friendly. He had reminded himself that morning that Zhuravlyov must be unhappy—and who could understand it better than he could himself? Perhaps, after all, he had misjudged him altogether. A lot of people thought well of him, and Koroteyev knew he was conscientious, hard-working, and devoted to the factory. You had only to remember how well he had behaved when the fire had broken out. Everybody had his weaknesses. It was difficult to keep a check on oneself. Could he be sure that he had not been less than fair to Zhuravlyov through jealousy? In any case, he would be friendly to him now.

Zhuravlyov was touched by Koroteyev's manner. He thought: "I always knew he was a first-rate worker. He is a good comrade as well. He isn't an intriguer; he doesn't try to undermine me, like Sokolovsky. I wonder if somebody has told him about Lena, people love to talk. He knows her. He was rather attracted to her, but he knows what she is like—'yes' today and tomorrow 'good-bye, you needn't come again.'"

When they got up he said: "I'd like to have a serious talk with you. Only not here. Would you perhaps come and have dinner with me on Sunday? Then we wouldn't be disturbed." He smiled unexpectedly: "I'm like you now. I am also a bachelor these days."

Thinking over this sentence afterwards, Koroteyev told himself: "Obviously he is suffering. He wanted to show me he is keeping himself under control. I always knew he had a strong will, but he must be fonder of her than I thought . . . What can he want to talk about? Surely not Lena? It can't be. I'm so crazy myself, I begin to think other people are out of their minds, too. Must be about some directive from the head office, to do with Brainin's project . . . But why didn't he want to talk in the canteen, or in his office? Anyhow, it doesn't matter . . . I wonder what Lena is thinking about."

He worked through the afternoon. Afterwards he again tried to control his thoughts, but his heart rebelled. As he was going home he suddenly thought he saw Lena ahead of him. He hurried on; it was an elderly woman with a bundle. And yet repeatedly in the bluish mist he seemed to catch a glimpse of Lena. It made no sense. But where could she be?

That night he went to the club—Brainin was to read a paper on world affairs; it would be interesting to know what he had to say on France. He hid from himself the thought: "Suppose Lena comes?"—she occasionally came to lectures. He arrived late and when he entered the long, darkened hall, Brainin had done with Europe and was talking about Asia: "India is, so to speak, disturbed by the existence of American bases in Pakistan." Soon the light came on; Lena wasn't in the audience.

The following evening he went again, though this time he had no excuse. The show was an old film he had already seen twice.

The third night there was an amateur program—some guitarists, a couple doing a Bulgarian dance, and a poem on the struggle for peace recited by Katya Stolyarova. Koroteyev sat motionless, unable through embarrassment to look around him, knowing that he would see Lena and that the "nonsense" had got the better of him.

All week he searched for her. He would go and stand outside the school, as though in contemplation of the snowdrifts, his ear cocked for the creaking of the garden gate. Knowing that she sometimes called on the Pukhovs, he discovered their address and waited for two solid hours outside their house in the biting cold.

Finally he realised that he could no longer endure such exhaustion and such anguish and promised himself to stop. That was on Saturday. After the factory he went home and started reading Chekhov. Savchenko came in.

"Dmitry Andreyevich, what luck to find you in! Come to the theatre. It's the first night of *Hamlet*, and I've got two tickets. You said you liked Shakespeare."

He had had the tickets for a week. In the meantime there had been the scene with Sonya and the extra ticket was now useless. Noticing the light in Koroteyev's window, he thought of asking him, though without much hope, so that he was almost startled when Koroteyev said:

"Why not . . . I haven't seen *Hamlet* since my student days."

It was not, of course, of *Hamlet* that he was thinking. Lena had told him that last season she had not missed one first night. "Though she has other things to think of now . . . All the same, you can't tell—everything is possible . . . Anyway, it isn't fatuous to accept such an invitation. It's not like hanging around outside people's gates."

Savchenko was entranced by *Hamlet*, by the decor, by Koroteyev's company. Koroteyev seemed to follow the play with interest. During the first intermission he refused to leave his seat and sat on, without even glancing at the audience, his eyes fixed on his program. At his tenth reading of the words, "Produced by Meritorious Artist . . . ," he told himself with shame: "I'm as bad as Savchenko. In fact, he's got more sense."

At the next intermission he made up his mind to go out with

95

Savchenko and smoke a cigarette. On his way down he passed
Lena on the stairs. He was not thinking of her at that moment;
he was so startled that he went by without speaking. She was
with some woman, who he thought was Dr. Scherer. He turned
sharply and ran after her:

"Yelena Borisovna!"

She stopped and said quietly:

"Good evening, Dmitry Sergeyevich. I thought you hadn't
recognised me."

He turned to say good evening to Vera, but she had vanished.
He stood wordlessly. Lena, too, was silent. At last he said with
difficulty:

"I wanted to come to see you, but I didn't know where you were
. . . I never thought I'd meet you here."

She laughed. "Why not? I told you I was a theatre fan. Now,
more than ever—I am feeling so well. I'm so relieved. I told
you I was having trouble with the seventh grade; well, now
they're making tremendous progress. Pukhov has helped me a
great deal. On the whole, things are working out beautifully. I
am living at Vera Scherer's. I've been promised a room but not
until autumn. Anyway, Shura adores Vera and hates the thought
of leaving her. You won't know her, she has grown so much.
Today I bought her some coloured pencils. Please don't think I
feel depressed; on the contrary, I've never been so cheerful.
Of course, I shall be very glad if you drop in some time, but
don't think I have to be visited. I have lots of friends. Last night
I was at a students' party, and I even danced. I have a lot of
work, and I've been made an agitator [1] as well; I'm in charge of
three blocks. I wasn't even sure I would have time to come tonight. I don't like the acting. Ophelia is affected and Izumrudov

---

[1] This word has not the connotation that it has in English. In the
Soviet Union the role of an agitator is to explain to the population
official policies and points of view in short-term matters (such as
elections), as distinct from the role of the propagandist, who deals
with general principles and long-term matters.

has made Hamlet a neurotic. I think Hamlet is a strong character. Do you agree with me?"

She spoke unusually fast as though afraid of stopping, and without waiting for Koroteyev's view of Hamlet, she held out her hand:

"Good-bye, Dmitry Sergeyevich. Vera must be looking for me."

He kept her hand a moment longer.

"Yelena Borisovna, I have been thinking so much about you . . ."

She felt that in another moment she would start to cry, but pulling herself together, she said in the same hurried way:

"Thank you, but don't worry about me. I've told you, I'm all right, quite all right."

She fled.

Koroteyev saw the last act and walked home silently with Savchenko. Savchenko was shaken by the play. Its poetry was still ringing in his ears. Koroteyev thought wryly: "Now everything has more or less been said. I needn't stand in front of Pukhov's gate and dream of happiness. It's strange—how did I ever live before I met her? I don't understand it now. And yet I lived, I studied, worked. I must live again as though she didn't exist. Life has to be simple, bare. Happiness is for the young, for people like Savchenko. Now—my room, the desk light, the designs, and no one with me. I am not just going home. I am returning to myself, to my own life. I'll try not to be a fool, not to dream."

Lena talked all night to Vera Scherer. She had come home animated and spoke about the play and even entertained Vera with an imitation of Ophelia—Tanechka had been no good at all in the part. Suddenly she burst out crying. Vera was alarmed. She gave her drops of some kind and, sitting down beside her, took her in her arms. Then Lena told her everything.

"I know it's madness. He warned me that he didn't love me— he could not even imagine such a thing—he said I was an empty-headed flirt and that we hadn't anything in common. It isn't my fault I'm in love with him, but I wouldn't dream of thrusting my-self on him. And I don't want his pity. Naturally, he has made up his mind that I have left my husband because of him; he said he'd come to see me. I won't let him in . . . You must think I'm behaving like a schoolgirl, but I assure you this is something very serious. It has never happened to me before; it's the first time . . . But I don't want people to be sorry for me. I know you'll understand: you've been through so much . . . It's so terrible . . ."

When she had calmed down a little, Vera said: "Lena, why are you so sure he doesn't care for you?"

"Oh, I know that for certain. That's why he made that speech at the club . . . Now he's sorry for me, he wants to cheer me up. I can't bear people to be sorry for me. And I love him, I know that only too well. Tonight when we were going up the stairs and all at once I saw him, everything went spinning round me, I almost fell . . ."

Vera, for some reason, thought of Sokolovsky's story about the desert plant. "How happy you must be if you can love and suffer and weep like this . . ."

11

ZHURAVLYOV TRIED NOT TO THINK of Lena. It upset him and he was afraid, as he put it to himself, that his production record would be upset. Last Sunday she had brought their daughter to the apartment. He took Shura for a walk, then played hide-and-seek, hiding in the attic while Shura shouted: "Daddy, I know where you are. You're under the bed." When Lena came to get her, he examined her intently; she looked extremely fit. What did she care! Probably she already had her eye on someone else. He would have liked to ask her if she wanted to go through with the divorce. In that case they would need to talk things over and settle on the official reason. But he decided: "It isn't worth it. She'll tell me if it comes to that. I can't talk to her, it's too upsetting."

He believed that he was quietly recovering from the break-up of his home, but the experience had left a deep impression on him. Until recently, when he thought about his life he pictured it as a straight wide road. It was true that he had had his troubles. At one time he had even been afraid for his career, but afterwards he had reproached himself with giving way to moods. He had got by. It couldn't have worked out otherwise for him. So in this situation, too, he told himself: "Why get upset? I can live without her." And indeed he did not often think of her: it had been, it was no longer. He would get used to it. He began, however, to be unsure. Things were somehow blurred; people seemed hostile. He lost something of his calm, spoke with too much heat, and at such moments said too much. He had been proud of his capacity to see the brighter side. Now he was suspicious and on the look-out for slanders and conspiracies.

On Monday Lena had been gone two weeks. On Tuesday there was a Party meeting. In his opening speech, Sibirtsev, the chairman of the Factory Committee, referred to housing: it was high time that the new houses were put up. Zhuravlyov nodded. He even said: "No doubt about it." He knew Sibirtsev had to raise this question at every opportunity, since it was he who, a dozen times a day, listened to the workmen's grievances. The hovels really were disgusting. Any moment they might fall to bits. But now everything was in order. The plans had been definitely approved and the work on the foundations would begin in the second quarter. Zhuravlyov would have let it pass if Sokolovsky hadn't butted in, unexpectedly siding with Sibirtsev to point out that the building of the three new blocks of apartments should have been started in 1952. At that Zhuravlyov boiled over: the foundry had been recognised as having priority; it concerned the country as a whole. Sokolovsky knew the position perfectly, and for him to raise the issue at a Party meeting was "demagogy of the first order." Sokolovsky answered quietly: "Comrade Zhuravlyov seems to be unaware of the functions of the Party organisation." After that the discussion switched to offices for the election campaign and ended peacefully.

Zhuravlyov went home and brooded. "Sokolovsky didn't bring up housing for nothing. He must be working up to something. The houses aren't the point. When I told him the new model had to be delayed, he flew into a rage: "So you're going to put the brake on the brakes!" That isn't a bit witty, it's just downright insolent. Something tells me he's up to no good. He's always been a busybody, in the Urals he tried to finish Sapunov—he failed to pull that off and they slung him out—now he wants to take it out on me. The best thing would be to forestall him, but what the devil can he have in mind exactly?"

He had a moment's hesitation—could he be exaggerating? Sokolovsky had a miserable disposition. He needled everybody, and how often had he twitted Zhuravlyov himself! But all the same, they had worked together for six years. He pulled himself short—it was not the same this time. "He must smell something; a fellow like that has a nose like a retriever. Why should he have brought up the housing matter, which was not his business anyway, if he didn't mean to do me in?"

"The factory is everything to me," thought Zhuravlyov, "especially now that Lena's gone. And will that trouble-maker really squeeze me out? I've never been a career man but I do appreciate the trust they showed by putting me in charge of such a factory. And when you think of it, that's all that's left to me."

For the past fortnight, Zhuravlyov had indeed worked longer hours than ever, almost frantically, visiting both shifts, inspecting every workshop, and talking to the workmen.

When on Saturday he reminded Koroteyev that he expected him on Sunday, Dmitry thought that it must concern Brainin's project. Zhuravlyov had talked about it ceaselessly. He must want to go over it once again.

Zhuravlyov received him warmly. At dinner the conversation ran at first on the day-to-day events at the factory. Then Zhuravlyov recalled the war and Koroteyev in turn told a story about the fighting on the Vistula. They began to feel that closeness which exists between two front-line veterans whose experiences were not shared by others.

After they got up from the table, Zhuravlyov said:

"You have only been with us two years but I feel you are really one of us. You have the interests of the factory at heart. For me now, it is my whole life."

His voice faltered: Koroteyev felt embarrassed. "How fond he must be of Lena! Still, it's understandable." Zhuravlyov went on:

"You know how it is. A factory is a big family; everybody has to pull together. On the whole we are a friendly lot. There is only one thing wrong. I assure you, it isn't a question of prestige with me. I am a plain man come of peasant stock. I don't care for discipline except at work. The way I look at it, once you're outside the gate, go ahead and say what you like. But you can't work in an atmosphere of suspicion. I admit, Sokolovsky has considerable experience, but his attitude is such that it is quite impossible for me to work with him. I've tried. I've closed my eyes to all sorts of things; but now it's reached the breaking point . . ."

"He's a difficult man but he's a good worker," Koroteyev said soothingly. "I really shouldn't put much weight on what he says. I don't know him very well—we don't meet outside the office— but Yegorov says his tongue is a bit sharp. Honestly, Ivan Vasilyevich, I shouldn't pay too much attention."

"It isn't a question of his tongue. Take this, for instance—why is he always snooping about the workshops? He's hardly ever in his room. He's suspicious somehow—of everybody—of Yegorov, of yourself."

"Surely not! A designer can't do his work shut up in an office—

he's got to watch out for practical snags. I often ask him myself to check up outside. If it weren't for his annoying personality, you would never think of such a thing."

"Well, how can you assess him without taking his personality into consideration? Do you know what happened in his last job? I'll tell you. The director was Sapunov, a young man, clever and energetic, who put the factory on its feet. Sokolovsky got it into his head that a project he proposed was deliberately shelved, so he started undermining Sapunov. This was in war time. You and I were freezing in the trenches, and he was looking after his career and trying to destroy an honest man. He was shown up. There was even an article in the local paper. But he managed to get by; he pulled some strings."

"It's hard to believe, somehow . . . He doesn't look like a trouble-maker."

"You're too trusting, Dmitry Sergeyevich. There are other things in Sokolovsky's past . . . I believe Voronin was still with us when you came. An excellent fellow; he was ill a long time, had something wrong with his liver and neglected it. But what really finished him off was the trouble with the spindle bearings —you remember? And whose fault was that? Sokolovsky's. Voronin got the blame, but the error was in the project—no doubt about it."

"I did not know Voronin. When I came he was in the hospital. It's difficult to imagine Sokolovsky letting such an error get by, though, of course, everybody makes mistakes. Anyway, he is a brilliant designer."

So far Zhuravlyov had spoken calmly, almost with complacency, but now suddenly he lost his temper and jumped up, his puffy, greenish-tinted cheeks flushed and shaking.

"Let me tell you, he is a brilliant trouble-maker, there's no doubt about it. Pity you weren't at the Party meeting; that was an instructive sight. Why do you think he raised the housing question? Do you think he cares how the workers live? He

doesn't give a damn. Sibirtsev—he cares. And do you think I
don't? Every time I look at those wretched huts it hurts me. I'm
terribly relieved that we'll soon be able to house the men like
human beings. It's my responsibility as director, not his. And
when I tell him that politely, he starts instructing me in Party
organisation. What right has he got to talk to me like that, will
you tell me?"

Koroteyev tried to pacify him:

"I don't think Sokolovsky meant to be insulting. After all, he is
an old Party member . . ."

By now Zhuravlyov was beside himself. Hardly conscious of
what he was saying, he shouted breathlessly:

"An old Party member! . . . Well, you know! . . . His record
is a bit off-colour . . . His family is abroad. In Belgium. You
think it's gossip? Nothing of the kind. You have only to look up
the records . . . I've never mentioned it, I stick to my work, I'm
not a trouble-maker . . . I've even stood up for him—why drag
out the past? If they've given him the chance to work, let him
work . . . But don't tell me he's so pure that he has the right to
tell me off . . . At best he's only fifty per cent trustworthy, no
doubt about it . . ."

Koroteyev was silent. He thought: "How strangely people are
made. A patchwork, all mixed up. When Zhuravlyov was telling
me about Rzhov I felt quite close to him. He spoke with real
affection of the men who fought with him. That wasn't oratory;
I'm sure he was quite genuine. But that was an hour ago . . .
And now he's insinuating, slandering. What did he want me for?
To drag me into it? I'll never believe that story about Voronin.
Sokolovsky is honest; and no one can touch him as a designer.
Not that I would like to live in the same room with him; everybody says he likes to needle people. And what does he have to
do that for?—As if life hadn't sharp enough teeth. Perhaps be-
cause he's been bitten himself? Anyway, he couldn't be more
honest. I teased Savchenko and told him he was a romantic, but

Savchenko was right—Zhuravlyov is worthless. I don't know how I came to have a friendly talk with him and drink his vodka. Why should I listen to his dirt?"

He got up:

"I have to go to work." At the door he stopped. "I don't agree with you about Sokolovsky. Bear that in mind."

For a long time Zhuravlyov could not get over his mistake. What a fool he had been! Koroteyev was obviously hand-in-glove with Sokolovsky. Scoundrels, the pair of them . . . "Could it really have been to talk philosophy that he used to visit Lena? I'm much too trusting all around. Look at Lena. Could I ever have suspected her? And yet she's turned out to be no good . . .

"All the same, it was more cheerful with her in the house. If Shura were here now, I could go and play with her. And the house feels empty, somehow . . .

"Koroteyev is right about the boiler brackets—it's a question of welding. Tomorrow I'll have to see Yegorov. It can still be put right . . .

"Sokolovsky must have pull in Moscow, no doubt about it. Will he really manage to get me out? Father used to say: 'Mind, Vanya, never stick your fingers into anybody's mouth.' A lot of things have changed since—factories have gone up; I used to look after geese, now I'm a director—but it's still true, you should never stick your neck out. Otherwise, what happens? I trusted Lena and she's deceived me; I trusted Koroteyev and he's turned out to be a scoundrel . . . Nice mood I am in! Can't remember ever feeling worse . . . And yet, when you come to think of it, nothing has really happened . . ."

Khitrov came in unexpectedly and Zhuravlyov brightened: "There's a real friend. Must have sensed what I was feeling like."

Zhuravlyov let himself go—Sokolovsky was torn apart, flogged, flayed. Khitrov broke in now and then: "You don't mean it!" "I never knew that!" "It's unbelievable!" "Can you imagine such a swine!" Thus encouraged, by the time he came to Sokolovsky's past, Zhuravlyov was shouting in a frenzy:

"Sent away his family, think of it! He's a Benelux, not a Communist."

Koroteyev also took a long time to recover from his conversation with Ivan. He was disgusted. Fortunately Sokolovsky was known at the head office. And the times had changed; Zhuravlyov could no longer destroy him. "All the same, it's horrible. Why didn't I tell him so? Must have got into the habit of keeping my mouth shut—used to seeing too much dirt. That's what is so bad. In the beginning, what could you expect?—You start building a house and there's bound to be a lot of trash left lying about. But now it's time we were getting tidier—the house is being lived in, after all. Now a Zhuravlyov sticks out like a sore thumb.

"And yet Savchenko isn't really right. You can't say Zhuravlyov is altogether worthless—he's devoted to his job and he seems to have been a good soldier. How can all these different things exist together in the same man? Lena has left him now, but there was a time when he attracted her. There must have been something in him that made her love him. He isn't a scoundrel—he's unfinished, incomplete, a reject of a man.

"It's easy to sort out a machine and replace the defective parts. But what do you do with a man? A year ago I would have said that Zhuravlyov was a useful worker—though, even then, I saw his seamy side. I tried not to think about it. But as a human being he's a mess. I feel as if I'd climbed out of a cesspool.

"A different sort of man is needed—people like Savchenko—romantics. The ascent is too steep, the air is too rarefied for people with rotten lungs. Age doesn't come into it. There are some contemporaries of Savchenko who could even outspit Zhuravlyov. And look what Lena says about old Pukhov. Yet here's a man who was brought up in the darkest time. There were always good and bad people. If a man is honourable he won't get lost; he'll come out on the right path. But what about the others? Knowledge doesn't get you far; it's feelings that must be trained. Take America—they've a world of education there; I can tell from their scientific journals. And the marvellous laboratories they put up! But just read what they do to Negroes and see how it depresses you—sheer savagery.

"But how can feelings be trained? It's difficult. It isn't difficult to grow grapes in the Crimea—that's like making a Savchenko grow up as an honest man. But take a wild vine—that's the young Zhuravlyov, and graft a conscience on to him—that's like cultivating grapes in the far north. Difficult, but possible—all you need is fervour, sensitiveness, determination. Our people have achieved unheard-of deeds. They're rightly called a heroic people. It's essential that each separate individual should be like that. Didn't Zhuravlyov take part in that universal upsurge— wasn't he caught up in it at Rzhov? And again here when the fire broke out? We have taken a lot of trouble over one half of the human being, but the other half is neglected. The result is that one half of the house is a slum. I remember that article of Gorky's I read long ago, while I was still at school; he said we needed our own Soviet humanism. The word has been forgotten; the task it still to be done. In those days it was only a presentiment; now it's time we tackled it.

"And what about myself? I swear at Zhuravlyov, but do I tidy up my own house? I, too, keep a partition between the way I reason and the way I live. Why did I condemn that unfortunate agronomist, Zubtsov? He'd have every right to say I am two-faced. How often do I say: 'That's all right in books but not in life' or 'Principles are one thing, experience is another.' That's hypocrisy. And yet it isn't that I mean to be dishonest. Why does it happen like that? It must be because we change, we grow so fast. Sometimes it's the mind that can't keep up; at other times it's the heart. Savchenko is much more whole. He hasn't been through the thirties or through the war. He demands more— that's his right. It looks as if we're getting near to what we once only vaguely dreamed of . . ."

Did Koroteyev fall asleep or did he only close his eyes and

drift with the rapid flow of thoughts, feelings, images? He remembered Zakharyev, killed at Stary Oskol, who said as he was dying: "All will be well." Then he heard Lisichkin, the welder, muttering crossly: "Silly giving me the prize. I didn't discover it by myself—we all thought of it together." And Savchenko saying: "They can't frighten us with bombs—we have ideas on our side, and we have our word, our honour." He was seeing wonderful people—warm, loving, harsh yet gentle—his own century's enormous tribe, and a kindly smile came across his face. Then he remembered Lena and for the first time the thought of her merged with his stubborn, virile dream of the future of mankind.

12

ZHURAVLYOV'S STORY MADE A DEEP impression on Khitrov. He told his wife and his eldest son that Sokolovsky had been discovered to be a double-dealer, a deliberate saboteur who had settled his family in Belgium.

"Zhuravlyov wouldn't have spoken carelessly. He's a cautious fellow, weighs his every word. Sokolovsky must have been unmasked up there," he raised his hand significantly.

He passed on the tale of Sokolovsky's exposure to Engineer Prokhorov, and to Dobzhinsky, the club manager, adding in each case: "Naturally, it's between ourselves." Prokhorov took the view that the whole thing was simply Khitrov's gossip—the story wasn't worth a rotten egg. Dobzhinsky, however, liked it. He was annoyed with Sokolovsky, who on some occasion had made fun of the club's activities, and he enjoyed startling people with sensational news. He garnished the dish and served it up to whoever cared to listen.

Khitrov's wife had a job in the bank and she naturally told her colleagues. And his son, who was in the tenth grade, informed his schoolmates during recess that Sokolovsky had been caught. He was a Belgian and there was going to be a trial soon.

Three days later, hundreds of people knew that something bad had happened to Sokolovsky. The only one who knew nothing was Sokolovsky himself. He continued working on the conveyor belt and in the evenings read a book on ancient Arabic manuscripts, telling himself gloomily: "No good calling on Vera for another two weeks—she'd say I come too often and two weeks is a very long time."

He had a talk with Zhuravlyov and told him he accepted his remarks about the signalling system and would make certain alterations in his project. He spoke calmly and Zhuravlyov thought: "Perhaps I overdid it. He certainly is a busybody, but that's chronic with him. He's agreed with me about most of the changes, says he is absorbed in work, and hasn't made a single wisecrack. Looks as if I needn't have upset myself. We'll get by all right . . ."

Gradually he regained his peace of mind and on the following Sunday went fishing with Khitrov. The water, where the ice was broken through, misted and bubbled merrily and Zhuravlyov kept saying: "Now we'll see what kind of fish there are." On the way home Khitrov asked him: "How are things with Sokolovsky?" and he replied just as though a week ago he hadn't cursed the chief designer: "He's busy altering his project. He's a nasty fellow but he knows his business."

Another week went by. Zhuravlyov had long forgotten that bleak Sunday when in his depression he had turned on Sokolovsky. Now the story of his exposure reached the schoolmaster Pukhov. He said at dinner:

"Never would I have believed Zhuravlyov to be capable of this. What a mercy Lena's broken with him! He's invented the story that Sokolovsky sent his family away to Belgium. If I were the public prosecutor I'd have him up for slander."

Volodya frowned: "What a nasty business! Father is so naïve —it isn't Zhuravlyov who'll get it in the neck, it's Sokolovsky. Haven't been to see him for ages; he probably thinks I am avoiding him. How silly . . ."

That same evening he called on Sokolovsky and found him working. The big table was spread with drawings; Sokolovsky was sitting at it in his fur-lined jacket. Volodya thought that he had aged and was looking wretched. Pushing over to him an album of construction photographs, Sokolovsky muttered:

"Have a look at that. I won't be long."

Volodya wasn't interested in construction but he pondered the inscription: "To Evgeny Vladimirovich Sokolovsky from his fellow-workers, in memory of the firing of the first blast furnace, 1931." In thirty-one Volodya was eleven; he was still keeping pigeons and showing off his Pioneer tie. He thought: "Actually, Sokolovsky is an old man. What have I got in common with him? Really, nothing. I thought at first he was a sceptic. I thought it refreshing to meet a man who believed in nothing. But what kind of a sceptic is he?—Loves his work, reads and re-reads regulations about cattle breeding—just a normal Soviet man, only a bit more intelligent than most. That may be why Zhuravlyov has picked on him. Nobody will take his part. With us, once you're down, you're not popular. It's the lucky ones who are trusted—like Zhuravlyov. I can imagine what Sokolovsky must be feeling. Lucky they haven't booted him out of his job yet. Though why lucky? They'll boot him out tomorrow."

"How cold it is," Sokolovsky said without looking up.

"It's very hot in here and you have your jacket on," said Volodya.

"Must have caught a cold," grunted Sokolovsky.

An hour later, putting away his work, he said morosely:

"Haven't seen you for a long time. What have you been doing? Working?"

"A little . . . I didn't want to bother you."

He was silent for a while. Then he forced himself to say:

"I heard you'd had some trouble at your office, Evgeny Vladi-mirovich?"

"Nothing much . . . Got to revise the project . . . Objections were quite reasonable."

Sokolovsky was annoyed at having a visitor. He was feeling ill; he wanted to lie down. He sat brooding silently. Volodya stayed.

"Well, did you like the photos?" asked Sokolovsky.

Volodya answered mechanically:

"Very much."

He thought: "Evidently he knows nothing. Perhaps it's just as well . . . Sits and works . . . Only if I leave it to him, Zhuravlyov will take him by surprise. I've got to warn him; he must have his answers ready." And Volodya said:

"I asked you about your job because I understand Zhuravlyov intends to ruin you."

"Does he, indeed . . . Is that in connection with the new model?"

Volodya got up and drew closer to Sokolovsky:

"He says you've sent your family abroad."

At that moment an absurd incident distracted both of them. You would think Fomka might have got accustomed to Pukhov, who was for ever bribing him with bits of sugar and slices of salami, but he hated anybody to be near his master and he now leapt from under the sofa and sank his teeth into Volodya's trousers. Sokolovsky grabbed him just in time.

"Fool! He goes for everybody," he muttered crossly.

Volodya wasn't sure whether these words applied to Fomka or to Zhuravlyov. He waited for Sokolovsky to deny the rumour Zhuravlyov had started, but Sokolovsky remained silent. He lay down on the sofa and mumbled with an air of surprise: "Is it really hot in here? My teeth are chattering."

Only then did Volodya notice that he was looking physically ill. He must really have caught a cold.

"Would you like me to make some tea?" he offered. "I could run out and get some brandy."

110

"I don't want anything. Just tell me, why didn't Leonardo da Vinci get his colours right? I read about it once but I couldn't understand. Were the pigments wrong, or didn't he mix them properly?"

"I don't know. In general, Evgeny Vladimirovich, I'm pretty ignorant."

They both fell silent. Volodya asked:

"Would you like to go to sleep? I'll go . . ."

"Stay, as you're here. You don't bother me. Tell me, do you like Leonardo's paintings?"

"I have only seen them at the Hermitage. It's difficult to judge."

"I like his mind. The things he was interested in! People used to be more many-sided. Did you know that Michelangelo wrote poetry? Now, could Einstein write poetry? Give me my coat; it's hanging over there."

Volodya thought: "He's trying not to show he is upset. He must think it's too degrading to deny Zhuravlyov's slanders. Perhaps he's right. I shouldn't have told him; it was the last straw. He was working quietly when I arrived; now he's lying down and talking gibberish. He's surely got a temperature. I ought to get a doctor; I can't leave him in this state."

Sokolovsky began again:

"I once read in some romantic story that the agave only blossoms once, after that it dies. All rubbish. There's one at the Botanical Gardens—it's blossomed and it's doing fine. It's just that while it's flowering it needs extra care."

Volodya became alarmed. Sokolovsky seemed to be delirious.

"I'll get a doctor, Evgeny Vladimirovich."

"Forget it! What's the date?"

"The nineteenth."

"How stupid. I thought it was the twenty-first. Don't take any notice of me, I'm talking rubbish. My head's splitting."

"I'll go and get a doctor. I'm sure you've got a temperature."

"What do I want a doctor for? I told you I've caught a chill."

Volodya stayed for another hour. Sokolovsky suddenly complained:

"My head is simply bursting. It's silly . . ."

Volodya got up:

"I'll get a doctor at once."

"Vladimir Andreyevich, wait a bit! . . . Mind you don't get Scherer. If you must call in somebody, call Gorokhov. But I'd much sooner not have anyone."

Gorokhov came and said it looked like the flu, but could be pneumonia, and the heart wasn't very strong . . . He would send Barykhina at once to give Sokolovsky injections of camphor and penicillin, and he would call again next morning.

Volodya stayed the night. Sokolovsky seemed to be asleep.

He was not asleep. It annoyed him that the fever prevented him from concentrating. His thoughts were chasing one another, running together, appearing and vanishing. It bothered him. He wanted to think over what Pukhov had told him. So that piece of ancient history was to be dragged out again! How many times had he explained it! In the end they always understood. They said: "Now it's clear." And then out crept a Sapunov or a Polish-chuk or a Zhuravlyov and it all began again—"How, what, why?" "In a month or two, when I am so done in that no amount of sleeping pills do me any good, Zhuravlyov will stroke his flabby cheeks and proclaim charitably: 'Now it's clear.' The funny part of it is that it isn't at all clear to me. Never shall I understand how my daughter, the granddaughter of an old bearded White Sea fisherman, comes to be called Mary. 'I drink to Mary.' Pushkin is beside the point. This is from the pen of Maya Balabanova, poor foolish woman who dreamed of tennis parties under California skies and died in the bleak suburb of Beaurivage to the sound of S.S. boots . . . What fools young people make of themselves!— Perhaps not only young people—I can't imagine how Masha can dress herself in that absurd tunic. She wrote she was a 'sympathiser.' But can you sympathise with a people's deed, sacrifices, labours? Either you lay the bricks yourself or you don't say anything . . . Evidently Zhuravlyov is determined to get rid of me. Nuisance—the new model has to be finished. The signalling will be all right; I'll cope with that . . . Perhaps tomorrow there will be a feature article, as there was in the Urals. What will the reporter think up now? 'Falcon proves to be a Belgian sparrow!' No, not now; now they wouldn't get away with it. There are a lot of things Zhuravlyov hasn't yet grasped . . . Why has he started this? Must have been annoyed because I spoke against him at the Party meeting. But how could I keep quiet? People work on marvellous machines and live in broken-down outhouses with leaking roofs. Where should it be talked about if not at a Party meeting? In Archangelsk there was a Nikita Cherny—an old Bolshevik, knew Lenin, worked with Innokenty—he used to say: 'The Party —that's our conscience.' Zhuravlyov will say: 'I'm a Party member, too . . .' Why do I keep thinking about Zhuravlyov? He isn't worth it. After all, the forms that you fill in aren't the most important thing in life. I'll write it all down again. Or, if I die first I won't have to write it. Everything is written down already.' What's the matter with my head? Never felt anything like it . . . I was sure today was the twenty-first; now it turns out it's the nineteenth. Mustn't go to Vera's earlier than the twenty-fifth. Six days. That's a long time . . . And suppose I'm really very ill? How long will it last? Vera was annoyed with me the other day. Shouldn't have told her about the aloe . . . Why is it that when we meet we so often seem to have so little to say to each other? It's as though our hearts were frozen through . . . It was very cold today—that's how I got chilled . . . Ought to drink a pepper brandy and sweat it out. Doctors always make things complicated. So does Vera . . . Gorokhov said 'infection.' You can't infect anybody with love. Neither Leonardo nor Pushkin managed that. I remember on the platform of the Kazan station, a soldier telling a girl who was seeing him off: 'They say Mayakovsky has shot himself.' She didn't know who Mayakovsky was. She grabbed his hand: 'Vanya, why must you go?' My head is literally splitting. I believe Pukhov has set fire to the house. That would be like him; he's always dropping cigarette ends. A huge fire! Suppose Pukhov gets burned? He says he's never painted anything. Ought to save the drawings . . . Why doesn't Pukhov know what pigments Leonardo used? Leonardo had a long beard; he was in love with Lisa. There is a pond near Simonov monastery where Lisa drowned herself. That was another Lisa. And the pond is no longer there—there's a Palace of Culture. It's a good plant but why do they still make those old-fashioned furnaces? They are too heavy and they gobble up a shameful amount of fuel. I believe the fire is spreading. There's a tap on the landing . . ."

Sokolovsky shouted:

"Put it out before it's too late."

Volodya shaded the lamp with a piece of cardboard. Sokolovsky was again quiet. Then he started muttering. Volodya caught isolated words: "Mary," "aloe," "succulents."

"Seems to be fond of botany," Volodya thought. "Talked about agaves. The things he wants to know! What difference does it make what paints Leonardo used? Saburov uses the same paints as I do; only the result is not the same . . . Wonder who Mary is. Must be an old love. Funny to think Sokolovsky at one time fell in love. It's a foreign name. Perhaps he's really been to Belgium. I shouldn't have told him; it was after that he lay down and started raving. It's all my fault . . ."

Although Volodya realised that pneumonia could not be due to an emotional upset, he now felt that Sokolovsky had been struck down by the piece of dirty gossip he had repeated to him.

Gorokhov called again the following morning. He frowned and said:

"I'd like another opinion. I'll get Professor Baikov."

The professor arrived from town. He explained something to Gorokhov at great length. Volodya could make nothing of the technical terms, but he could tell the doctors were worried. Gorokhov asked if it would be better for the patient to go to the hospital. Baikov shook his head:

"Better not move him. Can you get a nurse?"

Barykhina stayed with Sokolovsky. Towards evening Volodya went home. Sonya noticed his exhausted look:

"What's happened?"

He went to his room without answering.

Sokolovsky was unconscious for two days. On the third morning he opened his eyes. He thought he had overslept and would be late for work. He stretched his hand to his bedside table where he normally kept his watch and knocked over a medicine bottle. Then he remembered: "I'm ill. Gorokhov came . . ." He closed his eyes and tried painfully to remember more. "Pukhov came. I was feverish. Then there was a fire . . . No, I must have dreamed that . . ." Everything was jumbled up inside his head. For some reason only one thing stood out clearly: he had asked Pukhov what colours Leonardo used and he didn't know.

Gradually things came back to him. Volodya had told him about Zhuravlyov . . . Sokolovsky screwed up his face. His mouth was dry and there was an odd taste in it, as though he had been sucking rust . . . "I'm sick of that Belgian business . . . I'll get up at once and go to see Vera. There are moments when you can't be alone . . . Can't understand what time it is. It's light. That means she won't be in. I don't believe I'm well yet. My eyes hurt and my head feels as if it wasn't mine. I can't lift it . . ."

He moaned. Barykhina came over to him but he didn't see her: he was swallowed up again in the hot, dark whirlpool of unconsciousness.

When he again opened his eyes it was evening and Vera was bending over him. She was looking at him; never had he seen such an expression in her eyes. He tried to tell her something, found he couldn't, and only spoke her name. She said severely:

"You mustn't talk."

She moved away and whispered to Barykhina:

"He recognised me."

Sokolovsky lay with his eyes closed and asked himself dimly:

115

"Did I see Vera or did I dream it? Must find out—it's most important . . . I forgot she was a doctor. I must be ill . . . Can't work anything out . . . What's the matter with my head? Everything gets muddled . . ."

Barykhina came over to him:

"He's gone off again . . . Vera Grigoryevna, what's the matter with you?"

She handed Vera a glass of water. But Vera quickly pulled herself together and said quietly:

"Will you make a camphor injection? I'll telephone Professor Baikov."

13

SIBIRTSEV HAD SAID AS EARLY AS last November that people were needed urgently in the farms. He said it with conflicting feelings: he knew that the farms were asking for real workers, not loafers, and he also knew that Zhuravlyov would never let such people go. Indeed, how could he? The plant was manufacturing conveyor belts for two tractor factories and tools for Selmash;[1] it was doing essential work for agriculture. "The right thing," thought Sibirtsev, "would be not to urge anybody; but Zhuravlyov insists on a campaign."

Lashakov agreed to go to a machine tractor station. Zhuravlyov threw up his hands: "*He* can't go, whatever happens." Sibirtsev mumbled: "Then what are we to do, Ivan Vasilyevich?" Zhuravlyov said they must recruit among the newcomers ("among those who haven't got down to production yet, those who get under

---

[1] Selmash: Farm Machinery Trust.

your feet"). He thought a little and added: "Have a talk with
Chizhov. Incidentally, he used to drive a tractor." A year before,
Chizhov had been a Stakhanovite,[2] but he took to drink (his father was also an alcoholic). Zhuravlyov meant to fire him but
kept putting it off: "Gave him another chance. He's promised not
to touch a drop."

At the end of January the local newspaper photographer took
a picture of Chizhov and three young boys signing declarations
of their willingness to work on farms.

Sibirtsev had said frankly to Chizhov: "My advice to you is, go.
You're so fogged by drink, you don't know where you are from
one moment to the next. Zhuravlyov has been threatening for
ages to fire you, and he's right." Chizhov swore, thought a little,
swore again, then said limply: "So what? I'll go to my family. It's
a good Kolkhoz."

That autumn Belkin, too, went back to the Red Way Kolkhoz.
Since the war he had been kept at timber work in Lithuania. He
was a reliable man, a scowling giant who, whatever he was told
to do, said: "Wonder what they'll think up next," and then did it
perfectly. The news that he was back cheered Antonina Pavlovna. She often sighed that the Kolkhoz was short of hands.
Only think of it—twenty-two thousand acres, almost three thousand head of cattle, a poultry farm, an orchard, and a big apiary,
and only one hundred and sixty-three working members all told.
After Belkin came, her hopes soared: other people might come
as well.

Shortly after this, Radionov said to her: "My nephew Sasha
writes from Moscow that he wants to come to us. I don't rightly
know . . ." "Tell him to come," said Antonina Pavlovna. "We're
really short of people; that's our main trouble."

Sasha, when he came, said he had been a tally clerk in a small
co-operative. His health was poor. The doctor said he needed
more fresh air. The premises were in a semi-basement—it stank

---

[2] One who breaks production records.

117

of leather. He had no room of his own at all—he had to rent a corner in a chastnik's [3] room somewhere else. In a word, he had decided to transfer.

Sasha liked showing off. Within three days everybody knew that in the neighbourhood of Dresden where his battalion had been stationed a ewe had given birth to six lambs which ran after it like chicks after a hen; that in Moscow the foreman of the gang gave him a Chinese duck's egg—this egg was a hundred years old, a bit alarming but intriguing, and he'd eaten it up—that he'd been filmed while putting a bunch of flowers on Pushkin's tomb —he had to do it twice as the first time was no good, but on the screen the picture came out exceptionally well—that in a bus he'd got into conversation with Lysenko, who said the winter was very mild; Sasha asked him what the harvest would be like and Lysenko said he couldn't tell exactly but hoped that it would be exceptional.

Antonina began to worry: "Says his health is poor and he's a chatterbox as well. What can you do with such a fellow?" But when Sasha ran out of stories he settled down to work. He mended a table in the Kolkhoz common room and cleaned a cowshed. It turned out that he had served as a medical orderly, was good at carpentry, and could drive a truck. Antonina said to Radionov: "Thanks for Sasha. He's a good addition to our Kolkhoz."

But when she heard Chizhov was back she lost her temper: "The papers say the very best people are going on the land and we get Chizhov. Such a drunk I've never seen. Almost set fire to the club last summer. We don't want his kind here."

Chizhov arrived, sad and sober. His father, glad of a chance to celebrate, brought out two half litres. Young Chizhov immediately brightened up and started cursing Zhuravlyov. "That may be the reason I took to drink; he rouses such unutterable loathing in me. He's a damned pipsqueak, not a director. No wonder his

---

[3] Chastnik: a term used for the few individuals in the Soviet Union who engage in any form of private business.

own wife spat in his face." Chizhov's mother threw up her hands: "That's our Lena!" Chizhov nodded joyfully: "That's the one. I remember her when she was small; Uncle Pasha gave us both a hiding for stealing apples. Her father once made me a little animal, a pig with a snout like that—the spit and image of Zhuravlyov. It's luxury that tempted Lena—being a director's wife and all that. But in the end she couldn't stick it, and she moved out. It's the truth, I'm telling you."

(Lena often told herself: "I ought to write to Mother," but always put it off, knowing that it would upset her. She had written recently, saying everything was all right, she was busy, Shura was good at drawing. She had promised another letter soon, but of the big change in her life she had said nothing.)

Chizhov's mother called on Antonina early the next morning and reported with a sugary smile: "Our Genya is back."

She had never cared much for Antonina. "Bullies everybody. Gives out orders like a general. Who says I know less than she does? And even if she is the chairman, who gave her the right to ask why my husband's rolling drunk? That's my misfortune, not for her to enlarge upon. Her own husband hasn't even the brains to bring the cattle home—last summer we had to search all one night for Sobachnikova's cow. She'd much better keep quiet."

Still with the same smile, she asked if Antonina had any news of Lena. Antonina said she had had a short letter recently:

"She's busy, works two shifts, and she's been made an agitator [4] for the elections."

"Our Genya's told us she's getting a divorce—said she's left her husband. I meant to ask you how she's getting on, poor thing. Must be hard for her all by herself, with her little girl."

Antonina proved her power of self-control. She said nothing, but only asked Chizhova what Genya's plans were. Was he on a visit or did he mean to work in the Kolkhoz?

She did not say anything to her husband. All that night she lay

---

[4] In charge of explaining to the population official policies and points of view in short-term matters (such as elections).

awake, worrying about Lena. Chizhov was a good-for-nothing drunkard. All the same, he wouldn't dare invent a thing like that . . . Antonina remembered that Lena had told her she was disappointed in her husband. "Must be true. She's left him. But fancy not writing to her mother." She cried a little, quietly, then decided to go and see her daughter. "I'll bring Shura back with me. How can Lena manage by herself?"

When she arrived at Vera's, Lena had gone to the library and Vera to see a patient. The door was opened by Gorokhov's servant Nastya. Antonina pursed her lips and asked severely: "Does Lena room here?"

Shura didn't recognise her. When her grandmother called her she hid shyly behind Nastya. At last Lena came in.

Antonina cried and kept repeating: "Not a word to me, your own mother."

Then she calmed down and said:

"I'll take Shura with me. Anyway, till the autumn, till you're fixed up. Father will be pleased. He's poorly, but he still plays with the children. Still carves his little animals . . . You'll come to us for the holidays . . . Fancy not writing to your mother! Imagine, I had to find it out by chance, from Chizhova. Their Genya is staying with them. As though old Chizhov wasn't enough for us—you remember him, he used to frighten you, telling you you'd be a dwarf. He's still the same, works for a day and drinks for a month. Now Genya has joined him—he's his father's labour reserve. So Chizhova comes to me and says: 'Your Lena is getting divorced.' I only just managed not to howl in front of her."

"Do you blame me?" asked Lena.

"Don't talk nonsense. I'm just hurt that you didn't tell me, your own mother . . . Who am I to be your judge? . . . It's difficult to be on one's own, and with a child as well . . . Does her father come to see her?"

"He made it a condition that I should take her to see him every Sunday. The first time, I went. The following Sunday he sent a message that he was busy. Two days ago I called up to ask when I was to bring her over and he said he had too much work, he'd send her some chocolates—probably went fishing with Khitrov. And I thought he was so fond of her. That was what made me so miserable, trying to decide."

"You thought!" Antonina said crossly. "You thought a lot of things. You thought he was a wonderful worker, and that he was understanding and that he had a soul. Don't I remember how you used to talk about him!"

Lena's eyes filled with tears. Antonina was at once remorseful.

"Don't you take on . . . You were just mistaken in him, it happens to adults as well. I'm not reproaching you. But he isn't a good person, I've always felt it. I don't know your secrets, I'm not speaking about that . . . But when I stayed with you I took a good look at him . . . He's rough with people; he doesn't put himself in their place. I remember I asked him one day why the factory stores were so short of goods. People had to go to town to do their shopping—three hours there and back. You'd think he could have done something. He said he had his hands full running the factory and began boasting about his machines. Lied about the stores, too; said they had enough of everything, that they even had sugar. Another time I was there when a man came to ask him if his wife could get a lift on a truck to the maternity clinic. He said: 'That's not what the trucks are there for.' Afterwards I said, wasn't he sorry for the woman—he laughed: 'She'll slip the driver five roubles, why should I worry!' Those are the kind that make the people suffer—anything you tell them, they just brush it aside . . . When Chizhova told me, I couldn't sleep all night—it hurt me that I had to hear about it from a stranger —but I was glad for you—nobody could live with such a block of wood."

"Then why did you scold me when I told you I liked him less?"

"I didn't take it in properly. I thought—you've got a daughter, you'll settle down. It isn't easy to be a mother. You'll see for yourself when Shura's older. Sometimes you daren't give advice . . .

Anyway, you've managed all right without it . . . The only thing I still don't see is why you had to hide it from your own mother."

Two weeks had gone by since Lena's meeting with Koroteyev at the first night of *Hamlet*, but she was still thinking of her conversation with him. "Why was he sorry for me? He has a good heart, but that only makes it harder for me. If it weren't for Shura, I don't think I could stand it. Never did I believe such a thing could happen. The girls at college used to say they were in love; their boy-friends took them to the movies, and they all laughed about it. And I, too, thought I was in love with Ivan. How childish it all was . . . This is like a wound. I feel it constantly and it doesn't heal; it hurts more than ever now . . . Vera is a remarkable person. She has really helped me. She couldn't cure me, of course; there is no medicine for that. But at least I've stopped feeling ashamed. She has made me see there's nothing shameful in it, nothing wrong . . ."

Lena was afraid her mother would notice her state of mind but she told herself: "How could anybody notice? It isn't written on my face that I can't live without him . . . If I don't tell her she won't know. Besides, she isn't interested in that sort of thing . . . But it will be hard to part with Shura now. I'm more attached to her than ever . . . I can't imagine waking up and not seeing her in her cot, wriggling her toes and saying with that sly smile: 'I see you, Mummy. You aren't asleep.'"

Antonina had a long talk with her daughter. They recalled her childhood and together they cried a little over Seryozha. Then Antonina said she must go home the following day.

"I'll take Shura along."

"I don't know, Mother. It's particularly hard for me to do without her now."

Her mother looked at her and said nothing.

They talked about her father. Antonina smiled:

"He carved a rhinoceros the other day, a very good likeness, just like in the book . . . Let me take the child along, Lena darling, at least until the spring vacation. Your father will be happy. He's often poorly these days. He keeps saying: 'Pity little Shura isn't here.' "

"All right," Lena agreed sadly. "But I'll come for her in a month. Why are you in such a hurry, Mother? Couldn't you stay another day?"

"I can't, Lena dear. The spring is coming; we have a lot of work. We can do the sowing. I'm not afraid of that; but I'm worried about the vegetables—we're so short-handed. It's a mercy Belkin is back; he's a big help. And Radionov's nephew asked to come; he's a terrible show-off but he works all right. The one who is a real nuisance is young Chizhov. That's Zhuravlyov's present to us. Do you know what disgusts me most in Zhuravlyov? Suppose I were to go to him and say: 'Why did you send us Chizhov?'—he wouldn't bat an eyelid; he'd say Chizhov was a hero of labour. You show him a pigsty: he'll say it's a house, it's habitable. Or tell him a road isn't fit for driving. He'll grin and say: 'Isn't it a main road?' People are sick to death of that kind of man. How sick they are! You remember Dasha Kargina? Her Misha used to gather nuts for you—remember? He was killed in the war. She's a clever woman, Dasha. I often ask her advice. Well, when the papers published the report of the Plenary Session [5] she walked into the common room and said: 'It says here the country is short of cattle. Mark my words, that means there will soon be plenty. They are trusting people now—that's the main thing.' When you come to us you'll see, Lena. Everybody is in better spirits."

Early next morning Lena took her mother and Shura to the station. In the taxi Shura fell asleep at once. Lena was thoughtful. Suddenly Antonina said:

"What are you hiding from me, Lena?"

Lena was startled. Was it really written on her face? "Shall I

---

[5] This is a reference to the Central Committee's decree of September 26, 1953, on "measures to develop the raising of livestock and lower the compulsory delivery of animal produce to the State."

tell her?—No, that's a thing she'll never understand. Her mind works differently. Anyway, I couldn't bring myself to. I'd die of shame."

"I am not hiding anything. I'm just sorry you are going."

Her mother left it at that and Lena hoped she had set her mind at rest. But as they were saying good-bye, Antonina whispered:

"Again your mother will be the last to know. It doesn't matter, so long as you're all right. And you have your own mind; you don't need anybody else's."

14

ON THE EVENING OF THE NIGHT that he was never to forget, Zhuravlyov was full of cheerful confidence. Yegorov had been afraid that Sokolovsky's illness might hold things up, but now even Koroteyev, who was always one to think of difficulties, agreed that the new model would be ready by the first of May. On that day it would be released. That was an event of country-wide importance; it would be publicised in the newspapers and would probably be reported on the radio.

Zhuravlyov had dinner at home by himself. He ate with appetite, spreading butter thickly on chunks of bread and topping them with cutlets. Grusha was a good cook . . . Suddenly he smiled. He remembered the year he was appointed to the factory. What a difference between the conveyor belt and the machines that were in production then—it was like comparing a Zim [1] to an old pre-war crate. Each new model seemed to him to

---

[1] Like the newer Volga, a medium-sized Soviet car.

be a phase in his own life and he told himself: "We're growing—no doubt about it. It's wonderful how we're growing." It occurred to him, this was a fine evening to take off. He picked up the *Ogonyok* and read a short story about a store manager who wished to marry a college girl, but nothing ever came of it because they both changed their minds. "Why do they have to write about such things?" thought Zhuravlyov. "It isn't in the least amusing. It would be nice to know what that manager was like at work. Must have been a nincompoop—never had a thing in stock . . . At that rate, it looks as if our Borisenko must be in love. Khitrov said he had seen Dutch herrings on sale in town and we have still only got crab . . . I suppose I'll have to marry again—a director of a factory can't go in for love affairs." He laughed a little, thinking of himself arranging rendezvous and giving flowers like Pukhov, the artist. Smiling, he thought: "I'll take my time. They say that for a woman to be sensible she must be ugly, but that's all nonsense. Khitrov's wife must have been most responsible when she was young. Lena, on the other hand, is extremely irresponsible. I can't imagine how she can be good at teaching children. For a time she got me right out of step. It might have caused grave damage to the State. Lucky I'm not a weakling. I came to just in time."

It was ten fifty. Zhuravlyov turned on the radio. He listened with half an ear. Miners in Czechoslovakia had undertaken a new Socialist obligation; in Bolivia the output of precious metals had declined sharply; the Egyptian press was in favour of closer trade links with all foreign countries. This was followed by the weather report. Normally Zhuravlyov heard the weather report every Saturday, although he distrusted the forecast and would tell Khitrov: "They said clear and dry. That means you and I will get soaked to the skin." But this was Monday and he wasn't interested in the weather. "*In the next twenty-four hours fine weather, with moderate frost and strong gales, is expected in the middle and lower Volga districts.*" "Lies again. It's cold, no doubt about it, but when I was coming from the factory there was no wind at all." He listened to some songs by Soviet composers and was pleased with one of them, even humming the refrain:

Boldly forward we go,
Despondency we do not know.

Then he yawned loudly, hung his coat over a chair, and began slowly to untie his shoelaces.

The gale rose an hour before dawn and was unusually severe. It uprooted a big silver birch in front of Zhuravlyov's house and the tree fell on a watchman's lodge. Zhuravlyov leapt out of bed. Fresh from sleep, he couldn't understand the noise and thought that somebody was breaking in his door. He dressed hastily and ran out into the street. The night was clear and cold. He started for the factory, but the wind impeded his progress, almost knocking him off his feet. Near the hospital he saw Yegorov, hatless and with a frightened face, shouting inaudibly. At last Zhuravlyov heard: the third hutment had blown down. The storm grew in violence. There seemed to be a blind, angry, hopeless passion in it. It pulled up trees, tossed aside posts, boards, struts, tore off roofs, and sent unfortunate people spinning—just as if they weren't people at all but chips of wood, sweeping up the dry, sharp, bitter snow and flinging it in one's eyes with a mocking whistle.

Afterwards people said: "That certainly was a storm . . . Never has there been a storm like that." Old Yershov protested he had seen an even worse one on his wedding day in 1908. Ever after, at the memory of that fearful night Zhuravlyov shrank into himself superstitiously. Never could he quite believe that the gale had swept impartially over a number of districts, causing damage everywhere, and that there was nothing supernatural about it—it had even been predicted by the weather bureau. It seemed to him that the forces of nature, in conspiracy with mean and envious men, had advanced upon him, resolved to fell him, to uproot him, like the old birch tree outside his house.

The moment he came out he knew—this meant disaster. He

trembled for the unfinished frame of the assembly shop. As soon as he set eyes upon Yegorov, he thought: "This will all be blamed on me. Now they'll say: 'Where are the three new blocks of apartments, why were they delayed?' The victim will be Zhuravlyov."

All that day he worked as one possessed. Nine families and two single men from hutment B had to be rehoused. Zhuravlyov called on Ushakov, the secretary of the Town Committee, and asked for temporary housing. "What were you thinking of before?" shouted Ushakov. Zhuravlyov made no attempt to justify himself: "We've put some of the people in the assembly shop. Please help us, Stepan Alexeyevich." The gale had torn the roofs off six small houses. Furniture, trunks, bundles, were loaded on trucks. A woman was sobbing loudly. Semyonov, the machine operator, said nastily: "Satisfied?" Zhuravlyov let it pass. He put up the foreman, Vinogradov, with his wife, children, and old mother-in-law, in his own house. He went to see the chairman of the Town Executive: "Let us have three tons of corrugated iron. We'll patch up the roofs." He telephoned, got hold of slates, comforted the women, did all he could. But whether he was talking to the chairman or reassuring Vinogradov's mother-in-law or reckoning with Sibirtsev how many families could be put up in the hostel for single workmen, his mind only held one thought: "I'm finished. They're counting how many people have been left homeless, how many have suffered damage, how much wood and iron will be required, and I, Ivan Zhuravlyov, statistically a unit, I, an honest Soviet man who has given all his life to the service of the State, I am wrecked. The storm has wrecked me, and no one cares."

Six days went by in an agony of waiting. On the seventh, the secretary of the Town Committee telephoned: "There's a message for you from the Central Committee. You are asked to report in person." Zhuravlyov had been preparing for the worst, but was so taken back that he dropped the receiver. It dangled from its cord, buzzing plaintively, but he heard nothing. "Why didn't Ushakov call himself? He doesn't want to talk to me. It's catastrophic. I expected a query from the Ministry, but 'report to the Central Committee!' 'Report.' What is there to report? There was a storm; you'd think everybody knew that. I'm finished, that's what it is. But where's the justice of it? Do I control the weather? Without the precision-casting foundry we could never have fulfilled the quota. And look at what we've saved the State . . . First they pass the building plan; then they congratulate me twice on exceeding the quota; now they sink me. And why? Just because there was a storm. If there hadn't been a storm they'd have wired to congratulate me on the first of May. There's no logic in it. I am not a child, I shall soon be thirty-eight, and what am I being ruined by? The weather!"

He made many guesses as to who had sent a report to Moscow on the delay in building. "The most likely one is Sokolovsky. Pity, after all, I didn't finish him off. At the right moment and with such a trump card as his family in Belgium, I could easily have got rid of him. It's always a mistake to be too fastidious. Now he's got his own back. Perhaps it wasn't him—Yegorov says he's still in bed. Then, who can it be? Not Sibirtsev; he wouldn't have the nerve. Must be Ushakov; he's been pestering me about those houses. What business is it of his? I'm responsible for the factory. But no, he has to show his zeal, he's aiming at promotion . . . I haven't yet heard from the Ministry.[2] Of course, it must be Ushakov. And Sokolovsky put him up to it. It's quite possible to be in bed and still invent a slander and telephone the Town Committee . . . After all, who cares which of them it is—whichever it is, the one who is being ruined is me."

Travelling to Moscow, he sat brooding in his compartment, not even looking at the view nor replying to the conductor, who asked if he would like some tea. Normally he liked trains. He immediately put on striped pyjamas, played drafts or dominoes

---

[2] Ushakov is a Party official, and since Zhuravlyov has heard nothing from the Ministry he assumes that a report on the delay in building has gone through Party, and not the government, channels concerned with his industry.

with his fellow-passengers, smacked his lips over a chicken, sipped glass after glass of tea, listened to the radio, talked about his successful output, and laughed aloud as he read the *Krokodil* ("they've given so-and-so a good hiding"). Briefly, he enjoyed life. Now he was nauseated by all he saw. The railway engineer who shared his carriage was a chattering fool; the radio broadcast idiotic songs which made his head ache; the dilapidated stations, the little houses peeping out of snowdrifts—all of it was sickening. And there wasn't even enough snow; the harvest would be bad. In the restaurant the cutlets were underdone and the tea smelled of herrings. In the compartment it was intolerably hot and a draft blew from the window.

At night, while the railway engineer gave occasional little cosy snores, Zhuravlyov lay in his upper berth and thought and thought, trying hard to understand what had occurred. The window-blind let in a thin blue light. The engineer coughed, turned, and lit a cigarette—Zhuravlyov still went on thinking. Suddenly he understood: "It all began with Lena. That unfortunate woman stuffed her head full of silly novels and jolted to its foundations the life of an honest Soviet man. What will become of the factory! We have promised the new model for the first of May— what will happen now! It is true that Sokolovsky isn't bad as a designer and Koroteyev is satisfied now he has completely altered Sokolovsky's signalling—criticism is a great thing!—All very well, but the factory will have no unifying principle. Yegorov is an experienced engineer. He has had a lot of practice. But he is weak, and ever since his wife died, he has been going downhill. All the slackers will let themselves go. Koroteyev has a future, no doubt about it, but he's much too young. I simply can't conceive of the factory without me! It's unheard of—to think that slip of a girl has pulled all this down. Koroteyev was three hundred per cent right in that speech he made at the club—the moment you pull out one brick, the whole house falls down. What can you expect?—People are badly brought up; silly books are published—nobody knows why—now they've started talking about feelings—and this is the result . . . What you need is a firm line. Nobody can accuse me of having lived for myself; I lived for the factory. And now there is nothing, absolutely nothing left, just scattered beams and broken glass and litter, that's the life of Zhuravlyov."

The engineer unwrapped a package and offered Zhuravlyov a piece of pie:

"Home-made. My wife baked it."

Zhuravlyov refused; he couldn't swallow anything. He thought maliciously: "What are you so pleased about, I'd like to know. To-day she bakes you pies; tomorrow she'll find some agronomist and you'll be out. Sits there smirking; says he's summoned by his Ministry; must be counting on promotion. And suppose there is a railway accident—one-two-three and out you go, no nonsense about that. Nobody can be trusted."

Before he left, Zhuravlyov had told Yegorov he was going only for a day or two—this was not the time to be away, with the new model having to be ready by the first of May. But a week went by and Zhuravlyov was still not back. Then Yegorov received a call from the head office. They said a new director, Golovanov, had been appointed. He would be there by the second week of April.

Yegorov told Brainin. Brainin was delighted:

"I know Golovanov. I worked with him in Sverdlovsk. A sensible man and knows his job."

"That's good . . . I don't see why we shouldn't finish the new model by the first of May."

"Of course we shall."

Brainin suddenly remembered:

"And what about Zhuravlyov?"

"Clearly, he's been fired. I've been told they meant to fire him long ago; they were looking for another man . . . It's an odd thing—Sokolovsky told me last winter that Zhuravlyov was going to be fired. I thought then that he was joking—you know Sokolovsky; he likes to have his fun . . ."

I · The Thaw

Brainin laughed and unfolded his *Pravda*.

There was still no government majority in France. That, so to speak, was symptomatic.

It occurred to Yegorov that Sokolovsky had said long ago that Zhuravlyov would be removed. Must have known something . . . Then he gave no more thought to Zhuravlyov.

Khitrov's wife said to him:

"It's a nuisance for you. You were used to Zhuravlyov."

Khitrov thought it over and said:

"Not at all. Nasty piece of goods, Zhuravlyov; wanted everybody to agree with him. I couldn't stand him. I don't mind the change at all. Of course, we'll have to wait and see what sort of a bird this Golovanov is. Anyway, he can't be worse."

All the talk was of Golovanov and nobody so much as mentioned Zhuravlyov. Only Grusha, his cleaning woman, kept asking, when would Zhuravlyov collect his luggage—all the rooms were cluttered up and she needed to clean out the apartment; the New One was expected soon.

As before, the siren hooted, the lathes chirped, people went on working, joking, arguing, and nobody felt the absence of Zhuravlyov. Those who had been made homeless by the storm cursed him briefly and then forgot him.

They watched happily the foundations of the first of the three new blocks of apartments being dug in Frunze Street. Vinogradov's wife said: "Two rooms, bath, and kitchen—there's a new life for you. Let them get on with it."

Where was Zhuravlyov? What had become of him? Not a living soul remembers. A storm comes, gives a lot of trouble, and passes over. Who remembers it once it has stopped roaring?

Those were the last days of winter. One side of the street was still frozen (twelve degrees below zero) but already, along the other, the icicles dripped loud drops.

For the first time since his illness, Sokolovsky got out of bed, crossed to the cloudy, unwashed window, looked out at the soft grey snow, and thought: "Spring is only a step away."

15

Sonya had often thought about her future, pictured to herself the factory where she would have to work, and wondered whether she would be successful, but those had only been vague thoughts and daydreams. Now, when she learned that she was being sent to Penza, she was suddenly faced with the realisation that her youth was over. Student friendships, exams, lectures, quarrels with Savchenko, all that was in the past. Before her lay the unknown city, the plant, and her immense responsibility. True, her work had been praised at college, but what had she ever done other than school exercises? What would she amount to when it came to practice? How easily you could lose your head and make mistakes. Her practical course last year had shown her the enormous difficulties.

She told her father: "I'm afraid I won't know how to cope with things." He tried to reassure her: it was always like that, you felt you'd never manage, then you got into it. He recalled the year he had spent in Penza a quarter of a century before—a nice town, a number of gardens, great traditions. Saltykov-Shchedrin had lived in Penza and outside it there was Tarkhany, Lermontov country. Sonya smiled and felt still more frightened. "What do I care where Lermontov lived? It is true his poetry moves you, although nowadays we experience things differently. But does Father think I'll sit daydreaming in the town park? The factory is what interests me, and how I'll prove myself at work."

She was still living with her parents and still wondered whether Savchenko would come to see her (he didn't even know where she was being sent). She was still in her familiar world but all her thoughts had already fled from it to remote, enigmatic Penza.

She was to leave at the end of February. Then her departure
was put off as there was some talk that Borisov might be sent instead and that she would get a job at the Farming Machinery
Trust. Now she was told to go to Penza after all. Her father said:

"We ought to celebrate."

She refused: "Not now. It will be time enough when I've done
some work and come back on leave. That will be different."

Her mother sighed over Sonya's leaving. "How will she get on
out there? She doesn't really feel like going. I am convinced she
is not indifferent to Savchenko. She is only hiding it; and he's a
good boy. I wish they'd marry. Instead of that, she is going off—
and she's so young. And he is staying here—he's young, too; his
head could easily be turned. I wish they'd come to an understanding. I should feel less worried."

A few days before Sonya was to leave, her mother could hold
out no longer:

"Sonya, why doesn't Savchenko ever come to see you? You
haven't had a quarrel, have you?"

"Why should I quarrel with him? He's just busy."

"Does he know you are going?"

"Of course he does. I met him in the street the other day. He
said he wanted to drop in on Father but he had an awful lot of
work."

Sonya blushed: how well she had learned to lie! "To think I
haven't seen him since that night . . . He hasn't even bothered
to find out where I'm going. He cares nothing for me. I just imagined it . . . But I am not going to tell Mother . . . Besides, it's
not her business." And Sonya added:

"Why do you keep asking about him? I agree with you that he
is nice, but he is not my ideal man. It is unpleasant to receive
attentions from a man you're not attracted to."

Andrey Pukhov had a bad night, worse than any he had ever
had before. He felt that he was dying and mentally took leave of
all his dear ones. Sitting up in bed and peering at the blurred
stain of the window, he wondered with a pity he could hardly

bear: "Poor Nadya! With Sonya gone, how will she stand it on her own?"

He took care not to wake her and said nothing to her in the morning, only stayed in bed until midday. Then he struggled to his feet but found he must lie down again, so that he did not go to see Seryozha, though he had promised that he would go.

Andrey suddenly had a glimpse of himself and became thoughtful. "Perhaps Sonya really has some grounds for making fun of me? It does seem funny—straining myself desperately to go and see Seryozha. It does seem a tiny world . . . But what can you do: you have to fight, you can't live if you don't. When I was young I fought shoulder to shoulder with all the others. That was not only during the Revolution—long before. And also later —I struggled in my work. And with myself—nobody knows that. After all, there have been heavy blows, sorrows, failures, doubts; I had to fight to keep my faith in men. And I am still fighting— even when I'm talking to Seryozha, trying to pass on to him a lit- tle of my experience, feelings, thoughts. I'm fighting death. It en- circles me; it lies in wait for me. At night, in the dark and quiet, it tries to get the better of me and I struggle as best I can. In his old age a man dries up and shrinks: his mind sees further but his world gets narrower, tighter. I try to think of the lives of others, to break out of this room where every night I have to struggle all alone with death. But even there, I'm doing what I have done all my life. It's too soon for Sonya to understand that, and to explain it would be useless."

In the last few weeks his attitude towards Volodya had changed. He used to get indignant with him, but now, looking into his mocking eyes, he thought: "Poor Volodya. He has brains, gifts, he isn't a bad boy, but there is something lacking in him. He slouches through life like a grown-up waif." He knew he couldn't influence his views and he no longer argued with him or took no- tice of his cheerless jokes, but only tried now and then by some chance word, or without words, to convey his tenderness. Volo- dya felt this, and was careful not to show that he was moved.

134

I · The Thaw

With Sonya, Andrey had one more long conversation after she confessed to him her diffidence about her job. During this talk there were again moments when they ceased to understand each other. Sonya suddenly broke in: "Why do you keep talking about people? People don't frighten me. Even if my chief turned out to be some kind of Zhuravlyov, it wouldn't be all that frightening . . . It's the change from textbooks to machines—how will I manage that? That's the trouble." Pukhov felt lost. But immediately there arose again between them that inward contact which they both welcomed. What made it easier perhaps was their awareness that in a few days they would part. (Each thought with sadness: shall we ever meet again?)

That conversation convinced Pukhov that Sonya's business-like dryness of manner was put on and hid a young, proud, passionate, and timid heart.

On the eve of her departure, Sonya was sitting in her room. It was tidy and it looked empty. She had burned her schoolgirl diaries, letters from her college friends and from Savchenko, and had thrown away a mass of trifles that because of their connection with events in her past life had until recently been dear to her. The house was quiet—Nadezhda Yegorovna had gone out shopping. Volodya hardly ever stayed at home—he had been commissioned to decorate the foyer of the caterers' club. Sonya strained her ears: who was with her father? Gorokhov? No, it was a different voice . . .

"Andrey Ivanovich," said the unknown voice, "can you understand it? When she told me, I felt so afraid I thought I couldn't go on living. Later on I laughed it off. I had other interests. Everything returned to normal—I simply thought that there had been a myth and now the myth had vanished. And now, suddenly, it has all come back again of itself, for no reason I know of . . ."

"That has happened to me more than once." (This was her father.) "They say a human being is forgetful. It isn't true. A man forgets when he wants to forget, but what is real stays with him till the end—I can say it now, until he dies . . ."

Sonya, her curiosity aroused, looked through the half-open door. She saw an adolescent, freckled and red-haired, wearing large glasses. Pukhov noticed her.

"Is that you, Sonya? Come in and be introduced. My young friend, Seryozha. My daughter, a mechanical engineer."

Sonya went to her room. "How strange he is. He was talking to that boy as to an adult. What an absurd scene . . . I don't believe he has ever spoken like that to me. I felt sure it was some old friend of his." Then she grew thoughtful. "Perhaps he's right. That boy was gazing at him positively with adoration. That time we had an argument, Father said he wanted to pass on something of himself to others. He could hardly do that with Volodya. And I always pretend I don't need teaching, I have my own point of view. So he has trained these boys . . . I often used to ask him how I should behave. But I couldn't ask him what to do about Savchenko! To begin with, it would be humiliating. And, then, nobody can give advice on a thing like that. Anyway, none of that is relevant now—I'm leaving and Savchenko is not in love with me. The problem is liquidated. I have even burnt that photo of us together. I want to start a new life—without any rubbish trailing after me."

The day she left, her mother and Volodya took her to the station. Her father remained at home—Sonya said firmly it was too far for him and much too cold, and it would only be upsetting. As she was afraid of being late, they arrived an hour in advance.

Sonya was now feeling briskly cheerful—she thought she must have invented many of her difficulties. She had her training and her character; she would do all right.

In the stuffy waiting room a baby was howling. Volodya made depressing jokes. His mother, to conceal her nervousness, chattered about home-made cakes. She had meant to bake some for Sonya's journey, but owing to some misfortune, the pastry had failed to rise.

"*Announcing the departure of train 176, for Rtishchevo, Kirsanov, and Tambov. Passengers please take their seats.*"

"Rtishchevo—that's mine."

Halfway up the platform Sonya stopped; her face had a look of fear. Her mother exclaimed delightedly:

"You've come to see her off. How very nice!" Savchenko joined them.

Sonya said nothing. Volodya took his mother's arm.

"Come, Mother, let's go look at the train."

They moved away.

"How did you find out when I was going?"

"Your brother told me."

"I see. Why didn't you come to see me?"

"I thought you didn't want me to. Did you?"

"That wasn't what I said. It wasn't nice of you not to come."

"You spoke that time in such a way . . . I thought you didn't want me to."

"And did you want to?"

"Why do you ask? When we stood by the gate . . ."

"Don't let's quarrel at the last moment. I thought you understood. Why didn't you come in when I asked you to that time?"

"You asked me in to tea with all the others."

"And you suppose I always mean what I say?"

"Sonya, when will you come back on leave?"

"You must be mad! How can I take leave? I'm only just starting work."

"Do you know, I didn't take my leave last year. I'll come to Penza."

"On no account . . . When do you want to take your leave?"

"Soon. So you forbid me to come?"

"What would you do all day? You'd be terribly bored. Penza is not the Caucasus."

"I'd come to see you, not just the town."

Volodya and his mother now came back from looking at the train. Nadezhda said it was a very long train and suggested, after a glance at Sonya, that they should walk a little more; it was too cold to stand.

Savchenko asked diffidently:

"Sonya, you won't forget me?"

"One forgets what has no importance. The important things remain."

"And you consider this important?"

"How am I to know? I haven't tested it; I may forget!"

"But what do you think at this moment?"

Sonya looked at him; her eyes darkened. She was grateful that there was a crowd. Otherwise she might have kissed him.

Volodya said: "Didn't you hear? The conductor says you must get in."

She kissed her mother, then Volodya. Savchenko waited for her to say something. She held out her hand, her eyes shining: "I'll write . . . Can you hear me, Mother? The moment I arrive . . . Kiss Father for me."

Now Savchenko was on the bus going to the factory. He felt bewildered. Sonya had told him nothing. He didn't even know whether they had quarrelled in the end or made up. At one moment she had seemed to say that she would write to him, but apparently she had meant her mother. "Obviously she doesn't want me. When I said I would come to Penza, she said: 'On no account.' And yet she looked at me in such a way that I could hardly keep from kissing her. I can't stop thinking of her nowadays. It's all romanticism, as Koroteyev says. But then, it's easy for him to talk. He is an old man—well, not old exactly, elderly, he must be nearly forty—at his age one doesn't think about such things. I can't keep my mind from her. And the extraordinary thing is this: as it never comes to anything between us, I ought to be feeling miserable, and instead of that I'm happy. Just seeing off a friend should make you sad—and yet at this moment I feel gay. Still, I am quite sure I love her. Then why should I be feeling gay? Of course, there are many reasons. Koroteyev said I'd make good. That's most important. Our factory is wonderful. I like seeing it all as in a picture-book. First our conveyor belt—that's easy, I see that every day; then another factory where our machines are making tractors; then huge tractors rushing out into the steppe; then corn, lots and lots of corn, and the country growing richer, stronger; and then Communism . . . Anybody would feel happy in such a factory. And there are other things: there's *Hamlet*. And it's the end of winter; soon it will be spring—everybody's gay in spring. And there is Sonya. Does she love me? I don't know. But she exists and I've just been talking to her; that's marvellous in itself . . . Will she write to me? If she does, I'll go to Penza. If not, I won't—not for anything. I won't take my leave at all . . . Now I have to tell Koroteyev that the welding system is all right—there won't be any more surprises—we were checking on it all day yesterday. Only I'd better comb my hair or he'll notice something."

Outside Koroteyev's door he took out a comb, looked in the mirror, and slicked down his bristling hair. His eyes looked strange, staring. "That's from thinking about Sonya. Now I'll think of welding, and my eyes will get back into their sockets."

Sonya remained standing in the corridor. She was still living in the world she had just left. "He said he'd come . . . Well, if he really means it, let him . . . Father was right—you forget what you need to forget. Perhaps he'll forget me in a month. I must write to him that if he really means to come he mustn't until the summer. But if I write he'll come. Better not decide anything—let it decide itself . . . The snow is grey—so it should be, it will soon be April . . . I think everything will be all right in Penza."

She went into her compartment. A stout man in a rust-coloured jacket was saying to an army doctor: "We have a wonderful system of ventilation in our workshops."

Sonya thought: "Perhaps he comes from the factory I'm going to. That would be lucky; I'd hear about it now. I wonder what machines they have . . . No, it's a watch factory, not mine . . . What awful cigarettes he smokes . . . All the same, it was nice that Savchenko came . . . Funny, it's only three o'clock and I feel quite sleepy. Didn't get much sleep last night; it was the ex-

139

citement . . . Have to change at Rtishchevo, but Rtishchevo won't be for some time . . ."

Sonya slept, her head inclined a little to one side. Her face was peaceful, happy. The man in the rust jacket was saying they had intended to have showers, but hadn't put them in because the budget was cut—when suddenly he stopped and became absorbed in looking at her.

The long train puffed slowly and busily through the limitless fields blanketed with soft spring snow.

16

SOKOLOVSKY LOOKED AT HIS watch. Four o'clock . . . too early to get up.

It was a week since he had returned to work. But since his illness his nerves had gone to pieces, he slept less well than ever, and no drugs did him any good.

While he was still running a temperature, all the details of Volodya's story about Zhuravlyov came back to him. He felt neither astonished nor indignant. He thought: "Here it comes again," and yawned anxiously. He was himself puzzled by his calm—after all, Zhuravlyov had behaved outrageously. After six years of working together . . . "And what difference does that make? I'm past being surprised. As Vera would say, I've developed an immunity."

When Volodya told him of Zhuravlyov's removal, he merely said: "I see . . . well, it was to be expected." Volodya did not ask him why. He had realised that, for all his apparent cynicism, Sokolovsky was naïve, just like his father; they both believed in justice.

Sokolovsky had spent two weeks in bed. During that time,

I · The Thaw

Vera came to see him every morning. By evening he was tensely awaiting her return; but she had told him from the beginning: "You mustn't talk," and he had never ventured since that day to speak to her of what was in his heart. Volodya dropped in now and then to cheer him up and talked of trifles. One day Sokolovsky started a conversation about the Spanish school of painting. Volodya grinned: "My last commission was for pedigree hens. Now I am portraying a young citizen full of the joy of life, holding in her hand a box of mixed chocolates, naturally of the most expensive kind. It is most important that each variety of sweet should be exactly represented. And you want me to think of Goya."

The days were long—no work, no sleep, no people—and Sokolovsky thought of many things: of his youth, of the signalling system, of his friends who had fallen in the war, of Mary, of new welding methods, of Zhuravlyov, of life on other planets, of Filatov's operations, of the awakening of Asia, of the struggle for peace. But, whatever he was thinking of, his mind ceaselessly returned to Vera. He remembered that in a conscious moment between bouts of fever he had seen her eyes. Their look had been extraordinary and nothing that Vera could say now would ever sober him completely. At times he asked himself: "Did I imagine it?—I had a frightful fever—did I really see her then, or only later when I could plainly hear and understand her ordinary voice and everyday expression? I don't believe it; I am sure it was her eyes I saw and that they were full of tenderness."

Half past four. Sokolovsky began to feel a rising tenseness. To-day, for the first time since he had been ill, he would go to see her. He would thank her for looking after him. She would ask him how he felt and would try to keep to her role of doctor a little longer. After that she would be silent, and he, too, would have nothing more to say. "No, that won't do. Silence is worse than anything; I must constantly fill the room with words. Anything. I'll tell her about Fomka tearing Pukhov's trousers. And about Pukhov painting mixed chocolates. And in this connection—or in no connection—I'll start talking about Chinese sculpture of the Tang period. Then perhaps Vera will also tell me something . . . She said Zhuravlyov's former wife was staying with her—Yelena Yegorovna, or was it Yelena Borisovna?—she may be there. That will make it all much simpler—ordinary teatime talk. Then Vera will be called away; and if she isn't I shall get up and say goodbye. There won't be anything to wait for . . . But why did I see her looking at me with that expression? Nothing will ever efface that. And after all, do we really need words, explanations, scenes between us? In the evening all the brilliant colours vanish; everything seems muted, almost dulled. But what depth—stillness—it makes your head spin . . ."

At five he got up. Fomka stretched himself and crept forward on his stomach, offering his morning greeting. Unlike any ordinary decent dog, he never fawned or leapt, barking cheerfully, or wagged his tail. He only pressed himself to Sokolovsky's feet and looked up at him with eyes full of love, pain, and fear.

"What is it, poor little one?" Sokolovsky asked. "Did you have a nightmare? Did they beat you in your dream?"

Fomka stared at him unwaveringly; his eyes were as sad as a human being's. "Poor devil, wants to tell me something. It's a shame he hasn't got words. I expect they gave him a good hiding. The idiot isn't any wiser since I've had him—still watchful to the point of madness. A good thing I grabbed him in time when he leapt at Barykhina. Pukhov says I must get rid of him or I'll get into trouble. But who would have him? They'd shoot him. You can see he trusts me, the way he looks at me. I understand it's his life that's twisted him, but not everybody would."

By six Sokolovsky had finished shaving and had taken Fomka out. Coming in, he stopped to see if the paper had been delivered. Instead of it, a long, narrow envelope fell out of the box—a letter from Mary.

Dear Father,
　　Congratulate me. There have been big changes in my personal life. In Paris I had no luck: there are too many new things;

142

it is difficult to find a public. I tried to give a performance, got
into debt, and in the fall went back to Brussels. Here a performance was arranged for me. Felix Vandervelde, the art critic—
now my husband—wrote about my dancing. That was how we
met; he proposed and I accepted him. Naturally he can't live
only by his writing. He has to spend all day working in a bank,
but he is a sensitive person and we understand each other perfectly. Recently he told me that an important newspaper might
send him as a correspondent to Moscow, to write about the Moscow theatre and to report on the possibilities of trade relations
between East and West. Of course, this is still far from certain,
but now I dream of going with him. It would give me a chance
to see you and to show my dances to the Moscow public. Felix
is far from being a Communist, but he is a man of crystal-clear
integrity; he listens to what I tell him, and I never forget that I
was born in Russia. I don't suppose my views are the same as
yours, but on the whole I am a sympathiser. I don't altogether
understand how you live out there, but if I come with Felix I
will understand at once. After all, I know the language; that's
the most important thing. And so, if there are no new diplomatic
conflicts and if the paper doesn't change its mind, we may see
each other soon.

Your daughter,
MARY VANDERVELDE

Sokolovsky turned the sheet of lilac paper over and over in his
fingers and gazed in wonder at Mary's photograph. There was
something of her mother in her . . .

Six thirty. Too early to go to work. He opened a book, the life
of Benvenuto Cellini. Then he shut it again and surprised himself by sitting down and writing:

Dear Mary,
   I congratulate you. If you come to Moscow I will try to see
you. I can't imagine what you are like. In the old snapshot of
you as a student I recognise something, but the other one, in the
Greek tunic, I don't understand at all. Nor do I understand your
letter. You speak too lightly of big things. I understand that you
wish to see Moscow. I doubt if anything will come of your plan
to dance. We have a good ballet; you must surely have heard of

143

it. Of course, both you and your husband, if he is an honest man, will find it interesting to see a different world. But don't think that because you were born in Moscow you will find it easy to understand. I remember you as a little girl playing in the sand-heap on the Gogol Boulevard; there were other children playing with you. Those children know how we live and why: they have grown up here, worked here; they have been through many sorrows, joys, and hopes. It is not your fault that your mother took you away to Belgium, but you must look at this thing sensibly. You must realise that in our country you will feel a tourist, a foreigner. You say yourself that you don't understand how we live. Even if you spent some time here, if you looked at how I work and how my comrades work, and saw what makes us happy or indignant, you would still understand nothing. It is a different world; it is altogether different! Why did it all begin here, and not, let us say, in Brussels? Probably because we had less bread and more heart. It's all very complicated; it's part of a long, hard life. Think about it some time. There are times when I forget your tunic and your letters and think simply, "My daughter," and call you little Masha. Miracles do happen; perhaps under the shell is hidden . . .

Sokolovsky put down his pen and stared astonished at the long, closely written sheet. "I've lost my mind . . . who am I writing to, and why? . . . How could I explain anything to her? As if she needed my instruction. Let her live peacefully with her Felix, if he really is an honest man and if he sits in his bank because he has to and not because he's playing the market . . . I'll send her a wire—just congratulations, that's enough."

He tore the unfinished letter into small pieces.

An hour later he was discussing Brainin's project with him. He had stopped thinking of Mary and of the abyss that separated their two worlds. In front of him stood the model lathe constructed according to Brainin's design. Some of it was good, but there were certain weaknesses. Brainin lacked imagination; that useless valve there was a legacy from an older model . . . In his absorption with his favourite work, Sokolovsky forgot everything.

At eight that evening he went to Vera's. He had been afraid

144

that Yelena Borisovna (or was it Yelena Yegorovna?) would be there, but she was out. He thought Vera looked annoyed with him for coming and greeted him coldly.

"Perhaps you are busy?"

"No."

What was he to talk about? There simply was no subject and he knew it was too late to think of one. It would almost have been better if Lena had been there. "All the same, we did talk in the old days. Sometimes there was a silence, but we talked, and now —nothing. Something has changed. Vera feels it, too. How long can you sit in silence?"

He tried to start a conversation:

"Pukhov the painter used to come and see me when I was ill. Last time, we talked about Goya. There are two pictures of his, 'Youth' and 'Age': Death, like a porter sweeping out a yard, sweeps out with a broom those who have stayed too long . . . Well, so then Pukhov told me he had to paint a picture of mixed chocolates. He's in a complete muddle, Pukhov. He hasn't grown up. Sorry, that wasn't what I was talking about . . . What I meant to say was that I asked him about Leonardo . . ."

He stopped half way through the sentence. After all, it was not so very interesting, what pigments Leonardo used. Vera would be annoyed; she'd say she was tired. Better say nothing.

Vera straightened the cover on the table, shifted the lamp, pulled the blind down, and snapped it up again. She must make an effort to entertain her guest.

"Today I went to see old Pukhov. He had a pupil with him, an interesting boy, fond of anatomy, wants to be a doctor . . . You're not tired, Evgeny Vladimirovich? You shouldn't do too much after your illness . . ."

He said nothing. A clock struck in the next room; nine. Suddenly he got up and said tonelessly, almost inaudibly:

"Vera Grigoryevna, last time I was here, you didn't understand what I told you about the aloe . . . When I was ill . . ."

She broke in hastily:

"Don't! You mustn't!"

Again there was a silence. Vera had turned away; Sokolovsky could not see her face. He was thinking of how she had looked at him when he was ill.

She dragged out, almost voicelessly:

"Evgeny Vladimirovich, we are not children. Why talk about it?"

The bell rang: Vera was needed at the Kudryavtsevs'.

Vera hurriedly put on her coat and tied a scarf over her head. He knew that they were parting for many days. He said listlessly: "Good-bye, Vera Grigoryevna."

She shook her head, embarrassed:

"No, Evgeny Vladimirovich, wait for me. I'll be back soon."

She smiled. Now her face looked young and lost. If Lena had seen her then, she would have thought: "She's younger than I am." But Lena wasn't there. In the dark hall Sokolovsky could see neither Vera's smile nor the expression of her eyes. But it seemed to him that she was looking at him exactly as she looked that night he caught the glimpse of her when he was ill.

He waited for her patiently, standing by the window.

And outside the window there was a disturbance, excitement. At last, winter was on the run.

Along the pavement, the snow had melted and turned into a stream. Only over there, in the front garden, a little was still left. The casement was open but you couldn't feel it. Pity the window was still sealed so that you couldn't open it. Through the casement came the sound of voices.

Everything was all at once alive and resonant.

"Funny thing: now Vera will come in, and I'm not even thinking of what I'll say to her. I won't say anything. Or I'll say: 'Vera, the thaw has come.'"

17

THE LAST PERSON TANECHKA EX-
pected to see was Volodya. He had not been near her since January. Twice she had run across him in the street. He told her he
was mouldering away; he might drop in one day but really it was
better for them not to meet. They only upset each other. Tanechka understood that he wanted to break off and cried a little,
then agreed that he was right—better a clean break than to drag
it out.

And now, there he was again out of the blue. She felt annoyed.

"You needn't expect me to be moved to tears. You said we had
to break off and I agreed with you completely. It's silly to go back
to what isn't there any more."

Volodya smiled wryly:

"I won't try to persuade you. It's only that I am in a wretched
mood, and it's spring outside. I was going past your door and I
thought perhaps you were bored as well and would come for a
walk with me. We might go to the town park."

Volodya had guessed the truth. Tanechka was depressed; she
had little in her life to make her cheerful. When she had stopped
seeing him, the actor Griftsov had become attentive. She didn't
like him. He had no talent; he was eaten up with envy and he
had sweaty hands. She told him straight out that he was not to
count on her. On her free evenings she stayed home alone, sew-
ing, reading Dickens, or lying in bed, crying into her pillow. On
the stage she had had nothing but flops recently. Ophelia was a
disaster; though the audience clapped, she knew that she could
hardly have been worse. Then she acted in a Soviet play in the
part of a laboratory assistant who unmasked the professor for

subservience to foreign ideas. It was terrible, not a live word in it. When she made her speech flaying the professor, the audience laughed and she longed to cry: why do I have to grimace and shout these imbecilities? Soon it would be summer. Kashintseva would spend her leave in the country with her mother and Danilova in Yalta—she was having an affair with some geologist. Tanechka thought of her own summer with misery—touring in July and her leave in August. She would apply to go to Zelenino; that suited her purse. But she could see it all in advance: conversation at lunch on the benefits of steamed cutlets for those who were taking the cure; picking worm-eaten mushrooms in the afternoon; somebody getting drunk at dinner and making a scene that everybody else would go on chewing over; then the crossword from the *Ogonyok*, with twenty people torturing themselves over a mineral of six letters starting with B.

"All right, let's go . . . What do you think, shall I put on a coat or a rain cape?"

"Cape. It suits you better, and it's quite warm. Haven't you been out today?"

"I have, but I don't remember. I didn't pay any attention."

The street was gay and shining, with wet pavements. At the kiosk, there were still some old paper bouquets, but small bunches of violets, freshly sprayed, sparkled among them. Tanechka, however, walked along dejectedly. She felt as if Volodya had invited her only to hurt her feelings. "All he wants is to show that he need only beckon and I'll forget everything. Well, he's wrong. Perhaps I did once have some sort of feeling for him, but that's quite gone."

She felt like being nasty:

"You're quite a stranger. Have you been keeping well? Or rather, to speak your own language, have you been earning well?"

"Not very. I was unlucky. I did a portrait of Zhuravlyov, the Leader of Industry, and he was fired. They say he is now in charge of a unit that manufactures office seals. The portrait won't fetch ten roubles."

"Are you very sorry?"

"On the whole, no. It was good that he was fired."

"All the same, what are you doing?"

"I have done a panel for the caterers' club, and I hope soon to be commissioned to do something else along the same line."

"That means you are doing hack work as before . . . And what is Saburov doing?"

"Painting. I was there night before last. Apparently they came to him from the union and chose two pictures for the exhibition. He says they chose the two worst, but all the same, it's a good sign. I'm pleased for him."

"How strange. You used to try to prove to me he was a schizophrenic."

Volodya said nothing. Walking ahead of them were a couple whose very backs showed that they were in love and engaged in a stormy conversation. Volodya grinned:

"You and I are like a couple who have celebrated their golden wedding."

"I don't see that. Personally I have nothing special to remember."

"I have . . . But it doesn't matter. Saburov has done another picture of his cripple, this time in a pink blouse."

"You didn't like it?"

"On the contrary, I liked it a lot. But it is not the kind they'll take for the exhibition."

"And what do you conclude from that?"

"Nothing whatever. Or if you like, I conclude that I am a hack, but that's nothing new."

"You used to tell me everybody was. Why the minor key?"

"I don't know."

"Odd that you haven't made a single wisecrack. I hardly know you!"

"I often hardly know myself. Father used to tell me I was going in the wrong direction. I thought so myself. Now it turns out that I'm not going anywhere at all. However, that's not an interesting subject for discussion, especially on a fine day . . . I heard you played Ophelia."

"Yes, abominably."

"Savchenko was in raptures. He said you were very moving and he had always imagined Ophelia just like that."

"Well, he must be easy to please, because I really did act abominably. It happens sometimes; I simply couldn't get into the part . . . In the old days you used to laugh and tell me none of that mattered. Have you changed your mind about that, too? Is there such a thing as art, after all?"

"I haven't thought about it. What I have been thinking about chiefly is that *I* do not exist in art; that, regrettably, is a fact. Either I have never had a kopeck's worth of talent, or else I had five kopecks' worth and I gambled it away at the first street corner. But why talk about it? . . . Look at our pair of lovers. They've had a quarrel. She ran away from him across the street. He followed her and now they are back again on our side."

"You mean he won?"

"No, but this side is sunny. Sonya and Savchenko used to quarrel all the time and make up like that."

"Are they getting married?"

"No. She's gone to Penza. They'll quarrel and make up by mail. Father misses her badly."

"How is he?"

"A little better these last two days, but the doctors aren't hopeful. I believe he only keeps alive through sheer strength of will, fights it out day by day."

"Your father is a very remarkable man, do you know that?"

"I know everything, Tanechka. Even things I'll never tell."

His voice was so melancholy that Tanechka felt ashamed. "I shouldn't tease him all the time. He's not himself—no airs, no epigrams. He must be feeling very low. Like me . . ."

"Don't lose heart, Volodya. I often do myself. But then, I think suddenly everything might change. Don't laugh; I am really sure that it can happen. Do you believe in miracles?"

"What do you mean by a miracle?"

"Well, for instance, you are feeling terrible, and then suddenly you are all right; everything is changed. I mean everything is the same—the town and people and things—and everything is different. Do you understand?"

"Anything can change a mood. Any nonsense. I saw Sokolovsky yesterday. Do you remember I used to tell you about him? A gloomier guy I've never met. Well, yesterday I arrive and there he is, laughing, joking, talking. I even asked him what had happened to him. He said: "Nothing. It's the spring." He must be close to sixty. How many times has he seen the spring? If that's what you call a miracle, then I believe in miracles."

"No, I'm not talking about the weather. It can go much deeper than that. You'll meet somebody, and you'll really fall in love. Or you'll begin to work and find that you're absorbed in it. Like Saburov. Didn't you say yourself that he was happy? Perhaps Sokolovsky has done something that pleased him in his work. You used to tell me he was devoted to it."

"He's capable of being devoted to the astronomer's discovery of the existence of life on Venus. That's all he needs in life. Look, Tanechka, our lovers are going to the park, too."

"Naturally. It's always full of lovers. They'll sit and kiss. And what shall we be doing? Cursing or snivelling?"

"Neither. We'll wish them happiness. Pity we can't see their faces, but we'll assume that they are very, very charming."

In summer the park is hot, there is music, the trees stifle in the dust and soot, and there are people on all the benches reading newspapers and talking over their everyday affairs. But at that time of the year it was almost empty; there were only lovers and eccentrics—there was too much slush for anybody else. Here and there the snow still lay in sweaty patches and in the shadows the puddles glimmered with ice, but in the sun you could already see the bright sprouting grass. A wide lawn in the distance was black all over; only one corner was beginning to be faintly green. The old pussy willow had fat silver buds on it. The birds were fussing,

151

shouting, searching—presumably for food or lodging, but it seemed that they had started a most interesting conversation.

"Look, Tanechka, there is your complete assortment of miracles."

"I don't know what you are talking about."

"Winter is over—that's one miracle. Please don't contradict me. I see you are too hot even in your cape, and you meant to put on a coat. The pussy willow is coming out—that's two. The grass— three. And here you have the chief miracle of all, just look! That small thing . . . As white as white . . . It's literally burst through the icy crust."

Volodya picked the snowdrop. Tanechka held it cautiously in her hand and laughed:

"It's quite true. A snowdrop."

The lovers who all this time had kept ahead of them now sat down. Volodya smiled: "It's nice that he thought of spreading out his raincoat; the bench is very wet. You see, I was right—they really are very sweet. He must be a student in his first year, and she is probably still at school. The final exams are near. But at the moment she is not thinking of that. At the moment she is sitting for another kind of exam, perhaps the hardest of all . . . I like it that they're so happy."

"It's nice that you dragged me out, Volodya. It was so dark and sad in my room. I was sitting, snivelling all to myself . . . And here it's lovely."

"Wonderful! I've never been so happy to see the spring as I am now. You know, when I was a boy I had a passion for breaking the ice on puddles. Once I fell in up to the knees, got an awful scolding at home. It's a delightful occupation. I now propose to commit a prank: Vladimir Pukhov, aged 34, member of the Artists' Union and flatteringly reviewed in the now defunct *Soviet Art*, is about to conduct himself like a schoolboy in a public place."

Volodya ran up to the big puddle covered with sparkling ice and kicked the crust. Getting more and more excited, he kicked it harder and harder. Tanechka sat watching him and laughing. And from high up in the spring sky, the sun warmed Tanechka and Volodya, and the lovers on their wet park bench, and the black lawn, and the whole winter-chilled world.

18

LENA, WALKING ALONG THE street, saw neither the sparrows bathing in the puddles nor the patches of blue sky nor the new cheerfulness in people's faces. She was herself astonished at her state. "Look at Vera," she thought, "she is transfigured. And I am like a mole that can't wake up. I must have turned to stone."

Her past doubts, hurt feelings, pride now seemed absurd. What had happened to her was what she had read about in books: she had come to love Dmitry with a love that cut across the whole of life, and he did not love her. There was nothing to be done in such a case.

The sun, the laughter, the noise breaking in on the winter silence frightened her. She walked along, isolated by her grief.

"And what happened then?" she asked herself afterwards. She could find no answer. Everything was transfigured and resolved by a single word, a word she had heard all her life.

It was at the corner of Soviet Street, near the bus stop, that Koroteyev saw her. He shouted at the top of his voice:

"Lena!"

It was the first time that he had called her by her name and not her patronymic, and it was this that settled everything.

Had anyone told him a moment ago that he would shout and run across the street, he wouldn't have believed him. He was a man who knew how to control himself; his whole life showed him to be that. He had had no thought of meeting Lena. When he glanced round distractedly he was saying to himself: "It was last spring I got to know her, so it was a year ago. Now I know it's useless to count the months or the years. Whatever happens, I can't forget her. Life has become cramped and empty. And yet what happiness it is that she exists! She has made me over; she has changed me altogether. Now I find it strange to think that last winter I could come forward at the readers' meeting with those absurd opinions! Everything has proved to be so much more complex. But I will never see Lena again . . ."

Now they were walking side by side, confused, hurrying, speaking without thinking.

"I was walking along. Suddenly I saw you by the bus stop."

"It's strange, I knew your voice at once . . . I don't know why I happened to go out . . . I sit at home all day . . ."

"You are not in a hurry?"

"No. Are you?"

"I?"

Koroteyev raised his eyebrows and peered with a surprised expression: yes, it really was Lena.

A woman was standing on a window-sill, washing the window panes, and the glass shone, reflecting the blue light. A little boy was eating ice cream. A girl carried a bunch of pussy willows. That tree they passed—Lena remembered it, she had seen it being planted one autumn evening, with the people crowding round to watch. It was still quite bare; but if you screwed up your eyes, you could just see a little covering of green down. "What day is it? I can't remember anything. I don't understand. What has happened? Where are we going?"

"Where are we going?" she asked herself aloud.

They came to a brown house with four stories and a tower. It was the house where Koroteyev lived. They walked in quickly. The hall was still cold; winter had not yet left it. How dark it was! One could hardly see the stairs. Neither Lena nor Koroteyev

154

felt the cold. Lena raised her head and her green eyes shone in the half light. Koroteyev kissed her. From the street came children's voices, the hooting of traffic, and all the noises of a day in spring.

II. THE SPRING

PRINCIPAL CHARACTERS

In Russian *a person may be addressed or referred to by his surname (e.g.* KOROTEYEV), *his first name (Dmitry), a diminutive of his first name (Mitya), or his name and patronymic (Dmitry Sergeyevich). For the convenience of the reader, the main characters in the novel, particularly those whose names appear in several forms, are listed below.*

KOROTEYEV, Dmitry (Mitya), Dmitry Sergeyevich, engineer
    His wife Lena, Yelena Borisovna, schoolteacher
    Her daughter by her first husband, Shura
    Vyrubin, Leonid Borisovich, Dmitry's stepfather
SOKOLOVSKY, Evgeny Vladimirovich, chief designer
    Mary Vandervelde (Mashenka), his daughter
    Fomka, his dog
PUKHOV, Volodya, Vladimir Andreyevich, a painter
    Sonya (Sonechka), his sister, a young engineer
    Nadezhda (Nadya), Nadezhda Yegorovna, their mother
    Andrey (Andrushka), Andrey Ivanovich, her deceased husband, a teacher
SAVCHENKO, Grigory (Grisha, Grigulya), Grigory Yevdokimovich, a young engineer
SABUROV, a painter
    Glasha, Glafira Antonovna, his wife
SCHERER, Dr. Vera, Vera Grigoryevna, physician
GOROKHOV, another doctor
DMITRIYEVA, Yekaterina Alexeyevna, new school principal

SEROV, English teacher
STEIN, mathematics teacher
VASYA, pupil of Lena
SERYOZHA, former pupil of Andrey Pukhov
TANECHKA, former actress friend of Volodya Pukhov
GOLOVANOV, Nikolay Kristoforovich, the new factory director
ZHURAVLYOV, Ivan Vasilyevich, the previous factory director
BRAININ, Nahum Borisovich, an elderly engineer
    Yasha, his son
YEGOROV, chief engineer
SAFONOV, engineer
KHITROV, engineer
ANDREYEV, a foreman
DOBZHINSKY, club manager
BUSHAGIN, an accountant
TRIFONOV, head of the production department of the Party Town
    Committee
    Marusya, his wife
OBUKHOV, secretary of the Party factory group
DEMIN, new secretary of the Party Town Committee

Surnames often take *a* in the feminine (e.g. Pukhov, Pukhova).

1

AT THE MEETING OF THE PARTY
Bureau, Dmitry Koroteyev, who had just come back from a cure
at Kislovodsk, looked so upset that Brainin asked him quietly if
he felt all right.

It was not that Sokolovsky, the head designer on whose account the meeting had been called, was a friend of his. Like most
other people, Dmitry was wary of his temper, but he admired
him and had been horrified when the year before, the manager,
Zhuravlyov, had slandered him. What depressed him now was
that Sokolovsky seemed to have given grounds for the new
charge against him. Dmitry was influenced in particular by the
speech of Brainin, whom he knew to be an honest man and incapable of accusing anyone unjustly. Brainin had spoken with
restraint, admitting that he felt embarrassed: "No one would
deny, so-to-speak, Sokolovsky's long record of useful work." All
the same, he "felt obliged to qualify the head designer's refusal to
submit to the instructions of the management as unworthy of a
Soviet citizen and a Communist."

Dmitry thought: "Pity I was away when Sokolovsky's project
was discussed. Savchenko said the idea was interesting. It was
Sokolovsky's temper that spoiled everything. As a designer he's
brilliant. The year I worked with him was the best possible training for me. It's sickening to think that Zhuravlyov tried to damage him by inventing that ridiculous tale about Sokolovsky's
sending his family to Belgium. Zhuravlyov was capable of any

161

dirty trick and he loathed Sokolovsky. I said at the time, I did not
believe a word of it. And I didn't believe that Zhuravlyov would
bring it off. After all, times have changed.

"All the same, Sokolovsky has been very rash. You can't walk
out of a production meeting. Pig-headed man. . . . He was determined to force his scheme through although, clearly, Golovanov and Yegorov were opposed to it. He should have given in.
Instead of that, he banged the door and was rude to them as
well . . .

"I don't like Safonov; he's stupid and he's jealous. Not that he's
a bad engineer. Not a match for Sokolovsky, of course, but he
does know his job. It's difficult to argue with him when he says
that discipline has to be the same for all. Though even if he said
that two times two make four, I would still want to argue with
him. It looks as if Golovanov doesn't altogether trust him either.
But Brainin is a different matter—no one could suspect him of ill
will towards Sokolovsky. He is incapable of trying to harm anyone; all he wants is to be left alone. All he's interested in, apart
from his job, is his family—where will Yasha be directed to work
and will Lyubochka be admitted to the Institute. Savchenko calls
him the 'so-to-speak ladybird.' And yet even Brainin, for all his
kindness, has come out against Sokolovsky.

"It's no use Savchenko getting excited. Golovanov isn't a Zhuravlyov; he does not abuse his privileges. But a manager's opinion can't be disregarded; he's got all the threads of administration
in his hands. And he can't call an ordinary workman to order for
being rude to an engineer and not insist on at least a minimum of
discipline from the head designer.

"Savchenko talks well, though I think this time he's wrong. I
always thought he had a lot in him. It's wonderful how quickly
he has got into his work. He's changed in the past year; he's
grown up. I remember how he used to come to talk to me about
his love affair, blushing and stammering. Now he has a new self-
confidence. It must be because he's happy. They say it's always
like that. And yet with me it's just the opposite: I used to be more

self-assured. Now, sometimes, when Lena asks me something, I feel quite lost, I don't know what to say. . . . But I must listen to what is going on."

The speaker was Andreyev, a foreman whose standing at the factory was very high. He said that Sokolovsky was an old Party member; the workers respected him; he was never too busy to help them, to explain a thing when they were in a difficulty. It wasn't comradely to pick on a thoughtless word . . .

Safonov objected: it was not a question of Sokolovsky's gifts as a designer or of his character in general. "Sokolovsky's work is first-rate. All the more reason for him to control himself and to admit that he was wrong. For without discipline, comrades, I can't conceive how any factory can get on, nor indeed how any man can get on in his own life, at any rate if he is a Communist . . ." Chief Engineer Yegorov sighed sadly. He liked Sokolovsky, yet he nodded, as much as to say: "It's true, you can't do without discipline."

Savchenko spoke again.

Dmitry suddenly felt tired to death. "What are they all arguing about? Everybody knows that Sokolovsky is wrong, but nobody can think of the factory without him. So what was the point of starting all this row? And what's the use of Savchenko's shouting? He won't convince anyone. A moment ago he was talking like a specialist, an adult. Now he's lost his temper like a schoolboy. He doesn't know what life really is . . ."

Dmitry was no longer listening to the speeches. Pictures from his past flickered before him like the scattered pages of a book. The autumn night when his stepfather was arrested—rain, reddish footmarks on the floor, his mother biting her handkerchief and weeping. The steppe, the retreat towards the Don, Panchenko by his side. Panchenko couldn't walk; he said he had rubbed a blister on his foot, but his foot was oozing blood. He didn't say he had been wounded by a shell splinter; he only begged: "Don't leave me behind." Natasha, blushing and smiling, smoothing Dmitry's creased forage cap with her fingers and saying with tears in her eyes: "After the war you'll forget me." Natasha's funeral in shattered Dresden. The fire in the assembly shop; Zhuravlyov's face black with soot; Dmitry congratulating him and Zhuravlyov, out of breath, excited and worn out, embracing him. . . . "So many happenings, mistakes, losses! You have to know how to survive everything. Savchenko doesn't understand that yet . . ."

Three months earlier, when Sokolovsky had submitted his project, no one dreamed that the affair would take such a dramatic turn. It was a question of metal cutting tools for a big factory on the Volga. It was true that Safonov had at once called Sokolovsky's scheme "a risky adventure." This was in Golovanov's office. Sokolovsky, though he might by now have been accustomed to Safonov's running down whatever he proposed, lost his temper and began to talk about red tape and being always out of date. "Our technique develops faster than you can keep up with it," he said crossly to Safonov. "That's all there is to it." Golovanov took Safonov's side: "It's ridiculous to be personal in a business discussion." He said that he did not deny the advantages of the electro-erosion processing of machine tool parts, but the factory had its own line and the customers were not asking for machine tools of this sort. He reminded the meeting that "innovation has to be combined with a degree of caution" and told them that, at the factory in the Urals where he had worked before, "some highly plausible schemes had failed to produce results and had only swallowed a mass of capital." Sokolovsky lost patience altogether and, instead of defending his proposal, shouted: "I am amazed at you, Nikolay Kristoforovich. You look at things from your own local point of view and refuse to take the customers' interests into account. And a long way your caution will get you! We've found that working in a groove costs even more. . . . It's a shameful thing to say: we're living in the atomic age, people are performing miracles, and you hang on to an antediluvian machine!"

Golovanov had criticised Sokolovsky's project not because Safonov had convinced him that it was no good but because he wished to know what Sokolovsky had to say. It was his habit, when in doubt, to provoke a discussion. People who did not know him well were surprised to hear him first objecting to a plan and afterwards defending it. But Sokolovsky had worked with him for a year; he should have realised that it was useless to lose his temper, that he must argue with Golovanov, and that if he succeeded in convincing him Golovanov would himself overrule Safonov. Yet he did not even bother to reply and only said curtly: "Think it over. And consult the customers. My scheme speaks for itself." Golovanov answered drily: "All right. We'll think about it." He was not easy to provoke—he was known for his almost unshakable calm—but they all realised that this time he was angry.

When Golovanov was sent the spring before to replace Zhuravlyov, he thought he would find the factory in a neglected state. But it turned out that the basis of production was sound, the engineers were capable men, and the quota had always been fulfilled. Everyone he questioned confirmed that Zhuravlyov had been good at production and had worked unstintingly. What they had against him was that he had been indifferent to the workers' needs, had neglected to build houses for them, and had in general been rude, conceited, and unfair.

Golovanov had started on his first factory job at the time of the first Five Year Plan. He had had no special training, but had been sent to the Urals simply as an organiser who had drive. In the twenty years he had spent at a big engineering works there, he had studied technical production methods, followed the current literature on the subject, and was now considered to be an outstanding specialist. As soon as he took over Zhuravlyov's work he hastened the building of the workers' dwellings, changed the personnel manager, obtained six new buses for the route that linked the workers' settlement with the town, and saw to it that a complete overhaul of the hospital and the maternity ward was included in the plan for the following year: in fact, he did everything that his predecessor had been unable or unwilling to do.

After weighing all that he had been told about the former manager, he had come to the conclusion that Zhuravlyov, though a poor administrator, had been a good technician, and he had reported that the condition of the works was satisfactory. He believed now that all Zhuravlyov's mistakes had been corrected. The workers' houses were being built; indeed, two blocks were already in use. And there had not been any breaks in production, even in Zhuravlyov's time.

Yet although Zuravlyov had held his job as manager for only six years and was now hardly remembered by anyone, those years had left their mark on the community. Zhuravlyov liked people to agree with him in everything and had favoured several sycophants and intriguers who had been eager to guess what was in his mind and ready, when it suited them, to slander anyone. Needless to say, these were just the men who had been loudest in abusing him when he was dismissed and who had done their best, by flattery or intimidation, to keep their place at his successor's side. Not much harm had come of this, for Golovanov was a modest man and had a wide experience of life. But a few honest people such as Brainin and Durilin, who had lived in constant fear of slander under Zhuravlyov, had somehow wilted. Thus, if Golovanov asked Brainin's opinion on a problem, he hardly ever got a straight answer: Brainin would say nothing until he knew what Golovanov's own opinion was.

Zhuravlyov had expected the factory to suffer by his dismissal. In fact, however, a year had passed and not only had the quota been fulfilled but people were more gay, more spirited, more friendly when they were at work. You could hear more laughter, more cordial conversation, and more happy whispering of lovers after work was done. It was perhaps just because of this that certain unhappy traces of what Andreyev called jokingly "the years of the crane" [1] leapt to the eye.

---

[1] This is a play on Zhuravlyov's name: *zhuravl* means crane.

II · The Spring

When Sokolovsky's project was first discussed, Brainin, seeing that the manager was hesitant, said cautiously: "You could hardly call it an economic certainty, so-to-speak. There are other concerns which go in for this sort of thing. And our customers haven't brought the matter up. . . . Though it's true, in point of fact, that orders have been falling off. But it would take a very long time to get familiar with the new process . . ."

Brainin had a high regard for Sokolovsky; he was himself a gifted engineer and it could not be said exactly that he had got into a rut. A quarter of a century before, he had been thought of as an innovator. But for a long time now he had distrusted any new proposal that involved a radical change in production methods. This was perhaps because he had seen several projects, which at first had looked attractive, come to grief; or perhaps he was merely getting old. He did add, however, that it might be worth considering the scheme and asking what the customers thought about it.

But Safonov had declared resolutely at once that the electro-erosion process could not possibly pay off. "The project," he said, "shows that comrade Sokolovsky has read the new books on the subject but not that he has a realistic attitude towards production."

Yegorov kept silent until Golovanov asked him for his opinion and then said vaguely: "It's complicated. . . . Very complicated."

It was Safonov who led the campaign against Sokolovsky. He was an ambitious and embittered man who, though Zhuravlyov had favoured him and Golovanov had treated him well, remained convinced that Sokolovsky stood in the way of his advancement. He was friendly with Khitrov, who had been one of Zhuravlyov's yes-men, and together they would often curse Sokolovsky's project and his character and what they called his "carrying-on with the woman doctor." "Of course, Zhuravlyov was a fool," Safonov would say, "but he did see through

Sokolovsky." As for Sokolovsky's new plan, he never mentioned it except as a "pathological symptom."

Sokolovsky was jumpy; he snapped at people and managed to turn even Golovanov, who was usually so equable, against him. At the end of two meetings Golovanov asked Safonov to revise Sokolovsky's project. Everyone realised that the manager thought the scheme too risky as it sood. A month later Safonov presented his own version.

Sokolovsky listened attentively to his explanations, nodding as if he agreed with everything Safonov said, but afterwards laughed rudely: "I can't think what you've been wasting your time on. There is no difference between your machine and the ones we're using now. Obviously you don't give a damn for the customers. Have it your own way, but don't expect me to play ball . . ."

Golovanov tried to pacify him but Sokolovsky left the room without waiting for the end of the meeting.

An hour later Sokolovsky felt so ill that he could hardly remain sitting at his desk, but when he left he mulishly trudged home on foot instead of asking for a car. He went to bed but did not send for a doctor, thinking irritably: "What can doctors do for me? So far as I know, they haven't yet found a way of making a new heart."

No one saw him at the factory for a week. Safonov told the manager that he had called him up but Sokolovsky had been rude to him and had refused outright to work on the approved version of the project. "Of course, we can do without him," said Safonov. "But it does undermine discipline. Obukhov says the matter ought to be put before the Party Bureau." (Obukhov was the secretary of the Party group.) Golovanov did not care for the idea—why make so much of it?—But he felt that he was not sufficiently familiar with the life of the factory to take a stand either way.

Sokolovsky realised that he had acted stupidly. "I'm getting irritable. That's the trouble. And then my health let me down.

I should have called up Golovanov and told him I was ill and
I should certainly not have walked out of the meeting . . ."
Every evening he made up his mind: "Tomorrow I'll go to
Golovanov and say: 'Let's have a serious talk. We are neither of
us schoolboys and this is an important matter . . .'" Why did he
not do it? It was not his pride that stopped him, but he was always put off at the last moment by sheer annoyance. "All right,"
he told himself. "I was wrong, I talked a lot of nonsense. But what
has that to do with my project? Why don't they think about the
machine? Surely Golovanov can't have taken Safonov's arguments seriously!"

At the Party Bureau meeting he sat—a tall, stiff, sullen figure—
silent and tapping the table with his pipe. Asked to speak, he
said briefly that as a Communist he submitted to Party discipline
but he thought the management's decision was wrong. After
a short silence he added angrily: "It's wrong and it's untimely,
and what's more it's unintelligent."

When Safonov had first spoken to Obukhov about Sokolovsky's
un-Communist behaviour, Obukhov had frowned. "They're exaggerating," he thought. "Sokolovsky is hasty and bad-tempered,
but it's a long way from that to refusing to work." Both Safonov
and Khitrov, however, had insisted: Sokolovsky had walked out
of a production meeting, he had stayed away from work for five
days, now he was pleading sickness but he hadn't called a
doctor, he had sworn at Safonov. Obukhov was fed up with the
two of them; all the same he told himself: "It does look as if
Sokolovsky has gone too far . . ." He consulted Trifonov, the
head of the production department of the Party Town Committee, and Trifonov had said without a moment's thought:
"How can there be any doubt? Of course he's got to get a shaking
up." So now Obukhov proposed that Sokolovsky should be reprimanded.[2]

Sokolovsky evidently wanted to say something; he actually got

---

[2] The lowest penalty imposed by the Party.

up but sat down again at once and, when the chairman asked him if he had any comment to make, answered that he had none.

Andreyev protested: "I don't understand. What's he to be reprimanded for? And I'm bound to add that no one will understand it at the plant."

Savchenko got up and began to talk about the new project but Obukhov interrupted him: the issue was not the project but Sokolovsky's refusal to submit to discipline. All the same Savchenko insisted: "You can't separate the two things. It was his scheme that Sokolovsky was defending. Admittedly he was abrupt . . . but say that tomorrow his proposal is accepted, how will it be possible to justify the reprimand?"

"It's true," thought Dmitry. "Why the reprimand? Sokolovsky isn't a boy; we're not likely to reform him. He's been snapping at people all his life, but he's never yet been in trouble with the Party."

The meeting was adjourned for a quarter of an hour. Conversation started up: the Chelyabinsk plant was pressing for delivery; there was a rumour that the Moscow Maly Theatre would come in August; Durilin had been sent to the hospital— the doctor feared he had an ulcer; there was trouble in the assembly shop again . . .

Brainin was explaining to someone: "The treaty with Austria is a serious blow to the position-of-strength policy, so to speak."

Sokolovsky asked Dmitry in a friendly tone: "Did you enjoy your leave, Dmitry Sergeyevich? We're having a late spring— last week there were two hard frosts."

Obukhov took Dmitry aside: "Savchenko is confusing the issue . . . What has the project to do with it? I quite realise that this is all very unpleasant, but you can't do without discipline. . . . Trifonov considers that Sokolovsky has gone too far. It seems to me that a reprimand is the best he can hope for."

After the adjournment, Savchenko once again asked leave to

speak but the chairman said that a motion had been made to close the discussion.

"It's a pity to hurt his feelings," Dmitry told himself. But seeing that all the others except Andreyev and Savchenko voted for the reprimand, he, too, reluctantly put up his hand.

At dinner that evening he was so upset that he could eat nothing; he said that he had a headache and sat silently until he could bear it no longer and then told Lena all about it. She asked him in astonishment:

"Why on earth did you vote for the reprimand?"

"Obukhov told me it was the only way out—he had had a talk with Trifonov. . . . It's a horribly unpleasant business. I realise that Sokolovsky has antagonized everybody, but it's disgusting to see Safonov posing as a champion of Party ethics. Savchenko was boiling; he went on protesting right up to the end. He's a romantic . . ."

"And is that a bad thing to be?"

He had never seen such an expression on Lena's face. Her eyes, usually gentle and affectionate, were staring at him sharply; her lips moved as if she were repeating something over and over to herself.

"I never said it was. I only meant that Savchenko is young and reacts differently from the rest of us . . ."

"Never mind that. Answer my question: why did you vote for it?"

"I don't really know . . ."

Lena went quickly out of the room. She picked up a book and tried to work. She forced herself to read a page, but she broke down and big tears fell one by one upon the book. She remembered that bright May morning, the dark staircase, the hooting of the cars outside. "How simple and straightforward everything seemed then! What's the matter with him? I trust him. I love him, so of course I trust him. But I don't understand. . . . He's been through so much, he can hide his feelings, he's got great self-control, and yet suddenly he gets muddled, he says what he doesn't really think, he repeats what other people say. . . . No, there's something in it that I simply don't understand. There he is in the next room, and I'm sure he's worrying, too. He's next door and yet he's miles away. It's dreadful that we can't talk it out! I'm crying like a schoolgirl; it's idiotic. If he came in I wouldn't even be able to explain what's wrong with me . . ."

From behind the other door Shura whispered loudly:

"Mother! Mother!

"Why aren't you asleep?"

"Teddy's paw has come off."

Lena sewed on the teddy bear's paw. For a minute she felt easier: nothing had changed after all—Shura, Mitya,[3] happiness . . .

Dmitry was dozing in his armchair. His face, usually stern, looked childish, or perhaps elderly; the lines at the corners of his mouth, which gave him his resolute, almost stubborn expression, were smoothed out. Lena looked in at him and tears once more filled her eyes—tears of pity, perhaps, or of a love for which she had no words.

2

TRIFONOV ARRIVED HOME, PREOCcupied as usual. His wife, Marusya, did not notice that he had come into the room.

"What's the book you're so deep in?"

"Chekhov."

Trifonov was surprised.

---

[3] Diminutive of Dmitry.

"Is it still the Chekhov Jubilee? I thought it was over long ago."

Marusya said nothing. She went out into the kitchen to warm up the semolina. Trifonov had chronic kidney trouble and was on a strict diet.

He thought gloomily: "Reading! She's got nothing to do but kill time. She has no idea of what responsibility means. The trouble is that people won't mind their own business. Look at Demin, for instance."

Trifonov had got on with the former first secretary of the Town Committee, Ushakov, although occasionally Ushakov had scolded him: "That Zhuravlyov of yours is an obstinate fool. Where are the workers' houses? He's been leading us up the garden path for three years now."—"They'll start on them in the summer," Trifonov assured him; "it's true that Zhuravlyov's at fault—he's neglected the living quarters. But there's one thing you've got to take into account—there's never been a single hold-up in production."

So when Ushakov was transferred to another job and Demin arrived, Trifonov was on his guard at once. Why was Demin so self-confident? ". . . man's only been here a couple of hours and he wants to turn everything upside down."

Very soon after he came, Demin heard that Krasnov, who was on the Housing Committee, had put his brother-in-law and three of his friends ahead of their places on the list. "We must make sure there are no other abuses," he told Trifonov. "All the lists will have to be checked. Do you remember how many names there are on them?" Hardly able to conceal his irritation, Trifonov replied: "A hundred and fifty families and thirty single people. But you can't go through the lists again.—People will start squabbling and it will affect their work." Demin raised an eyebrow: "What do you mean? Don't you trust the workers? That doesn't seem right."

Trifonov said to his wife: "Demin will soon be transferred. You'll see."

"Why? Isn't he doing all right?"

Trifonov was annoyed; Marusya didn't understand the simplest thing. "I've been here for eleven years, haven't I. . . . He could take that into consideration. But no, he's got to come and turn everything upside down. That's not the way to work."

This had been in November; and more and more frequently since then Trifonov had wondered: "Who knows? Perhaps it's me they'll transfer. It's impossible to understand a thing. . . . In the old days, if you asked Ushakov, he would say, do this or do that, and if he didn't know the answer there and then, well, he would call up Moscow. But Demin says: "You're the head of the department. It's your responsibility. Why don't you decide for yourself?" And who'll take the rap?—Trifonov. And another thing, Demin doesn't know how to pull a man up. So naturally people are getting slack. Like Nikitin bursting in on me and shouting: 'My son got twenty-two points and he didn't pass and Khitrov's girl only got seventeen and they passed her! I'm not going to let them get away with it!' Things are getting out of hand, that's what it is."

Trifonov was neither greedy nor ambitious. His wife always wore the same pleated lilac dress. They did not keep a maid. Trifonov read no books. He rarely went to the theatre, and when he did, he sat in his box yawning and asking his wife: "Do you think it'll soon be over?" Most evenings he sat in his room and worked.

He was, on the whole, good-natured; he sympathised with young couples who were kept waiting two years for their room and was sorry for anyone who lost his job unjustly. At the same time, such cases annoyed him: "Why must they come to me? Why not to the Trade Union or to the Housing Committee?" He looked on people's unsatisfactory circumstances rather as on ruts in a well-made road. You shouldn't pay too much attention to individual cases: that would be harmful to the general interest.

For Trifonov life was an uninterrupted succession of cam-

174

paigns and each new campaign crowded out the one before it. A few years earlier he had devoted himself to planting trees in the factory settlement. Then he had transferred his interest to the manufacture of the workers' clothes—their coats were ugly, the shoulders were too narrow—and when he was told that the acacia saplings he had planted had been eaten up by goats he looked up in surprise: "Well, what if they have?"

Last spring, when Ushakov had been concerned with recruiting people for collective farms, Trifonov had urged Golovanov to release factory workers for this purpose. Recently Obukhov had told him that seven people had asked to go to farms but by now Trifonov's mind was on something else. "How's the assembly shop?" he asked. "We'll have to put on the screws or they'll be getting us into trouble."

His present hobby-horse was the struggle against old-fashioned methods of production. "Just look at the campaign the government has put on!" It was true that the position at the works wasn't bad—you had only to look at the production figures: 104.7 instead of the 100 in the plan. But you didn't really feel that things were expanding. Golovanov was a knowledgeable man and he got on with everyone. All the same he didn't have Zhuravlyov's grasp. Yegorov was getting old, he'd given up . . . The campaign to develop new techniques was going ahead, a report would soon have to be made, and what would the factory have to show?

In his zeal, Trifonov was able to forget his personal dislikes. He considered Sokolovsky a nuisance but when he first heard of his scheme he wondered: "Who knows? Perhaps there's something in it." Then he read Safonov's report and smiled, half disappointed and half pleased: what else could you expect? Sokolovsky liked to dazzle people. He was determined to be a public figure. What was the Ministry for? And why should Golovanov be obliged to think about the customers? They had their own managers, their own Town Committees. Let them do their own worrying. . . . "Our factory has its own line."

And when Safonov said that Sokolovsky's scheme would involve a lowering of output and actually produced figures, Trifonov really lost his temper: "So not even the customers will be pleased. It's all eye-wash!" He never quite trusted words, but figures struck him as infallible.

When he heard that Sokolovsky had walked out of the production meeting and was behaving provocatively, he told Obukhov: "It looks as if you'll have to rap him over the knuckles."

Today the Party Bureau was holding its meeting. Sokolovsky would have an opportunity to be reasonable, and if he didn't take it he would have only himself to blame.

After dinner Trifonov opened his newspaper but he felt too nervous to read it. It was two hours since the meeting had begun. Obukhov had promised to telephone as soon as it was over. Sokolovsky was probably trying to get back into favour and dragging things out.

At last Obukhov called; the reprimand had been administered; only Savchenko and Andreyev had voted against it. Trifonov thought: "Andreyev is a good worker but he can't think straight; he's getting a bit above himself."

Calmer now, he looked at the headlines. "Difficulties over the spring sowing in the Petrovsk area." He smiled: he could just imagine Kharitonov's face as he read that! "By the first of May the glass works will be fully equipped to produce the planned output." "That was my idea, to push Petrichenko . . ."

"Home and School." He read the feature article by Merzlyakova: "I'd never have thought she could write such a good piece . . . I think Marusya is spoiling Petya—he's getting slack."

Petya was Trifonov's son, a lively, mischievous boy. Trifonov was fond of him but left his upbringing to his mother: it was her business; he had enough troubles of his own. In the previous autumn Petya had fallen ill; Trifonov had panicked and sat up with him all night; but in the morning the doctor came and diagnosed measles. Trifonov remembered that he had once had

measles, calmed down, and even shouted at Marusya when she
spoke of possible complications.

He put down his paper.

"Marusya! Has Petya been getting bad marks at school? What
do you mean, 'It just happened'? Nothing 'just happens.' A boy
that age ought to have a sense of responsibility. I've been thinking for a long time that he needs a good talking-to."

He called the boy in. Petya, looking down at the floor, repeated in a monotone: "I'll try harder, I promise. I really will try
harder . . ."

When Petya had at last gone to bed, Trifonov told his wife:

"Whatever you may say, it does no harm to shake him up now
and then. . . . Oh, by the way, I forgot to tell you, Sokolovsky
has been reprimanded. I told them ages ago they'd have to do it.
. . . It's really too bad, the way everything falls on my shoulders."

Looking at her husband's face, puffy and unhealthily pale,
Marusya could not resist telling him:

"You should take some leave. As far back as last summer the
doctor said to me that you needed to take a cure. It frightens me
to look at you."

Trifonov shook his head.

"And who would do my work? Demin, do you imagine?—
Don't you worry, I'll stick it out a bit longer. It's a good thing
they've given Sokolovsky a shaking. It's a load off my mind; better than any treatment.

3

A RAY OF SUNSHINE HAD LONG
pierced the blinds. It darted over the ceiling, then glanced down,
settled on the bedside table, and finally woke Lena. She raised

the blind and smiled. It was as if yesterday's tears had never been. Now everything seemed simple and astonishing: the spring, Mitya, life.

Her mother, whom she had been to see the summer before, had told her, laughing: "You're quite unrecognisable."

"Do I look more settled?"

"Oh no, you've got my nature—always ready to boil over. But you've got more life in you; happiness is fairly oozing out of you."

Only now did Lena understand the meaning of love. The years with Zhuravlyov now seemed a distant, horrible nightmare. The newly woken passion, the unspent tenderness, the wonder—almost like a girl's—and the maturity of feeling in a woman of thirty, all this had fallen to Koroteyev's lot. Once, thoughtful and happy as she lay half dozing beside him, he had said to her: "In winter, how could one imagine what lay under the snow?" She put her arms round him and said: "I can't even remember when the snow melted."

Her wonderful, fortuitous happiness helped her face the fear that every now and then swept across her life like a blast of wind. In December, after a long interval of silence, Zhuravlyov had written her a letter. She had gazed at the familiar handwriting for a long time, trying to make up her mind to open the envelope. Zhuravlyov wrote that he had been having a bad time; that was why he had not written earlier. Now he had a new job and was pleased with it. He often thought of their daughter. Perhaps Lena would agree to let her come to stay with him in summer, if only for a month. It would be bad if Shura were completely to forget her father. The letter was unexpectedly gentle, and Lena was the more upset by it because of this. "It will be hard to refuse," she thought, "but I don't trust him. It would be like him to try to set Shura against me and against Mitya."

During the past year the child had grown attached to Dmitry and although Lena, whenever she spoke of him to her, called him "Uncle Mitya," Shura stubbornly insisted: "He's my daddy!"

II · The Spring

Perhaps she had been prompted to this by the maid, Dunyasha, but she may well have decided independently to promote him to the status of father. Lena thought, amused but also a little jealous: "I do believe that Mitya would confide in Shura sooner than in me!" Dimitry's bearing, usually reserved and with a hint in it of irony, concealed a childish sense of fun. He delighted in repeating words from Shura's private language. He spent a lot of time looking at her drawings, and improvised such noisy games to play with her that Lena would say laughingly: "Take yourselves off! I can't do my work!"

Letters now came from Zhuravlyov every two weeks; they were gentle but insistent. Lena answered them punctually, writing in detail about their daughter. But she shied away from the thought of the summer: would she really have to let Shura go? Dmitry was rather shocked: "How can you help it? After all, he's her father . . ." Lena realised that he was taking an objective view, but all the same she felt indignant: "He hasn't the least idea of what Zhuravlyov is like." Before this she had thought more calmly of him: "After all, it was I who upset his life." But in these past months, either because she had become more fully aware of the horror of the years she had spent with him or because she was alarmed by the affectionate tone of his letters, she kept saying to herself: "I simply can't meet him, I can't. What will happen if he comes back into Shura's life?"

There were difficulties, too, about her work, to which she devoted herself more intensely than ever. To Lena, with her sensitiveness and her sense of duty to each child, school was not just lessons, classwork, and examinations; it was a skein of destinies that had been entrusted to her. She suffered such agonies over the dramas of their half-childish hearts—dramas not deep perhaps but containing an element of danger in their simple poignancy—that Dmitry tried to calm her: "Aren't you making too much of this?" he asked.

The year before, when the headmaster had retired, she had

179

taken heart. He had been a pedant, interested only in marks, who used to say: "You can always tell from the figures what they will become!"

Unhappily, the new headmistress, Dmitryeva, did not fulfil Lena's hopes. She was fifty-three, very tall, thin, with grey hair piled on top of her head. She dressed in black with a small lace collar and her thin lips were constantly pursed in a half smile. She came from Voronezh and her private life had been unfortunate. During the war her husband had left her for a girl in the signal corps and returned home only to collect his belongings. Her only daughter had married a successful builder and gone with him to Sakhalin; they spent their leave in the Crimea and the girl never visited her mother. Dmitryeva considered that she had stood up to all the blows that life had dealt her, but her heart had grown hard. She could not endure expressions of emotion because they seemed false to her, nor young women since they reminded her of the laughing, curly-haired signalwoman who had shattered her life.

She had a great fund of experience to draw on and liked doing so. "My dear Yelena Borisovna, why get so upset? Exactly the same thing happened to me in Kaluga, in '32, or was it '33, and it came out all right in the end." If Lena said that Alyosha Neverov could not be judged by normal standards (it was true that he was bad at mathematics but his essays were remarkable), or that Kolya Zarubin had an impossible home background (one room, drinking parties, and fights between his parents), or that Shura Zarchenko who was always telling tales ought not to be quoted as an example to the class because that was just the way to turn him into a sneak for life, Dmitryeva would answer with her invariable smile: "Yelena Borisovna, don't get so excited. I assure you, it isn't worth it. I've been up against that sort of thing myself, hundreds of times. Believe me: children are all alike. You've got too much imagination. Why don't you write something? Novels about school life are the fashion."

She was outwardly polite to Lena, but she told the other

teachers that Yelena Borisovna had become a teacher only through sheer chance, that her whole approach to school work was theatrical: she was always looking for conflicts and for violent sensations. And wasn't it odd to entrust the education of children to a woman who had made a failure of her own family life? These views were sometimes passed on to Lena, who blushed scarlet with annoyance. The break with Zhuravlyov, the torments she had endured before she achieved her present happiness, had taught her self-restraint; but, like many women with golden-red hair and a delicate pale skin, she blushed very easily.

Stein, the mathematics teacher, said to her one day: "I know Dmitryeva well. I worked with her for eleven years in Voronezh. In '49 she went for the history teacher—wrote a six-page report about him, labelled him 'a rootless cosmopolitan' and implicated some woman or other. She's a real pest and one who knows how to get in with the authorities. She's been here less than a year, but she's got pull with the LEA.[1] They've asked her to take the chair at the Chekhov evening at the club. You'd better keep clear of her."

Examination time was approaching and, as usual, Lena was worried about her class. To make matters worse, there had been an unpleasant incident. Someone had cut out a huge heart and above it the initials "L.A." on Masha Khitrova's desk. Ever since, Dmitryeva had nagged at Lena: "You're always talking so much about sensitiveness towards people, Yelena Borisovna, I was sure you had the confidence of the children. After all, you're their home-room teacher. It's extraordinary you haven't yet discovered who mutilated the desk. In Voronezh in '48 we had a fearful state of affairs—all the walls along the hall were scrawled with drawings—but I spotted the culprit right away. Apart from the fact that the desk is State property, what bothers me is the children's unhealthy minds. If they daydream about amorous

---

[1] LEA: Local Education Authority.

adventures at that age, they're bound to end up in jail. I don't like saying it, Yelena Borisovna, but I'm beginning to think you haven't sufficient control over your class."

Lena blushed up to her ears, but was silent. She had schooled herself to endure Dmitryeva's strictures with calm. What grieved her was the thought that the children did not trust her. For several days she tried to guess who could have carved the desk. It must have been a boy, but which of them could it have been? Petya Stasov was good at carving: he had shown her two boxes he had made, the Kremlin on one and some hares on the other. But Petya wouldn't spoil a desk; besides, according to him, only idiots made friends with girls. "L.A." told her nothing: there wasn't an L.A. in the class.

Dmitry laughed when Lena told him her trouble: "It reminds me of a foreign novel I read in translation as a boy. A man killed a banker and made off with his property, but afterwards he threw away his diamond cuff links because they had initials on them and the banker's initials were the same as his own. Thanks to that, the clever detective got on to him. It was wonderfully silly but I've remembered it ever since. You'll have to get re-classified, Lena, from school work to counter-intelligence."

In spite of Dmitryeva's grumbling about the "unheard-of breach of discipline in class seven," Lena concentrated on her real problems: Shura Lebedyeva was behind in all her subjects; Kolya Grushenko could not spell; and what had happened to Vasya Nikitin? He was clever and had always had top marks, but now he was only getting two's and three's [2] in mathematics and in English. And the exams would be in a few days . . .

In moments of stress Lena was sustained by her love for her husband. Neither the workaday sameness of their lives nor the occasional flashes of anger, such as had made her weep the day before, weakened her affection. On the contrary, the sadness which invaded her at the thought that she might never com-

---

[2] Maximum for each subject is five.

pletely overcome the barrier between Mitya and herself gave her love an added poignancy.

It might have been expected that at the end of a whole year spent with Dmitry she would have felt that she really knew him. Of course, she had found out a good deal. Reluctantly, warily, in fits and starts, he had told her about his past: his frustrations as a boy; the war, Natasha, the dreams which had comforted him in the trenches. She knew the facts about him, his tastes, his habits, but she often thought: "There's something in him I still cannot understand."

A big event in Lena's life was the arrival of Dmitry's stepfather. His mother had been widowed early. Alone, she had brought up Dmitry; but when she was thirty-eight and her son was sixteen she had married again. Her second husband, Vyrubin, was a professor of agronomy, two years older than she. Dmitry was at first distrustful of his stepfather and they had no time to become friends: within a year Vyrubin had been arrested. Dmitry seldom thought of him and never asked his mother anything about him. It was now two years since he had been to see her in Ulyanovsk and she had told him that Vyrubin's case was being re-examined: it appeared that he had been falsely denounced. Eighteen months later she had fallen ill with pneumonia and had died. Koroteyev went to her funeral; on his return from Ulyanovsk he told Lena: "Almost the day before she fell ill, Mother heard that Leonid Borisovich had been rehabilitated. A neighbour told me that she took his snapshot out of her trunk and sat up crying all night. If you don't mind, Lena, I'll write and ask him to come to us—after all, he's got no one left." Lena replied warmly: "Of course! Write at once! How can you ask? It's dreadful to think that your mother didn't live to see him . . ." She was silent for a while and then said: "Seventeen years! I can't begin to imagine it . . ."

Lena expected to see an old man, crushed by circumstances and perhaps embittered. "Will he want to talk to us?" she wondered. But the door opened and a tall man, with a suitcase in one hand and a package in the other, asked: "Is Dmitry Serge-yevich at home?" He had a red, weather-beaten face with straggling white eyebrows sticking out of it. Lena was particu-larly struck by his youthful, resonant voice. When she took the package from him, he cried: "Careful, Yelena Borisovna, these are plant cuttings that I want to acclimatise here—medlars, mulberries, and peaches. . . . I tried them out there in moun-tain conditions—the winters were very hard, worse than here . . ."

Lena thought at once that here was an unusual man and the more she saw of him the more she was impressed. Dmitry was no less astonished than she was. On the very first day he said to Lena: "I begin to think that compared with him I'm an old man."

Of course the conditions in which Vyrubin had lived had affected his health. He once admitted: "Even now I can't look calmly at a cigarette. After I had my coronary thrombosis I had to give them up." However, he carried on cheerfully. Soon he be-gan to teach at the agricultural school and got down to writing an article. Occasionally he would frown: "I'm terribly out of date; they've gone a long way ahead in all these years."

The day after his arrival he said to Dmitry: "Have you perhaps got a photograph of your mother? I have nothing left." Dmitry gave him an old photograph of his mother and himself as a small child; she was holding him in her arms. Vyrubin took it, went quickly to his own room, and did not reappear until eve-ning.

He never spoke of what he had been through. Only gradually and with difficulty did they learn that he had spent ten years in the far north, then two "marvellous" years in Tashkent; after that he had been posted to a remote mountain settlement. He thought for a little while and said: "When the notice came that my con-viction had been reversed, I looked at it but I couldn't read the letters. Seventeen years I'd waited, and now I was as stunned as if a frightful noise had been going on and was suddenly cut off. . . . Then I pulled myself together and began to think about work, where I should go and what I'd still be fit for . . ."

In the first days he would sometimes fall silent in the middle of a conversation and stay sunk in his own thoughts; or he would question the others in surprise when they mentioned things that were well known to everyone else. He would walk about the streets alone for hours and then say: "I'm trying to get acclimatised." And indeed he got accustomed to his new life very quickly. One day he came home looking very cheerful and said: "I've been reinstated. My Party membership is to count from 1919. I was still a student then, at Timiryazevka . . ." [3]

Lena soon made friends with him. He asked her questions about her school and eagerly listened as though what she told him was of immense interest. He'd say: "Ah, well done," or "You certainly can't put up with that." He was pleased with his own students and talked to her about them: "Of course, there are some poor specimens. I said yesterday to Golovin: "I see you are wearing the latest narrow trousers, but do broaden your mind a bit. You won't go far on your appearance alone." A few are career men. There's Nikolayevsky, for instance; he told me he didn't intend to get stuck at the bottom of the ladder. He's got nothing in his head but he attacks the Weismannists and he's got an uncle in the Ministry, so he's quite determined to become a scientist. But how many are there like that?—five or six at most. On the whole, they're splendid boys, interested in everything; they lap it all up and sometimes they even have an idea that isn't in the textbook."

One day Lena could no longer resist saying to him: "Leonid Borisovich, please don't be annoyed. . . . Perhaps it's a stupid question. . . . But you've endured so much. . . . How is it that you have kept your spirit? Not only your interest in life, but your faith?" He smiled: "I'm not the only one, Yelena Borisovna. I've seen quite a few people to whom the same thing has happened.

---

[3] The Timiryazev Academy of Natural Science.

185

It was rare for anyone to despair completely. . . . If you think about it, it's not possible to jettison everything you have lived by. To tell the truth, even in the most terrifying moments I never lost hope—sooner or later it would all work out. And, of course, I wanted to live till then. . . . And now you see—I'm living a second life."

At night Lena thought over Vyrubin's words. "Mitya says that his outlook is different from mine because of all he's been through. It's true he has been through much more than I have. It must be dreadful to lose one's friends—Natasha. . . . And then for three years his own life hung by a thread. All the same Leonid Borisovich must have had a much worse time. Why is it that he doesn't ever say, like Mitya, that I exaggerate? Mitya doesn't like talking about the bad side of things, though actually he's more aware of it than I am. Perhaps it's too painful for him to think about it and so it annoys him when I insist. I don't know. . . . I can't get to the bottom of it."

She was determined, at whatever cost, to understand the contradiction which she sometimes felt in Dmitry's words. She was trying to do it now. By morning she had forgotten their short conversation and even her tears of the night before, but when she came home from school she began to think about it again. "I was in the wrong: he came back tired and on edge, and then I flared up. But all the same, why didn't he answer me? He's told me that when last year Zhuravlyov slandered Sokolovsky in front of him, he said straight out that he did not believe a word of it. Then why didn't he take his side yesterday? I'm sure that in his heart he doesn't agree with the decision. And I know he's incapable of cowardice. I don't understand anything!"

Suddenly she remembered Dmitry's speech at the readers' conference two years earlier. "I thought then that he was aiming his speech at me, that he meant, by showing how badly the hero of the novel had behaved, to get me to wake up in time. But he told me the other day that no such thought had ever crossed his mind. He only spoke because he had been asked to speak, and he didn't know himself why he spoke as he did. And when I asked him why he had insisted that no such feelings as the hero's could exist, when in fact they were his own feelings at the time, he was upset and said I didn't trust him. But I do trust him—more than I trust myself. Only there are moments when I can't understand him."

Dmitry brought Savchenko back with him from the works; he said they had a lot to discuss: he must catch up with things after his leave. They went into the next room. Lena spread the school exercise books on the table and forgot everything in her pleasure at Alyosha Neverov's good essay on Lermontov.

Savchenko gave Dmitry the full details of Sokolovsky's scheme.

"It's a pity you weren't there when it was discussed. For a long time Golovanov couldn't make up his mind. I can't understand how he can take Safonov's report seriously. You know what Safonov is like."

"But Brainin agrees with Safonov."

"They say that a man who's taken a beating is worth two who haven't. But to my mind it's just the reverse. Brainin's taken a beating, and now he is always looking over his shoulder. It wouldn't really be so complicated to train a certain number of hands."

Dmitry thought: "Two years ago it was I who used to lecture Savchenko. It looks as if we've exchanged roles. . . . Of course, the problem isn't as simple as he makes out, but Brainin does exaggerate the difficulties. Zharov was telling me that at their works the electro-erosion method had given good results."

"I agree with you," he said aloud. "It's an interesting scheme. All the same, we can't disregard the objections of the technical people. After all, the plant isn't a laboratory: our job is mass production. And by the way, having a row with Safonov won't do any good. My opinion of him is the same as yours, but you can't deny that he's had a lot of experience."

Savchenko gave a slight shrug. Was it possible that Dmitry had become a coward?

Outwardly Savchenko had much more self-control than he had had a year ago; he no longer jumped up to interrupt, but his heart still burned with the fire which at their first meeting had made Dmitry call him a romantic. Now he was possessed by Sokolovsky's scheme, and Dmitry's words seemed to him to show such impotence that he looked at him with pity: how could an intelligent and honest man repeat Safonov's arguments like a parrot?

"Shaposhnikov will tell you about our chances of adapting ourselves quickly to the new process. As for Safonov's point about low output, it's simply unscrupulous. He doesn't mention that there would be less wastage, and that we're not at the moment getting maximum accuracy. Even Yegorov has nothing against the principle. The quarrel is really about something else: should the interests of the customers be our concern? Even a boy in the Pioneers knows that he should think about the interests of the country as a whole."

Savchenko went on defending the project with enthusiasm. Finally Dmitry said:

"I'll have a word with Golovanov. I must hear what he has to say. The matter will certainly have to be reconsidered . . ."

Savchenko was on the point of leaving when he turned to Dmitry, saying: "I meant to talk to you about the personal angle. Of course, according to the book Sokolovsky's behaved badly. But we all know what he's like. I am convinced that the reprimand has had a terrible effect on him. He is looking ill, he might even crack up. . . . Safonov has really gone too far this time. Suppose Sokolovsky were really to get fed up and leave? Frankly, I don't understand why you voted for the reprimand."

For a moment Dmitry was taken aback, as he had been the day before with Lena, but he recovered at once and said calmly: "We all appreciate Sokolovsky's qualities and no one's dreaming of letting him go." He called out: "Lena, aren't you going to give us some tea? We've had a long talk and it's getting late."

Savchenko thought: "He doesn't want to talk about it. He must have voted as he did out of fright—he didn't like to be in the minority. I used to think he was straight. Perhaps I was mistaken . . ."

He said he couldn't stay: he was in a hurry because he had work to do; but Lena refused to let him go.

At supper he forgot the unpleasant argument with Dmitry and carried on a lively conversation with Vyrubin. There was nothing they did not touch on—the Asian Conference, books, isotopes, the transplanting of trees.

Dmitry, tired and upset, sat in silence and only joined in when Savchenko mentioned a new novel. He said gloomily: "It may be well written but the hero is too good to be true. None of it is convincing."

He fell silent again and did not seem to hear the argument that broke out between Savchenko and Vyrubin.

Lena smiled to herself: "Savchenko has forgotten all about the urgent work he said he had to do. How well these two understand each other! They are both interested in so many things. Yet there is thirty years' difference between them. But what's wrong with Mitya? He isn't himself . . ."

When she and Dmitry were at last alone, she put her arms round him timidly and said: "You are very sad today. What's happened?"

He shook his head and went over to the window. Dawn was breaking. The lamps of the factory, turning pale, looked like lights painted on a backcloth. The poplars by the fence were green with that first, puzzled greenness which catches at one's heart. The spring was late here, Sokolovsky had said. In Kislovodsk all the flowers were out before he left.

He stood at the window for a long time. Then he let down the blind and said quietly:

"When I came back it was as cold as November. Now it's spring.
. . . Don't take any notice of me, Lena. I haven't got used to
working again; I get tired and then I say silly things."

4

VOLODYA PUKHOV, THE PAINTER,
had been out of sorts for some time, even though his picture,
"The Pioneers' Campfire," had been given a flattering notice in
the local paper. Sometimes he would shut himself up in his room
and work all day; at other times he would disappear for weeks
on end. When his friends asked for him, his mother sighed: "I
really don't know what to say. You can never get a word out of
Volodya."

It had all started in the autumn. Volodya often recalled that
bright September day. The day before, they had asked him to
come to the exhibition. A Moscow journalist had been enthusiastic about his picture and had promised to write it up. It
had not yet entered Volodya's head that he'd go chasing after a
damned willow tree. But in the morning when he woke up, he
suddenly longed to paint something good. Not for any special
reason—just because he wanted to.

Every morning he had trudged through the greasy, sticky
mud to Sparrow Island. There, sitting on a damp tree stump, he
had painted an ancient, round-topped willow that hung down
over the river. It put him in a rage. Looking at it, he thought:
"What on earth do I want with this idiotic tree? Is it just that I
saw something like it at Saburov's? I'm aping him, and the worst
of it is that I can't bring it off.

"What sort of a sky is this? I've painted it according to all the rules: bluer near the earth, paler higher up. But there's no air, no autumn light." Angrily he spat out his chewed, bitter cigarette butt. "It's fifteen years since I've painted from life. I did arrange for sittings when I had to do a portrait, but that was only to impress the model—people like Zhuravlyov. Actually I painted from a photograph. It seems to be very easy to unlearn . . ."

He tried to convince himself that he had no talent. "Perhaps I'd have made a decent engineer. But no, I'm no good at mathematics. I could have been an economist or a lawyer. Why should one have to have a sense of colour? It's not compulsory. Every man should know his limitations. It's time to come to terms with facts, Vladimir Andreyevich.[1]

One day when he was looking for a canvas he came across an old still life—a bunch of nasturtiums that he had painted five years earlier at Saburov's. The jug wasn't very good and the way the background was filled in struck him as revolting, but the flowers hadn't come out badly. "Now I think of it, Saburov was in raptures. It's really odd to think it was I who painted that. The flowers glow, they're sad and disturbing. I can't be as ungifted as all that. But in that case, why does nothing I try come off nowadays? Not that I am a Saburov. But I need to know that I *could* have painted like him. I suppose it's a question of pride."

One November morning when the snow had gently covered the melancholy street (dug up because the Town Soviet had at last decided to asphalt it), Volodya sat brooding on his unsuccessful sketch until dusk; then he turned its face to the wall and realised that he must go out at once. He was feeling giddy. He ran out into the street. Even the light frost did not sober him. He forced himself to collect his thoughts. Today was Sunday; he could go to see Sokolovsky. He hadn't been to see him since the spring.

He came home late and looked disgustedly at his easel and

---

[1] Volodya's name and patronymic.

palette just as in Moscow, after a violent drinking bout, he had looked at the mess of empty bottles, the remains of food and cigarette butts. He lay down at once. When he looked at the canvas next morning he lost his temper completely. Well, you couldn't say he hadn't tried! "There's a tree for you! Green, pollarded, cheerful! It should move the editor of the art review to tears of joy. Elegant, feathery clouds. For some reason, I've even put in a seat. I know—it's there for people to sit down and rest on. Savchenko, for example, the pioneer of new methods of production—he's a nature lover but why should he sit on a rotten stump? Come to think of it, I might paint Savchenko sitting on the seat and submit the picture for exhibition. Now where can that grey willow have got to? And the autumn light? Not that there's anything to be surprised at. What can you expect of an expert in the art of pot-boiling who is suddenly seized with an urge for real, true art? It's silly. It's positively indecent. Like a bun-faced chorus girl trying to play Tatyana: 'But I am promised to another and shall be true to him for life.' She's learned her part; the only trouble is, her voice doesn't sound quite right— she's been swigging beer laced with vodka all night. Last spring, when I dragged Tanechka into the park, I told her I was down and out. Roughly speaking, that's true. I wonder how Tanechka is now? There was some talk of her getting married. Some schoolboy like Savchenko must have fallen in love with her. Well, she's no Ophelia and anyway Hamlets don't grow around here."

He smiled, and suddenly forgot about his painting and his worries. Tanechka, chilly, muffled up in a grey knitted shawl, seemed to be looking at him sadly, and he felt such tenderness that it amazed him. He remembered his evenings with her, and later the thaw and the first snowdrop in the park. "I thought then that everything was going to be different. Probably because Tanechka was beside me. It's no use pretending, I clutched at her like a drowning man at a straw. Not because she could save me—she herself didn't know how to live. But with her I could feel. Afterwards I turned to stone—that's a fact. I'm glad she's fallen in love. All that about Hamlet—that was just spite and jealousy. I do want her to be happy. Just because I've got a stone around my neck, there's no reason why she should drown, too. Of course, if Tanechka were here, beside me now . . ."

He was exasperated with himself. Tanechka was not the point. "I've let everything that matters slip through my fingers—love, art, life. What on earth have I been dreaming about? Only about prizes, I suppose. But that's just what art doesn't forgive.

"It's not my fault, it's the times we live in. It doesn't matter how you paint. What matters is the subject: the right subject at the right time, not a year too early or a year too late. Suppose, for instance, there is a campaign against drunkenness. Well, there you are—drunken father can't get the key into the keyhole while the daughter—in Pioneer uniform, of course—looks on disapprovingly. The critics want it all streamlined. You've only got to get excited about real painting and they'll roar at you at once: 'Colour worship. Cult of form. Impressionism. Objectivism.' Just try showing them that tree by the river—they'd burst out: 'What's the good of that messy willow? We are planting avenues of lime trees. It's all right to paint the autumn if you put in plenty of apple trees, or the golden forest, or a holiday at the collective farm, but Pukhov's landscape is merely demoralising.' I know the form by heart. I thought things had changed when they put Saburov's pictures on show, but who wrote about them? There wasn't a word. Instead, they all went into raptures about my 'Pioneers' Campfire.' It's ages since I've seen Saburov but I bet he's still in the same state—living on enthusiasm and the earnings of his crippled wife. You have to be a madman to work as he does.

"There's no real artistic milieu, that's the trouble. It's true, I did know plenty of painters in Moscow. One day they'd all beam and congratulate you—that was when you'd had good notices in the papers. Another day you got a bad press and one of the men would say: 'I rather like your work myself but the others don't approve.' They're not looking for anything new, they won't let themselves get excited. It's a hard time to live in."

Then he would start to argue with himself. A hard time? Of course it was. But had any time been soft? "There are no soft times, only soft people—people like myself. Take Galileo—it wasn't easy to do what he did, and no one put up a memorial to him in his lifetime. Nothing that's worth doing has ever been easy. And there, it seems, lies the essence of art. You'd think literature was easy to understand—after all, you learn to read at school—and yet, they say, people laughed at Mayakovsky. The public didn't understand him and the poets resented him. And now there's a Mayakovsky Square in Moscow. . . . It's not a question of the times. Some people will always make for the fleshpots: there you are, the banquet is laid, there's vodka, there's hors-d'oeuvres.—No, I've overlooked cultural progress—it's champagne now, vases of artificial flowers, and greetings in leatherette frames.—As for the outsiders, well, Saburov's not the only one. In Moscow I saw how Shumov worked, and Dolichenko, and Granovsky. . . . Where the dickens do they get their perseverance? I don't understand it. I suppose you've got to have a special personality. When Father said 'the people,' his voice changed. Saburov believes in the people, too. He once tried to comfort me by telling me that 'our people are really marvellous.' It's funny, what could Father and Saburov have in common? They were poles apart. And yet Father liked Saburov and got cross when I said he was a schizophrenic. Of course, Father was a remarkable man, everybody knew that. Look at the way they cried at his funeral. They say there is something in heredity: Mother swears I've got Father's eyes, but what else have I inherited from him? So far as I can make out, absolutely nothing. A man makes his own life, he's only got himself to blame. I am to blame for myself—I've got myself into the soup. I've forgotten how to work. What's worse, I've forgotten how to feel. Did I feel anything when I was painting that willow by the river? I felt the damp and it made me sneeze. All told, there's nothing inside me. The fact is I've spent a lot of time trying to crack a nut and it's turned out to be quite empty. And then I set myself up as a judge and condemned 'the times' . . ."

Once again he tried to work. He chose a small house he liked the look of on the outskirts of the town and began to paint it; every now and then he looked round guiltily. "That's a funny thing," he thought, "who is it I'm afraid of? I feel as if I were sixteen, and had gone out to meet Mira and were frightened of being caught by Mother."

The house was a failure, too. He painted it out and started on a still life, a bowl of apples. He worried over that for a week and then gave up.

The manager of the club called unexpectedly to tell him there was an urgent job. Volodya decided not to go.—"I've had enough of it."—Then he wavered: "How long can I go on playing the fool? I seem to have lived in a daze these past six months, as though I'd been drunk. Why did I sweat over those blasted apples? I'll never be a real artist, but I've got to live. It's a good thing really that Dobzhinsky called. It's high time I got back to reality. I can't afford not to, anyway. The money for 'The Pioneers' Campfire' went long ago. Like this I'll be able to help Mother; it's not easy for her these days, poor thing; she's only got her small pension and she is always feeding those boys Father used to fuss about. But that's probably a good thing; it comforts her. . . . The long and the short of it is, I'll have to go to the club."

It turned out that Dobzhinsky was preparing a Peoples Friendship exhibition. Volodya got some books out of the library. The Bulgarians were easy—there was even a book of illustrations—but how did Albanians dress? "Never mind, I'll think up something." He worked diligently. Everything seemed to be all right again. He got an advance and asked Nadya, a cheerful, freckled girl who worked as a typist at the club, to dinner at the Volga Restaurant. "She's rather nice," he smiled sadly to himself. At dinner he told her some old chestnuts and Nadya giggled; Volodya wondered silently why she thought them funny. Afterwards he saw her home, kissed her hand decorously, and decided not to take her out again. "She's a good girl, she ought to get married—not go falling in love with me." He liked to think of her surrounded by her family. "It's nice that I don't want anything from her. The fact is, I don't need anything from anyone."

He spent his mornings looking through the paper, talking to his mother, and drawing; in the evenings he sat in his room reading Dickens and sometimes fell asleep over his book. His life was dull, but it was on an even keel and not unpleasant. His mother was less worried about him: she had been afraid that he was ill.

Winter passed. The streets were chattering again, noisy with spring. Volodya yawned cosily, watching the patches of sunlight creep across the red-stained floor. Offered a new commission—a portrait of Andreyev—he grumbled: the exhibition panel would take him at least another month, how could he be expected to go straight on to a portrait? It was true that the fee was good and there was no risk. He could not forgive himself for having offered to paint Zhuravlyov. "You should never bank on anyone's position being safe. Zhuravlyov was here one day and gone the next and I was left with his stupid portrait on my hands. But Andreyev is a different matter: it's a firm order, there's even an advance. They're enthusiastic about him at the plant; there was an article on him the other day. Savchenko never stops talking about him. Should I, perhaps, take it on? I could give some of the money to Mother and go to Moscow for a month. I can't go on reading Dickens for ever! I left Moscow like a boy who'd had a beating, I'll go back as an important artist from the provinces. I can relax for a bit. And then, in Moscow there are always prospects. You have to be mad, like Saburov, to squat in this dump and meditate on art! . . . So that's settled, I'll take it on.

Life isn't hard after all, though it's a fact that I'd sooner sleep than be alive."

5

VOLODYA WAS WRONG IN THINK-
ing that nothing had changed at the Saburovs'. It was true that they still lived in the same cramped little room, now more crowded than ever with canvases, and Glasha's modest pay was still the basis of their budget. All the same, there had been a considerable change in Saburov's life.

It had all started at an exhibition where Savchenko was struck by a landscape and a woman's portrait by Saburov, an unknown painter. They seemed to him remarkable. He remembered meeting Saburov at the Pukhovs' and determined to seek him out.

When he did, he stood for a long time in front of the canvases in the little room, saying nothing and smiling vaguely, and finally summed up his impressions in the one word that was always on Glasha's lips: "Marvellous!"

Later on, he took Andreyev to see them and asked if he might come again and bring some of his other friends, and now on Sundays the Saburovs' room was always full of enthusiastic visitors.

Saburov liked having them and talked with them for hours, but he treated their praise with reserve. He would say: "I don't like that picture myself. It began all right but afterwards I spoiled it," or "You see, the light is wrong in this one." Saburov combined humility with confidence in his chosen way. He believed that real art was bound to reach people in the end and

197

that it was not for him to struggle for recognition but to get on with his work.

Glasha's reaction to the visitors' enthusiasm was different. She never worried about their cramped quarters or the other difficulties of their life, but she could not reconcile herself to the fact that her husband's work was not properly appreciated and was hardly ever known. There had been a time when she had dreamed of miracles—a telegram summoning him to Moscow, an article entitled "Birth of an Artist" in her morning paper. . . . She disliked Volodya and thought him a careerist, yet she often thought of his unexpected visit: hadn't he admitted that he was envious of Saburov? So for Glasha these Sundays meant the triumph of justice. How long had she not waited for these admiring looks and for that deep silence which comes over people in the presence of genuine art!

Saburov became friendly with Andreyev. At their first meeting they discovered that they had both been in the fighting at Mozhaisk in '42, Andreyev as a gunner and Saburov as an infantry lieutenant. As often happens, their memories of the war years at once drew them to each other. What Andreyev remembered best was the snow; it was astonishing how much snow there had been that year. The dead lay in the bare woods which hid nothing and the winter crept under your shirt until it reached your heart. Villages burned and ragged women and children warmed themselves at the blaze. It made you choke with anger to think of it. . . . And those endless processions of people walking past. . . . At the end of this talk Saburov said: "You've got a good job—you're always among people. I'm painting on my own, day in, day out. For me the war was an escape, an excursion into the world—for four whole years we griped together, we shared our hopes, we shared everything, even our letters—we had in common whatever gave joy or sorrow to each one of us."

Andreyev lived not far away, in the same narrow street which ran down to the river, slippery in rain or frost and with acacias flicking the passers-by from behind the fences. Whenever he came, Glasha put the kettle on the stove and they would talk till long past midnight.

"You know why I like you?" Andreyev said laughing to Saburov. "You're a stubborn man; you love your work and you don't give in. To me that's real, it's important. Sometimes when I get an idea at the plant they laugh at me and say it won't do; but if I'm sure I've hit on something useful, then I stick to my guns."

Andreyev was a thick-set man with a shaven head and clever, inquisitive eyes. He had been brought up in a children's home; he had finished the ten-year school and had meant to train as an electrical engineer, but then the war came. He had been twice wounded, once by a shell splinter in the belly; he had had to have a "complete re-fit" after that, he said. He had taken part in the fighting for Prague, seen Czechoslovakia and Hungary, and had vivid memories of ancient castles perched on hills, of vineyards and of well-built peasant houses. When he was discharged he decided to go to a technical college, but unexpectedly fell in love and married. They had a daughter and he took a job at the plant. He assumed that this was only for a time, that he would get back to his training later, but he became attached to his job; in his free time he sat over a text book or stayed on in the workshop and invented technical improvements.

His prestige at the works went up after he made, in his spare time, a pneumatic device that increased production. He had one great sorrow—his second daughter had died. He had also had troubles: Zhuravlyov, who couldn't stand him, had accused him of being responsible for some damaged product and entered it in his report. But now things were easier. Golovanov thought highly of Andreyev; he said: "That's a man who likes to find everything out for himself, he's got real ability—just the fellow to put the shoes on the flea."[1]

Saburov had once said to Glasha: "Andreyev has a real feeling

---

[1] Feat of a legendary smith in a short story by Leskov.

for painting. He never likes anything shoddy. I've always noticed it about him. Now, Golikov has no opinions of his own; he just repeats what Savchenko says. But Andreyev is quite different. He told me yesterday that he liked the landscape with the little pink house and sand in the foreground—you remember the one? And he's quite right, I think it's the best thing I've done in the last year."

Andreyev asked Saburov: "Why is it they don't give you a show? It's very odd. What's wrong with your trade union? Must be bad organisation somewhere."

Saburov said: "It's like this, you see. It's difficult for us to organise, we're not a factory. You were talking the other day about parts with a one-tenth of a millimetre aperture; if it's made a hundredth of a millimetre less, then it's no good. Such accuracy seems to me miraculous, I said so at the time. But miracles of that sort are visible through a magnifying glass. But how can you demonstrate scientifically that Raphael is a better artist than So-and-So? You can feel it, you can know it, but you can't prove it. You say 'bad organisation'? Perhaps . . . but it's hard for a painter to tear himself away from his easel and sit at a director's desk. And what sort of a judge is he likely to be? The more original his own talent, the more likely is he to be mistaken in judging the work of others. So you get a natural division: some produce art, others classify it and hand out the laurels for one picture or throw out another."

"All the same, I don't understand. You're a resolute man, and your approach is the same as ours, it's the Soviet approach—you want to work for the people. And yet here are your pictures, as good as buried away in a cellar. . . . It happened that Savchenko told us about you and we came. But you can't bring everyone to a private apartment as you can to an exhibition. Why don't you put up a fight?"

Saburov smiled.

"Fight? I get on with my work—that's my fight. I keep on trying to do better . . ."

II · The Spring

One Sunday, after a lot of people had been to the Saburovs', Glasha said to him:

"If you only knew how happy I am! They've discovered you— at last!"

He put his arms round her and answered thoughtfully:

"I think really that I've discovered them. Can you understand? I've broken through the ring . . . and I'm glad these people aren't artists or critics, but engineers, workers, people from a larger world. D'you know, Glasha, I'd like to paint Andreyev's portrait. I'm always thinking about it. It wouldn't be easy."

"He's got an extraordinary face. Everything seems to stick out, everything looks larger than life: mouth, nose, eyebrows. Yet it all goes together somehow."

"Yes, it would be almost too easy to get a good likeness. Perhaps the main difficulty would be just that—because the likeness is not the point. You know how you sometimes look at a portrait by a well-known painter and you're really amazed—the moustache is right, the medals are all in their right place, it's even a fair likeness, but there's nothing there—no art and no man—it's just a bad still life. I believe the structure of the face has to be related to the man's personality and to his clothes, and to the background and the light—everything must be significant. It's sometimes said about a man that his appearance is deceptive: he doesn't look like what he really is. But that's because he isn't really like the first impression you get of him. There is always a connection, only you can't always find it. The danger is what is called 'expression' —something passing, changing, which obscures the form. That's for the photographer, not for the painter. Though it's true that if you look at *Ogonyok*[2] you can't always tell if the reproductions are of paintings or of colour photographs. But you couldn't mistake a Rembrandt for a photograph. I know you so well, Glasha, I'm so aware of you that when I paint you I can sometimes hit it off. But I'd have to think hard about Andreyev: I'm

---

[2] Popular magazine.

sure there's a big subject for me there. It's true what I've told you: I've discovered him. Now I must say what I've discovered in a painting."

Andreyev gladly agreed to sit. To begin with, he stayed quite motionless, afraid to move his head even a hair's breadth.

"I'm not a photographer," laughed Saburov. "You'll soon tire yourself out sitting like that, and I work slowly. Talk about something: Glasha always chatters when she sits for me."

So Andreyev began to talk and was soon carried away. As it happened, Sokolovsky had explained his scheme to him the day before. The electro-erosion treatment of metals was not unknown to him: he had read and thought about it, and he had at once grasped the importance of the project. He told Saburov at great length what electrical impulses and erosion were.

"It's his portrait you ought to be painting. Golikov says Sokolovsky is like an old sea-captain who knows the seas like his village pond. That's true, but it's not the whole truth. You've never seen him? He's got a bronzed face, grey hair, and clear blue eyes. But what is remarkable about him is his enthusiasm. When he is possessed by an idea, he talks of nothing else. They hurt his feelings the other day, and quite unjustly. Really hurt him. I told him how indignant we all were about it, but he didn't listen—in one ear and out the other. I don't know—perhaps he didn't want to show that he minded. Or perhaps he really didn't mind; he's an odd guy. Our workers are very angry; you know he was reprimanded by the Party Bureau. Everyone is talking about it. I've discussed it with several people and we're not going to leave it at that. There's going to be a meeting of the Party group. . . . Am I sitting right? You said I could talk, but I've been twisting and turning and making it difficult for you."

"Not in the least! For the portrait, everything that concerns *you* is important to me."

Andreyev burst out laughing.

"So you weren't listening. And I was afraid I was distracting you. I wasn't talking about myself, you know."

"I heard what you said about Sokolovsky. And about yourself, too."

Three days later Andreyev arrived in a rage.

"Do you know what Dobzhinsky's thought up? He's commissioned Pukhov to paint my portrait! I won't have him painting me. I hear he did a portrait of Zhuravlyov—that's just the right model for him. Yershov's article says that his picture in the exhibition is a work of near genius, but I think he just wastes canvas . . ."

Saburov was silent.

"Don't you agree?"

"It's not as simple as that," Saburov answered at last. "Pukhov was at school with me; we used to see a lot of each other at one time. Believe me, he's got real talent; but he's done everything in his power to destroy it. I think he must be very unhappy. If you'd only seen his work when he began! He still hadn't learned to draw, but looking at his sketches, you couldn't help believing in him. I felt then that I myself might never do anything important, but that Volodya was a born artist. I remember he painted the slope of a hill on a summer day, before a storm: it was all so lowering, so strained—the heavy sky, the still trees. . . . His misfortune is that he's forgotten about art. You know, people often think that the only thing that matters is the subject. But the truth is, you can paint a small still life and convey more than in a conversation piece ten yards square. Don't judge Pukhov by the show. He might find you stimulating, and then he'd paint a good portrait."

Andreyev shook his head.

"I told them that in any case I can't sit now. I'm too busy. I don't like your Pukhov."

Saburov eventually showed Glasha the portrait of Andreyev in a dark blue jacket sitting on a stool, a silvery, pale green wall behind him. He had succeeded in suggesting the beauty of Andreyev's homely, heavy face, a beauty that perhaps no one but Andreyev's wife had ever seen before. It was a face the stubbornness and passion of which were softened by a knowing look, as of a man who is keeping to himself the end of some fantastic, complicated story.

"I've never imagined him like that," said Glasha. "Do you know what he looks like? An alchemist . . ."

Saburov was amused.

"Of course! Just as Sokolovsky is like a sea-captain." He turned the face of the canvas to the wall. "I'll look at it again tomorrow. I can't see it any more now."

He went to the open window. There was a high wind; sheets hung out to dry were bellying like sails; a girl held down her dress with one hand; in the grass were the first dandelions, dazzlingly golden. Spring. . . . He looked at this view every day, and was still charmed by it. "That would be something to paint! What a lot there is still to paint! Sokolovsky . . . Savchenko. I've never before seen a smile like that. . . . And Glasha —I haven't yet brought out a hundredth part of what I know about her . . ."

He looked around. Their eyes met, and they both felt shy.

6

WHEN VOLODYA WOKE UP HE WAS at once conscious of an intolerable emptiness. It was inexplicable: everything was in its normal place—the panel, Mother, the puddle under the window, the novel by Dickens. But he did not know what to do with himself. He opened the book. No, he didn't feel like reading about sentimental debtors . . .

After dawdling through the day he trudged off to Sokolovsky's in the evening. He knew from Savchenko that Sokolovsky was having a bad time and did not feel like seeing people; but he

had to talk to someone because the emptiness was ringing in
his ears and he couldn't breathe.

They discussed the Bandung Conference, ancient Indian archi-
tecture, the Dresden picture gallery. Volodya was jumpy and
talked at random. What had he come for? Sokolovsky was feeling
sick enough without him. At last he asked tentatively:

"I hear you've been having more trouble . . ."

Crossly, Sokolovsky knocked his pipe on the table.

"Nothing special. I've got an awful temper, as you know: I'm
always cursing myself for it. My dog Fomka bites his friends:
luckily that's not one of my habits, but I growl at them. But
that's beside the point. What matters is: I've proposed a scheme
that I think is interesting. . . . You know what electrons are?"

Volodya laughed.

"I've studied about them but I don't remember much."

"Extraordinary man you are! You seem to think that atomic
energy is an impenetrable mystery. Why not get a book and
read about it? You'll find it absorbing, I promise you. In our day
anyone who doesn't understand physics is like a blind man. . . .
At least you have an excuse, you're an artist; not like some
engineers I know—quite prominent ones too—who haven't an
idea of the progress physics has made. However, that's another
matter. . . . My scheme has met with serious objections. All the
same, I'm still hoping they'll come back to it. A lot of things
have changed lately, you know."

Volodya said with polite indifference:

"You mean things are better without Zhuravlyov?"

"It's not just Zhuravlyov. I tell you: there have been a lot of
changes. Haven't you noticed?"

"On the whole, no. Four streets have been asphalted. They're
building a new theatre. Dobzhinsky has promised us two French
films—one's supposed to be amusing. They've taken away the
stuffed bear at the entrance to the Volga and put up a long
mirror—now there'll be something to smash. That's all I can
think of . . ."

"I'm really sorry for you if you don't see what's going on under your nose. The trouble is, you don't meet anyone. People are beginning to hold up their heads. They grumble, but that's a healthy sign. I listened in to London yesterday—it's useful for learning the language; it's extraordinary how they pronounce things. I'll never learn. They were talking about us. They don't understand a thing. They argue from wishful thinking. They talked about our weakness, whereas we've never been so strong . . ."

After a pause Sokolovsky asked:

"Why are you looking so miserable? Are you doing any painting?"

Volodya was embarrassed.

"Well, yes—that is, strictly speaking, no. I've practically finished a panel for the club—only the Hungarians left to do. A little while ago I was commissioned to do a portrait of Andreyev, but they say it has to wait—he's very busy just now. So actually I'm free . . ."

Then he surprised himself by adding:

"I told you the other day I wanted to do some real painting. I don't know why I felt like showing off to you. I suppose it's because I respect you. Schoolboy stuff. . . . You know, I've never really tried to do serious work, and there wouldn't be much point in it. . . . Take you, for instance, when you're working at a new machine—that's something everybody needs, everyone is interested. But have you ever thought what a man like Raphael would be doing if he lived in these days?"

Sokolovsky looked up in surprise.

"What has my machine got to do with it? One has to know how to make a machine as one has to know how to paint a picture . . ."

"There's a time for everything. Nowadays Raphael would be carrying out Dobzhinsky's commissions. Though perhaps they'd pay him at a higher rate, in view of the popular success of his 'Madonna' . . ."

Volodya talked to hide his embarrassment. Sokolovsky was annoyed.

"You're too fond of money, that's what it is! Perhaps you think everyone is like you. That's nonsense. Savchenko was telling me he saw some remarkable landscapes at the exhibition. He went to see the artist and he was enchanted. . . . And he's not the only one. Several people have told me about those paintings. I shall go and see them for myself as soon as I have time. So kindly don't . . ."

He stopped abruptly. "What's the point of dressing him down?" he thought. "He just acts the cynical old man but he's only a boy really, and a bit neurotic at that . . ."

However, Volodya did not take offence. He felt something altogether different—was it jealousy perhaps, or envy? He forced himself to smile.

"Don't get annoyed. All I meant was that technology is more important nowadays than art, and that's a fact. As for Savchenko, I admit he's completely honest and a good technician . . ."

"He's remarkable! You'll hear more of him. He's really gifted."

"So much the better. Nevertheless, he doesn't understand painting. I know the man he was telling you about—Saburov, he's an old school friend of mine. It's true, he's got great ability: great talent, if you like. Incidentally, I did all I could to get his work into an exhibition. But, honestly, there's nothing to rave about: he works in his own little corner. He's been painting the same tree for years—that and his wife. However, don't let's bother about that: I'm very glad for his sake that he's been recognised. He's been treated most unfairly: the Union used to say he was nothing but a schizophrenic. Any kind of genuine appreciation is good for him. Even Savchenko's . . ."

He shot this out in one breathless salvo, afraid of betraying himself if he stopped for a second. Sokolovsky turned away, muttered something, and poured out some wine. Then he went on to talk about Andreyev.

"I'm glad they've commissioned you to do his portrait. Have you met him yet?"

"Only for a moment. He came to see my father last winter. He's got an interesting face."

"Not only his face: he's a most interesting person. He reads a lot; he thinks for himself. He's not a man to get into a rut. . . . That's a man of tomorrow, if you like."

When Volodya got up to go, Sokolovsky said:

"Come again, soon. Our talk today went wrong somehow. It happens. . . . The great thing for you is, don't lose heart. There are moments when one feels that everything is finished—one's come to a full stop. But in fact it's a new beginning. It's a new chapter. Do you see what I mean?"

On his way home Volodya thought over Sokolovsky's words and smiled sadly: Sokolovsky was an elderly man but he reasoned like a child. "A new chapter, for heaven's sake. . . . A caterpillar is transformed into a butterfly, but a man can't change. I've only got one life: I shan't be given another. . . . But that's not the point. The truth is, I'm slipping. For some reason, I had to pretend I'd helped Saburov to get his masterpieces shown, and then I had to go and abuse him. As it happens, I am just as excited about Saburov's work as Savchenko is. Obviously I'm envious. Disgusting . . . I wonder who else spoke about him to Sokolovsky. Though, what does it matter who it was? Savchenko himself could sweep anyone along with his enthusiasm. And on the whole, he's right: Saburov's canvases do stand out at the show. I can't seriously claim that my 'Pioneers' Campfire' is painting. It's revolting really—why did I start doing that kind of thing? I suppose it was because Savchenko wanted it—well, not he, but others like him. And now he turns around and goes into ecstasies over Saburov. There I am again, trying to turn everything inside out. After all, I got the money, so there's no injustice. The real bore is that that's what's made me bankrupt."

When he got home he sat down to work—he had promised to

finish the panel by the 10th of March and now it was April—
but nothing would come right; he fidgeted and yawned dejectedly.

It had seemed lately as if life were going better, but now it
had fallen to pieces again. He caught himself thinking constantly about Saburov. He had meant to go and congratulate him
on his success, but he hadn't done so. "Why should he be a hypo-
crite? Of course Saburov was talented—Volodya had always said
so, but there was no need to exaggerate. Savchenko was a born
enthusiast. Sonya wasn't just a girl to him, she was a goddess.
Probably he'd never seen a picture gallery, so Saburov's pictures
had bowled him over. Oh well, it wasn't worth thinking about."
But he could not get rid of his importunate thoughts. He remembered Saburov's paintings sometimes with excitement and
sometimes with rage: "How monstrously I've been had."

When Volodya at last delivered the panel to the club,
Dobzhinsky said:

"I was just going to call you. We're holding a discussion about
the exhibition on the 24th. Criticisms have been pouring in. We
kept putting off the meeting—we were afraid we couldn't cope
with it. But Shishkov came down the other day from Moscow
and told us the Ministry was very interested in the show and had
promised to send a correspondent from *Soviet Culture* to attend
the discussion. We're having great arguments here. Especially
about the pictures by the local man, Saburov—you know him, of
course. I'm not really up in these matters myself, but some people
are raving about him. Not everyone, of course. Khitrov, for
example, thinks they're daubs and that we shouldn't have shown
them. On the other hand, Koroteyev likes them very much.
Anyway, it ought to be a lively affair. I'm not going to ask you
to read a paper, but you simply must speak. If the date doesn't
suit you, we'll change it. You know how popular you are. I personally think 'The Pioneers' Campfire' wonderful. And lots of
people are saying yours is the best thing in the show. Of course,
you've got a wide outlook; you've lived in Moscow; one can say

that your ideas are on an All-Union [1] scale. And Saburov most likely can't see beyond the end of his nose."

Volodya felt uncomfortable. He would have been better pleased if Dobzhinsky had cursed him. But a moment later he reflected: "Why should it annoy me to be praised? Of course Dobzhinsky knows nothing about art—no more than Savchenko does. Still, he is praising me sincerely, and it shows that there are lots of people who like my work. That's the chief thing. I can't work like Saburov. And what's more, I don't want to. That's just it: I don't want to."

So Volodya shook Dobzhinsky vigorously by the hand:

"You shouldn't praise me: I consider I'm still learning. But I don't want to produce work like Saburov's. That's just it: I don't want to. Anyhow, thank you for what you said. It makes a lot of difference . . ."

He left the club in a more cheerful mood. He walked to Lenin Street and then on to the Town Garden. After weeks of cold and rain it was a fine May day. Children were playing in the sand-pit. A tall soldier whispered something to a girl and she turned away and smiled. The narcissi in the flower beds were like white butterflies about to fly away. Volodya remembered Tanechka and felt sad. It was true that they had often quarrelled, but still she had been there with her warm, sad lips, the fair down on the nape of her neck and her naïve sorrows—a new line on her face or a few grey hairs. Now there was no Tanechka. In fact, there was nothing.

He turned back towards the centre of town and paced along endless Pushkin Street.

It was astonishing: three hours earlier he had been in splendid spirits. One had really to be at sea to feel so upset by Dobzhinsky's compliments.

"It's a year ago since Father died. Father must have had his difficult moments but they were different from mine. Father re-

---

[1] The All-Union Society for Cultural Relations with Foreign Countries.

gretted all the things he hadn't had time to do. But when I think of the things I have done I feel sick. . . . Everybody loved him. There was that dark little girl who used to come to see him. . . . Just now I pretended not to notice Rumyantsev—he'd have started a long conversation about justice or philistinism or how one must remember Korchagin,[2] or how schoolboys nowadays don't give up their seats to him. But Father would have stopped and listened and even been moved by what he said. . . . Or there's Smolyakov sitting on the bench smoking his pipe. According to Father, he blew up a tank during the war and reported that two of his comrades had blown it up, so that they should get the medals. 'A very fine man,' Father said. . . . When he nodded to me just now I was terrified in case he might come up and speak to me. No wonder nobody gives a damn for me, not even Dobzhinsky . . .

"There are too many people in the streets. It's the warm weather that's brought them out like a rash. And they're not even enjoying themselves strolling about; they're just shoving and pushing. . . . There was a rumor that Sokolovsky was going to marry Dr. Scherer. I meant to congratulate him. But he's still alone with his dog Fomka. He's probably so used to living alone that he likes it. But for me it's a new thing. In Moscow there were always all those painters and movie people I went around with. And afterwards there was Tanechka. Now there's nobody.

"In Dickens, if a character starts at the bottom, he's sure to swim up to the top in the end. I used to notice just the opposite in life: people getting up to the top story in no time and then shooting down. In those days people sat on the edge of their chairs, now they seem to sit down properly, but what about me? Well, nobody's trying to trip me up. I can go to Moscow if I like. Even if they do print Glasha's portrait in *Ogonyok*, that won't mean the end of me: haven't I a line in social themes? The trouble is, I don't want to go on with that stuff . . .

---

[2] The hero of a novel, *How the Steel Was Tempered*, held up as an example for children.

"Why did I think Saburov mad and the way he'd chosen frightening? Certainly, he doesn't make much money. But does that matter? He loves painting and he paints the way he wants to. He isn't only gifted, he's got nothing on his conscience. His cripple is devoted to him. Compared to me, he's a millionaire!

"I should never have taken up art. If a coach is coupled to the wrong train, it can be uncoupled. But if the train is on the wrong track, that's worse. It can't leave the track—there'd be a crash. I can neither be a Saburov nor change my profession. It looks as though there's nothing I can do about it.

"According to Sokolovsky, people are beginning to hold their heads up. Who's holding his head up, I'd like to know? Savchenko, perhaps? But then he's always had his eyes fixed on the stars or on the ceiling. As for me, if anything, I'm more round-shouldered than ever.

"A few days before he died Father said to me: 'I'm getting a bit dotty. Look how green the grass is—I've never seen it so green as that.' He was so glad to see the spring.

"It's spring now, and it makes me feel sick. Well, I've had enough of pacing the town! It's narrow but it's long. Just like life. I'd better go home—there's nothing else to do."

7

VOLODYA'S MOTHER SAT AT HER desk sorting papers. She was trying not to cry: it was a year today since Andryusha had died.

He had died as he had lived. In the morning he had looked cheerful and joked over his tea. It was a marvellous spring day and his wife did not stop him when he said he wanted to go for a walk. He returned late, about three o'clock. "You shouldn't walk so far," she scolded him. "See how ill you look." He explained that he had had to see Seryozha whose exams were coming on and who had fallen in love—there were complications of some sort; Seryozha was a good boy, but he'd lost his head. "Go and have your dinner," said his wife, but he replied that he was too tired; he would rather lie down. He was biting his lip and she realised he was in pain. She cried out: "I'll fetch Dr. Scherer at once." He said quietly: "Don't, Nadya. You'd better stay with me . . ."

Afterwards she reproached herself. How could she have left him? She had meant to help him, and all she did was to let him die alone. The telephone had been out of order and there was no one in the house. Perhaps he had called out to her and she had come too late. The hospital was a long way off.

Just a year ago. She had tried hard not to give way, but her loss was very great. She kept feeling as if he were still beside her; she would turn to speak to him and her glance would fall upon his empty place at the table.

Now she was sorting his letters, manuscripts, all the odds and ends that it had been his habit to slip into the drawers of the desk. There was a gnawed cigarette-holder. He had stopped smoking after his first heart attack, but when he was working he would often put the holder between his teeth and laugh and say: "Look, Nadya, I'm smoking. Don't be cross with me—it's only a dummy."

Some pages of an article, with notes in the margins: "Must mention Zamyatin. . . . Family influence not taken sufficiently into account at school. . . ." He had wanted very much to finish it, but had only written the beginning.

His album, given him by his pupils at Penza in '24. A line of verse in a child's handwriting on the first page:

Tell me not that he is dead: he lives . . .

A newspaper clipping tucked in: Lenin's funeral.

Pebbles—he and Volodya had collected them on the beach in the Crimea. Cufflinks. The certificate of his degree.

An invitation to the Victory Celebration. An old yellow newspaper with a Stalingrad communiqué . . .

The beginning of a letter to Volodya: "This may upset you—I'm sorry—but I don't like the tone of your letter. I think you are attaching too much importance to your first successes."

"He was always worrying about Volodya," thought Nadezhda Yegorovna. "I felt that he didn't like his pictures, though he never said so. I told him once that we were old, young people had different tastes, and he agreed. Sometimes he spoke too sharply to Volodya, but in his heart he loved him. He'd say: 'Volodya is much better than people think he is.' And that's true. People think Volodya is selfish, but really he's very sensitive. This morning he offered to come with me to the cemetery. I could see what he felt.

"A chestnut. Now why did Andryusha put a chestnut in that drawer? Did it remind him of something? Or did he simply bring it home with him from the south and it got in here by accident?

"A letter from the head of the Institute about Kostya. An old electricity bill, can't think what it's doing here, it can be thrown away.

" 'Thank you, dear Andrey Ivanovich, for the interest you have taken in my affairs. If I managed to prove my innocence it was only thanks to your active intervention . . .' signed Vetnikov or Venshikov—no, Veshnyakov; 1929. I don't remember Andryusha telling me about him. He was always ready to intercede for anyone: if they'd all written to him, there'd be a whole volume.

"An eyeglass case. I brought him that from Moscow. He said it was too good for him and he hardly ever used it.

"A photograph of his father. I don't think Andryusha was like him. Perhaps just the eyes a little. He said his father was kind but timid: he worked for some miller or other. A photograph of Andryusha stamped 'by M. I. Kolesnikov, Oryol.' That's where he went to school. I once suggested our visiting Oryol, but he said he had no one left there. Though when the papers reported there'd been a lot of destruction at Oryol, he was terribly distressed.

"A photograph inside an envelope; it's so faded it's difficult to make it out. Oh yes, it's one that Balashov took when the Whites were driven out of Rostov. There's Andryusha. And me in a greatcoat. Andryusha said I looked like a boy, with my hair cut short. What a ragamuffin I was! How extraordinary it all was then. It's frightening to remember, the happiness we had, such happiness! And we were so young! Andryusha must have forgotten he'd put that photograph into an envelope. He was looking for it once—he rummaged everywhere and couldn't find it.

"A telegram from the men who served with him at Atkarsk: 'On your fiftieth birthday.' Three months before he died I suggested we should give a party for his sixty-fifth birthday but he wouldn't have it. Many people sent greetings all the same. I collected all the letters and telegrams in the right-hand drawer.

"A photograph of Sonya at Atkarsk—she's only four but you can see she's got character, she's wilful, always has to have her own way; and she's the first to suffer from it. When I die she'll be quite alone. All her friends got married long ago. When Savchenko came to Andryusha's funeral she told him she was glad he was there and asked him to come to see me sometimes; she treated him as one of the family. He's a good man, he's straight. Andryusha used to like talking to him; he came nearly every day after Sonya left. But it doesn't seem to come to anything between them. Last autumn he told me he'd take leave and go to Penza to see her but he never went. He looks so sad nowadays when he comes, and he always asks what Sonya says in her letters. I'm sorry for Sonya, too.

"Here's the snapshot I was looking for—Andryusha, when we first met. A student in a high-necked shirt. He was just back from the front, in '18. He was twenty-eight. How funny his hair was—he used to say he needed a rack for it, not a comb. How long ago that was! Of course, Andryusha changed over the years but his expression remained the same. He always looked like that to me. He was extraordinarily young. Right up to his death. I still keep thinking he'll walk in and start talking about Kostya or Seryozha . . .

"But this is all that's left of him. He didn't even finish writing that article. Lots of people came to the funeral, but who remembers him now? It's dreadful that a man should vanish! Everything is as it was but he's gone without a trace!"

She turned her head to keep the tears from falling on her mementos.

The bell rang. She hastily wiped her eyes. Who could it be? In the doorway stood red-haired Seryozha. He looked upset and mumbled that perhaps he'd come at the wrong moment—it was nothing urgent. She made him come in. He had been one of Andryusha's favourites.

Seryozha was nervous. He took off his glasses and blinked his kindly grey eyes. He muttered something but seemed not to know how to begin and at last said:

"Nadezhda Yegorovna, Ninochka and I have felt like this about each other for a long time now. Andrey Ivanovich said we ought to give it time and make quite sure, that if it wasn't real we'd soon forget each other. I promise you, we are quite sure. Three years is a very long time, you know."

Nadezhda Yegorovna couldn't help smiling.

"How old are you, Seryozha?"

"Nineteen."

"And Ninochka?"

"She'll be nineteen in four months. Nadezhda Yegorovna, we're prepared to wait—a year, even two. But what am I to do? Her father has forbidden her to see me. That's the tragedy. Will you speak to him? He'll listen to you. Nina says that your family is always held up as an example in their house. Andrey Ivanovich once said to me that trials should make one stronger, and that's

true enough: I feel I've become enormously strong. But I met
Nina at the library yesterday and she's fretting dreadfully. And
she's got exams coming, too. I'm terribly worried about her,
Nadezhda Yegorovna!"

"I know Ninochka. She's a sensible girl and she's always done
well at school. I'll go and see her father tomorrow. Perhaps he
doesn't know you very well. Now then, Seryozha, mind *you*
don't fail. When's your first exam?"

Seryozha beamed. Of course he would pass his exams. So
would Nina. When he finished at the Institute, they'd go together to the Urals, or Turkmenia, or some other place. He
talked away of different factories and of the distant regions
where his fellow students came from. In fact, his head was clearly
spinning with joy—there was plenty of room in their country
and plenty of life ahead.

His visit distracted Nadezhda Yegorovna from her melancholy
thoughts and after he had left she went on smiling for a long
time. "He says he's strong, but his lips were trembling," she
thought. "He very nearly burst into tears. He's a good boy. . . .
And Kostya comes to see me too, and Sannikov, and Pavlik. Of
course, Andryusha's goodness made them what they are. Somehow I feel better when they are around. Sonya's so far away;
and Volodya goes about with a hang-dog look and never says a
word. But that's the way he's always been. After he'd come back
from Moscow I once said to him: 'What are you? A son or a
tenant?' He laughed and said that on the whole he thought he was
a prodigal son, but that he was grown-up and ought really to
look after me. I'll go to see Ninochka's father tomorrow without
fail. Andryusha always spoke highly of Seryozha and you can
see he's a responsible boy. You can't treat first love so harshly.
He is so comic with his huge glasses and his freckles—I've never
seen so many. Ninochka's a wise girl not to go chasing after good
looks . . ."

Savchenko came that evening and Nadezhda Yegorovna was

glad to see him. She was alone. Lately Volodya had not been
home much. She got out Sonya's last letter and read parts of it
aloud and paraphrased the rest.

"She writes: 'I like the work, and I'm really feeling fine. I've
already written to you about Sukhanov.' " She explained hastily:
"That's her boss; he was very kind to her when she first arrived—
not a young man, apparently. . . . There's more about the
factory: 'You'll never guess who I suddenly saw in our shop:
Zhuravlyov! I couldn't believe my eyes. Volodya told me he'd
been sent as a foreman somewhere, but I didn't realise he was
being funny as usual. It seems that Zhuravlyov did get into real
trouble; he waited around in Moscow for eight months but
finally he was sent to us—as head of production. He's been here
more than two months now—I meant to tell you long ago but
kept forgetting. Savchenko used to say all sorts of dreadful things
about him—I was afraid he'd start throwing his weight around.
But whether Savchenko was exaggerating or Zhuravlyov has
changed, I don't know; he seems all right to me. He's polite to
everybody; he listens to complaints and tries to help. Savchenko
said his invariable reaction was: "Let's have no argument about
it," but twice he's said to me: "It's possible I've been mistaken."
He's got very much thinner, not a bit like Volodya's portrait of
him.' Then she goes on about me. The poor girl's worried about
my health. She asks about her brother, why he never writes to
her. But Volodya doesn't like writing letters. I often write to her,
though she complains that my letters are short. I don't know
what to write about. Anyway when she comes home we shall
have plenty of time to talk. She asks after you and wants to be
remembered to you."

She put away the letter and thought regretfully: "Poor Sonya.
And I'm sorry for Savchenko, too. I'm sure he still feels the same
about her."

Savchenko stood up to go and she did not try to keep him.
When Andryusha was alive, he used to stay for hours, but what
did he have to talk to her about?

"Nadezhda Yegorovna, I wasn't sure whether I ought to come today or not. It's exactly a year today since . . ."

She could hardly hold back her tears. So he had remembered after all!

"Andryusha was very fond of you . . ."

"He did a great deal for me. And not only me, of course— we all learned from him . . ."

She made him sit down again and put the kettle on and sliced up cheese and salami.

"You like it strong, Grigory Yevdokimovich?" she smiled. "I'd better call you Grisha, I expect your mother does."

Confused, Savchenko replied:

"My mother called me Grigulya."

He told her his mother had died in Leningrad during the siege. An aunt had taken him in and then they were evacuated to Tomsk. Twice he ran away to go to the front, and once he got as far as Minsk, but he was sent back. He pretended he was seventeen but he was only fifteen at the time. His uncle was killed near Königsberg. Now his aunt was alone. He had invited her to live with him, but she was a Leningrad woman, she said, and would die in her native city.

Nadezhda Yegorovna asked for news of the plant: Yegorov hadn't been to see her for a long time.

"But Yasha Brainin came in yesterday. He's being sent to Karaganda; his father's unhappy about it but Yasha himself is delighted. He told me they'd been after Sokolovsky again, but I couldn't believe it. Why should they, now Zhuravlyov's out of the way, and they all speak well of Golovanov?"

Savchenko told her that Sokolovsky had lost his temper, that he had proposed a marvellous project, and that Andreyev had backed it. It had to be admitted that the official attitude had been too rigid. After all, Sokolovsky wasn't a young man.

"It's all very well your telling me, but have you said all this to them?"

"Of course I have!"

Nadezhda Yegorovna thought: "Andryusha was never afraid to tell people the truth. Savchenko remembered him and he came. . . . So something remains. It flows on from one to another; it doesn't disappear completely."

"Grisha, what does Sonya write to you?"

"She hardly ever writes. She's terribly busy, of course. Maslov was in Penza not long ago, and he says they're pleased with Sonya at the factory."

He tried to smile, but it was a sad smile.

"I must go, Nadezhda Yegorovna. I've stayed much too long. It's nearly twelve."

He had hardly gone when she heard Volodya's step. Thinking his mother was asleep, he went quietly towards his room, but she called out:

"Volodya! There's a letter from Sonya. It's in the drawer."

"Why aren't you asleep?"

"Savchenko's been to see me—he left just before you came in. I'm worried about Sonya."

"Why? She writes that she's getting on well."

"I don't mean that. She and Savchenko aren't hitting it off."

"What makes you think that? He's always asking about her."

"I just feel it. You should have seen him today; such a hang-dog look."

Volodya laughed:

"So what? If Savchenko's depressed, what can I do about it?" He got hold of himself. "Don't pay any attention to me, Mother. I'm talking like an idiot." He kissed her. "Don't worry about Sonya; she can stand on her own feet."

He thought: "It's true, too. Sonya's like Father. She's got principles; she's tough. Not like me."

Aloud he said: "You know, Mother, I've been thinking today how everybody loved Father. Almost everyone I come across knew him—either they came here, or else I remember Father talking about them. Sonya's very like Father. She's a strong person."

"Still, I'm sorry for her. She has no one. She's an obstinate girl."

"Perhaps there's someone she likes at Penza. She writes about this Sukhanov."

"It's the third time she's mentioned him. 'An interesting man' —but what are we supposed to make of that? Perhaps he's married? Well, anyhow, I dare say it doesn't mean anything. But you must write to her, Volodya. She feels hurt."

Volodya smiled sadly.

"Write about what? Nothing's been happening, either to me or in general. Good night, Mother."

All the same he forced himself to write:

> Dear Sonya,
> Mother is well, and your letter cheered her up a lot. She keeps on saying that you are in good spirits and that's been enough to make her look twenty years younger. She does a lot for Father's boys. Do you remember red-haired Seryozha? He's having an unhappy love affair, and he's always running to Mother for advice. On the whole, it's a good thing. It keeps her mind off her own grief.
>
> I personally have no news. I handed in the panel today, and I've been asked to do a portrait of Andreyev. I work, sometimes I sulk, sometimes I make jokes. I've been reading Dickens; now I'm going to switch to Stendhal. Occasionally I have a chat with Sokolovsky—he's been trying, unsuccessfully, to make me understand physics. Talking of which, I envy you for knowing about such things. Savchenko says that Sokolovsky's project is terrific; he explained it to me, but I didn't understand much; it has to do with some way of treating metal in a tempered form and other equally mystifying matters.
>
> I often think about you. You mustn't feel I'm a bad brother. Of course, I've often said stupid things to you, but that's just my charming character! Please don't be sad. Remember when you're in a bad mood that things may be different tomorrow. I've been told by someone that it's always possible to begin a new chapter, even when there seems to be nothing left in life. It might be true. I'm sure you're not losing heart—you're like Father. Whenever I think of you, I always remember him.

A Change of Season

It's a year ago today, Sonya. I went with Mother to the cemetery this morning. I wish I could write to you about Father, but there's so little one can say in words, except that everybody loved him, and that's a rare thing. You and I have suffered a great loss, and we must stick by each other more closely.

Do write to me, and I promise I'll often write and tell you about Mother. She says she finds it hard to say what she wants in a letter, but I cheer her up by reminding her it'll soon be July and then you'll be here. Perhaps you could take your leave in June?

Of all your news about Penza, I was particularly ravished by your description of the change in Zhuravlyov! I really don't know which is more difficult to imagine—Zhuravlyov slim and svelte, or modest and kind. In any case, remember me to him. By the way, I've still got his portrait. If he gets any thinner, I'll send it to him as a present, to remind him of his pompous past.

Be cheerful and happy, Sonya. All my love.

He thought no more about his own troubles, or Saburov, or what to do about his life. He suddenly felt better. He went to bed and fell asleep with a slight smile on his face.

8

IF SOKOLOVSKY SEEMED CALMER, perhaps even more cheerful than usual, this was not because he wished to hide that he felt hurt but because he struggled with himself and was afraid of giving way to his depression.

When Savchenko told him he thought the reprimand had been unjust, he said: "Don't you bother your head about that. It's true they needn't have rubbed my nose in it, I'm not a puppy. But by and large, I'm the one to blame. When you're fifty-eight you shouldn't behave like a child. . . . What I'm worried about is my project—they were so busy fussing about me that they forgot about what mattered. If they'd said: 'Sokolovsky is an old fool, it's time he was pensioned off, but there's something to be said for his proposal,' I'd have hugged them. But like this it makes no sense. There was I telling them about the electro-erosion process, and all they bothered about was my manners."

He was again suffering from his old trouble, insomnia, and he had plenty of time at night to think of what had happened. Part of his exasperation, he thought, was due to his unsettled personal affairs. A week before the Party Bureau meeting Vera had told him it would be better if they did not see each other again. It was true that this was not the first time it had happened: now he, now Vera would decide in moments of despair that they must part, that they were nothing but a torment to each other. Then, after a few days or weeks would come the reconciliation and with it such joy that it wiped the memory of the quarrel from their minds.

They loved each other with a passionate, jealous, and sad love, the kind that flares up like an autumn storm and makes the evening of life vivid and uneasy. Each had for a long time lived alone and become accustomed to a hard and shut-in life: "We've got used to our shells," Vera had once said. She was afraid lest Sokolovsky came to realise that she was weak and anchorless— she did not want to be pitied. Once she had kept away from him for weeks because she was trying to save the mechanic, Sukharyov, in spite of having diagnosed cancer: Sukharyov was dying painfully and Vera told herself: "This is *my* trouble, why should I involve him in it?" At other times she kept away simply because she felt depressed; the long years of sorrow rose before her—her husband's death, loneliness, February '53. Then she would call up Sokolovsky and say: "Don't come. I'm on duty." Sokolovsky felt hurt and jealous; but he, too, was afraid of letting Vera see him when he was feeling out of sorts and only confided to his dog, Fomka: "What a pair of lunatics we are, you and I!" When he and Vera did meet again, either they were as happy as children or they quarrelled. Sometimes the smallest thing led to a wretched scene that they would both interpret as a final break. But in reality nothing could now separate them: too many things bound them together and the happiness that had come to them fortuitously was too great.

There was another reason for Sokolovsky's nervous state. He had recently had a letter from his daughter. Mary wrote that she hoped to see him, as she and her husband were soon coming to Moscow; they had put their name down at the travel agency and would probably arrive in June. The letter had excited him, though he tried to convince himself that he and Mary had nothing in common. She had dropped eurhythmics and had taken up painting instead: she wrote that she believed in nothing but abstract art. "It doesn't interest me," he thought, "and it doesn't even sound as if she means it. What on earth shall we talk about? We'll sit looking at each other and get upset." All the same, deep in his heart he thought of her with tenderness and longing. He searched her letters for simple, human words and blamed himself for his distrust: it was impossible that Mashenka [1] should be a stranger. He was both impatient to see her and afraid.

But neither the thought of Mary nor his differences with Vera could have destroyed his equilibrium. He was too accustomed to solitude, to doing without tenderness or care, to give way to his feelings. The reason for his outburst at the factory lay in that fever of the spirit which had possessed him in recent years. He was overjoyed to see the change in human relationships; it delighted him that the people were livelier at meetings and spoke louder, that the workers had moved into the new apartment houses, and that Dmitry's stepfather had come back. Remembering his youth, the civil war, the years of famine and of ardour,

---

[1] Diminutive of Mariya, the Russian form of Mary.

he would say to Savchenko: "We're making strides. We talk less and do more." But whenever now there was a hold-up, whenever a Khitrov or a Safonov crawled out to accuse someone or to recite his set piece about how everything in life was achieved, "more than achieved," or when Brainin, who had himself suffered injustice under Zhuravlyov, said cautiously at the sight of thieving, bribery, or boorishness that it was not his business but that of the management or the police, then Sokolovsky was beside himself with rage. He realised that he was too impatient, that it was useless to want everything at once. "Nothing happens all at once," he told himself in his calmer moments. "We built our house with sweat and tears, and it will take us a long time to make it fit to live in."

Sometimes he attributed his state of mind to his age: he had no time left to waste on weighing and measuring everything he did. In winter he was often ill, but he did not tell Vera. It had started with ordinary flu but there had been complications that affected his lungs and in the end Dr. Gorokhov had said gloomily: "Your heart is in a bad state. Overwork and neglect. . . . You can't go on like this; you're not a young man." Sokolovsky listened attentively to Gorokhov's instructions and made up his mind to follow them, but soon forgot. On the occasions when he felt a sudden, sharp pain in his chest and lost his breath, he forced himself to go on working, talking, smiling; he struggled with his illness as he had always struggled with the difficulties of his life. Now and then he reminded himself angrily that he hadn't long to live, but he never in his heart felt old, and listening to Savchenko or some other youngster, he noted with amusement that though they had the whole of life before them they were just as impatient as he was: "So it isn't a question of age."

After the meeting of the Party Bureau he felt like going to see Vera but decided not to.

They had not seen each other for a long time and their last meeting had been painful to both. Vera had said: "Better make

a clean break. . . . It doesn't seem to work. . . . You can adjust
a screw or rub down a cork to make it fit, but hearts are not
adjustable."

The unwitting cause of their latest quarrel was Volodya
Pukhov, the artist. Sokolovsky had told Vera about his talk with
him and Vera was indignant: "I could never understand why
you allow him into your house. It's not true about Saburov. I
went to the show myself. Pukhov's just envious. He's got a mean
mind." Sokolovsky took Volodya's side: "But you don't know him.
Of course it's disgusting that he turns out pot-boilers, but he's
the first to suffer from it. His cynicism is all put on." Vera lost
her temper: "It's funny you should be so exacting with some
people and forgive others everything they do."

They went on to talk of others. Sokolovsky, who was known to
be difficult, was capable of saying exceedingly unpleasant things
in the heat of the moment; but he soon cooled down and from
being too harsh became sad and tolerant. Vera could not understand this: she was consistent in her likes and dislikes.

"What about Zhuravlyov?" she asked angrily. "Is he a swine or
isn't he, according to you? He ruined Lena's life, he behaved
abominably to his subordinates, he left his workers in miserable
barracks that rotted over their heads, he planted a man who took
bribes on the housing committee—that case is before the prosecu-
tion at this moment. Not to mention the lies he told about you.
And then you tell me I'm unjust to people!"

"I don't in the least intend to whitewash Zhuravlyov," Sokolovsky objected stubbornly. "In point of fact, I haven't given him a
thought since his dismissal. But if you want to bring him up, all
I can say is that Zhuravlyov worked conscientiously; he wasn't a
thief; nor did he lose his head at the time of the fire; and they
say he had a good war record. Of course, it was wrong to let a
man like that do whatever he liked. But why blame only
Zhuravlyov? What about Obukhov? And Trifonov? And indeed,
what about Comrade Sokolovsky, the head designer? Why didn't

II · The Spring

I go to Moscow and complain about the housing? All I ever did was to shout at the Party meeting. Zhuravlyov isn't the real point. I've no doubt he's been hauled over the coals. But you can't brand a man as if he were a thief or a boot-licker from the day he was born. A lot depends on education and environment. There aren't many born villains, though I agree there's plenty of wickedness in the world."

It was not that Vera was convinced of Pukhov's wickedness, nor was Sokolovsky a great believer in Zhuravlyov's virtues, but neither would give way. The real quarrel was not, of course, about either Zhuravlyov or Volodya; its roots lay buried in old misunderstandings, reservations, grievances. They were both tired and failed to understand each other. Every word caused pain. They were frightened for the future of their love but in trying to defend it only dealt it terrible wounds.

Yet, needless to say, it was not the memory of this bitter conversation that prevented Sokolovsky from going to see Vera. He thought about her ceaselessly and longed to hear her voice, press her to his heart, reassure himself that he was not alone. What held him back was something else. He was afraid of betraying his own wretchedness, of infecting Vera with his own sadness. His constant solicitude for her was almost superstitious: she had suffered enough, he felt. He must never add to her distress. He knew that if he saw her he would not be able to conceal his trouble. "Thirty-four years in the Party, and now a reprimand! Even in the Urals, when they wrote their lies about me in the papers, no one thought of such a thing. Certainly I'm at fault, but that doesn't make it any easier to bear." He felt deeply wounded. Vera would want to help him and he knew that there was nothing more bitter than to feel powerless to help.

A week went by. No one told Vera of the decisions of the Party Bureau and she had no idea of Sokolovsky's state. The bitterness of their last meeting had long vanished from her mind. Every evening she waited for him. But she could not make up her mind to call him. Could he be offended? No, he was surely busy with his project—if not, he would have come. He could not seriously believe that it was all over between them because of some silly words . . .

One evening she told herself: "It's too humiliating—here I sit as if I were chained up." She decided to go around to Lena's. She had not seen her for a long time, and she might as well have a look at Shura: Lena had said that she was pale and had no appetite.

Vera and Lena met often; they were bound by a strong friendship born in a time that had been difficult for both. Two more different people could hardly have been imagined: Vera so reserved, Lena gay and sociable. Yet their standards, which were high, and their opinions, always held with passion, often coincided.

Lena was delighted when Vera came, but she felt embarrassed. Several times she had meant to visit her but had put it off: suppose Vera asked her why Dmitry had voted for the reprimand. "It's a mystery even to me," she thought, "I don't want to judge him but I can't understand it."

Vera examined the little girl, said there was nothing seriously the matter, and wrote out a prescription. Then they had a long talk about Vyrubin and about Lena's mother, who had recently been to stay with Lena. "Mother likes Dmitry," Lena said laughing. "She gave me strict orders: 'Mind you're always considerate to him—he's very sensitive.' "

Lena expected Vera to tell her how Sokolovsky had taken the reprimand and twice started to speak of him, but Vera seemed not to notice. At last she asked:

"How is Sokolovsky, Vera?"

"He's all right. He's working very hard."

"Is he very upset by what has happened?"

Vera had no idea what Lena was talking about but she realised at once that Sokolovsky had kept something from her. She managed to say calmly:

228

"You know what he's like. When he's wrapped up in his work, he can't think of anything else."

For politeness' sake she stayed another quarter of an hour and said good-bye cheerfully; then in great distress she ran through the dark empty streets to the house where Sokolovsky lived.

She was alarmed and hurt but she could not help smiling as she came into his room: after all, she had told Lena the exact truth—there he was, sitting at his desk working. But her smile vanished at once.

"What's happened?"

Sokolovsky's face had cleared at seeing her, but now he frowned, realising that he would have to tell her.

"Wait a minute. Sit down. It's so long since I've seen you."

"Tell me," Vera insisted. "What's happened?"

He began with the project and got carried away as he explained the details. Vera became so angry that she could hardly control herself. At last he came to the meeting of the Party Bureau.

"It's my fault. I walked out of the production meeting. I didn't explain to Golovanov. I acted like a child. But it's not that important. I feel sure they'll come back to my project sooner or later, that's what matters."

"I don't believe you. What's worrying you at this moment is not the project but the reprimand. Why pretend?"

There was a long silence. Each was thinking: "How useless words are." Then Sokolovsky talked about Vyrubin.

"I went to see him day before yesterday. He's writing a long article. It seems that while he was still 'out there' he began to work on chemical fertilisers and got astonishing results, especially with tomatoes. Needless to say, some of our clever people didn't want to hear about it. According to them, chemical fertilisers were a negation of the influence of natural conditions, the idea was anti-biological, it was almost metaphysics! Now, naturally, they've come to their senses."

Vera interrupted him:

229

"I don't want to hear about that. Why do you talk to me as if I were a stranger? You know you're not thinking about fertilisers at this moment."

"I'm thinking about Vyrubin. Compared to what he's been through, what do my troubles amount to? And yet he's working, not spending his time thinking about his past. He talks about fertilisers and I believe he's right—I don't mean about agronomy but about life, about the human condition. You're wrong, Vera; I'm not pretending. Of course I find it hard, but I told you the truth—what's important to me is the project. What matters in the long run is not whether Engineer Sokolovsky was upset; there are plenty of engineers and plenty of things to be upset about. What matters is the project."

He spoke with such conviction that Vera was shaken.

"Why didn't you tell me? Don't you trust me?"

He came up to her, put his arms round her, and was at once filled with the peace he had been dreaming of for days.

"I do more than trust you. You're my life, Vera. Don't be angry. I didn't want to upset you; that was the only reason I didn't come when I wanted to so much."

Vera smiled.

"There's such a lot you know—about machines and botany and painting. And yet I'm a closed book to you. Can't you see that it's my happiness to share your troubles? I want to live your life. Can't you understand?"

Rain pattered on the window, the first warm spring rain that makes everything unfold and blossom; the drumming of the big raindrops on the glass was friendly. Sokolovsky saw that there were tears in Vera's eyes. He kissed her wet cheek, gazing long at her. She looked like a girl who experiences the joy and pain of love for the first time.

She stayed with him until morning. As she was going away he said: "I used to think that only young people had to struggle for their love and only until they'd straightened things out be-

tween them. But it's not like that. You have to struggle for it all
your life, not to let it come to harm. You have to carry it safely
over many obstacles and go on doing it till the day you die. Vera,
my love."

9

VOLODYA HIMSELF COULD NEVER
explain afterwards why he went to the discussion on the exhibition. Although Dobzhinsky had insisted, had called three times
to tell him that Fokin was coming from Moscow—"It's a great
event"—he had been firmly determined not to go: he would be
sure to get annoyed and talk a lot of nonsense. In his present
state of nerves the discussion seemed to him a humiliation: if they
must set themselves up to judge the artist Pukhov, then let them
pass sentence in his absence.

Why then did he go?—His vanity flared up: "They can say
what they like. I've no reason to hide."

The hall was crammed. Volodya thought: "It's all one to them
—Brainin on foreign politics, amateur theatricals, space-travel,
painting—they'll swallow the lot."

Brainin rose to speak. People fidgeted, coughed, and whispered.
Even Brainin looked bored to death. He praised Volodya's work.

"Pukhov's picture deals, so-to-speak, with a most important
educational problem."

His son Yasha said loudly to the girl sitting next to him: "Father
has learned Yershov's article by heart."

Volodya thought: "There's Brainin praising me, and it doesn't
give me any pleasure. Why did I come? I'm sure Saburov never
goes to these discussions: he sits at home and paints. But I have

to come on the double and torment myself about what Brainin will say or Fokin write about me. Brainin talks as if he were at a State funeral. Next moment we'll hear: 'Vladimir Pukhov, so to speak, honourably followed the creative path.'"

Khitrov got up. He spoke pompously, clearing his throat and making significant pauses, as if to show that he knew a lot more than he could say to such an audience.

"It is not by chance that Saburov avoids socially important themes and takes to by-paths. No one denies the artist's right to paint a landscape. But what does Saburov show us in his landscapes? He has painted a house in our workers' settlement. Why is it so unattractive? Not by chance, Comrades—the picture shows a clear intention to throw doubt on our achievements. Saburov's other painting is the portrait of a woman. Here surely was the artist's opportunity to show us a specifically Soviet type. But what have we here? Can we believe that this woman plays a part in building Socialism in our country? It is a face without expression; in the eyes there is neither the flash of inspiration nor the glow of reflection; and her clothes are deliberately shoddy. What can be the appeal of such decadent productions? It is the harder to understand when side by side we see the remarkable painting by Pukhov, dedicated to the happy life of little Soviet children. Year by year Pukhov interprets for us the most urgent problems discussed in our newspapers. His paintings were selected for special comment at the All-Union exhibition— this, Comrades, did not happen by chance either . . ."

It was more than Volodya could bear. He yawned unhappily. He should never have come. . . . Even his father had said that Khitrov was "slimy," and he had hardly ever spoken ill of anyone. No one liked Khitrov. Dobzhinsky seemed to be the only one who applauded.

Savchenko was asked to speak. Volodya started. The audience brightened up. Savchenko spoke badly, skipping from one subject to another, but with warmth.

II · The Spring

"I remember coming out of the Hermitage. It was a grey, misty day but everything before my eyes seemed to blaze . . ."

Volodya too thought of the Hermitage. "Who knows," he wondered, "perhaps Savchenko really does care for art."

"It seems to me that when a man looks at a painting, the landscape or the face the artist has portrayed comes alive—the one who's looking at it gives it a new life. And when the landscape or the portrait reaches the onlooker, it's he who changes. . . . Saburov's portrait of a woman has helped me to understand a lot . . ."

Volodya was astonished at himself: he had been afraid of getting angry if Savchenko praised Saburov, but he found that he was not. "Actually, it's a very good thing that he is fond of painting. Only I don't want him to talk about me. It wouldn't be fair: for one thing, he's one of the people whose fault it is that I do this stuff, and for another—you don't hit a man when he's down."

Savchenko was still talking about Saburov. He spoke of what he had seen at his house:

"You can't convey the quality of a picture in words; even a poet couldn't do this, and I'm a bad speaker; but I wish you could see one particular landscape. It's the very beginning of spring, there's still snow on the ground, but you know that at any moment now the earth will burst into green. And a small portrait—it's of a woman in a grey shawl, her face glowing as if it had the light of sunset on it. And a still life—also in the spring—grey pussy willows in a glass jar. It takes great love to reveal so much of life . . ."

When Savchenko finished, everybody clapped. Volodya clapped, too: "On the whole, it was a stupid speech; but if I sit like a stuffed pig they'll think I'm jealous of Saburov. And that I'm not. . . . I remember that still life with the pussy willows. It's good . . ." He could see Fokin in the first row. "He must be laughing to himself: 'What oddities these provincials are.' He

233

wrote about me very nicely last autumn. He can't possibly like Saburov. Though who knows? Why shouldn't he change? He's never had an opinion of his own."

Embarrassed by his success, Savchenko went quickly back to his seat. So long as he was talking, he had looked to Volodya tall and arrogant, but now he was again the Savchenko who had spent hours waiting for Sonya at the gate. "Mother says he's discouraged. I'm rather sorry for him. Sonya is difficult, and she's the one who will suffer. They might have been married long ago, but it's all gone wrong . . .

"How long will they go on chattering? I'd have done better to go to the Volga."

Dmitryeva spoke in high praise of "The Pioneers' Campfire."

"Pukhov shows a wonderful delicacy in observing the eagerness to learn and the sense of discipline of Soviet schoolchildren. As a teacher with thirty years' experience, I should like to say to him that I am deeply grateful . . ."

Many people clapped. Volodya smiled. "Dmitryeva's not Khitrov," he thought. "She's a teacher, she isn't young, she's got a good face. And she really likes it! It's true, she doesn't know a thing about art, but neither do most people. Fokin will probably mention what she said. Perhaps after all I'm tormenting myself for nothing."

He stopped listening. Neither of the two speakers who followed said anything about him. "Why was I so sure I'd be attacked? I must be off my head. It's awful that there's no one to talk to. . . . Last night Mother asked why I didn't get married. Apparently it's indecent not to be married by the time you're thirty-five. And by fifty you should have had a decoration. But it won't be I who will be decorated—it will be Saburov. It's odd—here am I wondering what will happen in fifteen year's time, and I don't suppose I'll drag on till forty."

Suddenly he heard his name. It was Andreyev, whose portrait Volodya was about to paint.

"I cannot agree with Comrade Khitrov when he praises Pukhov

and attacks Saburov. Of course, I'm not an expert in this sort of thing. But when I saw Saburov's paintings, they made me feel like living, working, struggling. He has offered to paint my portrait."

Involuntarily, Volodya shouted:

"It's impossible! That must be a mistake."

Either Andreyev did not hear him or he did not understand what Volodya meant. He went on:

"I'm happy and honoured. Some of us often go to Saburov's. We've even written to the paper asking why his work is shown so seldom. I may say that the letter was sent two weeks ago but so far the editors haven't seen fit to reply. But that's beside the point. In my opinion, Saburov's paintings are inspiring. As for Pukhov, I remember a painting by him of a group of workers reading a newspaper. I'm a worker myself, Comrades, and I'll tell you frankly—it filled me with depression, and it even made me angry. The whole conception is false. Our people are not like that; they don't have those artificial expressions. It's like at the photographer's: 'Smooth your hair, please. Head a little higher, just a moment, now smile . . .' There's no beauty in it, no truth, no heart. And his Pioneers are unreal, too. Our children are lively and mischievous; every one has his own expression. But Pukhov's children are all the same: every one is at the top of his class and the hero of a moral tale. In the exhibition you've probably seen Saburov's portrait of a woman. It's a portrait of his wife. Honestly, I couldn't take my eyes away from it. I don't know how long I'd been standing there when I heard them saying it was closing time. Now that, Comrades, is real art."

Volodya wrote feverishly on the back of his invitation:

"May I speak? V. Pukhov."

He began calmly, saying a few words in a monotonous voice about the value to the artist of criticism and of such discussions as the one held today, and suddenly burst out:

"It's fantastic! It's Andreyev's language I was using in my paintings, it's him I was addressing in words he could understand, and it's for that he is attacking me now! I'll never believe that Saburov's paintings can mean anything to *him!*"

He stopped, at a loss for words. Everyone was silent. Then he began again, tonelessly reiterating the text-book words stocked in his memory:

"Saburov is a formalist—the desire to escape into colour values is a dereliction of idea-content in art. We artists know that the people expect us to portray great themes. Saburov's painting is an alien manifestation and it is my duty to give warning to the public . . ."

In the end he was shouting again:

"I don't want to paint like him! That's just what I don't want to do! He has alienated himself from our Soviet life! His aim is to undermine it! It's he who stands in the dock! Such painting is nothing less than an attack on our way of living."

A few people applauded noisily. Someone shouted: "Bravo! He's hit the nail on the head!" Dobzhinsky did not know whether to be delighted or indignant and looked inquiringly at Fokin, but Fokin said nothing. He was thinking: "Pukhov must have knocked back at least three glasses. They don't waste their time in the provinces, any more than we do!" Yasha Brainin said to his companion: "There's a nice case of crime and punishment for you." The girl replied: "I don't believe a word he said."

As Volodya went towards the door, everybody turned to look at him.

Afterwards he had only a vague memory of how he made his way to the Volga. It was still light but for some reason the street lamps were lit. Someone was trying to overtake a girl in a light blue dress. In the bus people were saying it was warm, it would soon be summer. A woman was telling her neighbour that she had a permit to go to Adler: "You can't think what the sea is like out there; it's wonderful! And such roses around the ve- randah—thousands of them, and of every colour." At the back, a student was learning by heart: "Giordano Bruno attacked the classifications of the schoolmen and the analyses of the logicians."

II · The Spring

The doorman at the Volga bared his yellow teeth: "Lovely day." Volodya was surprised: "Is it?"

The accordion sobbed. At the end table, a drunken clerk with red hair and a bristly chin was muttering angrily to himself: "Who gave her the right to spit on me?" Volodya thought: "I know him. Twice when I've been to my publisher for money he's told me it wasn't pay day. What are all these people doing here today? Is it Saturday? But really, it's surprisingly empty. I must get drunk or I'll go mad."

Wrinkling up his nose, he swallowed a glass of vodka.

"Is this home-brew?"

The waiter replied indifferently:

"It's Moscow vodka—it's what you ordered."

Volodya felt like smashing the glass, cursing, shouting at the red-haired clerk that people are always spitting on each other, but he only said tamely:

"All right. Give me the same again."

The next morning he woke up late, and for a long time could not remember what had happened. When he did, he thought: "Andreyev is a normal type, so he's sure to be married. If his wife wasn't at the club he'll have told her at teatime: 'Pukhov's not only a bad painter, he's a complete swine—he's jealous of Saburov.' On the whole, that's true. I know that Saburov is an honest artist but I did my best to slander him. Like Khitrov. . . . Why? Evidently I'm frightened that when they get a look at real painting they'll see that the Emperor has no clothes on, after all—they'll see me for what I am. It's not a question of money—that can always be earned somehow. It's not even a question of prestige—for Yershov, and even perhaps for Fokin. I'll go on being a 'leading' painter for a long time. What frightened me was that Andreyev had understood.

"Anyway, all that's immaterial now. I've been a bad painter and now I've become a swine. I can avoid Khitrov, but how am I to live with myself?"

His head was aching. He went out for a breath of air but only walked as far as the corner and turned back: "Suppose I run into someone I know . . ." He told his mother he had urgent work to do and stayed shut up in his room all day. "I knew I oughtn't to go to that meeting. But what's done is done. Dare I go to Sokolovsky? No—he'd only turn me out. The whole town must know. If only I'd been seeing Tanechka, this wouldn't have happened: I'd have been ashamed in front of her. But what's the good of talking. I'm at a dead end. I've reached rock bottom."

For several days he was in a fever, obsessed by one thought: "What does Saburov think of me? Andreyev will have told him, and he's sure to remember that I used to visit him and admire his pictures. He must think I'm a real swine."

He stopped thinking about art and what to do with his life. A thousand times he told himself: "I must go see Saburov. I must tell him straight out: 'I lost my head; I came out with a lot of filth. If you can, forgive me. I'm very ashamed of myself.'"

Several times he started out but turned back, stopped by shame or pride. Or he would say to himself: "What's the good? —He wouldn't let me through the door."

But at last he did make up his mind to go.

Saburov welcomed him as usual, but Volodya could find nothing to say. Glasha pretended to be tidying up. They all three felt awkward.

Saburov looked at Volodya: he had changed, he seemed older. "He must be torturing himself. I told Glasha he is his own executioner. He's got real talent and he's suddenly realised that he's been treading it underfoot. Glasha can't understand that. If only I could paint his portrait!" Forgetting everything else, Saburov gazed with admiration at Volodya's narrow, greyish-green face, with its heavy chin and brilliant, almost luminous eyes under high-arched brows. It gave an impression of tension, of great inner torment. It reminded him of a portrait by El Greco with a background of red rocks. "Goodness, it's very rude of me to stare at him."

"How are you, Volodya? It's ages since we met. I was afraid you weren't coming to see us any more."

Volodya started. "Here we go now," he thought. But try as he might, he could not utter a word: only his lips moved soundlessly.

Saburov fussed over him, asked whether he'd like some tea, recalled their schooldays, trying to cheer him up.

Glasha remained silent.

Volodya stood up and for some reason said:

"Spring is late this year. . . . I'd better go . . ."

All at once he noticed the landscape Savchenko had spoken of: early spring, snow here and there, and a patch of young green. He thought: "It's like the Town Garden that day I was mooning about with Tanechka. Then it seemed that everything might really change. But it hasn't . . ."

"That's my latest sketch," said Saburov.

Volodya thought absent-mindedly: "Now she'll say: 'Isn't it marvellous?' " But Glasha was silent.

"I'd better go," Volodya repeated, and this time he actually went to the door.

Glasha stood up.

"I'll see you to the gate. It's terribly muddy in the yard."

At the gate she said:

"One thing I beg of you—please never come here again."

He had never seen her eyes like this, either in real life or in Saburov's portraits of her: such was the anger in them that he turned away and walked quickly down the steep, slippery street.

10

TRIFONOV HAD HAD A TALK WITH
Golovanov and was going towards his car when he saw Dmitry.
"Dmitry Sergeyevich! I didn't know you were back. How are
you? Did you take the baths?" And without waiting for an
answer, he began to talk about work. "How do you like Safonov's
project? They say output will go up by four per cent."

Dmitry replied that he had not yet had time to study either
Safonov's project or Sokolovsky's.

"Oh well, Sokolovsky's project is not a serious proposition. You
know I've always backed progressive ideas, but this is a lot of
eyewash, if you'll forgive my saying so. Laboratory experiments
are one thing, but a great industrial enterprise is another."

"Opinions differ. It needs thinking about."

Trifonov agreed perfunctorily and would have walked on; but
Dmitry stopped him.

"Naturally you know that the Party Bureau gave Sokolovsky a
reprimand?"

Trifonov sighed.

"Of course, it was most unpleasant: an old member of the
Party; been at the plant for years. But he had to be pulled short.
It's very easy to let things get slack. I gather there were eleven
in favour and only two against."

"Yes, I voted in favour."

"You were right, Dmitry Sergeyevich. I know you think a lot
of Sokolovsky, but this was a matter of principle."

"But I think we made a mistake. Our approach was too
formal. In any case, at the Party meeting, I'm going to propose
that we don't confirm the reprimand."

Trifonov was furious. He had a pale, parchment face and when he was angry his cheeks, which hung down in folds, quivered.

"I cannot understand you, Dmitry Sergeyevich! What possible explanation have you got? This is undermining authority . . ."

"It's never too late to correct a mistake. It's not as if we didn't know our Sokolovsky. He's quick-tempered. But he's never refused to work, and it's not true to say he has. He didn't deserve to be reprimanded and I'm going to say so."

"That's your right. And the Party meeting has the right not to confirm the reprimand. As you know, I always stand up for the principles of Party democracy. And I don't want to quarrel with you about Sokolovsky. You may know best. But a fact's a fact: at the Party Bureau you voted in favour, and in your place I wouldn't go back on that. It'd be inconsistent. Anyway, the Party meeting would confirm it just the same. You'd only find yourself in an awkward position."

"I'm in an awkward position already. Or rather, I'm in a nasty position: I didn't vote according to my conscience. I meant to talk to Demin about it. He came to the plant yesterday, but I was in the workshop and didn't know. Well, good-bye . . ."

Trifonov drove away in his car, but it was a long time before he could calm down and his cheeks went on quivering angrily.

"Koroteyev has a very high standing at the works. But if he's going to be for one thing today and for another tomorrow, who is going to respect him? What we need is a firm hand. Golovanov is an honest man and he knows his job. But he's too soft, he's spineless. Obviously Sokolovsky needed a dressing down. If they think he's infallible, then what was all the fuss about? Safonov swore to me that they were all against him. I'm not interested in their quarrels, but it's very easy to get disorganised. . . . It's not by chance that Koroteyev mentioned Demin. If Ushakov were still here, I wouldn't worry. Of course, he was too soft with Sokolovsky, but as things are now, he'd have told Koroteyev it's best to drop it. . . . I can't answer for Demin . . ."

Back at his own office at the Town Hall, he went on thinking about his conversation with Dmitry. It was a bad business, very bad. He remembered the rumours at the time of the row over Krasnov and the dozen complaints about the inefficiency of the administration. Golovanov didn't know how to keep order; he was incapable of establishing his authority.

It was true that there had been more chaos in Zhuravlyov's time, but in those days people grumbled to their wives or to their friends: now they went straight to Golovanov, or Obukhov, or the Town Soviet.

"It's very easy to let people get slack," thought Trifonov, "and once that happens, output goes down and none of these new methods can help. . . . Koroteyev is a member of the Town Soviet. He makes reports; he writes articles—one in *Trud* [1] last week—he shouldn't undermine authority.

"Before it was simple: the Town Party Committee would have confirmed the Party Bureau resolution and that would have been that. Now it's all more difficult. Besides, Demin isn't Ushakov, he won't do it. Queer fellow he is. I talk to him about production and he says: 'You can't talk about production without talking about people.' He likes to be clever. He ought to be a writer, but in the Party apparatus he's out of place."

Everything about Demin got on Trifonov's nerves. Although he ate a lot, he was nothing but skin and bones and as tall as a beanstalk. You'd take him for a sprinter; you could just see him running races. And run he did—to the plant, the Meat Combine, the building site—and never a hat or a cap on his head—nothing even to take off when people greeted him! According to Khitrov, he had behaved disgracefully at the circus. The clowns had sent him into fits and he had laughed louder than anyone. Not a thought for his position! And what stupendous self-assurance!— Even a top-form schoolboy who has to address a meeting at his school has the sense to think about it in advance and write

---

[1] "Labour," the trade-union newspaper.

his speech and read it out, but on the first of May Demin spoke impromptu and even told the audience from the platform that "people don't listen to a speech which is read out." It was getting impossible to work: twice a week Demin received anyone who wished to see him and even asked each one of them to sit down. So now, when Trifonov's secretary, Zoya, tried to keep people out, reminding them that he was a busy head of a department, they shouted: "So what? Why will Demin always see us?" Demin said the newspaper was dull and criticised the editor, Yershov. A man had only to make a violent speech for Demin to say: "That's a sensible fellow." "It's asking for trouble," thought Trifonov. "Whatever made them send us a man like that?"

"All the same, Koroteyev is going too far. Even Demin will be annoyed. It's a serious business; the authority of the Party Bureau is at stake. Of course, Demin gives himself airs—he likes to show off—but nobody can say he's stupid. I'll have to have a talk with him before Koroteyev gets to him."

Demin's secretary said he was alone working.

Demin was indeed sitting in front of a pile of papers.

"I've only come for a minute. This won't take long.—Have they spoken to you about Sokolovsky at the plant?"

"That's just what I'm on now. It's complicated. I don't know much about machine tools yet. I spent four years in cotton. What do *you* think about his project?"

Trifonov would have liked to say: "Eyewash!" but controlled himself. It was a good thing that for once Demin had admitted his ignorance; there was no point in sticking one's neck out.

"Yes, it's a complicated business."

"I wonder what Koroteyev has to say about it."

Trifonov was silent, then made up his mind to get down to brass tacks.

"I was at the plant this morning—I'm worried about the assembly shop. They're behind schedule again. I ran into Koroteyev and he told me quite casually that at the Party Bureau he'd voted in favour of reprimanding Sokolovsky but that now he was going to speak against it. Could you perhaps give him a hint?"

"What sort of a hint?"

"That he'd better not speak—not undermine authority."

Demin shrugged his shoulders.

"I don't see anything wrong with it. If he thinks he's made a mistake, why shouldn't he admit it?"

"That's all very well. . . . But what will in fact happen? The Party meeting quashing a decision of the Party Bureau—that's bad enough. And then, what will people think of Koroteyev?— They'll say he's a weathercock!"

"If he thinks he was wrong, it's better he should say so. As for the reprimand—the Party organisation has the right not to confirm it.—Know the rules?"

Trifonov thought sadly: "Now he's putting on his act. And to think he's first secretary!"

"It could affect output. Once things get out of hand, anything can happen."

Demin smiled.

"You're talking about Sokolovsky? I spent a couple of hours over there yesterday and I got the hang of it more or less. All Sokolovsky can be blamed for is walking out of the discussion— he lost his temper. He's sorry for that himself. All the rest is a lot of lies. Safonov has been running every day to Golovanov, and Khitrov has done his best, too. They cooked up a story that Sokolovsky refused to work on Safonov's project.—Bunkum? He's made a whole lot of corrections—they showed me in the design room. You can go have a look—seventeen pages of typescript. It's all a put-up job. It's disgusting! Of course he sticks up for his own plan, but that's another matter. Golovanov says they've got to think it over. . . . The reprimand was ridiculous. I can understand how Koroteyev feels!"

It was a good hour after he was back in his office before Trifonov could bring himself to open the file that Zoya had put on his desk. Then he called her in.

"Why have you typed 'utilisation'?"

"It's what you dictated."

"I'm asking you why you've spelled utilization with an 's' instead of a 'z'?"

"But it can be spelled either way."

"There's no such thing as either way. Look up *Pravda*—it's always 'z'."

His cheeks quivered.

At home, he would not touch his food. Marusya said pityingly: "Do have something. It's steamed and it's without salt; it can't hurt you."

He did not even hear what she said. "It's easy to upset things," he thought aloud gloomily, "but who's to put them together again? Trifonov, as usual."

That night he could not go to sleep; he had pains in the small of his back and his legs felt numb. The room was stuffy. Marusya slept, her face tucked into the pillow, while Trifonov thought and thought:

"Tomorrow I'll drop a hint to Obukhov—if that's their mood, he'd better not say much at the Party meeting. It's the only way now. . . . Sokolovsky will get completely out of hand. To hell with him. So long as they don't get disorganised at the plant. They're a pretty strong team. A bit more pressure on the assembly shop and they'll come out on top. . . . What's Demin up to? You'd think he'd be the first to worry. But all he does is to strike attitudes. Even when he talked to me, he might have been addressing a meeting. And who's the one to worry about output?—Trifonov, of course. And then some noisy character like Savchenko will jump up with accusations: 'Trifonov showed partiality. He was unjust to Sokolovsky. His approach is too formal. He takes no account of people. He was inconsiderate to Koroteyev.' And who am I working for, I'd like to know? Certainly not for myself. Dr. Gorokhov told me straight out I ought to take at least six months off and have treatment. I don't need a doctor to tell me I'm in a bad way. But I keep it to myself and I begged

Gorokhov not to tell anyone. I'm not like Demin; I'm not playing to the gallery. All I want is that things should go better . . . "It's half past three. Oh well, I shan't get any sleep now . . ." The dazzling May morning burst arrogantly in at the window.

11

DMITRYEVA WAS SPEAKING AT THE Teachers' Council: "Some of the younger teachers—of course, I have no particular colleague in mind—fail to establish their authority. They let the children get out of hand and thus encourage their bad traits. Yet the presence of a morally defective boy or girl is immediately reflected in the behaviour and the academic achievement of the whole school. Unfortunately, the questionable 'hero' of the regrettable incident in class seven has not yet been found . . ."

Lena had long forgotten about the carving on the desk. Her mind was taken up with Vasya Nikitin. He had been at the top of the class: why was he doing so badly now? He was absent-minded and he looked ill. Yet the doctor said there was nothing the matter with him . . .

She decided to go to see Vasya that evening, to have a look at his environment. He lived not far from the school. His father had been killed in the war; his mother worked as cleaning woman in a canteen. She never came to the parents' meetings, but she had once been to see Lena and Lena thought she was a grumbler but kind. She had complained that her son read books at night instead of going to sleep.

Lena found a bare, clean little room. There was a pile of pillows on the high bed; a lot of photographs; paper roses in a vase.

II · The Spring

Vasya's mother was not home. The boy was writing something but when he saw Lena he quickly pushed the exercise book into the drawer of the kitchen table.

Vasya was shy at first: he did not understand why she had come and tried to anticipate her questions: "I know I've been doing very badly at math lately and I only got a two [1] in English. But that just happened." Lena tried to draw him out, she joked with him and told him about her own schooldays: "My father liked carving animals out of wood. I remember he once made me an elephant." Vasya was interested and said: "I've tried to carve, too, but I can never get the proportions right. I tried a rhinoceros once!" He wanted to tell her that his mathematics teacher was very like a rhinoceros, but he didn't dare say so. He said he was interested in zoology: "It's a pity we haven't got a zoo here. I've watched animals a lot—goats, squirrels, birds. Near school last spring a thrush stole a nest from some starlings, and after that not a starling came near it—they're frightened of thrushes."

There was a silence. Then he asked: "Have you read Durov's book? It's fascinating, especially about sea lions. They are born jugglers."

As soon as Lena spoke of lessons, Vasya's face clouded. He said he'd try to catch up. "I have a lot of worries, you see. In class I often find myself thinking about something quite different." Lena tried in vain to discover what his worries were, he would not tell her. But as he was seeing her out, in the porch he suddenly said: "You mustn't think I was hiding something away from you when you came in. That was my diary. I write in it every day. . . . But I couldn't show it to anyone—I just couldn't —it would be like going out naked into the street." Lena answered: "I'm glad you're keeping a diary, but do make a real effort with your mathematics and English. Otherwise, you'll make me look foolish: I've always been proud of you, and all of

[1] Maximum for each subject is five.

247

a sudden you're getting low marks. I know you can do it. You've got plenty of determination."

When Lena came out of school next day, Vasya was waiting for her. He walked beside her in silence but finally, as they neared her house, he said:

"Yelena Borisovna, it was I who carved on the desk. If you only knew how I've been worrying about it!"

"I'd never have believed it of you. You're thoughtful enough to keep a diary; then you go and do such a stupid thing . . ."

"I don't understand it myself. It was a mood that came over me. You might say I went blank—had a momentary lapse of memory . . ."

"That was bad!"

"Yelena Borisovna, please let me explain. The day before, you see, Lyuba Gorshenina and I had a quarrel. I told her I didn't like the film of *The Charterhouse of Parma,* and she said I didn't understand anything and had an exceptionally coarse nature. But it's not true, because I like the novel, and I was only talking about the film. And then she said I was the kind of person who never listened to music on the radio, but only to sports—and she said a lot more like that. Well, to make a long story short, she told me definitely she wouldn't speak to me again and I was to give her back her photo. I was classroom monitor at the time. I wanted to write to her—of course, give her back her photo, but also to let her know that *my* feelings didn't change so quickly. But then I decided that it would be humiliating to write after all that, so I just gave her the photo. And then, you see, after they'd all gone, I went blank—had a black out. I assure you I did the carving quite mechanically—I simply wasn't thinking of what I was doing. And the result has been this very unpleasant situation. That is why I've been so odd lately."

"But why didn't you own up when I asked? Somebody else might have been blamed."

"Yelena Borisovna, hundreds of times I've made up my mind

248

to tell you. You can't begin to imagine how I've suffered from concealing it!"

"Then why didn't you own up?"

"Because Yekaterina Alexeyevna said that the person who'd done it would have to pay for repairing the desk, and I haven't got any money. I can't tell Mummy: it's hard enough for her as it is. Later when I go to technical college she won't have to take in washing. Every morning I've wanted to tell you. And when you came yesterday, I was longing to all the time you were there. When you left, I made a note in my diary that our conversation had been extraordinarily interesting—but that my mind had been miles away from the subject . . ."

Lena just managed not to smile.

"Her name is Lyuba Gorshenina—why did you cut out 'L.A.'?"

"Her patronymic is Alexandrovna. Nobody calls her by it, of course, but then, I tell you, I did it automatically. I suppose unconsciously I didn't want her to be involved . . ."

Lena told him that he had behaved very badly, that Lyuba would look down on him if he failed in his examinations, and that he must get down to mathematics at once—even, if necessary, give up his diary for the time being. And she promised not to tell anyone about the desk.

How then did the story reach Dmitryeva? Vasya only told Lyuba, having of course made her promise not to tell anyone else. But the next day Lyuba quarrelled with Vitya. Vitya had said that not a single teacher was to be trusted—they didn't care how they put you to shame in front of the whole class. Lyuba replied: "That's not true! I can't think why you go on like that. If you promise to keep it a secret, I'll tell you something . . ." Vitya told only Sasha, who was his only friend and from whom he had no secrets; they had sworn to tell each other everything. Then Sasha's mother scolded him and he told her that Yelena Borisovna understood how people felt even if his mother didn't. Now Sasha's mother was rather taken by Serov, the English teacher, who was a snob and a cynic; and one day she said to him: "You're wrong to say there's no romance in our way of life. Feelings do exist. The other day a child confessed to Yelena Borisovna—he's a friend of my son . . ." As Serov's ambition was to be head of a school, he went with the whole story the next morning to Dmitryeva.

At the next Teachers' Council meeting Dmitryeva said: "At last the facts of this wretched affair have come to light. Naturally the boy must be punished. But now I want to touch on the function of a home-room teacher. I cannot approve of teachers angling for cheap popularity with the worst elements in the class. When I was in Voronezh a teacher in the ninth grade pandered to the base instincts of a youth and the public prosecutor had to intervene. Of course, I'm not comparing the two cases: Nikitin is only a boy and however revolting his behaviour it has not gone beyond the limits of ordinary naughtiness. But we know how easily naughtiness can lead to criminality. It is our duty to warn Yelena Borisovna. We all like her and we must put her on her guard against conduct that is contrary to our progressive principles of education. She must realise that children cannot be brought up successfully unless the teacher has a clear conception of Soviet ethics."

Lena found the strength not to take up Dmitryeva's hints. She only made a heated plea for Vasya. She described his background, said how worried he had been and that this accounted for his bad marks: indeed, in the past two weeks he had improved noticeably.

The mathematics teacher backed her up but Serov sneered: "It's true I gave him a four yesterday, but you know perfectly well, Yelena Borisovna, that a child can make an effort once and still remain an incorrigible idler."

Later Stein told Lena:

"Dmitryeva says she won't leave it at that, she's going to take it up with the Board."

Lena smiled: "Let her."

But she was far from feeling as calm as she looked. Of course she had been right. But not only Serov but another teacher had backed up Dmitryeva. They were working up a hostile atmosphere. And Merzlyakova, who was on the Board, loathed Lena. She went about saying that a woman with a child had no right to leave her husband, that if Zhuravlyov had failings it was her duty to re-educate him, and that any mother would be frightened of entrusting her children to such a flighty creature. "She's hand in glove with Dmitryeva," Lena thought. "They'll start an inquiry. They'll do their best to poison my life."

She thought bitterly: "I won't tell Mitya; he's upset enough as it is. Anyhow, I've no idea what he'd say to me. It's terrible that I don't always understand him. Last winter when I told him about my row with Dmitryeva he said: 'Why do you argue with her, Lena? You won't change her and you'll only wear yourself out. You've got to realise that she's the one with access to the authorities. It's her they'll believe, not you. You're like a child, you won't face facts.' Of course, he only wanted to keep me out of trouble, but all the same, I don't understand. I could never have told *him* to keep quiet if he felt indignant about some nasty mess. There are a lot of things we react to differently. He told me once it's a question of age, but I don't know . . . He still hasn't told me why he voted for the reprimand. Sometimes I'm at my wit's end about him."

At home she found a letter from Zhuravlyov. He was counting on coming for Shura in the last part of June. Lena flared up: "What makes him so sure I'll let her go? If he wants to see her, let him come here for the day, and I'll go out. I can't bear the idea of listening to him talk. I hate him. I know it's wrong but I can't help it."

Vyrubin told her that Dmitry had telephoned to say he would be back late; he had to go to a meeting. Lena thought: "Now this is someone I can talk to: he'll understand."

Vyrubin listened to her with interest.

"He's a good boy," he said. "Of course he is a fool, but who isn't

251

at his age? When I was a schoolboy I fell in love with an actress at the Korsh Theatre—I'd seen her on the stage and knew she was my ideal. Every night I used to wait for her outside the theatre and follow her as she walked home—she lived quite close to us, in Gazetny Alley. Sometimes she was escorted by a man, but I didn't mind that. I only gazed at her from afar—and thought she was perfect. But one night she stopped and shouted at me: 'You impudent boy! How dare you? I'll report you to your school.' You can imagine what I went through. I even thought of suicide . . . Vasya's the same as any other boy. Now, about repairing the desk—that's a problem. But if you gave it to me, I'd do it in a couple of hours. I learned to do a lot of things when I was 'out there.' I'm not just an agronomist, I'm a miner and an electrician and a carpenter and an organiser of concerts . . . But your headmistress, she really is a case . . ."

"Unfortunately they think very highly of her at the LEA."

"Who does? Probably people who are her kind. I've been told that Stepanov, who is on the LEA, is an honest, energetic man. Don't *you* lose heart, that's the main thing. I'm seeing a lot of things these days with fresh eyes—as though I'd been asleep for seventeen years and had just woken up. Sometimes it depresses me, but more often I feel glad. I had a talk with Demin today—he's a splendid man. He was interested in my work. He said he would set up an experimental plot and asked if our hot-house was big enough. I was with him for an hour and a half. It turned out that he knew all about me. In '34 his elder brother passed his examinations at my Institute. I don't remember him, of course, but the brother told Demin about me. Demin told me they don't go in much for research at the technical college and said it was a pity: it's when you are young that you're curious, and you don't develop your mind just by learning things by heart, but by trying to have your own say . . . I came away very pleased. People like Demin can do a lot. But one's got to stick to one's guns. *You've* got to stick to your guns. It may be a bit nerve-racking, but you'll fight your way through in the end. This is a good time for young people who want to do things. If only I had another ten years!"

Dmitry came home unexpectedly early; his meeting had been postponed. At once Lena broke off the conversation about her troubles. But when she looked at Dmitry she marvelled: "How cheerful he looks today! It's a long time since I've seen him look like that." He played the fool with Shura and told her funny stories, and they both laughed so much that Lena pretended to stop her ears.

She caught his mood: she stopped thinking about the headmistress and the LEA and Zhuravlyov's letter. All at once everything seemed different and delightful. "I've been unfair to Mitya. What made me think I couldn't talk to him about the Teachers' Council? I'm stupid! Of course I can tell him and he's sure to agree with me." But she felt too happy to do so, and anyway she wanted to forget about Dmitryeva.

It was Vyrubin who brought the subject up.

"We were just discussing a problem before you came in. Lena's principal is a strange creature, and Lena's afraid she's going to complain to the LEA—to Merzlyakova. But I don't think anything will come of it. They can't find fault with Lena: she's acted quite rightly. And after all, there are other people besides Merzlyakova on the Board. I've been hearing about Stepanov, for instance."

Dmitry smiled and said:

"This sounds like a detective story about a plot against the main office. Come on, Lena, tell me, what's your Dmitryeva been up to now?"

So Lena told the whole story again, but now she felt cheerful. She mimicked Dmitryeva. She took off on some of the other teachers and made Dmitry laugh by repeating Vasya's favourite, affected phrases: "I am positively incapable," "I absolutely assert."

Dmitry agreed that Lena could not go back on her word: the boy must not be hurt. And it was true about Stepanov. He'd met him at the Town Soviet: he had plenty of life and courage.

Dmitry's eyes had recovered their old sparkle and gaiety. Only for a moment did a faint shadow cross his face, when he said thoughtfully:

"Perhaps your Dmitryeva's not such a hag at heart. Perhaps she's been badly hurt some time . . ."

Shura was put to bed. Vyrubin went out to a Party meeting at the technical college.

"Shall we go for a walk?" Dmitry asked Lena. "It's a marvellous evening."

They strolled to the Town Garden. It was crowded. Dmitry smiled: how much better everything seemed in the spring! In winter people looked gloomy, muffled up in their sheepskin coats and furs and shawls. But now all the women were smart in their gaily-coloured dresses, and their faces looked contented. People were laughing. Lovers walked down side streets. There was a smell of freshly dug earth and of rain and of bird-cherry blossom.

"Lena, do look!"

Below them, in the half-light of midnight, the wide river moved slowly, ashen, bluish-grey, silver—the moon was breaking through the clouds. There were lights on the farther bank. Somewhere far away a woman's voice was calling.

Lena pressed close to her husband.

"Mitya, here's the spring again. Do you remember?"

He smiled; he was remembering the dark staircase in Lena's house, and Lena's lips. How stupid they had both been in those days! How they had doubted and tormented themselves and run from each other, when all the time happiness had been there and could not wait.

On the way home, Dmitry told her of his talk with Trifonov. Lena stopped short. Joyfully, but with a vague distrust that she could not herself understand, she questioned him:

"And you told him you'd speak against it?"

"Yes, I did. Of course, he was glum about it—said the Party meeting was bound to confirm the reprimand in any case. I don't know: it's equally possible they won't. But at least I'll have spoken against it."

"Mitya, what made you decide to do this now?"

He did not reply. Lena took a sidelong glance at him. He had a look of concentration, as if, gazing at the tattered clouds pierced by the pale, bluish light, he were searching for the answer to her question.

Much later, in the small hours, he told her what he had been thinking as they had walked home along the high riverbank.

"My grandmother was a believer. She used to tell me Bible stories: about the Ark, and the plagues of Egypt, and how the water turned into wine. She'd say, admonishing me: 'That's what it says in the Scriptures . . .' She told me how God took one of Adam's ribs and made a woman. But we all know that. What made me think of it now is that something's always been lacking in me— let's call it a rib—whether it was removed or I was born that way, I don't know—but what I do know is that you've given it back to me." He laughed outright. "Not Eve but Lena . . . Seriously, though, it's not simply that I love you, there's more to it—I can live fully. Do you understand? There's no weight on my shoulders —I was so used to the weight that now my head spins. I expect I'm talking nonsense. Go to sleep—it'll soon be time to get up. How short the nights are!"

12

THE TELEGRAM CAME EARLY IN THE morning. Volodya's mother waited for him to wake up to tell him the good news. She listened at his door: there were sounds of movement. She called softly and Volodya came out.

A Change of Season

"Up already? You work all night; you ought to sleep late."

"I promised to hand in some drawings today. There, have a look at them—that's a prize-winning melon, and this is a *Komsomolka*." [1]

"There's a wire from Sonya—she's arriving the day after tomorrow."

"Pleased?"

"What do you think? . . . You know, Volodya, that Sukhanov she wrote about—she's mentioned him three times. I don't think that can be by chance. Perhaps she's changed? . . . I must tidy up her room. The trouble is, there are no curtains."

She set about her domestic chores. Volodya put several sheets of paper into an envelope: he had spent the night writing to Sokolovsky. He took the letter around by hand and slipped it into Sokolovsky's letter box.

This is what it said:

> Dear Evgeny Vladimirovich,
> I realise that you no longer have the time nor the desire to bother with me. All the same, I beg you to read this letter to the end. After what I have done, I dare not come to see you, but I must speak to someone about certain things. And except for you I have nobody.
> I expect you have been told about my speech at the club, which must have made many people angry. The truth is, there's no real difference between me and Khitrov; in fact, Khitrov is less to blame. He probably hadn't even looked at Saburov's paintings, and if he had, he wouldn't have understood them. But I know his work well, and in my heart I've always admired it.
> Some days after the discussion, I went to see Saburov, meaning to say to him what I am writing to you now, but I said nothing—either I just lost my head or I was held back by childish vanity. I only came to myself later and then I couldn't go back. But it's not worth going into all that now.

---

[1] Girl in the Komsomol (Young Communist League).

II · The Spring

I've been thinking a great deal about what has happened to me, and now I think I've understood. The main trouble is my character. At school Saburov and I were friends. We both used to draw and dream of becoming painters. I liked reading, particularly poetry. The other boys used to laugh at us—they were interested in mechanics and sports, and adventure. Saburov was friendly with everybody, but I despised the others. I used to think: "A football match is everything to them." Even when I was older, I didn't take in what other people lived for; I missed a lot. So it was a revelation to me to discover that Andreyev could appreciate Saburov's work.

Many of the people who were at the club that day knew my father. They must have wondered how a son of his could have grown up into someone like me. They say that an apple always falls near the tree, but it's not so. I've met some remarkable people who were remarkable in spite of everything they had seen at home as children. And talking of apple trees, I remember being told at school that a crab-apple tree could grow from the seed of a very good apple—apple trees need grafting. I wouldn't listen to my father: he wanted me to be a teacher or a doctor or an engineer, but ever since I was a child I only wanted to paint.

You've often talked to me about painting and it surprised me. You are a specialist in your own field, and you are interested in so many other things, not only art but many things of which I haven't the least notion. But I have never been attracted to anything but painting. Unfortunately for me, I showed a certain aptitude. I went in for imitation because I saw there was a demand for it. I have met painters who were no better than myself, but fortunately for them they had no eye, no genuine sense of art. They were convinced that even if their pictures were not perfect they still had a certain social and artistic value. When people of that sort attack real artists like Saburov, they are probably being honest. I have no such excuse. I have known all along that I was doing pot-boilers and I soothed my conscience by telling myself: "It's impossible to do anything else."

I am not looking for extenuating circumstances, but if the picture is to be complete I must admit that no one stopped me when I took the wrong turn. When I say "no one," naturally I

257

am not thinking of you, but you, like my father, were to me a being from a different world. I told myself that though you understand art, you don't—and cannot—understand the circumstances under which artists work. Four years ago, in Moscow, I suddenly let down my hair and said publicly just what I thought about the work of certain well-known artists. I must tell you that it was not my conscience that made me do this, but only spite— my feelings had been hurt. After this they got to work on me and I decided to be more careful in the future. Please don't think I'm trying to put the blame on others. I know that I am myself to blame the most. As for the rest, I remember your telling me that many things had changed, and I hope that this applies to the closed circle of those who are concerned with art. I do remember that bacteria and fungi need nourishing broth.

I never intended to go to the discussion. Until five minutes before I stood up I hadn't dreamed of making a speech and if beforehand I had been shown a typescript of my speech I would have denied that I could ever speak like that in my life. All this is true, but all the same my crime was to some extent premeditated. It was not by chance that I accused Saburov: I was defending my right to pot-boilers. These things have their own logic: it starts with ironical smiles and "what can I do for you?" and it ends in monstrous filth.

The punishment is equally inevitable. A woman has told me the whole truth about myself. Believe me, I have been more punished than if I had been publicly condemned.

I have been considering for a long time what I am to do now. It would be simplest to go far away somewhere—to the Arctic, or Sakhalin, where nobody knows me, where I could set myself up as a draftsman and start a new life. Unfortunately, for family reasons, I cannot go away. And it would be difficult for me to change my profession here. I am known, I am labelled as a "leading artist." If I were to go to your plant and ask to be taken on as an unskilled labourer, they'd think that either I was being funny or I had gone out of my mind. So I am faced with a much more difficult task: that is, changing not my circumstances but myself. As far as my mother and my acquaintances are concerned, my way of living is unchanged, but I am determined to have nothing more to do with art. I am now doing some illustrations for a book on melon growing—making detailed drawings of melons and watermelons. But since I've always drawn cows and chickens in between painting, no one as yet guesses what I have decided.

I don't know if the new chapter you talked about will in my case be successful or come to a bad end. But I am sincerely trying to live as other people do who like me are not gifted but who are still necessary and dear to someone. If I succeed, I shall come and see you, but meanwhile I must confine myself to this confused letter, which is much too long.

Allow me, my dear Evgeny Vladimirovich, to thank you for all you have done for me, and to wish you the best of health.

Yours sincerely,
V. Pukhov

After he had read the letter, Sokolovsky sat frowning and drumming his fingers on the desk. Then he said moodily to Fomka:

"He's a good chap. You have to understand . . . But it's impossible to understand, that's the trouble."

In the evening Demin telephoned to say that he had now studied the project. If Sokolovsky had an hour free the next day, would he come to see him at his office. If not, Demin himself would manage to be at the plant the day after that.

Sokolovsky was excited. This must mean that it was not all over with his project. Demin seemed all right. He didn't go in for stock answers; he listened attentively and tried to understand. Today Savchenko had insisted that the Party meeting couldn't possibly confirm the reprimand, and even Obukhov had been doubtful. Sokolovsky had told them it would be a great relief to him if it were not confirmed. "Certainly I gave them some cause to complain," he thought, "but all the same I think it was unfair. Safonov dislikes me; that's his right. But why be personal in a thing of this sort? It hurts, all the same, that people like Brainin knuckled under. You can't really blame Golovanov: he's new here. But I'm glad that hardly anybody at the works could believe his ears. All this time they've been coming to my office to tell me—it's even been difficult to work. Yegorov says he disagrees with the decision, and so do some others. If the Party meeting does refuse to confirm the decision, it'll make it easier for me to get on with my work and to see people again. Safonov makes me out to be an old badger buried in a mound of earth—I who can't spend a day without seeing people. But what I told Safonov was the truth: what really bothered me was having my project turned down. If they'd said: 'We've got to take time to think it over, to consult the customers, to collect more data . . .' But no, they just shelved it, and approved Safonov's version. But that's only the old lathe with a few tiny improvements. It's lucky that Demin's taking an interest in it: he's the one to get things moving."

Sokolovsky decided to telephone Vera and tell her the good news. For a long time he listened to the dreary buzzing. Then Dr. Gorokhov's maid (Vera had a room in the doctor's house) answered and said Vera had gone out to see a patient.

Sokolovsky put a batch of drawings and diagrams into a file, together with clippings from newspapers and pages covered with his sprawling, indecipherable writing, which looked like cuneiform script. "I'll show this batch to Demin; he might be interested. My goodness, this is a piece of good luck. I never really expected anybody to give another thought to my project."

Suddenly he saw Volodya's letter on the table, and his expression changed. Carefully and sadly, he put away the small sheets in the lower drawer of the desk, where he kept his daughter's photographs.

"Vera can't understand why I have anything to do with him. I can't explain it myself. I've got attached to him . . . And then why should people point at him as if he were a monster?—He isn't at all. He says he's got no talent—that may be true . . . But he's got a heart—that I'm certain of."

13

At the Party meeting Trifonov
sat in silence, thinking despondently: "I told Demin that he
mustn't let it come to this, but he wouldn't listen."

Obukhov briefly explained why the Party Bureau had decided
to administer a reprimand to Sokolovsky: the head designer had
walked out of a production meeting, had given offensive and sar-
castic answers to official questions, had ignored the claims of
comradeship, and had conducted himself in a manner unbecom-
ing to a Communist. His lapse was made all the graver by the fact
that he was known and respected as a good worker and a man of
experience.

Obukhov spoke hurriedly, in a low voice, and as if he did not
believe his own words. This was indeed so. Just before the meeting had begun he had whispered disgustedly to Brainin: "We
must defend our resolution. We've made our bed and we must
lie on it."

Sokolovsyk was invited to defend himself. Briefly and drily, he
agreed that he ought not to have left the meeting, but added
crossly:

"As for what's comradely and what isn't, I'd better not touch on
that."

Trifonov's cheeks quivered. "This is what comes of spoiling
people! A kopek of penitence and a hundred roubles of pride!
Where's the self-criticism? I said long ago: 'If they aren't shaken
up in time, people like Sokolovsky will soon be sitting on our
heads.'" In spite of everything, he had been counting till the last
moment on Sokolovsky's getting a rebuff. Now his hopes were
shattered. Andreyev stood up to speak and it was clear that neither the engineers nor the hands agreed with the Party Bureau

resolution. Sokolovsky was popular at the plant in spite of his sharp tongue, perhaps even because of it: for if he lost his temper it was usually because of poor work, or because a dirty trick had been played, or because somebody had attacked a comrade behind his back, or because of some piece of callousness or injustice. He was respected not only for his great knowledge and hard work but also for his warmth and responsiveness.

An enormous impression was made on the meeting by Dmitry. He said it was he who had deserved a reprimand, for in voting at the Party Bureau he had acted against his conscience.

Trifonov turned away. He thought indignantly: "I've never heard anything like it! Fancy castigating himself like that in front of everyone! What will become of authority? The really frightening thing is that Demin likes these music-hall turns. How will it be possible to work in such conditions?"

Safonov spoke in favour of the reprimand, assuring the meeting that he had the support of several other members of the Party Bureau. As he said this, he glanced at Khitrov, but Khitrov had turned aside and was whispering to his neighbour.

The three speeches that followed Safonov's sounded less like a discussion as to whether Sokolovsky should be reprimanded than like a celebration in honour of an old, popular, and valued comrade.

Savchenko was smiling and did not ask to speak.

"Why doesn't Khitrov say something?" Trifonov thought furiously. But Khitrov was determined to say nothing because two days earlier he'd heard from Zoya, the typist at the Town Soviet, that Sokolovsky had spent two hours closeted with Demin. Of course, nobody knew what they'd been talking about, but Demin was quite capable of taking Sokolovsky's part. Khitrov thought: "Trifonov looks ill and says his kidneys are not well; but perhaps what's eating him is Demin. You've got to take everything into consideration . . ." After much thought, Khitrov came to the conclusion that it would be best to abstain.

Sokolovsky sat in a brown study, as though the discussion was no concern of his. He was remembering his conversation with Demin. "It's obvious he knows what it's all about; he's even gone over the plant where the electro-erosion machines are installed. There's no question that he's taking the project seriously. But even he talked about the difficulties and the need for more advice and additional consultation with the customers. That's fair enough. What frightens me is that they might still pigeonhole the project for good."

At one moment Sokolovsky did sit up and take notice—that was when Andreyev, after talking at great length about the principles of Party democracy, wound up in his simple, homely way: "How did all this begin? Sokolovsky was talking about new machines, and then other people turned the whole thing upside down and began discussing his character. Now, comrades, what's that got to do with it?" Sokolovsky smiled ruefully.

Only Obukhov and Safonov voted for the reprimand. Four people abstained and all the rest raised their hands against it.

In the hall Sokolovsky was surrounded by friends who shook his hand, congratulated him in simple, ordinary words but so cordially that he was embarrassed. He mumbled: "Now then, what is all this about . . . ?" Brainin came up to him, too, and blinked his kindly, shortsighted eyes:

"I must confess, Evgeny Vladimirovich, that we were all very hasty at the Party Bureau. I'm very glad that it's all wiped out now."

He pressed Sokolovsky's hand firmly.

"Thank you, Nahum Borisovich. I think you didn't take into account that by using the electro-erosion method with care you can reach a very high degree of precision."

Trifonov was doing his best not to show his feelings. He said to Obukhov: "Anyway, it's a good thing it's all over and done with—there are more important matters to think about. I'm still worried about the assembly shop . . ."

In reality, he was thinking of something quite different: life. For the first time he felt dead tired and thought: "I wish I could

go to sleep and never wake up!" In this mood he arrived home,
roared at Petya, and told his wife that he still had work to do.

He sat late over his papers, hardly distinguishing one letter
from another. Then he shuddered: "I think I'm going to pieces.
I must pull myself together! If I give way, what's going to happen? I've always said it's very easy to let things get disorganised
. . ." So he concentrated upon a note from the manager of the
glass factory.

Savchenko walked home, smiling all the way.

"It went off very well. Better than I dared hope." Then his
face clouded: "How could I think that Koroteyev was a coward?
That was disgusting of me. He had been on leave, he didn't know
what had happened, and anyway he was misinformed. When I
spoke to him, he didn't see why he should give me an explanation. And why should he make a confession to me, indeed? He'd
heard enough hot air from me. It's funny to remember how that
time long ago I asked him whether one ought to fight for one's
personal happiness! He must think I'm still only half out of the
egg!

"Besides, he must think me terribly tactless. When I think how
I used to pester him with silly questions about Yelena Borisovna
and Zhuravlyov! Of course, I couldn't know he was in love with
her. But I must have seemed stupid and boorish."

Savchenko was amazed when he thought of the recent past. "I
was twenty-five and I behaved like a schoolboy!" It seemed to
him a very long time ago that he had seen Sonya off at the station, still hoping that she would say she loved him. Yet little more
than a year had passed since then.

Sonya had come back for her father's funeral but had left again
almost at once. For some time she had written to Savchenko, but
her letters were reserved. She wrote about her work, about the
town of Penza, about the plays she went to, but did not reply to
Savchenko's passionate declarations. As time went by, he realised
that it was useless to press her and his letters became calmer and

less frequent. Her last letter to him had been a New Year's greeting. After that, he had written twice but Sonya had not answered. He often thought of their meetings, of their quarrels, of Sonya's resistance to his pleas. He had thought at the time that she was too cautious, too sensible, but now he told himself: "She's never been in love with me, that's all there is to it. Sometimes she gave way before the strength of my feeling for her—that time in the woods, when she kissed me of her own accord, she may have thought that she could love me, but that was only because she had no experience of love. She's probably grown up in the past year, just as I have. That passage from the letter her mother read to me, about someone called Sukhanov—perhaps she's fallen in love with him. Well, the only thing is to look the truth in the face. She never had more than a childish infatuation for me, that was all. But I love her more than ever. They say first love is soon over, but not with me. I keep catching myself talking to her, or thinking: 'That would make Sonya angry' or 'This would make her smile' . . ."

He often looked at the small photograph of Sonya he kept in his wallet. She had had it taken for some identity paper: she looked straight into the camera with a strained expression. Savchenko had often seen her like that. Her features seemed to have been traced with a sharp pencil. Her big, wide-open eyes had a clear, intent, almost stern look; but at moments of great emotion they shone softly and then she would pale and turn away. He also remembered her like this and would sometimes speak her name aloud sadly to himself.

Savchenko was gay and sociable. He had always had a lot of friends. He liked going to see them or calling at the club. He belonged to the Drama Society and had acted in *The Proposal* on the Chekhov evening. Women liked him; with his dark, curly hair, he had a Southerner's good looks and lively character. Natasha, supposed to be the prettiest girl in town and haughty with all the other men, made such eyes at him that he sighed, embarrassed. There was no room in his heart for anyone but Sonya and he could not conceive that there ever could be. "Don't you like Natasha?" asked young Golikov, a fellow engineer. Savchenko laughed: "How could anyone not like her?" He liked looking at her as he might look at a beautiful statue or a flower. But at night he saw Sonya, as he had once seen her in the wood, flushed, her hair tousled, her eyes shining with a light that she tried in vain to hide from him.

His friends believed Savchenko to be the most open of men. Didn't he say just what he thought, argue eagerly about books and plays, make fervent speeches at meetings, bursting with enthusiasm or indignation? He had been more upset than anyone when Sokolovsky was attacked and no one had done more to get the reprimand annulled. Demin, whom he had seen twice about it, thought of him: "There's a real man who takes things to heart —not smug, not a rubber stamp—if we had a few more like him it would be easier to work."

Whatever he did take to heart, he needed to infect others with his enthusiasm. He had spent two evenings on end converting Golikov to Sokolovsky's project: according to him, its adoption would mean the beginning of a new era for the factories that their enterprise supplied.

Yet there were some things which Savchenko did keep locked up in his heart: he had learned not to reveal his innermost thoughts. How could he ever admit, for instance, that he had recently suspected Dmitry of cowardice? He had realised for the first time in his life how difficult it was to understand others. It distressed him, but it was also a landmark in his life.

Jealously he concealed his unhappy love from his companions. If anyone mentioned Sonya, he listened quietly or would refer casually to their friendship. Only to Sonya's mother would he sometimes inadvertently betray himself: her gentle solicitude seemed to throw him back into the past. But not even to her did he admit his real feelings. When she asked him outright, his face darkened but he replied calmly that everything passed with time and that he hoped Sonya would make a happy marriage.

II · The Spring

Even now, when her mother told him as she opened the door: "I'm so glad you've come; Sonya arrived yesterday," he found the strength to keep his composure. Neither embarrassed nor upset, he greeted Sonya with a friendly smile and told her how well and sunburned she looked. She replied that she had been swimming in the river every day. Then they had a lively talk about many small things that they seemed to find immensely interesting.

Nadezhda Yegorovna went into the kitchen to get supper ready and also to leave them alone for a while. "Really, it's impossible to understand her," she thought. "Yesterday she asked twice where Savchenko was and why he hadn't come, but when I said I'd telephone him, she wouldn't let me—'Why telephone? There's no hurry. He'll come when he feels like it.' And now, when he came in, her face didn't alter a scrap. No, she feels nothing for him. Perhaps there's someone in Penza? . . . If anyone knows how to cover up, it's Sonya . . . Savchenko is different—he meant to show it's all one to him, but I could see he hadn't changed."

Left alone, Sonya and Savchenko went on talking about this and that. *Nora* had been produced in Penza but the leading lady had been bad. Yasha had gone to Karaganda. It was said that the Americans were willing to come to terms—they seemed to be behaving more sensibly. Our people would go there, Americans would come to us—that was what Sukhanov thought, though Brainin, who was older, was doubtful. There was a lot of truth in Granin's *Seekers* but the ending was contrived. Golikov was desperately in love with Natasha but she was going to Moscow in the autumn, to the Conservatoire. There was a wonderful park in Penza.

Out of the blue, Sonya asked:

"Are you married yet?"

"No. Why do you ask?"

"I just asked. Can't I take an interest in your life?"

"I'd have written and told you . . ."

"You never write."

"I stopped writing because you didn't answer . . . Go on, tell me about Penza. Who is this Sukhanov?"

"He's the head of the instrument shop. Why do you want to know?"

"You mentioned him just now—you said that he took a favourable view of the international situation. Is he a good technician?"

"Very. And he's an interesting person. He reminds me of Koroteyev. Tell me, is Koroteyev happy with Lena?"

"I think so. How does he remind you of Koroteyev?"

"I don't know. Just generally . . . Do you often go to the Koroteyev's?"

"Very often. I work with him, you know."

"Do you think Lena's nice?"

"Yes, I like her. Do you remember how you argued with me and said she ought never to have left Zhuravlyov?"

"Do you remember everything I've ever said?"

He flushed, and for a moment forgot his determination not to show his feelings.

"Yes, I do—I remember everything. I remember your saying at the station that what's real can't be forgotten . . ." Then he pulled himself up and said lightly: "We used to quarrel all the time, but now we've met again, we can laugh about the past. We've each got our own life to live . . ."

Volodya came into the room. Sonya said:

"Here's someone who's changed in the last year. Can you believe it? I've been home two days and he hasn't made a single joke."

Volodya smiled.

"*You* tell us something funny, Sonya. Has Zhuravlyov really become slim and languid?"

"There's really nothing funny to tell. I still don't seem to know how to size people up. Though, as a matter of fact, nobody at our place saw through him to begin with. He was particularly polite to me, as pleased to see me as if I'd been an old friend; told me you'd been painting his portrait. 'My former wife used to visit your late father . . .' He never calls Lena anything but 'my former wife.' It was true, what I wrote then: everybody liked him. I was beginning to believe that miracles do happen. But evidently they don't. He got his bearings, felt firm ground under his feet, put his troubles at the Ministry out of his mind, and off he went. He told Sukhanov off in public very rudely. Naturally Sukhanov answered back, though he's very self-controlled. So Zhuravlyov started to bait him; he removed four mechanics and now he says the instrument shop is wrecking the schedule. I told Zhuravlyov he'd been disgustingly rude to Sukhanov, so he went for me. It's a good thing we've got a sensible manager who stood up for Sukhanov. But you see what the trouble is: Zhuravlyov is perfectly good at his own job. So the manager says: 'He's a splendid worker.' But as a man he's impossible. Oh yes—I forgot to tell you the latest news: he's married again—he found some idiot with a permanent wave. He invited me to the wedding. Of course I didn't go. My opinion of him now is just the same as Savchenko's."

"His personality is now crystal clear," said Volodya smiling. "But all the same, tell us what he looks like now—is he thin? Does he look romantic?"

"Not in the very least. He's got fat again. It makes me furious to think of your portrait of him. Why did you flatter him so? You made him look like a hero, and really he's got the most repulsive face."

Volodya laughed.

"Bang goes another illusion. I really did think he had got thin in earnest and for good."

"Leopards don't change their spots," said Sonya. "Don't you know that?"

Volodya frowned: "No, I suppose not."

At dinner she went on talking gaily about her life in Penza, the factory, and her work. Her mother thought: "Not a word about Sukhanov. It's not natural. Or has she broken off with him as she's done with Savchenko? What a difficult girl she is. And there's nothing you can really get at . . ."

It was late when Savchenko left. The streets were empty. Only here and there couples were whispering in gateways. He bore his sadness with him through the bright night with its pale stars and the gentle fluff falling from the trees like a summer snowstorm.

"So we've met again," he thought. "How odd it is: I've lost Sonya, and yet my love is still alive."

For a moment he tried to comfort himself, or perhaps to probe his pain with the thought that she had reproached him with not writing, but he checked himself: "For Sonya, everything there ever was between us now belongs to the distant past. She thought of it and fell into her old way of speaking, but it sounded odd even to her. It's as clear as can be . . .

"One shouldn't be weighed down by sorrow. It ought to lead one onward, as light-filled as this night, as Sonya's eyes—not the Penza Sonya—the one who kissed me in the wood and told me softly I must wait."

Next morning, the moment he got to work he was called to the manager's office. Golovanov said, smiling:

"I've got a surprise for you. Moscow's just telephoned to say you've been included in a delegation of technicians. You are going to Paris. It'll be a fascinating journey. You know a little French, don't you?"

"Very little. I can read it but I haven't had a chance to practise speaking. I can't think why they should have chosen me."

"When I was in Moscow as far back as last autumn they asked me to recommend a few young technicians. I gave them your name among others. There are fourteen people in the delegation. Ryabtsev is the leader. They want you to be in Moscow no later than the second—there are various formalities to go through there. So you must be off in a week."

Back in the design room, Savchenko said to his friend Golikov:

"Do you know why I was sent for? I'm to go to Paris . . . It's so unexpected, I don't know what to make of it . . ."

"You have the devil's own luck, haven't you! Well, go on, say something. You'll be seeing Paris."

Savchenko thought: "What can it be like?" Images rose in his mind: the Eiffel Tower, a wide avenue, a stream of cars with an archway in the background. "Golikov's right, it will be interesting. The only trouble is that they might start reconsidering the project while I'm away. Sokolovsky's gloomy; he believes they've shelved it for good. He says he's off to Moscow for a few days. I hoped he was going there to promote the plan, but it seems it's on some private matter. All the same, I'm sure they'll come back to it in the end.

"And Sonya? She's come home and I'm going away. Well, I wouldn't have seen her again anyway. Or perhaps I would have gone to see her once, just before she left. If I didn't show myself at all she'd think I was jealous or offended. But now I won't be here when she leaves. I could just go in now and say good-bye. No, I'd better call, or I'll get upset like yesterday and tell her everything. What right have I to disturb her? Paris I'll see—the cars, the Eiffel Tower, the Arc de Triomphe—but not Sonya . . ."

He took the snapshot out of his wallet and looked at it for so long that his eyes blurred. Then he smiled sadly and got down to his blueprints.

14

THE RECEPTIONIST SAID:

"Madame Vandervelde? Room 116."

Sokolovsky had a moment of bewilderment. He knew, of course, that his daughter bore her husband's name and was a foreigner, but all the same it seemed absurd that Mashenka should be called Madame Vandervelde. For some reason he felt obliged to explain: "I am her father."

The receptionist answered indifferently:

"Please go right in. It's at the end of the corridor, the last room on the right."

Outside the door he stood a moment before knocking. He told himself absent-mindedly: "I must get my breath back," though in fact he had come up in the elevator.

The door was opened by a young woman, dressed rather quietly, he thought. She said cheerfully:

"I've been waiting for you all evening. Felix has gone to the theatre, and I've been sitting here looking at the clock."

Sokolovsky still stood by the door.

"Why don't you come in and sit down? Haven't we got a nice room? But isn't it funny—it seems so old-fashioned!"

Sokolovsky looked around; it was a typical hotel bedroom with satin-covered easy chairs and a Chinese vase and a huge bronze paperweight on the desk. He caught himself thinking: "I'm afraid even to look at her."

"Let me have a look at you. You were only so high when they took you away. And you can't tell anything from photographs."

Mary laughed.

"I don't remember you a bit. I was only three. You look very young and athletic. There seems to be a craze for sports in Russia, too; our people are mad about it. I play tennis sometimes, but Felix doesn't care for games. He prefers going to concerts or seeing his friends. I'm sure you'll like him; he's not a bit what you call 'bourgeois.' "

Sokolovsky was surprised: "How well she speaks Russian," he thought. "And what a chatterbox she is. But perhaps she's feeling shy. Of course she must be. Her manner is very simple. But why does she wear those high heels? It's odd she should be Madame Vandervelde—she could be taken for a Moscow student."

"You speak Russian very well."

"Does that surprise you? Mama used to talk nothing but Russian with me. The hotel people were surprised, too. The interpreter said I had no accent. But I make dreadful mistakes—she had to correct me twice today. I said I was interested 'to every-

thing Russian' and that I wanted 'to acquire the metro.' Wasn't
that funny?"

At last he really looked at her. "She's pretty. Like Maya . . .
She's got her mother's nose—slightly turned up. But she's more
serious and has intelligent eyes. She talks without stopping—she
gets that from Maya, too."

As if she had guessed his thoughts, Mary said:

"You know, Mama had a very bad time. She really made a
mess of her life. My stepfather is a nice man but terribly inconsiderate. He's very fond of women, even now when he's sixty-six
—or is it sixty-seven—I don't remember. Before the war he was
madly in love with an Egyptian lady. I don't blame him, but it
was hard for Mama. He moved to this lady's house. I was only ten
at the time, but I knew what it was all about. My stepfather gave
Mama money and she bought a wool shop—they go in a lot for
knitting in our country; it's supposed to be good for the nerves. So
Mama worked all day, which wasn't much fun for her, of course.
You remember what Mama was like? She was always dreaming
of going to Mexico or to India—she was meant for quite a different kind of life. She died of pneumonia. We had a terrible time
during the Occupation. We had to stay with my stepfather's sister in Mons—it's a small town, and in winter it was like being in
Siberia, with no heating. That's how Mama caught a chill. She
told me then to be sure to find you . . ."

The distant past rose before Sokolovsky's eyes: the Tverskoy
Boulevard, the statue of Pushkin, the girl student, and himself
talking to her about happiness . . .

"Mama was always floundering about—she could never get her
bearings. I think I'm the same kind of person—I blow hot and
cold. I told you I'd given up dancing, though everybody thought
it was silly of me. They said in Le Soir that I was promising. But
it came over me suddenly that it was a mistake for me . . . Do
you like eurhythmic dancing?"

"I've never seen any. You sent me photographs but I couldn't
judge from that."

273

"It's an entirely new genre. I used to think that you had had a revolution in every field, but now it seems to me that you prefer what's old-fashioned. So does Felix. Yesterday we went to the Bolshoi Theatre: technically of course the dancing is marvellous, but it made me laugh—it's so nineteenth-century. Like the furniture in this room . . . My dancing was completely different—no classical steps, the body just obeys the rhythm . . . But it isn't worth talking about now—my dancing is a thing of the past. Have you heard of Lepère?"

"No. Is he a dancer?"

"But I just told you I'm not interested in dancing any more. Lepère is a painter. Now that everybody says there won't be any more Iron Curtain, I'm sure he'll make a sensation over here."

"So you've decided to take up painting?"

"Yes, but you might say that I've gone back to it. I used to draw a lot when I was at school. That wasn't serious of course, but people said my work was good. I did a portrait of Mama at that time, and everybody said it was just like her . . . Later on I gave it up. I did a year at law school, and then I got enthusiastic about dancing. Now at last I've found my vocation—it's painting."

"Where are you studying?"

"I'm working more or less independently. Lepère occasionally gives me some advice, but he's moved to Paris and doesn't often come to Brussels. I've already had an exhibition, and it was quite successful. I've brought two small paintings and a photograph of another one to show you. I was so afraid you wouldn't come today, because tomorrow night we're being taken to Leningrad."

"I thought you'd stay longer. Why are you in such a hurry?"

"You can't imagine how expensive it is! Felix is earning a bit more than he used to, but even so, we had to save up a whole year for the trip."

"Where does your husband work?"

"At the Netherlands Credit Bank. But you mustn't think he spends his life as a cashier—he carries out financial operations. Of course, he used to dream of other things when he was a stu-

dent. He wrote poetry, and his chief interest was in literature. He
still reviews plays occasionally. But life has to be lived . . . I
can't complain—he earns a decent salary. But if you only knew
what prices are like at home! One can't afford fancies . . . However, don't let's talk about that. Tell me about your own life. I've
had four days—I've seen something of Moscow—but I can't
imagine what the town you live in looks like. At the post office in
Brussels, where I was sending off the telegram, they said at first
there wasn't such a place, but in the end they found it. Are there
many people there?"

"Not very many. About a hundred and sixty thousand."

"But that's a huge town! Like Liège. And what do you do
there?"

"I work in a factory. I'm an engineer, you know."

"I know. They wanted to show us a factory yesterday—industry seems to count more than anything else in your country. Felix
says you've made enormous strides. But I don't understand a
thing about machines. When I went to see the Renault plant in
Paris, I thought the noise would drive me mad. I only went because Felix dragged me. He's crazy about cars. We bought a little
Citroën last autumn and drove down to Nice. What kind of car
do you have?"

Sokolovsky wanted to say that he had none, that he preferred
not to use the plant car, but to walk; that if he wanted to go into
town, there were always buses. But he thought: "Why tell her?
She might think it was because of poverty." He was amused by
the thought that he should be practising diplomacy on his daughter. So he laughed and said: "I've got legs. They can still carry
me. As for you, I don't suppose you could walk a hundred yards
with those heels!"

Mary laughed, too.

"You're right. It's an absurd fashion. People go in more and
more for sports, and then all of a sudden you have to mince about
on Louis XV heels . . . You haven't married again?"

"No."

"Why not?"

"It hasn't worked out that way."

The thought of Vera came into his mind, and for a moment a happy smile lit up his grave face. Mary said:

"I'm glad I've seen you, too."

He felt ashamed. "She is Mashenka, my own daughter." He looked at her affectionately. "She rattles on with her nonsense, but who am I to say what she's really thinking behind it all?"

"I used to look at your photographs, trying to guess what sort of person you were," he said, "and how you were getting on over there. It's so far away from us. I'm glad you're happy and like your work."

"I don't suppose you ever thought your daughter would become a painter. Do you like paintings?"

"I think I do, but I haven't seen many. It's lucky you're going to Leningrad—you'll see the Hermitage."

"Felix loves the Flemish school. But, somehow, I am not moved by the old masters. They only show the external world, the outer shell. Now, I dream of conveying my conception entirely by colour values. That may sound silly, but it's very hard for me to express myself in Russian—I don't know the proper terms. I'd better show you my work, though in this light you won't see them to advantage."

In the right-hand corner of the canvas Sokolovsky saw spirals of an acid green; towards the middle and the left were greasy splodges of orange and dark blue against a mauve background.

"Lepère likes this one, though it isn't painted in his manner. He likes to fill the whole surface with dynamic forms, whereas here, you see, I've left dead space. The centre is empty."

"I don't understand it," said Sokolovsky, frowning. "What are you trying to represent?"

"The impact of dark blue on orange. It's like a blow, and it creates a vacuum. You cannot imagine how difficult it is to convey despair purely in terms of colour." She said this with such passion that Sokolovsky was bewildered.

"Why despair? You say you like your work. You get on with your husband. You're young . . ."

"I don't know how to explain it to you. You and I probably see things differently. You don't suppose I gave up dancing as easily as I would change a pair of gloves, do you? Of course I didn't. I've been trying to find myself. A writer I know said the other day: 'Despair is a certificate of maturity.' But don't let's talk about that. I'd better show you my other painting—How do you like it?"

"I really know nothing about this sort of thing. But I'm glad you enjoy your work—that's the main thing."

The photograph of still another painting showed circles, triangles, and commas rather like bacteria.

Sokolovsky was suddenly reminded of Volodya's letter. He thought: "The wretched fellow knows he's behaved like a swine, and I could very well tell him so and even refuse to have anything more to do with him. But all the same, he's much closer to me than she is. It's a mystery to me how that can be possible."

His face darkened. Mary was embarrassed and said:

"I can see you hate it. But tell me at least that you don't think badly of me."

"What nonsense! How could I? I tell you honestly—it's just that I don't understand it. You live in a different world. You know best what you have to do . . . I've just remembered how you cried when they were taking you away. It was cold and we wanted to wrap you up more warmly, but you wouldn't have it."

To Sokolovsky's surprise and alarm, Mary burst into tears.

"Have I hurt you?"

She shook her head. Then she wiped her eyes, powdered her face, and said in a low voice:

"Do you think it doesn't hurt me to feel what strangers we are to each other? That's why I've been chattering like this—I knew if I stopped I'd cry."

He wanted to take her in his arms, to comfort her, to tell her how much he thought about her—it looked as if she really were concealing genuine distress behind her gay façade. But he only had time to whisper "Mashenka." Then the door opened.

"Here's Felix. Let me introduce you. What was the play like? Let's go out and have dinner together, shall we? I'll interpret."

Sokolovsky took a good look at Mary's husband. "Seems to be a decent, solid sort of man," he thought. "I wouldn't have taken him for a financier—more for a violinist—wavy hair, bow tie, and that absent-minded look—almost a dreamer's look."

Felix said that he had been to see *The Cherry Orchard* and that although he did not understand Russian, it had moved him deeply. They talked of Chekhov, music, and old Flemish towns.

"You've no idea what the atmosphere is like in Belgium. Not too long ago, everybody was talking about nothing but the atom bomb, and where the first would fall and what would vanish from the face of the earth. But they've calmed down a bit now—they talk about business. The streets are covered with advertisements. The papers are full of murders and society gossip. For me, art is a breath of fresh air. Since I met Mary, I find it easier to live. Of course we have a lot of arguments; our tastes are different. But Mary is unusually sensitive, like all Russians. My colleagues' wives are philistines, but Mary never lets herself be stained by the sordid side of life."

"He really loves her," thought Sokolovsky. "That's good. They are good friends."

Sokolovsky asked Felix what his impression of Moscow was.

"It's hard to say straight off. There's so much that is unfamiliar to us. I've nothing against the system. When I was a student, I was very enthusiastic about Communism, but later I lost interest in politics . . . You have done a great deal—I had no idea Moscow was such a big city. An uncle of mine who's now dead used to work in Yekaterinoslav, and he used to say there were no towns in Russia except Petersburg. There are certainly things we need to know. It's nice to see the theatres so full, and with working people in the audience, judging by the look of them. At home, working people only go to the movies. We've talked with students. They seem cheerful, I suppose because they feel secure about the future. When I was a student, I was haunted by the fear of not making my way in the world. Some things have struck me as odd: for instance, you have a very large population but very few shops. It's not easy to find things to buy and there isn't much choice, especially in clothes. Of course, that's a temporary situation—I know what you went through during the war. I'm glad my wife is Russian. Who knows? Perhaps the future belongs to you."

"Of course the future belongs to them," cried Mary. "Look at my father: there's a strong man for you. He hasn't attempted to proselytise me, but I feel he's a real fanatic, and I like that." She was looking at the dance floor and said to Sokolovsky in Russian: "Don't be cross with me, but it's so funny. They waltz like our grandmothers."

When they got up to go, Felix told Sokolovsky that he had an appointment the next morning at the Ministry of Foreign Trade, and therefore could not go with the other tourists to Zagorsk. Mary did not want to go without him, as she was not interested in monasteries. Perhaps Sokolovsky would take her around.

As soon as he arrived the next day, Mary said:

"Were you surprised that Felix had business to do here?"

"Not at all."

"I got the impression that you were surprised. Please don't think there's anything wrong in it. It's just that he's got a commission from one of the clients at the bank who runs a textile mill at Verviers. Felix says they're going through a crisis there, and apparently you're short of good woven material. Naturally Felix would prefer not to have to bother with this sort of thing, but unfortunately we've got into debt over this trip. I expect you're thinking we're dreadfully bourgeois. If you could only see your daughter in Brussels . . . But that's of no interest. I was afraid you wouldn't come this morning."

"How could I not come? What would you like me to show you?"

"Oh, nothing. I'm sick of sight-seeing. Let's just stay here."

She was quite unlike the Mary of yesterday. She didn't laugh and hardly spoke. She asked him:

"Tell me about the way you live, and your friends, and the places you've been to."

For a long time he talked about the war years, and about the Ural forests, and Savchenko, and his own work; but he felt she was not really listening to him. At last he said:

"You seem sad today."

She replied almost irritably:

"Does that surprise you? While you've been talking, I've been thinking how strange it all is to me. Perhaps even more so than to Felix. He takes it for granted that I feel at home here. It's true I can speak Russian, but when you tell me about your life I don't understand anything. It's awful to be in the country where I was born and feel a complete stranger. It's enough to make one desperate. I thought about it all night."

Her voice shook. Affectionately, Sokolovsky took her thin, cold hand in his.

"Mashenka, why not stay on? Say, for a month. Come home with me and take a look around. Then you'll understand better. We'll be friends."

She took her hand away and spoke with unusual sharpness:

"How is it that you don't see that this isn't possible? I have my own life to live—and then . . . We've tormented each other enough."

She looked at the clock.

"Felix ought to be back soon. I realise that you can't be very interested in him. Though he liked you very much. But that's no reason for keeping you."

Sokolovsky stood up.

"Well, we'd better say good-bye."

She hugged him tightly, and said when he was at the door:

"Don't be cross with me. It's all been a stupid mistake. Look after yourself."

·   ·   ·

Instead of going home from the airfield, Sokolovsky went to see Vera. She was surprised.

"Back already? You said you were going to stay a week."

He said he was tired after the flight and sat silently in his arm-chair. Vera opened a book, not to disturb him. Occasionally he glanced at her, but she did not notice or pretended not to.

His mind was filled with the thought: "Mashenka doesn't exist: it was a stranger I met and I've been trying to persuade myself that she's my daughter . . . But perhaps she's not so absurd after all. Those heels—well, she herself admitted they were a stupid fashion. But the circles and the spirals? She really seemed to believe that they meant something. And why shouldn't she? She's been brought up very differently. It seems to me that she wears some sort of mask, but also that she's really thrashing around trying to find her place in life. She was quite right today when she said it's a terrible thing to find oneself a stranger in one's own country. I couldn't sleep all night worrying about her; and it seems that she was in the same state. I'm afraid she's a stranger in Belgium, too. There must be lots of people there with whom I could get on, but with her I couldn't. Perhaps it's because we both expected too much of each other. And the only result of our meeting is that I find she's a stranger to me. How can she possibly understand our way of life? What she noticed was the absurd paperweight in their room. She didn't take in anything about the people. Even her Felix understood more than she did."

At the thought of Mary's husband, Sokolovsky almost smiled. Felix had talked about Van Eyck and mysticism and Handel, and then today he had rushed off to make a deal on trousers. "But why should I be irritated by him? He doesn't seem a bad fel-low. They haven't much money. And she said he hates this work. The fact is, it's easier to condemn people than to understand them. He's somehow simpler than she is. Why does she have to talk in that superior tone? The famous Lepère—that's just what we were waiting for! The fact that we've built a new world in spite of every obstacle means nothing to her. 'Despair is a certifi-

cate of maturity.' What rubbish. If you're going to use that anal-
ogy, then hope is the first and last examination you've got to pass
in life. Certainly the last—if you have no hope left, then you can't
even die like a human being—you just kick the bucket."

He checked himself. "For heaven's sake, whom am I quarrelling with? I meet a young woman and she turns out to be a stranger, I don't understand her and I upset her and I upset myself,
and now I might be haranguing a meeting. Perhaps she really
feels desperate—how can I tell? I can't judge from her silly triangles. Now she's sitting in the train, and thinking: 'I had hoped
Father would understand me, but he turned out to be just a dry
old stick. I feel like hanging myself, and all he talks about is high
heels.' I don't know . . . But there's one thing that I do know:
you've got to work and suffer to achieve real intimacy."

He stood up and walked over to Vera.

"How did you get on in Moscow?" she asked.

"There wasn't a car at the airfield, so Maslov gave me a lift into
town. And from there I walked. No, as a matter of fact, the truth
is I ran here. I really did. And do you know why? I simply
couldn't wait to see you. No, just a minute—let me finish. You're
a doctor and to you the heart is just a muscle. But do you know
what a heart really is? Your heart—that's my home. That's all.
Now let's have some tea."

15

SONYA WAS SETTING THE TABLE
for three. Her mother said:

"Volodya's not in. He's gone to see Bushagin."

"Who's Bushagin?"

"He's the publishers' accountant. I can't understand Volodya. He never used to go and see anybody but Sokolovsky, but now it seems he's found a friend. Why doesn't he see Saburov any more? He's an artist and he's a nice fellow, and his wife is nice. Or he could call on Rachkovsky. But why Bushagin? I know the wife— I don't even want to mention her. Lena says the daughter goes about in rags, and the mother's never at home. I don't like the way Volodya's looking these days. He was never very cheerful, but now he's got a real down-in-the-mouth look."

"Perhaps he's in love."

"What are you talking about, Sonya? That wouldn't be like him. I went into his room yesterday to tidy it up—I thought he had gone out. But there he was, sitting and staring at one spot— he didn't even hear me come in. And his face was so queer—I can't describe it to you. I asked him if he had a pain, and he laughed and said he was as fit as a fiddle. D'you know what I'm afraid of? He's come in very merry several times. I'm sleeping badly and I always hear him. That never used to happen before. They say that Bushagin's a drunkard: he's had treatment but he hasn't been cured. I hope to goodness Volodya doesn't take to drink. I've gotten to know him better now. He pretends he's happy and there's nothing he wants. And he's become so considerate! He's always trying to cheer me up. And he was so worried about Sokolovsky. Now he's started saying what a wonderful person Tanechka is. Then why didn't he marry her?"

"I haven't even asked about Tanechka."

"She's married a doctor, and they've gone off to Kazakhstan. She came to see me before she left. You wouldn't have recognised her—she was radiant. But I don't know if it will last. She said it was a hard break to give up the theatre."

"She wasn't much of an actress anyway. Our repertory company in Penza has a much higher standard."

"Do you often go to the theatre?"

"No, not very often."

"Then what do you do in the evenings?"

"It depends. Sometimes there's a meeting. Sometimes I go out to see people—Kharitonova or Sukhanov. I can't ask anyone in: you have to go through Xenya Ivanovna's room, and she's always asleep by ten."

"Sonya, how old is Sukhanov?"

"I suppose he's nearly fifty. I don't really know. Why do you ask?"

"Oh, no reason. I was only asking. You like him, don't you?"

"He's a good engineer, and he helped me when I started. And he's interesting to talk to. He spent two years in China. In general, he's got plenty to say."

"He's not married?"

"Yes, he is, he's got two children; his elder daughter is in her second year at college. His wife's a frightful woman. All she talks about is clothes, or else she's swearing at the maid. She collects all the latest gossip when she goes out shopping. I can't imagine how he puts up with her."

"You talk as if he meant something to you."

Sonya laughed: "I don't believe Sukhanov notices whether he's talking to a man or a woman. That's probably how he happened to marry. His wife would have been perfect for Zhuravlyov . . . Savchenko said that Lena's very happy. Do you like her?"

"Very much indeed. Your father was very fond of her."

"I hardly know her."

"It's Brainin's birthday today. He's asked me; and you too, of course. At first I thought that as Yasha is away there would be nothing but old people and it wouldn't amuse you, so I said I thought you had an engagement. But he said the Koroteyevs and Savchenko were coming, so if you come you'll see Lena. You know, one of these days I'd like to ask Brainin here, and Yegorov, and the Koroteyevs and Sokolovsky. Perhaps Vera Scherer would come, too. You're here so seldom. But I don't know if I can arrange it before Savchenko leaves."

"Is Savchenko going away?"

"So Brainin said. I thought you knew."

"Where's he going?"

"To Paris, with a delegation."

Sonya was so furious that she forgot her pride.

"He might have told me! I suppose now he's being sent to Paris he won't talk to ordinary mortals! Anyhow, lots of people are being sent abroad now. One of our engineers was sent to Sweden the other day."

"I think it embarrassed him to tell you that he was leaving when you have just arrived. He is always asking about you."

"What makes you think I care about him? I only speak to him because he used to come to see Father, and now he comes to see you—Where does the lilac come from?"

"It's the first this year. Seryozha gave it to me."

"Look—it's got good luck all over it.[1] Seven, eight, nine—too many to count. What mad lilac!"

"It smells marvellous. I'll put it in your room. What are you doing this afternoon? It's lovely out."

"I want to read. I've been out this morning. Sukhanov's given me an interesting book."

In the evening her mother asked her:

"What have you decided? Are you coming to the Brainins'?"

"No, I'm in the middle of my book and I can't tear myself away."

The book lay open upon the table—it was about the electrical processing of tools. But Sonya was not reading it. She was thinking about Savchenko.

She thought: "It's my own fault, of course. But how was I to know? It's extraordinary how you can learn to know and understand all sorts of things but what's inside you remains a complete mystery to you. When I got to Penza I was convinced that my real life was beginning and that Savchenko belonged to the past —like examinations and school friends and my parents' house. I

---

[1] Lilac with more than four petals to the calyx is thought to be a sign of good luck.

thought: 'Now I must take life seriously.' At first I couldn't get the hang of the work. Sukhanov told me off. I kept forgetting where everything was. And the moment I sat down to read in the evening, Xenya Ivanovna would rush in and scold me for leaving on the light in the kitchen. And then there was the time when Kazin asked me out for a drive in the country and for some reason I went and he talked about lofty themes and then grabbed me and tore my blouse and it was all I could do to get away from him. It was all so different from what I had expected. And Savchenko went on writing that he loved me, as if nothing in my life had changed.

"Of course I hoped he'd pay no attention to my telling him not to come—I kept hoping he'd arrive. But I blamed myself for that. I thought I'd get over it. But it's happened the other way around—he's got over it and I'm going out of my mind. I'm ready to throw myself at him. But it's too late. He's going to Paris and he never told me! Just didn't think it necessary! And now I don't know what I'll do next . . . To think I gave myself away in front of Mother! But Mother thinks I'm in love with Sukhanov, so that's all right. What's happening to me? I can't read, I can't sit still—I feel like running to him now . . . But he's probably at the Brainin's, being the life and soul of the party.

"What a fool I was to treat him as I did—saying we must think it over, give it a fair trial, wait . . . I realise now how blind I was. I thought: a grown-up woman must be sensible. Father scolded me but I wouldn't give in. I told myself my vocation was mathematics, not poetry. I wouldn't have emotional scenes. I'm ashamed to think of it now—I even said we couldn't get married until we had an apartment! How he must despise me in his heart! Now I see how stupid it was—what do I care where we live or what it's like so long as I can be with him . . .

"I wouldn't have thought it possible for anyone to change so much in a year. He's suddenly grown up; he's sure of himself. I used to think of him as a schoolboy, but now when he came I sat paralysed, terrified of what he would say next. And he actually teased me, to get his own back for the past. He reminded me of how I quoted Father to him about real things being unforgettable, and then immediately made his point: 'You've got your life and I have mine.'

"Obviously, he's in love with someone else. That's what gives him his self-confidence. He probably laughs when he thinks about me. He probably thinks: 'I was only a boy, and for some reason I liked a practical young woman who was always counting and sizing things up.' I must stop thinking about him. But what else have I to think about? Mother says Volodya's troubles have driven him to drink. That's no way out. I can't stand drunks. When I'm back in Penza I'll work hard and I'll have less time to think of him. But here it's wretched—to know he's near and yet a stranger to me . . . Of course, I'll manage to hide my feelings. If we meet before he goes, I won't let him guess anything. Let him think I've got my own life. But I know I'll never be free of this . . ."

The doorbell rang. "Probably one of Father's boys come to see Mother. Perhaps it's that red-headed Seryozha, delighted because he's passed his exams and is seeing Nina."

Sonya opened the door—It was Savchenko.

Calmly she greeted him and took him to her room.

"Mother's not in—she's at the Brainins'."

"I know. I was asked, too."

"Why didn't you go?"

"I wanted to come to see you."

"How nice of you. Would you like some tea?"

"No, thank you. I can't stay long. I've got some work to do. What sort of a vacation are you having?"

"Fine. I'm having a good rest. But you can see, today I decided to do a little work."

"I've read that book. It's on the subject I'm studying now. By the way, I've got some good news . . ."

"I've heard already. You must be delighted."

"Yes, I am, but you don't know why. Golovanov told us today

that our buyers are interested in Sokolovsky's project, and they're sending over two engineers to look at it. There's to be a conference next week, and now even Golovanov is beginning to wonder. It's frightful that I won't be here."

"Yes, but to make up for it, you'll be walking about Paris—more interesting than coming to Penza . . . Why didn't you tell me you were going to Paris?"

"I had no idea myself when I last saw you. Golovanov told me the following day. And I only heard the news about the project today. Everyone at the plant is full of it. You realise what it means? Sokolovsky wasn't thinking only of our plant; he was also thinking of the buyers—and this will mean an enormous step forward for them. Demin understood at once. It's a pity I can't go into it in more detail."

"Why not? I'm very interested. Are you in such a hurry?"

"No, but I can't explain now."

"I see—your thoughts are already far away."

"On the contrary. They're too close at hand."

He stopped himself, thinking: "Why did I say that? And my voice has given me away . . . I shouldn't have looked at her." He wanted to tell her she had misunderstood him, that it was the plant he had in mind. He managed to say:

"You're thinking . . ."

But he could not finish. He stood in the middle of the room, confused. Sonya came up to him and said gently:

"I wasn't thinking anything . . ."

Then she kissed him, again and again.

In the dining room the clock on the wall struck ten, eleven, twelve. They heard nothing.

All of a sudden Sonya started: "There's Mother!" She jumped up quickly and turned the key in the lock.

The lilac gave out a strong scent and Sonya whispered to Savchenko:

"Earlier today I was thinking how mad the lilac was: nearly every flower says good luck."

288

16

Late at night Sonya led Savchenko down the dark hallway.

Two days later he left. As she saw him off at the airfield, Sonya
said:

"I won't say anything to Mother until you come back but I'll let
the director at Penza know at once. I hope they'll let me leave,
though naturally Zhuravlyov will make trouble for me if he can.
Yegorov says they'll take me on here. But write to me, that's the
main thing. When you're walking around Paris, remember that
I'm at your side. Whatever you are looking at, I'm looking at it,
too. I'm living with you every minute. Do you understand?"

Sonya's mother had in fact heard Savchenko leave in the early
hours but she had not asked any questions. Sonya looked so
happy that she needed no explanations.

The party she had planned did not take place until after
Savchenko left. From early morning on, Nadezhda Yegorovna
was busy shopping and cooking. Volodya got the wine and
helped her to pull out the table. His mother thought: "Perhaps
the party will cheer him up. Sokolovsky's coming and Volodya
likes him." But Volodya unexpectedly disappeared. Nadezhda
Yegorovna sighed: "I expect he's gone off to Bushagin's again
. . . Never mind, at least I'm happy about Sonya.

"Pity Yegorov's ill and can't come. He's never really been well
since his wife died. It's not surprising—they meant everything to
each other . . .

"I told them all it was a party for Sonya's homecoming. Now if
I could have said: 'Sonya's getting married,' that *would* have been
a party! But it's not in her character to tell me."

There were roses on the table. Vera Scherer was surprised:

"Roses already! Where do they come from? They're lovely—it might be summer."

"Vyrubin brought them," Nadezhda Yegorovna explained. "They're hot-house ones."

Sokolovsky poured the wine and toasted her health. He had been excited for days: the buyers were coming on the twenty-second. Yegorov had been over the project in detail and had promised to support it. "It's all turned out better than I could possibly have expected," thought Sokolovsky. "And it's nice that Vera's here tonight—it's so hard to get her to go out. It's the first time she's been out with me. It's a nice party—they're nice people, and for some reason they all look happy. That doesn't often happen."

Even Brainin, usually so gloomy, was cheerful. He had been afraid he had offended Sokolovsky and had cursed himself for giving in to Safonov. But now there was Sokolovsky sitting next to him and talking as if nothing had happened. "We've a lot of memories in common," thought Brainin. "All those years of work together, good years and bad." When the first conveyor belt was installed at the plant, Sokolovsky, Brainin, and Yegorov were mentioned in the order, and they celebrated by spending the evening at Yegorov's. "Pity Yegorov isn't here tonight," he thought. "He never seems to feel well nowadays . . . When Zhuravlyov was trying to fire Sokolovsky, he turned on me, too . . . What an idiotic speech I made at the Party Bureau. If they adopt Sokolovsky's project, I'll be delighted. He's a good man to work with. He was very helpful to me last year over the communication system. But it isn't easy just to sit and talk to him— he likes rubbing people the wrong way . . . But today he's in a good mood."

Another reason for the cheerfulness of both Brainin and his wife, a fat woman with frightened, prominent eyes, was that their son Yasha was happy. When he first heard that Yasha was to be sent to Karaganda in the far north, Brainin had been upset and his wife had wept. Only Yasha took it calmly: "What's wrong with Karaganda?" Brainin lost his temper: "You're a child. You don't understand anything! It's the back of beyond. There isn't even a town anywhere near, and the climate is abominable. And you're actually pleased about it!" But quite recently a letter had come from Yasha and his mother showed it to everyone she met. Yasha wrote that the work was even more interesting than he had expected, the communal quarters were quite decent, and he liked the people he worked with. On the way to Nadezhda Yegorovna's house Brainin had said to his wife: "It's a good thing that Yasha has a lot of character. He might have become a mother's darling—we spoiled him enough. But he isn't fussy. He likes his work, and he gets on with people. He'll always fall on his feet."

Lena, too, was in a good mood: that morning she had had a letter and a package from Zhuravlyov. He wrote that there had been some changes in his life: he had married again. Of course, he still looked forward to seeing Shura as soon as he could, but meanwhile unexpected difficulties had cropped up at the factory which made it impossible for him to take any leave before September. In the package were a box of candy and a knitted dress for a three-year-old girl. Lena gave the chocolates to Shura, saying: "This is from your father." At once Shura ran to Koroteyev: "Daddy, I'm going to give you a treat. Only you mustn't take the one with the silver paper—that's got to be eaten last, because it's so pretty." Lena sighed with relief. "September is a long way off. It's a good thing he's married. Now he has settled down I feel happier."

Lena was also happy to see Dmitry talking and laughing loudly. "I've been living with him for a whole year," she thought, "and I've seldom seen him so relaxed and talkative."

Two hours earlier, while Lena was changing, Dmitry had for some reason remembered his talk with Trifonov. "He was so sure I'd make a fool of myself, but now it's he who looks a fool. I'm not thinking only of the reprimand—he said that Sokolovsky's project was eyewash, whereas it's a practical plan. I told Golovanov that we mustn't think only about delivering goods on time—we must think about the wider interests of the buyers. It's lucky Demin intervened. And of course the buyers jumped at it. Trifonov is always behind the times. He only knows four verbs: prompt, correct, scold, and punish. But that's beside the point. A year ago all my worries came from Zhuravlyov. Now it's Trifonov I blame for everything. But what matters is: how is Comrade Koroteyev behaving? Lena realised this before I did. Perhaps because women are more sensitive? Or perhaps it's easier for Lena—she's been through less than I have." Dmitry's face darkened; but at that moment Lena came in. Her new, greenish-blue summer dress was very becoming. He put his arms around her. She laughed and said: "Don't crumple my dress. It's time we went." Once again she saw the slight but happy smile on Dmitry's face, which hardly ever left him now.

Vyrubin did not consciously think about his past: it was still alive in him. At times it weighed on him; but it gave him stability and strength. He explained to Sokolovsky how fertilisers could be successfully applied to prevent the early fall of fruit. The fact that he could devote all his energies to the work he loved, that he was sitting with his friends in a comfortable room, that in spite of everything he was alive—all this made him feel young again. Nedezhda Yegorovna thought: "It's hard to believe he's five years older than I am."

She asked Lena:

"How did your examinations go off? Wasn't there a boy you were anxious about?"

Lena laughed.

"Vasya got five in everything except English—there he got a four, and even there he deserved more. Don't you see how cheerful I am, Nadezhda Yegorovna? I was worried about him. But he's a good boy—he didn't let me down."

Sonya sometimes lost the thread of the conversation and answered at random. Brainin asked her:

"Do you prefer being in Penza or at home?"

II · The Spring

"We work on a very different schedule at our factory."

They all laughed, and Brainin said jokingly:

"You don't seem able to think about anything else. I believe you've left your heart in Penza."

Sonya blushed—"I'm behaving badly," she thought—while Brainin thought with surprise that he had hit the nail on the head.

Sonya was sitting beside Vera and they talked in undertones. "It's sad about your father," said Vera. "He'd have loved to be here this evening. I remember telling him a week before he died that I was pleased because the hospital was to be reconditioned, and you know, he felt better at once—And tonight everybody's pleased, I think; even Brainin."

Sonya thought: "I'd have told Father all about it. He used to say that I had tight bands around my heart. But there aren't any bands now: Savchenko knows that. How funny that Mother should call him Grisha and that I should always think of him as Savchenko—ever since the first day we met. Even that night . . ."

Brainin asked if he might listen to the radio: he was anxious to hear what they were saying about the forthcoming meeting of the heads of governments. But they were too late—it was the end of the last news bulletin. All they heard was that some tourists from Sweden intended to visit Leningrad, that the Dynamo football team had won three to nothing; the weather forecast for the next day was "occasional clouds, light wind, morning temperature cool."

This was followed by singing: the announcer explained that the singer was a well-known French soloist:

"O streets of Paris, streets of grey and blue;
I walk alone and sorrow walks beside me."

Sonya couldn't bear it and went to turn off the radio. What a miserable song! Somewhere far away there was Paris; Savchenko was walking alone, and sorrow was walking beside him . . .

293

Nadezhda Yegorovna said to Brainin, who was sitting at the other end of the table: "Did you know Savchenko's in Paris?"

"Yes, indeed, and what a good thing, too. All these top-level discussions about relative military strength and so on don't seem to stand in the way of cultural and economic exchanges."

Brainin's wife watched Sonya. She thought her husband had been wrong, as usual: she had always known Savchenko wouldn't give up.

They got up from the table. Sokolovsky, laughing, told Vyrubin about an American he had seen at the Moscow airfield. The American had had too much to drink and was wearing an enormous fur cap.

"It was boiling hot. We couldn't take our eyes off him and there he was explaining he was 'a Red Cossack.' "

Nedezhda Yegorovna asked Lena how Shura was and Lena showed her some snapshots. Nadezhda Yegorovna became sentimental:

"What a pretty little thing! Oh well, they're a terrible worry when they're small but it's even worse when they grow up. But she looks very gay."

"She's playing with Vyrubin's cat. He's just got a cat . . ."

Brainin went up to Sokolovsky with a wine glass in his hand:

"Here's success to your project, Evgeny Vladimirovich!" They clinked glasses.

Vera and Sonya were talking in a corner. They were gay but also a little shy. When Vera felt shy, she looked like a girl. Nedezhda Yegorovna whispered to Sokolovsky: "Look, you'd think they were telling each other their most intimate secrets." Sokolovsky smiled. "Perhaps they are."

Dmitry overheard Sonya saying: "I used to think everything was so complicated. Now it seems to me much simpler, but perhaps that's just where the complication lies."

On their way home, Lena said to Dmitry: "Vera is a great friend of mine, and yet when she comes to see me she always invents some excuse for it—either she's returning a book or Shura isn't looking well . . . Gorokhov calls her 'the hermit crab.' I could never imagine her going to a party. But did you see how gay she was? She never says what she feels about Sokolovsky, but this evening in front of Brainin I heard her saying to him: 'I'll come home with you.' I'm so happy for her. You don't realise, Mitya, what a wonderful person she is!"

Lena fell silent and they walked along holding hands like children. She thought about her husband. "I don't suppose I know all there is to know about his life, and perhaps I don't completely understand what I do know. Lately he's been so cheerful, but perhaps he'll be moody again tomorrow. Anyhow, I'm not going to fuss any more. I'm sure I won't, now I know that he has a strong character—he will make out all right."

"What are you thinking about, Mitya?"

He stopped, a little startled, and looked at her. Then, with that faint half-smile, he said:

"I really don't know."

A car came towards them and for a second the head-lamps lit up Dmitry's face, with its high forehead and stubborn mouth.

17

THE DAY BEFORE SHE LEFT FOR Penza, Sonya went to Volodya's room. He was at work, drawing a can of fish for a poster.

"You know, Volodya, I'm hoping to be transferred here. I've no doubt your friend Zhuravlyov will try to put a spoke in my wheel, but I think they'll let me go all the same."

Sonya was afraid her brother would try to find out why she wanted to be transferred, but Volodya only smiled.

"I'm very glad for your sake. Do you understand? I'm very glad." He paused and then went on:

"If you're going to be here with Mother, I shall be able to go away."

"You mean you're going to Moscow?"

"Under no circumstances. I don't mean anywhere in particular. I was really thinking in general terms."

"Volodya, have you got into trouble of some kind?"

"On the contrary, everything is quite all right."

"Then why are you so depressed?"

"I don't know. Probably because of the fine weather—it's the spring working in reverse."

"I've seen hardly anything of you since I've been here. Who's this Bushagin?"

"He's just a man."

"I know he's a man. But why do you go around with him all the time? Do you like him so much?"

"On the whole, I do."

"They say he is a drunkard."

"That's an exaggeration. You know he's an accountant. He has to count money—perhaps he couldn't if he didn't get drunk now and then."

"I'm afraid you're being foolish, Volodya. You know, you once wrote that we must always remember Father, and that we must never let go of each other. But here you are in this state and I'm going away. Promise me you will try to pull yourself together, and if anything happens you will write to me at once. Promise?"

"Of course." Then he burst out laughing. "It's easy to give a promise. I've made so many promises. But to keep them . . . that's another matter. Sonechka, don't be cross with me. I'll try, really I will."

Volodya and Nadezhda Yegorovna saw Sonya off. Just as they were saying good-bye, Sonya suddenly said to her mother:

"I may be back soon. *Au revoir!*"

II · The Spring

Volodya waved his handkerchief till the train was out of sight.

In Sonya's carriage were a woman and her little girl; a man, obviously travelling on official business, who was snoring cosily, an incredibly fat and shabby briefcase clasped tightly to his chest; and a young man, apparently a student. The little girl kept trying to go to Sonya, but her mother would not let her. The student said:

"This is certainly a fine, fast train! It's creeping along like a tortoise going backwards."

Sonya, deep in her own thoughts, made no reply. So the student opened a book and said no more.

Then Sonya took Savchenko's letter from her bag. She thought: "What a long time it took to get here! And I couldn't imagine why he didn't write."

She read the letter again though she almost knew it by heart.

Don't be offended, Sonya, and don't think badly of me. Several times I've begun to write to you, but I never managed to go on. Of course, we haven't much free time; either we're sight-seeing, or visiting factories, or being entertained. The French are very hospitable and they eat dinner twice a day. But that's not the real reason I haven't written to you. I've had time to wander about the city by myself, and to talk to you as I did so. But I couldn't get it down on paper, and I'm afraid this letter will be a failure, too.

I expect you want to know first of all what Paris is like. It's beautiful, even more beautiful than I'd imagined. I wasn't much taken with the Eiffel Tower or the Champs Elysées. A man who works here with our trade delegation took us to see them before anything else and he thinks they're the best sights of Paris. But along the banks of the Seine there are some wonderful places— by day the river is leaden, scaly, and at night it's full of coloured jewels thrown into it by the street lights, and there are barges on it and families living on them. And along the banks are book-stalls, and the booksellers look even more ancient than the books. And there are houses the colour of ash, and chestnut trees, with

297

benches underneath and couples sitting on them—people go by but the couples pay no attention and just go on kissing. Some of the alleys are so narrow I doubt if Zhuravlyov could push his way through them. There are many wonderful old buildings. And flowers everywhere, in the parks, in the shop windows, on street carts, and on nearly every woman. There is much that is interesting in the organisation and plants of the factories we've been to, but also a lot of rubbish. But what I like best are the people: they are alive and they like to joke. They work quickly and with ease.

In short, Paris is so beautiful that it clutches at your heart, and at the same time it's sad—it's difficult to explain why. Don't think the people in the streets look gloomy; on the contrary, they are rather gay. Of course, in the working-class areas there are some shabby patches here and there, and you can see some anxious-looking women. But in the same areas I also saw merry-go-rounds in the squares and people dancing. Yet, all in all, you're left with an aftertaste of sadness. If Saburov were here, he'd probably be able to explain why. I often think of him, perhaps because the town is beautiful and the French are fond of painting. Or perhaps for another reason. He taught me how to use my eyes. I've said that he'd be sure to understand the reason for this sadness, but I can't explain it myself.

Sokolovsky once told me that so long as he was working on a project or trying to push it through he was lost to the world, and whether he was pleased or furious he still felt splendid, but that once it was all finished and put into production he felt flat. I get the feeling here that the finishing touches were given long, long ago and now there are no new projects, no excitement—perhaps that's the reason for the sadness, but I don't really know.

I never realised before how the French live, and I've been surprised in many ways. As for them, they have the haziest notions about how we live. I was talking to an engineer—obviously he gets his information from the newspapers, which publish inconceivable nonsense about us. He was astonished at our technical knowledge. He asked me if I was married and was surprised when I told him that in our country you did not have to register your marriage. You could do as you wished. One worker assured me that everybody in the Soviet Union was happy all the time; he got quite excited about it and said that you never saw anything but smiling faces in Soviet photographs. Of course, that is a bit excessive. Was I able to smile, for instance, when I thought you had forgotten me, or when Sokolovsky was reprimanded? It is not like that.

What is true is this: when I think of our town, our plant, I at once feel happier, though I don't gloss over anything—I see the poor streets, the peeling façades, and all sorts of things that need improvement. Perhaps you're surprised, Sonya, that I say "our plant," "our town," when I know that in ten days you'll have gone to Penza. But already I see you at my side—you don't mind, do you? However, I haven't explained. When amid all the beauty of Paris I think about our town and feel that that is where I left my heart and life, it's not just because it's my native land, but because we've worked out something for ourselves, and we're going to work out still more in the future. I find I am more interested by life at home: there are more worries but there is more future.

Please don't imagine I'm playing the foreign correspondent, gathering material for a newspaper article: it's just that I find myself constantly thinking about our affairs at home. I long to know as soon as possible what was decided about Sokolovsky's project. It's rather odd that he's never been to Paris, for he told me in advance what my reactions would be. It's as if he were standing on a high tower and could see into the far distance. If you happen to meet him, tell him he's often in my thoughts.

Please remember me to your mother and Volodya. Tell Volodya that you meet painters at every step and there's a street in which there is an exhibition in every house. I've seen some very good canvases. Another thing—but don't tell him this: he's got a dash of French in his make-up. I've often noticed here that when a man is sad he laughs and jokes—On the other hand, one evening I was out with some French engineers and we had some drinks and got a bit merry, and that was when they started to sing melancholy songs.

As you see, I'd never make a writer. I've written six pages and I haven't said the important thing—and I'm a long way from knowing how to put it into words. But I think you know without my saying it. I want to be with you. If I tell Golovanov that I've been counting the days till we return, he won't believe I'm not making it up. But it's true. But what can I say? When I thought there was no hope for me, I could have written a hundred pages about love, and now I can't manage to say anything.

The lilac here is over now, but I remember everything. I am by your side, and if I didn't have to write but could talk to you, why then—! Yes, and I wouldn't have to talk either!

From Moscow I shall come to Penza, if only for an hour.

Your Grigory Savchenko

Sonya put the letter back in her bag and shut her eyes. The little girl toddled over to her again. She had a big head and large, astonished eyes.

"I've told you not to bother Auntie," said her mother. Sonya opened her eyes and smiled at the little girl.

A NOTE ON THE TYPE

THE TEXT of this book is set in CALEDONIA, a Linotype face designed by W. A. Dwiggins (1880–1956), the man responsible for so much that is good in contemporary book design and typography. Caledonia belongs to the family of printing types called "modern face" by printers—a term used to mark the change in style of type-letters that occurred about 1800. Caledonia borders on the general design of Scotch Modern but is more freely drawn than that letter.

Composed, printed, and bound by
Kingsport Press, Inc., Kingsport, Tennessee.
Typography and binding design by

WARREN  CHAPPELL

A NOTE ABOUT THE AUTHOR

ILYA EHRENBURG is equally well known in his own country and abroad as a novelist and journalist-foreign correspondent. Exiled in 1906 as a young student, he spent the next twelve years of his life on the Left Bank as a struggling poet. During World War I he became a war correspondent, and returned to Russia in 1918. Since 1940, while living and writing chiefly in the Soviet Union, he has traveled, and written of his travels, all over the world and has become the master of *reportage* in the U.S.S.R., as well as a major influence against conformity through his fiction and literary criticism.

Ehrenburg

A change of season.